The Dead Command

By

Vicente Blasco Ibanez

Double9
BOOKS

The Dead Command
by Vicente Blasco Ibanez

ISBN: 978-93-61156-69-4
Published by

DOUBLE 9 BOOKS

2/13-B, Ansari Road
Daryaganj, New Delhi – 110002
info@double9books.com
www.double9books.com
Tel. 011-40042856

ABOUT THE AUTHOR

Vicente Blasco Ibanez was born in Valencia. He studied law at university and graduated in 1888, but he never practiced because his interests were in politics, journalism, and literature. He was particularly fond of Miguel de Cervantes. In politics, he was a fierce Republican partisan in his youth, and he established the newspaper El Pueblo in his hometown, where he launched the Republican populist political movement known as Blasquismo. The journal caused so much controversy that it was brought to court several times. In 1896, he was caught and condemned to a few months' imprisonment. He created numerous enemies and was shot and nearly died in a single dispute. In 1909, he proceeded to Argentina and established two new communities, Nueva Valencia and Cervantes. He held seminars on historical events and Spanish literature. Tired and dissatisfied by government failings and inaction, he traveled to Paris at the start of World War I. He died in Menton, France, the day before his 61st birthday, at Fontana Rosa (also known as the mansion of Writers), the mansion he had built and dedicated to Miguel de Cervantes, Charles Dickens, and Honoré de Balzac.

·

CONTENTS

PART FIRST

CHAPTER I
A MAJORCAN PALACE

Jaime Febrer arose at nine o'clock. Old Antonia, the faithful servant who cherished the memory of the past glories of the family, and who had attended upon Jaime from the day of his birth, had been bustling about the room since eight o'clock in the hope of awakening him. As the light filtering through the transom of a broad window seemed too dim, she flung open the worm-eaten blinds. Then she raised the gold-fringed, red, damask drapery which hung like an awning over the ample couch, the ancient, lordly, and majestic couch in which many generations of Febrers had been born and in which they had died.

The night before, on returning from the Casino, Jaime had charged her most earnestly to arouse him early, as he was invited to breakfast at Valldemosa. Time to get up! It was the finest of spring mornings; in the garden birds were singing in the flowery branches swayed by the breeze that blew over the wall from the sea.

The old servant, seeing that her master had at last decided to get out of bed, retreated to the kitchen. Jaime Febrer strolled about the room before the open window almost nude. There was no danger of his being seen. The dwelling opposite was an old palace like his own, a great house with few windows. From his room he could see a wall of indefinite color, with deep scars, and faint traces of ancient frescoes. It was so near, the street being extremely narrow, that it seemed as if he might touch it with his hand.

Nervous on account of an important event which was to take place in the morning, he had passed a restless night, and the heaviness following the short and indifferent sleep led him to seek eagerly the invigorating effect of cold water. Febrer made a sorry grimace as he bathed in the primitive, narrow, and uncomfortable tub. Ah poverty! His home was devoid of even the most essential conveniences despite its air of stately luxury, a stateliness which modern wealth can never emulate. Poverty with all its annoyances stalked forth to meet him at every turn in these halls which reminded him of splendidly decorated theaters he had seen in his European travels.

Febrer glanced over the grandiose room with its lofty ceiling as if he were a stranger entering the apartment for the first time. His powerful ancestors had built for giants. Each room in the palace was as large as a modern house. The windows were without glass all over the house and in winter they had to be closed by wooden shutters which admitted no light except that entering through the transoms, and these were studded with crystals cracked and dimmed by time. Lack of carpets disclosed floors of soft Majorcan sandstone cut in small rectangles like wooden blocks. The rooms still boasted the old-time splendor of vaulted ceilings, some dark, with skilfully fitted paneling, others with a faded and venerable gilding forming a background for the colored escutcheons which were emblazoned with the coat of arms of the house. In some rooms the high walls, simply whitewashed, were covered by rows of ancient paintings, and in others were concealed by rich hangings of gay colors which time had failed to destroy. The sleeping room was decorated with eight enormous tapestries of a shade of dull green leaves representing gardens, broad avenues of trees in autumnal foliage leading to a small park where deer were frisking, or where solitary fountains dripped into triple basins. Above the doors hung old Italian paintings in soft brown tones representing nude, amber-hued babes fondling curly lambs. The arch dividing the alcove from the rest of the apartment suggested the triumphal order, its fluted columns sustaining a scroll-work of carved foliage with the softened luster of faded gilding, as if it were an ancient altar. Upon an eighteenth century table stood a polychrome statue of Saint George treading Moors beneath his charger; and beyond was the bed, the imposing bed, a venerable family monument. Antique chairs with curved arms, the red velvet so worn and threadbare as to disclose the white woof, jostled against modern cane-bottomed chairs and the wretched bathtub.

"Ah, poverty!" sighed the heir of the estate.

The old Febrer mansion, with its beautiful unglazed casements, its tapestry-filled halls, its carpetless floors, its venerable furniture jumbled with the meanest of chattels, reminded him of a poverty-stricken prince wearing his brilliant mantle and his glittering crown, but barefooted and destitute of underclothing.

Febrer himself was like this palace—this imposing and empty frame which in happier times had sheltered the glory and wealth of his ancestors. Some had been merchants, others soldiers, navigators all. The Febrer arms had floated on pennants and flags over more than fifty full-rigged ships, the pride of the Majorcan marine, which, after clearing from Puerto Pi, used to sail away to sell the oil of the island in Alexandria, taking on cargoes of spices, silks, and perfumes of the Orient in the ports of Asia Minor, trading in Venice, Pisa, and Genoa, or, passing the Pillars of Hercules, plunging into the fogs of Northern seas to carry to Flanders and the Hanseatic Republics the pottery of the Valencian Moors called majolica by foreigners because of its Majorcan origin. These voyages over pirate-infested seas had converted this family of rich merchants into a tribe of valorous warriors. The Febrers had now fought, now entered into alliances with Turkish corsairs, with Greeks, and with Algerines; they had sailed their fleets through Northern seas to face the English pirates, and, on one occasion, at the entrance of the Bosphorus, their galleys had rammed the vessels of Genoese merchants who were trying to monopolize the commerce of Byzantium. Finally, this family of soldiers of the sea, on retiring from maritime commerce, had rendered tribute of blood in the defense of Christian kingdoms and the Catholic faith by enlisting some of its scions in the holy Order of the Knights of Malta. The second sons of the house of Febrer, at the very moment of receiving the water of baptism, had the eight-pointed white cross, symbolizing the eight beatitudes, sewed to their swaddling-bands, and on reaching manhood they became captains of galleys of the warlike Order, and ended their days as opulent knights commanders of Malta recounting their deeds of prowess to the children of their nieces, being tended in their illnesses and having their wounds dressed by the slave women with whom they lived despite their vows of chastity. Renowned monarchs passing through Majorca would leave their sumptuous quarters in the Almudaina to visit the Febrers in their palace. Some members of this great family had been admirals in the king's armada; others governors of far distant lands; some slept the eternal sleep in the Cathedral of La Valette beside other illustrious Majorcans, and Jaime had done homage at their tombs during one of his visits to Malta.

La Lonja, the graceful Gothic structure near the sea at Palma, had been for centuries a feudal possession of his forefathers. Everything was for the Febrers which was flung upon the mole from the high-forecastled galleons, from Oriental cocas with their massive hulls, from fragile lighters, lateen-sailed settees, flat-bottomed tafureas, and other vessels of the epoch; and in the great columnar hall of La Lonja, near the Solomonic pillars which disappeared within the shadows of the vaulted ceilings, his ancestors in regal majesty used to receive voyagers from the Orient who came clad in wide breeches and red fezzes; Genoese and Provençals wearing capes with monkish hoods; and the valiant native captains of the island covered with their red Catalonian helmets. Venetian merchants sent their Majorcan friends ebony furniture delicately inlaid with ivory and lapis lazuli, or enormous, heavy plate-glass mirrors with bevelled edges. Seafarers returning from Africa brought ostrich feathers and tusks of ivory; and these treasures and countless others added to the decoration of the halls, perfumed by mysterious essences, the gifts of Asiatic correspondents.

For centuries the Febrers had been intermediaries between the Orient and the Occident, making of Majorca a depository for exotic products which their ships afterward scattered throughout Spain, France, and Holland. Riches flowed in fabulous abundance to the house. On some occasions the Febrers had made loans to their sovereigns, but this did not prevent Jaime, the last of the family, after losing in the Casino the night before everything which he possessed—some hundreds of pesetas—from borrowing money for a journey to Valldemosa on the following morning from Toni Clapés, the smuggler, a rough fellow of keen intelligence, the most faithful and disinterested of his friends.

While Jaime stood combing his hair he intently studied his image in an antique mirror, cracked and dimmed. Thirty-six! He could not complain of his looks. He was ugly, but it was a grandiose ugliness, to adopt the expression of a woman who had exercised a peculiar influence over his life. This ugliness had yielded him some satisfactory adventures. Miss Mary Gordon, a blonde-haired idealist, daughter of the governor of an English archipelago in Oceanica, traveling through Europe accompanied only by a maid, had met him one summer in a hotel at Munich. She it was who first became impressed, and it was she who took the first steps. According to the young lady, the Spaniard was the living picture of Wagner in his youth. Smiling at the pleasant memory, Febrer contemplated the prominent brow which seemed to oppress his imperious, small, ironic eyes. His nose was sharp and aquiline, the nose common to all the Febrers, those daring birds of prey who haunted the solitudes of the sea. His mouth was scornful and receding, his lips and chin prominent and covered by the soft growth of the beard and mustache, thin and fine.

Ah, delicious Miss Mary! Their happy pilgrimage through Europe had lasted almost a year. She was madly enamored on account of his resemblance to a genius, and wished to marry him; she told him of the governor's millions, mingling her romantic enthusiasm with the practical tendencies of her race; but Febrer ran away at last, before the English woman should in her turn leave him for some orchestra director or other Who might be an even more striking double of her idol.

Ah, women!... Jaime straightened his figure which was manly, though the shoulders bent somewhat from his excessive stature. It had been some time since he had taken interest in women. A few gray hairs in his beard, a slight wrinkling around the eyes, revealed the fatigues of a life which, as he said, had whirled "at full speed." But even so he was popular, and it was love that should lift him out of his pressing situation.

Having finished his toilette he left the dormitory. He crossed a vast salon lighted by the sunshine filtering through shutters in the windows. The floor lay in shadow and the walls shone like a brilliant garden, covered as they were by interminable tapestries with figures of heroic size. They represented mythological and biblical scenes; arrogant dames with full pink flesh standing before red and green warriors; imposing colonnades; palaces hung with garlands; scimitars aloft, heads strewed over the ground, troops of big-bellied horses with one foot lifted; a whole world of ancient legends, but with colors fresh and vernal, despite their centuries, bordered with apples and foliage.

As Febrer passed through the stately hall he glanced ironically at these treasures, the inheritance from his ancestors. Not one of them was his! For more than a year these tapestries, and also those in the dormitory, and throughout the house, had been the property of certain usurers of Palma who had chosen to leave them hanging in their places. They were awaiting the chance visit of some wealthy collector who would pay more royally believing them to be purchased direct from their owner. Jaime was only their custodian, in danger of imprisonment should he prove false to his trust.

Reaching the center of the salon, he turned aside, impelled by habit, but seeing nothing to obstruct his passage, he burst into a laugh. A month ago a choice Italian marble table which the famous knight commander, Don Priamo Febrer, had brought back from one of his privateering expeditions had still stood here. Neither was there anything for him to stumble against farther on; the enormous hammered silver brazier resting on a support of the same metal, upheld by a circular row of cupids, Febrer had also converted into cash, selling it by weight! The brazier reminded him of a gold chain presented by the Emperor Charles V to one of his ancestors which he had sold in Madrid years ago, also by weight, with the addition of two ounces of gold on account of its artistic finish and its antiquity. Afterward he had heard a vague rumor that the chain had been re-sold in Paris for a hundred thousand francs. Ah, poverty! Gentlemen could no longer exist in these times!

His gaze was drawn by the glitter of some enormous writing desks of Venetian workmanship, mounted upon antique tables sustained by lions. They seemed to have been made for giants; their innumerable deep drawers were inlaid in bright colors with representations of mythological scenes. They were four magnificent museum pieces, a feeble reminder of the ancient splendors of the house. Neither did these belong to him. They had shared the fate of the tapestries, and were here awaiting a purchaser. Febrer was merely the concierge of his own house. The Italian and Spanish paintings hanging on the walls of two adjoining rooms, the handsomely carved antique furniture, its silk upholstery now threadbare and torn, also belonged to his creditors—in fact, whatever there had been of value in his venerable heritage!

He passed into the reception hall, a cold, spacious room with elevated ceiling, in the center of the palace, which connected with the stairway. The years had tinged the white walls with the creamy shade of ivory. One must throw his head well back to see the black paneling of the ceiling. Casements near the cornice together with the lower windows lighted this immense, austere apartment. The furnishings were few and of romantic severity; broad armchairs with seats and backs of leather studded with nails; oak tables with twisted legs; dark chests with iron locks showing against upholstery of moth-eaten green cloth. The yellowish-white walls were only visible, as a sort of grill-work, between rows of canvases, many of them unframed. There were hundreds of paintings, all badly done, and yet interesting pictures painted for the perpetuation of the glories of the family, executed by old Italian and Spanish artists who chanced to be passing through Majorca. A traditional charm seemed to emanate from the portraits. Here was the history of the Mediterranean, traced by crude and ingenuous brushes; sea fights between galleys, assaults upon fortresses, naval battles enveloped in smoke. Above the clouds floated the pennants of the ships and rose the tower-like poops with flags bearing the Maltese cross or the crescents crinkling from the rail. Men were fighting on the decks of the ships or in small boats which floated near; the sea, reddened by blood and lurid from the flames of the burning vessels, was dotted with hundreds of little heads of men still fighting upon the waves. A mass of helmets and three-cornered Schomber hats mingled upon two vessels which grappled another where swarmed white and red turbans, and above them all rose hands grasping pikes, scimitars, and boarding-axes. Shots from cannons and blunderbusses rent the smoke of battle with long red tongues. In other canvases, no less dark, could be seen castles hurling firebrands from their embrasures, and at their bases warriors almost as big as the towers, distinguished by eight-pointed white crosses upon their cuirasses, were setting their ladders against the walls to clamber to the assault.

The paintings bore on one side white scrolls with the ends folded about coats of arms, on each of which was written in ill-formed capital letters, the story of the event; victorious encounters with the galleys of the Grand Turk or with privates from Pisa, Genoa and Vizcaya; wars in Sardinia, assaults on Bujia and on Tedeliz, and in every one of these enterprises a Febrer was leading the combatants or distinguishing himself for his heroism, the knight commander Don Priamo towering above them all, he who had been both the glory and the shame of the house.

Alternating with these warlike scenes were the family portraits. On the topmost row, crowding a line of old canvases depicting evangelists and martyrs in semblance of a frieze, were the most ancient Febrers, venerable merchants of Majorca, painted some centuries after their death, grave men with Jewish noses and piercing eyes, with jewels on their breasts, and wearing tall Oriental caps. Next came the men of arms, the sword-bearing navigators with short cropped hair and profiles like birds of prey, all clad in dark steel armor, and some displaying the white Maltese cross. From portrait to portrait the countenances grew more refined, but without losing the prominent forehead and the imperious family nose. The wide, soft collar of the homespun shirt became transformed into starched folds of plaited ruffs; the cuirasses softened into jackets of velvet or silk; the stiff broad beards in imperial style changed to sharp goatees and to pointed mustaches, which, with the soft locks falling over the temples, served as a frame for the face. Among the rude men of war and the elegant caballeros, a few ecclesiastics with mustaches and small beards, wearing tasseled clerical hats, stood out conspicuously. Some were religious dignitaries of Malta, to judge by the white insignia adorning their breasts; others, venerable inquisitors of Majorca, according to the inscription which extolled their zeal for the spread of the faith. After all these dark gentlemen of imposing presence and metallic eyes, followed the procession of white wigs and of countenances rendered youthful by shaving; of coats resplendent with silk and gold, showy with sashes and decorations of honor. They were perpetual magistrates of the city of Palma; marquises whose marquisate the family had lost through matrimonial complications, their titles becoming merged with others pertaining to the nobility of the Peninsula; governors, captain generals, and viceroys of American and Oceanian countries, whose names evoked visions of fantastic riches; enthusiastic "botiflers," partisans of the Bourbons from the start, who had been compelled to flee from Majorca, that final support of the house of Austria, and they boasted as a supreme title of nobility the nickname of butifarras, which had been given them by the hostile populace. Closing the glorious procession, hanging almost on a level with the furniture of the room, were the last Febrers of the early nineteenth century, officers of the Armada, with short whiskers, curls over their foreheads, high collars with anchors embroidered in gold, and black stocks, men who had fought off Cape Saint Vincent and Trafalgar; and after them Jaime's great grandfather, an old man with large eyes and disdainful mouth, who, when Ferdinand VII returned from his captivity in France, had sailed for Valencia to prostrate himself at his feet, beseeching, along with other great hidalgos, that he reëstablish the ancient customs and crush the growing scourge of liberalism. He was a prolific patriarch, who had lavished his blood in various districts of the island in pursuit of peasant girls, without ever sacrificing his dignity; and as he offered his hand to be kissed by some one of his sons who lived in the house and bore his name, he would say with a solemn voice: "May God make you a good inquisitor!"

Among these portraits of the illustrious Febrers were a number of women, grand señoras with great hoops filling the whole canvas, like those painted by Valasquez. One of them, whose slender bust emerged from her flowered bell-like skirts with pale and pointed face, a faded knot of ribbon in her short hair, was the notable woman of the family, she who had been called "La Greca" on account of her knowledge of Hellenic letters. Her uncle, Fray Espiridion Febrer, prior of Santo Domingo, a great luminary of his epoch, had been her teacher, and the "Greek woman" could write in their own language to correspondents in the Orient who still maintained a dwindling commerce with Majorca.

Jaime's glance fell upon some canvases farther down (the distance representing the passing of a century) where hung the portrait of another famous woman of the family, a girl in a little white wig, dressed like a woman in the full skirt and great hoops of the ladies of the eighteenth century. She was standing beside a table, near a vase of flowers, holding in her bloodless right hand a rose as large as a tomato, looking straight before her with the little porcelain-like eyes of a doll. This woman had been styled "La Latina." In the pompous style of the epoch the lettering on the canvas told of her knowledge and wisdom, and lamented her death at the tender age of eleven years. The women were as dry shoots upon the vigorous trunk of the soldierly and exuberant Febrer stock. Scholarship quickly withered in this family of seamen and soldiers, like a plant which springs up by mistake in an adverse clime.

Preoccupied with his thoughts of the night before and of the contemplated trip to Valldemosa, Jaime stood in the reception hall gazing at the pictures of his forefathers. How much glory, and how much dust! It had been twenty years, perhaps, since a merciful cloth had passed over the illustrious family to furbish it up a little. The more remote grandfathers and the famous battles were covered with cobwebs... and to think that the pawnbrokers had declined to acquire this museum of glories under the pretext that the paintings were poor! Jaime was surprised that it should be difficult to turn these relics over to wealthy people anxious to pretend an illustrious origin for themselves.

He crossed the reception hall and entered the apartments in the opposite wing. They were rooms with lower ceilings; above them was a second story occupied in other times by Febrer's grandfather; relatively modern rooms, with old furniture in the style of the Empire, and on the walls illuminated prints of the romantic period, representing the misfortunes of Atala, the love affairs of Matilde, and the achievements of Hernán Cortéz. Upon the swelling dressing tables were polychrome saints and ivory crucifixes, together with dusty artificial flowers beneath crystal bells. A collection of cross-bows, arrows, and knives recalled a Febrer, captain of a corvette belonging to the king, who made a voyage around the world near the close of the eighteenth century. Purplish bivalves and enormous nacre-lined conch shells lay upon the tables.

Following a corridor on the way to the kitchen he left on one side the chapel which had been closed for many years, and on the other the door of the archives, a huge apartment with windows opening upon the garden, where Jaime on his return from trips had spent many afternoons poring over bundles of papers kept behind the metal grating of many series of ancient bookshelves.

He peeped into the kitchen, an immense place where anciently were prepared the sumptuous banquets of the Febrers, who fed a swarm of parasites, and lavished generosity on all their friends who visited the island. Antonia looked dwarfed in this high-ceiled, spacious room, standing near a great fireplace which would hold an enormous pile of wood and was capable of roasting several animals at once. The ranks of ovens might serve for an entire community. The chill cleanliness of this adjunct of the palace showed lack of use. On the walls great iron hooks called attention to the absence of the copper vessels which used to be the splendrous glory of this conventional kitchen. The old servant did her cooking at a small hearth beside the trough where she kneaded her bread.

Jaime called to Antonia, to announce his presence and entered the adjoining room, the small dining room which had been utilized by the last of the Febrers, who, being in reduced circumstances, had abandoned the great hall where the old-time banquets used to take place.

Here, also, the presence of poverty was noticeable. The long table was covered with a cracked oil-cloth of blemished whiteness. The sideboards were almost empty. The ancient china, when it became broken, had been replaced by coarse platters and jars. Two open windows at the lower end of the room framed bits of sea, of intense and restless blue, palpitating beneath the fire of the sun. Near them swayed rhythmically the branches of palm trees. Out at sea the white wings of a schooner approaching Palma, slowly, like a wearied gull, broke the horizon line.

Mammy Antonia came in, setting upon the table a steaming bowl of coffee and milk and a great slice of buttered bread. Jaime attacked the breakfast with avidity, but as he bit into the bread he made a gesture of displeasure. Antonia assented with a nod of her head, breaking into speech in her Majorcan dialect.

"It is hard, isn't it? No doubt the bread does not compare with the tender little rolls the señor eats at the casino, but it is not my fault. I wanted to make bread yesterday, but I was out of flour, and I was expecting that the 'payés' of Son Febrer would come and bring his tribute. Ungrateful and forgetful people!"

The old servant persisted in her scorn of the peasant farmer of Son Febrer, the piece of land which constituted the remaining fortune of the house. The rustic owed all he had to the benevolence of the Febrer family, and now in these hard times he forgot his kind masters.

Jaime continued chewing, his thought centered upon Son Febrer. That was not his either, although he posed as owner. The farm, situated in the middle of the island, the choicest property inherited from his parents, that which bore the family name, he had heavily mortgaged, and he was about to lose it. The rent, paltry and mean, according to traditional custom, enabled him to pay off only a part of the interest on his loans; the rest of the interest due served to swell the amount of the debt. There were still the tributes, the payments in specie which the payés had to make to him, according to ancient usage, and with these he and Mammy Antonia had managed to exist, almost lost in the immensity of the house which had been built to shelter a tribe. At Christmas and at Easter he always received a brace of lambs accompanied by a dozen fowl; in the autumn two well-fattened pigs ready to kill, and every month eggs and a certain amount of flour, as well as fruits in their season. With these contributions, partly consumed in the house, and in part sold by the servant, Jaime and Mammy Antonia managed to live in the solitude of the palace, isolated from public gaze, like castaways. The offerings in money were continually becoming more belated. The payés, with that rustic egoism which shuns misfortune, became indolent in fulfilling his obligations. He knew that the nominal possessor of the estate was not the real owner of Son Febrer, and frequently, on arriving at the city with his gifts, he changed his route and left them at the houses of his creditors, awe-inspiring personages whom he desired to propitiate.

Jaime glanced sadly at the servant who remained standing before him. She was an old payesa who still kept to the ancient style of dress peculiar to her people—a dark doublet with two rows of buttons on the sleeves, a light, full skirt, and the rebocillo covering her head, the white veil caught at the neck and at the bust, below which hung the heavy braid, which was false and very black, tied with long velvet bows.

"Poverty, Mammy Antonia," said the master in the same dialect. "Everybody shuns the poor, and some fine day if that rascal does not bring us what he owes us, we shall have to fall to and eat each other like shipwrecked mariners on a desert island."

The old woman smiled; the master was always merry. In this he was just like his grandfather, Don Horacio, ever solemn, with a face which frightened one, and yet always saying such jolly things!

"This will have to stop," continued Jaime, paying no heed to the servant's levity. "This must stop this very day. I have made up my mind. Let me tell you, Antonia, before the news gets abroad: I'm going to be married."

The servant clasped her hands in an attitude of devotion to express her astonishment, and turned her eyes toward the ceiling. "Santísimo Cristo de la sangre!" It was high time!... He should have done it long ago, and then the house would have been in a very different condition. Her curiosity was stirred, and she asked with the eagerness of a rustic:

"Is she rich?"

The master's affirmative gesture did not surprise her. Of course she must be rich. Only a woman who brought a great fortune with her could aspire to unite with the last of the Febrers, who had been the most noted men of the island, and perhaps of the whole world. Poor Antonia thought of her kitchen, instantly furnishing it in her imagination with copper vessels gleaming like gold, dreaming of its hearths all ablaze, the room filled with girls with rolled up sleeves, their rebocillos thrown back, their braids floating behind, and she in the center, seated in a great chair, giving orders and breathing in the savory odors from the casseroles.

"She must be young!" declared the old woman, trying to worm more news out of her master.

"Yes, much younger than I; too young; about twenty-two. I could almost be her father."

Antonia made a gesture of protest. Don Jaime was the finest man on the island. She said so, she who had worshipped him ever since she led him by the hand, in his short trousers, walking among the pines near the castle of Bellver. He was one of the family—of that family of arrogant grand seigniors, and no more could be said.

"And is she of good family?" she questioned in an effort to force her master's reticence. "Of a family of caballeros; undoubtedly the very best in the island—but no—from Madrid, perhaps. Some sweetheart you found when you lived there."

Jaime hesitated an instant, turned pale, and then said with rude energy to conceal his perturbation:

"No, Antonia—she's a—Chueta."

Antonia started to clasp her hands, as she had done a few moments before, invoking again the blood of Christ, so venerated in Palma, but suddenly the wrinkles of her brown face broadened, and she burst out laughing. What a jolly master! Just like his grandfather; he used to say the most stupendous and incredible things so seriously that he deceived everybody. "And I, poor fool, was ready to believe your nonsense! Perhaps it was also a joke that you were going to get married!"

"No, Antonia, I am going to marry a Chueta. I am going to marry the daughter of Benito Valls. That is why I am going to Valldemosa."

The stifled voice in which Jaime spoke, his lowered eyes, the timid accent with which he murmured these words, removed all doubt. The old servant stood open-mouthed, her arms fallen, without strength to raise either her hands or her eyes.

"Señor!... Señor!... Señor!"

She could say no more. She felt as if a thunderbolt had crashed upon the house, shaking it to its foundations; as if a dark cloud had swept before the sun obscuring the light; as if the sea had become a leaden mass dashing against the castle wall. Then she saw that everything remained as usual, that she alone had been stirred by this stupendous news, so startling as to change the order of all existence.

"Señor!... Señor!... Señor! A Chueta! An apostate Jewess!"

She grasped the empty cup and the remnants of the bread, and ran to take refuge in the kitchen. After hearing such horrors in this house she felt afraid. She imagined that someone must be stalking through the venerable halls at the other end of the palace; someone—she could not explain to herself who it might be—someone who had been aroused from the sleep of centuries! This palace undoubtedly possessed a soul. When the old woman was alone in it the furniture creaked as if people were moving about and conversing; the tapestries swayed as if stirred by invisible faces, a gilded harp which had belonged to Don Jaime's grandmother vibrated in its corner, yet she never felt terror, because the Febrers had been good people, simple and kind to their servants; but now, after hearing such things——! She thought uneasily of the portraits hanging on the walls of the reception hall. How severe those señores would look if the words of their descendant should reach their ears! How fiercely their eyes would flame!

Mammy Antonia finally grew calm and drank the coffee left by her master. She had laid fear aside, but she felt profound sorrow over the fate of Don Jaime, as if he were in peril of death. To bring the house of the Febrers to this! Could God tolerate such things? Then scorn for her master momentarily overcame her old-time affection. After all he was nothing but a wild fellow, heedless of religion, and destitute of good habits, who had squandered what had been left of the fortune of his house. What would his illustrious relatives have to say? How ashamed his aunt Juana would be—that noble lady, the most pious and aristocratic woman in the island, called by some in jest and by others in an excess of veneration, la Papisa—the Pope-ess!

"Good-bye, Mammy. I'll be back about sunset."

The old woman grunted a farewell to Jaime, who peeped into the kitchen before leaving. Then, finding herself alone, she raised her clasped hands invoking the aid of the Sangre de Cristo, of the Virgin of Lluch, patron saint of the island, and of the powerful San Vicente Ferrer, who had wrought so many miracles when he ministered in Majorca—a final and prodigious saint, who might avert the monstrosity her master contemplated! Let a rock from the mountains fall and forever close the way to Valldemosa; let the carriage upset, and let Don Jaime be carried home on a stretcher by four men—anything rather than that disgrace!

Febrer crossed the reception hall, opened the door to the stairway, and began to descend the worn steps. His forefathers, like all the nobles of the island, had builded on a grand scale. The stairway and the zaguán occupied a third of the lower story. A kind of loggia in Italian style, with five arches sustained by slender columns, extended to the foot of the stairway, the doors of which gave access to the two upper wings of the building opening at either end. Above the center of the stairway, facing the street door, were the Febrer arms cut in the stone, and a great lantern of wrought iron.

On his way down Jaime's cane struck against the sandstone steps, or touched the great glazed amphoræ decorating the landings which responded to the blow with the sonorous ring of a bell. The iron balustrade, oxidized by time and crumbling into scales of rust almost shook from its sockets with the jar of his footsteps.

As he reached the zaguán Febrer stood still. The extreme resolution which he had adopted, and which would forever cast its influence on the destiny of his name, caused him to look curiously at the very places which he had so often passed with indifference.

In no other part of the building was the old-time prosperity so evident as here. The zaguán, enormous as a plaza, could admit a dozen carriages and an entire squadron of horsemen. Twelve columns, somewhat bulging, of the nut-brown marble of the island, sustained the arches of cut undressed stone over which extended the roof of black rafters. The paving was of cobbles between which grew dank moss. A vault-like chill pervaded this gigantic and solitary ruin. A cat slunk through the zaguán, making its exit through a hole in a worm-eaten door of the old stables, disappearing into the deserted cellars which had held the harvests of former days. On one side was a well dating from the epoch when the palace was constructed, a hole sunk through rock, with a time-worn stone curb and a wrought-iron spout. Ivy was growing in fresh clusters between the crevices of the polished rock. Often as a child Jaime had peered over the curb at his reflection in the luminous round pupil of the sleeping waters.

The street was deserted. Down at its end, near the walls of the Febrer garden, was the city rampart, pierced by a broad gateway, with wooden bars in the arch like the teeth in the mouth of an enormous fish. Through this the waters of the bay trembled green and luminous with reflections of gold.

Jaime walked a short distance over the blue stones of the street which was destitute of sidewalks, and then turned to contemplate his house. It was but a small remnant of the past. The ancient palace of the Febrers occupied a whole square, but it had dwindled with the passing of the centuries and with the exigencies of the family. Now a part of it had become a residence for nuns, and other parts had been acquired by certain rich people who disfigured with modern balconies the original unity of the design, which was still suggested by the regular line of eaves and tile-covered roofs. The Febrers themselves who were living in that portion of the great house which looked upon the garden and the sea, had been compelled to let the lower stories to warehousemen and small shopkeepers, in order to augment their rents. Near the lordly portal, inside the glass windows, some girls who greeted Don Jaime with a respectful smile were busy ironing linen. He stood motionless contemplating the ancient house. How beautiful it was still in spite of its amputations and its age!

The foundation wall, perforated and worn by people and carriages, was cleft by several windows with grilles on a level with the ground. The lower story of the palace was worn, lacerated, and dusty, like feet which had been plodding for centuries.

As it rose above the mezzanine, a story with an independent entrance which had been rented to a druggist, the lordly splendor of the façade developed. Three rows of windows on a level with the arch of the portal, divided by double columns, had frames of black marble delicately carved. Stone thistles climbed over the columns which sustained the cornices, while above them were three great medallions—that in the center being the bust of the Emperor with the inscription DOMINUS CAROLUS IMPERATOR, 1541, in memory of his passing through Majorca on the unfortunate expedition against Algiers; those on either side bore the Febrer arms held by fish with bearded heads of men. Above the jambs and cornices of the great windows of the first story were wreaths formed of anchors and dolphins, testifying to the glories of a family of navigators. On their finials were enormous shells. Along the upper portion of the façade was a compact row of small windows with Gothic decorations, some plastered over, others open to admit light to the garrets, and above them the monumental eaves, such as are found only in Majorcan palaces, their masses of carved timbers blackened by time and supported by sturdy gargoyles projecting as far as the middle of the street.

Over the entire façade extended cleats of worm-eaten wood with nails and bands of rusted iron. They were the remains of the grand illuminations with which the household had commemorated certain feasts in its times of splendor.

Jaime seemed satisfied with this examination. The palace of his ancestors was still beautiful despite the broken panes in the windows, the dust and cobwebs gathered in the crevices, the cracks which centuries had opened in its plaster. When he should marry, and old Valls' fortune should pass into his hands, everyone would be astounded at the magnificent resurrection of the Febrers. And yet, would some people be scandalized at his decision, and did he himself not feel certain scruples? Courage, forward!

He turned in the direction of El Borne, a broad avenue which is the center of Palma, a stream bed which in ancient times divided the city into two villages and into two hostile factions—Can Amunt and Can Avall. There he would find a carriage to take him to Valldemosa.

As he entered the Paseo del Borne his attention was attracted by a group of people standing in the shade of the dense-crowned trees staring at a peasant family which had stopped before the display windows of a shop. Febrer recognized their dress, different from that worn by the peasants on the island. They were Ivizans. Ah, Iviza! The name of this island recalled the memory of a year he had spent there long ago in his youth. Seeing these people who caused the Majorcans to grin as if they were foreigners, Jaime smiled also, looking with interest at their dress and figures.

They were, undoubtedly, father, son and daughter. The elder rustic wore white hempen sandals, above which hung the broad bell of a pair of blue trousers. His jacket-blouse was caught across his breast by a clasp, affording glimpses of his shirt and belt. A dark mantle hung over his shoulders like a woman's shawl, and to complete this feminine garb, which contrasted strongly with his hard, brown, Moorish features, he wore a handkerchief knotted across his forehead beneath his hat, with the ends hanging down behind. The boy, who was about fourteen, was dressed like the father, with the same style of trousers, narrow in the leg and bell-shaped over the foot, but without the kerchief and mantle. A pink ribbon hung down his breast like a cravat, a spray of flowers peeped from behind one of his ears, and his hat with a flower-embroidered band, thrust back on his head, allowed a wave of curls to fall around his face, brown, spare and mischievous, animated by African eyes of intense lustrous black.

The girl it was who attracted the greatest attention with her accordeon-plaited green skirt beneath which the presence of other skirts could be divined, forming an inflated globe of several layers which seemed to make still smaller her fine and graceful feet encased in white sandals. The prominent curves of her breast were concealed beneath a small yellow jacket with red flowers. It had velvet sleeves of a different color decorated with a double row of filigree buttons, the work of the Chueta silversmiths. A triple shining gold chain, terminated by a cross, hung over her breast, but so enormous were the links, that, had they not been hollow, they must have borne her down by their weight. Her black and glossy hair was parted over her forehead and concealed beneath a white kerchief tied under her chin, appearing again behind in long heavy braids tied with multi-colored ribbons falling to the hem of her skirt.

The girl, with her basket over her arm, stood looking at the strange sights, admiring the tall houses and the terraces of the cafés. She was pink and white, without the hard coppery roughness of the country women. Her features had the delicacy of an aristocratic and well cared for nun, the pale texture of milk and roses, lightened by the luminous reflection of her teeth and the timid glow of her eyes, under a kerchief resembling a monastic head-dress.

Impelled by curiosity Jaime approached the father and son whose backs were turned to the girl and who were absorbed in contemplation of the show window. It was a gun store. The two Ivizans were examining the weapons exposed with ardent eyes and gestures of adoration, as if worshipping miraculous idols. The boy pressed his eager, Moorish face against the glass as if he would thrust it through the pane.

"Fluxas—pa're, fluxas!" he cried with the excitement of one who meets an unexpected friend, calling his father's attention to the display of huge Lefaucheux pistols.

The admiration of the two was concentrated upon the unfamiliar weapons, which seemed to them marvelous works of art—the guns with invisible locks, repeating rifles, pistols with magazines which could hurl shot after shot. What wonderful things men invent! What treasures the rich enjoy! These lifeless weapons seemed to them animate creatures with malignant souls and limitless power. Doubtless such as these could kill automatically, without giving their owner the trouble of taking aim!

The image of Febrer, reflected in the glass, caused the father to turn suddenly.

"Don Jaime! Ah, Don Jaime!"

Such was his astonishment and surprise, and so great his joy, that, grasping Febrer's hands, he almost knelt before him, while he spoke in a tremulous voice. He had been killing time along the Paseo del Borne so as to reach Don Jaime's house about the time he should arise. Of course he knew that gentlemen always retire late! What a joy to see him! Here were his children—let them take a good look at the Señor! This was Don Jaime; this was the master! He had not seen him for ten years, but he would have recognized him among a thousand.

Febrer, disconcerted by the peasant and by the deferential curiosity of the two children who stood planted before him, could not recall his name. The worthy fellow guessed this slip of memory from Jaime's hesitant glance. Truly did he not recognize him? Pèp Arabi, from Iviza! Even this did not tell much, because on that little island there were but six or seven surnames, and Arabi was borne by a fourth part of the inhabitants. He would explain more clearly—Pèp of Can Mallorquí.

Febrer smiled. Ah, Can Mallorquí! A poor predio in Iviza, a farm where he had passed a year when he was a boy, his sole inheritance from his mother. Can Mallorquí had not belonged to him for twelve years. He had sold it to Pèp, whose fathers and grandfathers had cultivated it. That was during the time when he still had money; but of what use was that land on a separate island to which he would never return? So with the geniality of a benevolent gran señor he had sold it to Pèp at a low figure, valuing it in accord with the traditional rents; and conceding easy terms for payment, sums which, when hard times pressed upon him, had often come as an unexpected joy. Years had passed since Pèp had satisfied the debt, and yet the good souls continued calling him master, and as they saw him now they experienced the sensation of one who is in the presence of a superior being.

Pèp Arabi introduced his family. The girl was the elder, and was called Margalida; quite a little woman, although but seventeen! The boy, who was almost a man, was thirteen. He wished to be a farmer like his father and grandfathers, but Pèp had determined that the boy should enter the Seminary at Iviza since he was clever at his letters. His lands he would hold for some good hard-working youth who might marry Margalida. Many young men of the island were already chasing after her, and as soon as they returned the season for the festeigs, the traditional courtship, would begin, so that she could choose a husband. Pepet was destined for a higher calling; he would become a priest and after singing his first mass he would join a regiment or embark for America, as had done many other Ivizans who made much money and sent it home to their fathers with which to buy lands on the island. Ah, Don Jaime, and how time passes! He had seen the señor, still a mere child, when he spent that summer with his mother at Can Mallorquí. Pèp had taught him to use the gun, and to shoot his first birds. "Does your lordship remember?" It was about the time that Pèp married, while his parents were still alive. Since then they had only met once in Palma, when they arranged the sale of the property (a great favor which he would never forget) and now, when he presented himself again, he was almost an old man, with children as tall as himself.

As he talked of his journey the rustic displayed his strong teeth in mischievous smiles. It was a wild adventure of which his friends there in Iviza would talk a long time! He had always been of a roving and venturesome disposition—a vicious habit formed when he was a soldier. The master of a small trading vessel, a great friend of his, had picked up a cargo for Majorca, and had invited him just for a joke to come along. But it was risky to joke with him. As soon as the idea was suggested he accepted. The youngsters had never been in Majorca; in the entire parish of San José, in which he lived, there were not a dozen persons who had seen the capital. Many of them had visited America; one had been to Australia; some neighbor women talked of their trips to Algeria with smugglers in their feluccas; but no one ever came to Majorca, and with good reason! "They don't like us here, Don Jaime; they stare at us as if we were strange animals; they think we are savages, as if we are not all the children of God." And here he and his children had been subjected to the gaze of the curious throughout the whole morning just as if they were Moors. Ten hours of sailing on a magnificent sea! The girl had a basket of lunch for the three of them! They would return tomorrow at break of day, but before sailing he wished to speak to the master on a matter of business.

Jaime made a gesture of surprise, and listened more attentively. Pèp expressed himself with a certain timidity, stumbling over his words. The almond trees were the greatest source of wealth on Can Mallorquí. Last year the crop had been good, and this year it did not look unpromising. It was being sold to the padrones, who were bringing it to Palma and Barcelona. He had planted nearly all his fields to almonds, and now he was thinking of clearing and cleaning off the stones from certain lands belonging to the señor, and of raising wheat on them—no more than enough for the use of his own family.

Febrer did not conceal his surprise. What lands did he mean? Did he really have anything left in Iviza? Pèp smiled. They were not lands exactly; it was a stony hill, a rocky promontory overhanging the sea, but he might cultivate it by terracing the steep slopes. On its crest was the Pirate's Tower—did not the señor remember? It was a fortification dating from the time of the corsairs. Don Jaime had scrambled up to it many times when a child, shouting like a young warrior, flourishing a cudgel of juniper wood, giving orders for the assault upon an imaginary army.

The señor, who had hoped for an instant in the discovery of a forgotten estate, the last one of which he might be the real owner, smiled sadly. Ah! the Pirate's Tower! He remembered it. A bold limestone cliff, in the crevices of which sprung up bushes and shrubs, the refuge and sustenance of rabbits. The old stone fortress was a ruin, now slowly crumbling under the stress of time and wind. The stones were falling from their places, the corners of the merlons were wearing away. When Can Mallorquí was sold the tower had not been included in the contract, possibly through oversight because it seemed worthless. Pèp could do as he liked with it, Don Jaime assured him. Probably he would never return to the place, forgotten since the days of his youth.

When the peasant spoke of future remuneration, Don Jaime silenced him with the gesture of a gran señor. Then he glanced at the girl. She was very pretty; she looked like a señorita in disguise; the young fellows on the island must be wild over her. The father smiled, proud, yet disturbed by this praise. "Come, girl, what should you say to the master?" He spoke to her as if she were a child, and she, with lowered eyes, her face flushed, fingering a corner of her apron, stammered a few words in the Ivizan dialect: "No, I am not pretty. I am at your lordship's service."

Febrer brought the interview to a close, telling Pèp and his children to go to his house. The peasant knew Antonia, and the old woman would be very glad to see him. They must eat with her whatever—whatever there was to be had. He would see them again about sunset when he returned from Valldemosa. "Good-bye, Pèp! Good-bye, children!"

He made a signal with his cane to a driver seated on the box of a Majorcan carriage, a light vehicle mounted upon four slender wheels, with a cheerful canopy of white canvas, and drove toward Valldemosa and the wealthy Jewess whose dowry was to recoup his fortune.

CHAPTER II
BARTERING THE ANCESTRAL NAME

Having reached the outskirts of Palma and the open vernal fields, Jaime Febrer repented of his present way of existence. He had not been beyond the confines of Palma for a year, and he had been spending his afternoons in the cafés on the Paseo del Borne and his nights in the gambling hall of the Casino. It had never occurred to him to go forth where he might see the fields clad in tender green, the waters murmuring in the acequias; the soft blue sky dotted with white, fleecy islets, the dark green hills where stood the windmills swinging their arms upon the summits, the abrupt sierras forming a rose-colored background to a landscape which everywhere smiled and whispered sweetly, as in the days when, it astounded the ancient navigators, causing them to name Majorca "the Fortunate Isle"! When, thanks to his marriage, he should acquire a fortune, and could redeem the fine estate of Son Febrer, he would spend a part of the year there, as his forefathers had done, leading the healthy, rural life of a gran señor, munificent and honored.

The horses were going at topmost speed and the carriage whirled past a string of peasants trudging along the road returning from the city. There were slender brown women wearing over their braids and white rebocillos broad straw hats with streamers and sprays of wild flowers; men dressed in striped drill, the so-called Majorcan cloth, their hats stuck on the backs of their heads like black or gray nimbuses around their shaven faces.

Febrer recalled the characteristics of the road although he had not passed over it for many years. He was like a stranger returning to the island after a dimly remembered visit. Farther on the road forked; one branch leading to Valldemosa and the other to Soller... Ah! Soller... Scenes of his boyhood rushed through his memory! Every year, in a carriage like this, the Febrer family used to journey to Soller where they owned an old structure with a spacious zaguán, the House of the Moon, so named on account of a hemisphere of stone having eyes and nose, representing the luminary of night which adorned the upper part of the portalón.

They habitually went early in May. When the carriage rolled along a narrow pass high up in the sierra, the little Jaime would shout with joy as he beheld, lying at his feet, the valley of Soller, the Garden of Hesperrides of the island. The mountains, dark with their pine trees, and dotted with little white houses, lifted their crests bound about in turbans of vapor. Below, surrounding the village and stretching down the valley as far as the sea, were orange orchards. Spring burst over the happy land with an explosion of color and perfume. Wild flowers grew among the rocks; branches of the trees were decked in waving green; poor habitations of the peasants concealed ruinous poverty beneath canopies of climbing roses. Rustic families from towns far and near gathered at the fiesta of Soller: the women in white rebocillos, heavy mantillas, and with gold buttons on their sleeves; the men in gay waistcoats, homespun woolen cloaks, and hats with colored bands. Concertinas whined, calling to the dance; glasses of native sweet wine and of wine from Bañalbufar passed from hand to hand. It was joy and peace after a thousand years of piracy and of war against the infidel peoples of the Mediterranean; the joyful commemoration of the victory won by the peasants of Soller over a fleet of Turkish corsairs in the sixteenth century.

In the port, the fishermen, masquerading as Mussulmans, or as Christian warriors, held a sham naval battle on their little boats, firing off blunderbusses and flourishing swords, or pursuing one another up and down the roads along the shore. In the church a festival was celebrated to comemmorate the miraculous victory, and Jaime, seated in a place of honor beside his mother, thrilled with emotion listening to the priest just as he did on reading an interesting tale in his uncle's library in the second story of the great house in Palma.

The inhabitants of Soller had risen in arms against Alaró and Buñola on learning from a boat which had come over from Iviza that a fleet of twenty-two Turkish galiots with many galleys was heading for their coast, threatening this the richest town of the island. Seventeen hundred Turks and Africans, formidable pirates, attracted by the riches of the town, and drawn on by the desire to attack a convent of nuns, where beautiful young women of noble families lived retired from the world, had landed upon the beach. Divided into two columns, one marched against the Christians who had gone out to resist them, while the other, making a detour, entered the town, capturing youths and maidens, pillaging churches and killing the priests. The Christians realized the extremity of the situation. Before them were a thousand advancing Turks; behind them the village in the hands of looters, their families subjected to violence and outrage calling to them in despair. They hesitated only a moment. A sergeant from Soller, a valorous veteran of the army of Charles V in the wars of Germany and against the Grand Turk, urged them on to attack the enemy. They fell upon their knees and invoked the Apostle St. James, and then attacked with their fire-locks, arquebuses, lances and axes, devoutly expecting a miracle. The Turks faltered; then turned their backs. Their terrible chieftain, Suffarais, Captain General of the sea, an ancient Turk of great obesity, famous for his courage and daring, exhorted them in vain. At the head of his body-guard, a squadron of negroes, he attacked, scimitar in hand, felling a circle of corpses around him, but at last a native of Soller pierced his breast with a lance, and as he fell the invaders fled, even forsaking their standard. Then a new enemy barred their way. While trying to reach the coast and take refuge aboard their ships, a band of robbers that had witnessed the battle from their caves in the crags, seeing the Turks in retreat, came out to meet them, firing their flintlocks and brandishing their daggers. They had with them a troop of mastiffs, ferocious companions of their infamous career, and these animals, according to the chroniclers of the epoch, "gave evidence of the excellence of the Majorcan breed." The troops under the command of the veteran sergeant turned back to the desolated village from which the looters fled as best they could in the direction of the sea, or fell decapitated in the streets.

The priest became exalted as he related the victorious defense, attributing the greater part of the success to the Queen of Heaven and to the Apostle warrior St. James. Then he eulogized Captain Angelats, the hero of the day, the Cid of Soller, and also the valiant doñas of Can Tamany, two women on an estate near the village who had been surprised by three Turks greedy to satiate their carnal appetites after long abstinence on the solitudes of the sea. The valiant doñas, arrogant and strong, as are all good peasants, neither cried out nor fled at sight of these three pirates, enemies both of God and of the saints. With the bar used for fastening the door they killed one of them and then locked themselves up in the house. Hurling the corpse out of a window upon the assailants, they broke the head of another, and they drove the third off with stones, like true descendants of the Majorcan slingers. Ah, the brave doñas, the forceful women of Can Tamany! The good people worshipped them as sainted heroines of the interminable war against the infidel, and they laughed tenderly over the deeds of these Joans of Arc, thinking with pride how perilous was the Mussulmans' task of supplying their harems with new flesh.

Then the preacher, following traditional custom, brought his harangue to a close by naming the families who had taken part in the battle; a list of a hundred, to which the rural audience listened attentively, each nodding his head with satisfaction when the name of one of his forefathers was pronounced. This lengthy enumeration seemed short to many, who made a gesture of protest when the preacher ceased. "There were others whom he did not mention," murmured the peasants whose names had not been read. All desired to be descendants of the warriors of Captain Angelats.

When the fiestas ended and Soller recovered its tranquillity, young Jaime used to spend his days racing through the orange orchards with Antonia, old Mammy Antonia of the present, who was then a fresh young woman with white teeth, full bust, and vigorous tread, widowed a few months after her marriage and followed by the ardent glances of all the peasantry. Together they went to the port, a peaceful, solitary basin, its entrance half concealed by a curving rocky arm of the sea. Only now and then the masts of some sailing vessel coming to take on a load of oranges for Marseilles, appeared before this blue town with its surrounding waters. Flocks of old gulls, enormous as hens, fluttered with evolutions like a contredanse upon its glossy surface. The fishermen's boats came in at sunset, and beneath the sheds along the shore enormous fishes were left hanging, their tails sweeping the ground, bleeding like oxen; together with rays and octopuses from which dripped a white gelatinous slime like drops of palpitating crystal.

Jaime loved this quiet port and its brooding solitude with religious veneration. Then he recalled the miraculous stories with which his mother used to lull him to sleep—the great miracle wrought upon these waters by a servant of God to flout the hardened sinners. Saint Raymond of Peñafort, a virtuous and austere monk, became indignant with King Jaime of Majorca who was basely enamored of a certain lady, Doña Berenguela, and who remained deaf to holy counsels. The friar determined to abandon this recalcitrant, but the king sought to prevent his departure by laying an embargo upon all ships and vessels. Then the saint descended to the lonely port of Soller, spread his mantle upon the waves, stepped upon it, and sailed away to the coasts of Catalonia. Mammy Antonia had also told him of this miracle, but in Majorcan verse, in a primitive romance that breathed the simple confidence of centuries which clung trustfully to the marvelous. The saint, having embarked on his mantle, set up his staff for a mast and his hood for a sail; then a wind from heaven blew upon the strange vessel; in a few hours the servant of the Lord sailed from Majorca to Barcelona; the lookout at Montjuich announced with a flag the apparition of the prodigious craft, the bells of Seo rang, and the merchants rushed down to the sea-wall to welcome the sainted voyager.

Little Febrer, his curiosity aroused by these marvels, was eager to hear more, and his companion called the old fishermen who showed him the rock where the saint had stood while invoking the aid of Almighty God before setting sail. An inland mountain which could be seen from the port had the form of a hooded friar. Along the coast, at an inaccessible point, a cliff seen only by fishermen resembled a monk kneeling at prayer. These prodigies had been formed by God, according to the simple souls, to perpetuate the memory of the famous miracle.

Jaime still recalled the thrills of emotion with which he had listened to these tales. Ah, Soller! The epoch of holy innocence in which he had first opened his eyes upon life to the accompaniment of miraculous stories and commemorations of heroic struggles! The House of the Moon he had lost forever, and also the credulity and the innocence of youth. Only memories lingered. More than twenty years had rolled away since he had pressed foot on the paths of forgotten Soller; it now came back to his mind with all the smiling fancies of childhood.

The carriage reached the fork of the road taking the route to Valldemosa, and all his memories seemed left behind, motionless by the roadside, growing hazy in the distance.

The way to Valldemosa held no memory of the past. He had been over it only twice, after coming to manhood, having gone with friends to see the cells of the Cartuja—a once renowned Carthusian convent. He recalled the farmers' olive trees along the roadside, aged trees of strange, fantastic shapes which had served as inspiration for many artists, and he thrust his head through a window to look at them again. The ground was rising; here began the stony, unirrigated ground, the lowest of the foothills. The road wound steeply among the ancient groves. The first olive trees now passed before the carriage windows.

Febrer had seen them, had often spoken of them, and yet he felt the sensation of something extraordinary, as if looking at them for the first time. They were black, with enormous, knotted, open trunks, swelling with great excrescences, and the foliage was sparse. These were olive trees which had stood for centuries, which had never been pruned, in which age robbed the sap from the branches to distend the trunk with the protuberances of a slow and painful circulation. The region looked like the deserted studio of a sculptor littered with thousands of shapeless bulks, with monsters scattered over the ground, upon a green carpet dotted with bluebells and marguerites.

One of the trees resembled an enormous toad crouching ready to spring, holding a spray of leaves in its mouth; another was a great coiled boa with an olive crest upon his head. There were trunks open like ogives, through the orifices of which shone the blue sky; monstrous serpents coiled in groups like the spirals of a solomonic column; gigantic negroes, heads down and hands on the ground, the roots like fingers thrust deep into the soil, their feet in the air, grotesque stems with bunches of leaves springing from them. Some, vanquished by the centuries, were lying on the ground, sustained by forked branches, like old men trying to lift themselves with the aid of crutches.

It seemed as if a tempest had swept these fields, overthrowing and twisting everything out of shape, and afterward turning them to stone to hold this work of desolation under a spell forever. Some trees standing erect, and having softer outlines, seemed to have feminine faces and figures. They were Byzantine maidens, with tiaras of dainty leaves and trailing vestments of wood. Others were ferocious idols with protruding eyes and long flowing beards; fetiches of gloomy, barbaric cults capable of checking primitive humanity in its progress, forcing it to its knees with emotion as if at a meeting with divinity. In the calm of this frenzied, but motionless distortion, in the solitude of these fields peopled by startling and eternal specters, birds were singing, wild flowers crept to the foot of the worm-eaten trunks, and ants came and went, an infinite rosary, burrowing in the ancient roots like indefatigable miners.

Gustave Doré, according to report, had sketched his most fantastic conceptions in these olive orchards, steeped in the mysteries of centuries. Recollection of this artist recalled to Jaime's mind others more celebrated who had also passed along this road, and had lived and suffered in Valldemosa.

Twice he had visited the Cartuja merely to see the places immortalized by the sad and unhealthy love of a pair of famous persons. His grandfather had often told him of "the Frenchwoman" of Valldemosa and her companion "the musician."

One day the inhabitants of Majorca and the people of the Peninsula who had taken refuge on the island, fleeing from the horrors of civil war, saw a strange couple disembark, accompanied by a boy and girl. It was in 1838. When their luggage was landed the islanders were astounded by an enormous piano, an Erard instrument of which but few were to be seen in those days. The piano was held in the custom house while the tangle of certain administrative scruples was unraveled, and the travelers sought lodging at an inn, and later rented the estate of Son Vent, in the environs of Palma. The man seemed to be ill; he was younger than the woman, but wasted by suffering, pale, with the transparent pallor of the consecrated wafer, his limpid eyes glowing with fever, his narrow chest shaken by harsh and continuous coughing. A fine, silky beard shaded his cheeks; a black, shaggy head of hair like a lion's mane crowned his forehead and hung down behind in a cascade of curls. She was strong and vigorous and did all the work of the house like a good bourgeoise more willing than skilled in such labors. She played with her children like a girl, and her kindly, smiling face clouded only when she heard the cough of the "beloved invalid." An atmosphere of exotism, of irregular existence, of protest against conventional custom, seemed to surround this vagabond family. She dressed in fantastic gowns, and wore a silver dagger thrust in her hair, a romantic ornament which scandalized the pious Majorcan dames. Besides, she did not go to mass in the city, nor make calls; she did not go out of her house except to play with her children or to entice the poor consumptive out into the sunshine, leaning on her arm. The children were as extraordinary as the mother. The girl went dressed like a boy that she might run with greater freedom.

Soon island curiosity ferreted out the names of these strangers of alarming peculiarities. She was a French woman, a writer of books; Aurore Dupin, the illustrious Baroness Dudevant separated from her husband, who made a world-wide reputation through her novels, which she signed with a masculine given name, and the surname of a political assassin, George Sand. The man was a Polish musician, of delicate constitution, who seemed to leave a portion of his existence in each one of his works, and who felt himself dying at twenty-nine years of age. He was called Frederic François Chopin. The children belonged to the novelist, who was about thirty-five.

Majorcan society, bound up in its traditional preoccupations, like a mollusk in its shell, and hostile by instinct to impious novelties from Paris, waxed indignant over this scandal. They were not married! And she wrote novels which startled respectable people by their audacity! Feminine curiosity wished to read them, but only Don Horacio Febrer, Jaime's grandfather, received books in Majorca, and the small volumes of "Indiana" and "Lelia," belonging to him, passed from hand to hand without being understood by their readers. A married woman who wrote books and lived with a man who was not her husband! Doña Elvira, Jaime's grandmother, a señora from Mexico, whose portrait he had so often seen, and whom he imagined always dressed in white with her eyes turned heavenward and her gilded harp between her knees, called upon the retiring woman at Son Vent. She enjoyed overwhelming the ladies of the island who did not know French with the superiority of the foreigner; she listened to the novelist's lyric eulogies of the originality of this African landscape, with its little white houses, spiny cacti, slender palms, and aged olive trees, in such striking contrast to the harmonious order of the broad fields of France. Then Doña Elvira, in the social gatherings at Palma, defended the authoress with fervor—a poor emotional woman, whose everyday life was more like that of a Sister of Charity, more full of care and sorrow than of passion and pleasure. The grandfather took it upon himself to intervene and prohibit his wife's calls in order to quiet neighborhood gossip.

The scandalous pair was completely ostracized. While the children were frolicking like young savages in the fields with their mother, the sick man sat at his dormitory window, or peeped out of his doorway, seeking a ray of sunshine. In the small hours of the night came the visit of the muse, and the man, sick and melancholy, seated himself at the piano, where, coughing and moaning, out of the bitterness of his spirit he improvised his voluptuous music.

The owner of the estate of Son Vent, a bourgeois of the city, ordered the foreigners to move, as if they were a band of gypsies. The pianist was a consumptive and the landlord did not wish to have his property infected. Where should they go? To return to their own country would be difficult since it was in the middle of winter, and Chopin trembled like a forsaken bird, thinking of the chill of Paris. He loved the island, despite the inhospitable people, because of the suavity of its climate. The Cartuja of Valldemosa offered itself as their sole refuge, a building devoid of architectural beauty, with no other charm than that of its medieval antiquity, situated in the mountains with pine-covered slopes, having, like delicate curtains tempering the sun's ardor, plantations of almond and palm, through the branches of which the eye could make out the green plain and the distant sea. It was a monument almost in ruins, a monastery suggesting melodrama, gloomy and mysterious, in the cloisters of which camped vagabonds and beggars. To enter it one must cross the old cemetery of the friars with its graves disturbed by the roots of forest trees thrusting bones up to the very surface. On moonlight nights a white phantom stalked through the cloisters, the shade of a wicked friar who haunted the place of his misdeeds, while awaiting the hour of redemption.

Thither went the fugitives one stormy winter day, buffeted by wind and rain, traveling along the same route which Febrer now followed, but by an old road which barely deserved the name. The wagons of the caravan climbed, as George Sand said, "with one wheel on the mountain and the other in the bed of a gully." The musician, wrapped in his cape, sat trembling and coughing under the canvas cover, throbbing with pain as the vehicle jolted over the rough ground. The novelist herself followed on foot over the worst places, leading her children by the hand on this vagabond journey.

They spent the entire winter in the isolation of the Cartuja. She, wearing Turkish slippers, the little dagger always thrust into her ill-combed hair, courageously did the cooking with the assistance of a young peasant girl who took advantage of every opportunity to gorge herself with the dainties intended for the "beloved invalid." The urchins of Valldemosa stoned the little French children, calling them Moors and disbelievers in God; the women cheated the mother when they sold her provisions, and moreover they dubbed her "the witch." They all made the sign of the cross when they met these "gypsies" who dared to live in a cell at the monastery, neighbors to the dead, in constant communication with the spectral friar who stalked through the cloister.

By day, while the invalid was resting, George Sand prepared the broth, and with her slender, white, artistic hands, helped the maidservant to peel the vegetables; then, with, her two children she would race down to the abrupt, tree-covered beach of Miramar where Ramon Lull had established his school of oriental study. Only at the approach of night did her real existence begin.

Then the great gloomy cloister vibrated with mysterious music which seemed to float in from afar through the heavy walls. It was Chopin, bending over the piano composing his Nocturnes. The novelist, by the light of the candle was writing "Spiridion," the story of the monk who finally forsook his faith; but frequently she laid aside her work to rush to the musician's side and give him medicine, alarmed at the frequency of his cough. On moonlight nights, tempted by the thrill of the mysterious, in a voluptuosity of fear, she stole out into the cloister where the darkness was pierced by the milky spots of the window panes. Nobody!... Then she would sit down in the monks' cemetery vainly awaiting the apparition of the ghostly friar to enliven her monotonous existence with a novel adventure.

One night during Carnival season Cartuja was invaded by "Moors." They were young men from Palma, who, after having overrun the town disguised as Berbers, thought of the "French woman," ashamed, no doubt, at the isolation in which she was held by the townspeople. They arrived at midnight, with their songs and guitars breaking the mysterious calm of the monastery, frightening away the birds perched in the ruins. In one corner of the cell they danced Spanish dances which Chopin watched attentively with his fever-lighted eyes, while the novelist flitted from group to group, experiencing the simple joy of the bourgeoise at finding herself not forgotten.

This was her single happy night in Majorca. Afterward, with the return of spring, the "beloved invalid" felt relief and they began a leisurely return to Paris. They were birds of passage, who, after wintering on this "Fortunate Isle," left no other trace than an undying tradition.

Jaime could not even find out with certainty which room she had occupied. The changes which had taken place in the monastery had obliterated every vestige. Many families from Palma now spent the summer at Cartuja, transforming the cells into handsome apartments, and each one wished it to be understood that his was the one which had been occupied by George Sand, she who had been defamed and ostracized by their grandmothers. Febrer had visited the monastery with a nonagenarian, who had been one of the youths that had gone dressed as Moors to serenade the Frenchwoman. He could not remember any details nor could he even recognize her room.

Don Horacio's grandson experienced a kind of retrospective affection for that extraordinary woman. He imagined her as she appeared in her youthful pictures, with expressionless face and deep enigmatic eyes beneath fluffy hair, with no other decoration than a rose over one temple. Poor George Sand! Love had been for her like the ancient Sphinx: each time that she ventured to interrogate it she had felt its merciless blow upon her heart. She had tasted all love's abnegations and perversities. The capricious woman of the Venetian nights, the unfaithful companion of de Musset, was the same nurse who cooked the meals and prepared the cough syrups for the dying Chopin in the solitudes of Valldemosa. If only Jaime had known a woman like that, a woman who combined within herself the natures of a thousand women, with all their infinite feminine variety of sweetness and cruelty!... To be loved by a superior woman upon whom he could impose his masculine will, and who at the same time would inspire him with respect for her was his dream.

Febrer sat as if stupefied by this thought, staring at the landscape without seeing it. Then he smiled ironically, as if realizing his own insignificance. The object of his journey flashed across his mind, and he pitied himself. He, who had been dreaming of a grand, unselfish, extraordinary love, was on his way to sell himself, offering his hand and his name to a woman whom he had barely seen, to contract an alliance which would scandalize the whole island... worthy end to a useless, unbridled life!

The emptiness of his existence was revealed to him clearly now, stripped of the deceptions of personal vanity, as he had never seen it before. The nearness of his sacrifice stirred him to re-live the past in his memory, as if seeking justification for his present acts. What purpose had been served by his passing through the world?

He returned again to the childhood recollections which had been evoked on the road to Soller. He imagined himself in the venerable Febrer mansion with his parents and his grandfather. He was an only son. His mother, a pale lady of melancholy beauty, had been left an invalid as the result of his birth. Don Horacio lived in the second story, in the company of an old servant, as if he were a guest in the house, mingling with the family or isolating himself according to caprice. Jaime, in the midst of his childhood recollections, beheld his grandfather's figure in prominent relief. Never had he surprised a smile on that white-bearded face, which contrasted with his dark and imperious eyes. The members of the household were prohibited from ascending to his apartments. No one had ever seen him except when in street dress, which was always scrupulously neat. His grandson, who was the only one allowed in his dormitory at all hours, found him early in the morning in his blue coat with high, pointed collar and a black stock folded around his neck, ornamented with an enormous pearl. He maintained this correct old-time elegance until overtaken by illness. Whenever sickness compelled him to keep his bed he would give orders to his servant not to admit even his son.

Jaime used to pass many hours seated at his grandfather's feet, listening to his tales, and at the same time awed by the enormous number of books which overflowed the bookcases and littered the tables and chairs. He found him ever the same, wearing his coat lined with red silk, which seemed changeless, but which was renewed, nevertheless, once every six months. The seasons brought no other variation than that of converting the velvet winter waistcoat into another of embroidered silk. His pride was centered chiefly upon his linen and his books. He ordered from abroad dozens of shirts which frequently lay in the bottom of the clothes press forgotten and yellowing and never worn. The booksellers of Paris sent him enormous packages of recent volumes, and in view of his unceasing orders added "Bookseller" to the address, a title which Don Horacio displayed with playful satisfaction.

He talked to the last of the Febrers with grandfatherly kindness, trying to make him understand his tales, despite the fact that he was sparing of words and showed little patience in his relations with the rest of the family. He told of his journeys to Paris, and to London, sometimes in a sailing vessel as far as Marseilles and then by post-chaise; again by steam-engines along iron roadways, great inventions the infancy of which he had seen. He told of society at the court of Louis Philippe; of the great beginnings of the romanticist movement in which he had taken part; and he told of the barricades thrown up in the streets which he had watched from his room, not mentioning that, at the same time, his arm was encircling the waist of a grisette peeping out of the window beside him. His grandson, he would say, had been born in a glorious epoch, the best of all. Don Horacio recollected the disagreements with his terrible father that had compelled him to travel through Europe; that caballero who had gone out to meet King Ferdinand, to ask him for the reëstablishment of ancient usages, and who blessed his sons, saying: "May God make you a good inquisitor!"

Then he would display before Jaime great books containing views of splendid capitals in which he had lived, and which to the boy seemed like cities beheld in a dream. Sometimes he would remain lost in contemplation of the picture of "the grandmother with the harp," his wife, the interesting Doña Elvira, the same canvas which now hung in the reception hall among the other ladies of the family. He did not seem moved; he maintained the same grave demeanor which accompanied the jests to which he was addicted and the coarse words with which he sprinkled his conversations, but he said in a somewhat tremulous voice:

"Your grandmother was a great lady, with the soul of an angel, an artist. I seemed like a barbarian beside her. She was one of our family, but she came from Mexico to marry me. Her father was a sea-faring man, and he stayed over there with the insurgents. There is no one in all our race who resembles her."

At half past eleven in the morning he would dismiss his grandson, and putting on his tall hat, black silk in winter and beaver in summer, he would sally forth to take a stroll along the streets of Palma, always through the same locality and along identical pavements, rain or shine, insensible to cold and to heat, wearing his frock coat in every weather, continuing on his way with the regularity of a clock automaton which steps out, travels his little course, and then conceals himself at the stroke of certain hours.

Only once in thirty years had he varied his route through the white and deserted sunny streets. One morning he had heard a woman's voice issuing from the interior of a house:

"Atlota—twelve o'clock; Don Horacio is passing. Put on the rice."

He turned toward the door, saying with lordly gravity:

"I'm no wench's clock!" He jerked out the abusive words without sacrificing any of his dignity. From that day he changed his route to disappoint those whom he perceived had come to depend on his punctuality.

Sometimes he talked to his grandson about the ancient greatness of the house. Geographical discoveries had ruined the Febrers. The Mediterranean was no longer the highway to the Orient. The Portuguese and Spanish of the other sea had discovered new routes and the Majorcan ships lay rotting in idleness. There were no longer battles with pirates. The Holy Order of Malta was now only an honorable distinction. A brother of his father, knight commander at Valetta when Bonaparte conquered the island, had come to spend his last days in Palma with only the meagre pension of a half-pay officer. It had been two centuries since the Febrers, forgotten on the sea where there was no longer any commerce, and where only poor padrones and fishermen's sons now made war, had given themselves up to investing their name with a splendrous luxury, which gradually ruined them. The grandfather had witnessed the times of genuine seigniory, when to be a butifarra in Majorca was something which the people rated between God and caballeros. The arrival of a Febrer in the world was an event which was discussed throughout the entire city. The great parturient dame remained secluded in the palace forty days, and during all this time the doors were open, the zaguán filled with vehicles, the whole retinue of servants lined up in the ante-chamber, the salons filled with callers, the tables covered with sweets, cakes, and refreshments. Days of the week were set apart for the reception of each social class. Some were only for the butifarras, the aristocracy of the aristocrats, privileged houses, renowned families, all united by the relationship of continual inter-marriage; other days for caballeros, traditional nobility who were looked down upon by the former without knowing why; next the mossons were received, an inferior class, but in familiar contact with the grandees, the intellectual people of the epoch, doctors, lawyers, and scriveners, who loaned their services to illustrious families.

Don Horacio recalled the splendor of these receptions. The people of the olden time knew how to do things in the grand way.

"It was when your father was born," he said to his grandson, "that the last fiesta was held in this house. I paid a confectioner on the Paseo del Borne eight hundred Majorcan pounds for sweets, cakes, and refreshments."

Jaime actually remembered less about his father than about his grandfather. In his memory he was a sweet and sympathetic figure, but somewhat dim. When he thought of him he recalled only a soft, light beard like his own, a bald forehead, a happy smile, and eyeglasses which glittered as he bent over. It was said that when a boy he had a love affair with his cousin Juana, that austere señora whom everybody called the "Pope-ess," who lived like a nun, and who enjoyed enormous riches, making prodigal donations in former times to the pretender Don Carlos, and now to the ecclesiastics who surrounded her.

The rupture between his father and Juana the Popess was, no doubt, the reason why she held herself aloof from this branch of the family and treated Jaime with hostile frigidity.

His father had been an officer in the Navy, in accordance with family tradition. He was in the war on the Pacific coast of South America; he was a lieutenant on one of the frigates that bombarded Callao, and, as if he only desired to give a proof of his valor, he immediately retired from the service. Then he married a señorita of Palma, of meager fortune, whose father was military governor of the island of Iviza. The Popess Juana, talking with Jaime one day, had tried to wound him by saying in her cold voice and with her haughty mien: "Your mother was noble; of a family of caballeros—but she was not a butifarra like ourselves!"

The early years of his life, when Jaime first began to take notice of the things about him, were passed without seeing his father save during hasty trips to Majorca. He was a progressive, and the reform party had made him a deputy. Later, when Amadis of Savoy was proclaimed king, this revolutionary monarch, execrated and deserted by the traditional nobility, had been compelled to turn to new historic names to form his court. The butifarra, Febrer, through a party demand, became a high palace functionary. When he insisted that his wife should remove to Madrid she refused to abandon the island. She go to the Court! How about his son? Don Horacio, steadily growing more slender and weak, but ever erect in his eternal new frock coat, continued taking his daily stroll, adjusting his life to the ticking of the clock of the ayuntamiento. An old time liberal, a great admirer of Martinez de la Rosa for his verses and the diplomatic elegance of his cravats, made a wry face when he read the newspapers and the letters from his son. What was all this leading to?

During the short period of the Republic the father returned to the island, considering his career ended. The Popess Juana, despite the fact of their relationship, refused to recognize him. She was much occupied during that epoch. She made journeys to the Peninsula; it was said that she turned over enormous sums to the partisans of Don Carlos who were carrying on the war in Catalonia and the northern provinces. Let no one mention Jaime Febrer, the old time naval officer in her presence! She was a genuine butifarra, a defender of their traditions, and she was making sacrifices in order that Spain might be governed by gentlemen. Her cousin was worse than a Chueta; he was a shirtless beggar. According to the gossips bitterness for certain deceptions in the past which she could not forget was mingled with this hatred of his political professions.

On the restoration of the Bourbons, this progressive, he who had been a palatine under Amadis, became a republican and a conspirator. He made frequent journeys; he received cipher letters from Paris; he went to Minorca to visit the squadron anchored in Port Mahon, and taking advantage of his former official friendships, he catechized his companions, planning an uprising of the navy. He threw into these revolutionary enterprises the adventurous ardor of the Febrers of old, the same cool daring, until he died suddenly in Barcelona, far from his kindred.

The grandfather received the news with impassive gravity, but the neighbor women of Palma who awaited his passing along the streets to set their rice over the fire, saw him no more. Eighty-six! He had strolled enough. He had seen enough of this world. He retired to the second story, where he admitted no one but his grandson. When his relatives came to see him he preferred to go down to the reception hall, in spite of his debility, correctly attired, wearing his new frock coat, the two white triangles of his collar peeping above the folds of his stock, always freshly shaven, his side whiskers carefully combed and his toupee brilliant with pomatum. At last came a day when he could not leave his bed, and the grandson found him between the sheets, looking as usual, still wearing his fine batiste shirt, the stock which his servant changed for him every day, and the flowered silk waistcoat. When a call from his daughter-in-law was announced Don Horacio made a gesture of annoyance.

"Jaimito,—the frock coat. It is a lady, and she must be received with decency."

This operation was repeated when the doctor came, or when the few callers he deigned to receive were admitted. He must maintain himself "under arms" until his last moment, as he had been seen all his life.

One afternoon he called with a weak voice to his grandson who sat by a window reading a book of travel. The boy might retire. He wished to be alone. Jaime left the room, and so the grandfather was able to die in solitude, free from the torment of having to pay attention to the neatness of his appearance, with no witnesses to the grimaces and contortions of the last agony.

Febrer and his mother being left alone, the boy grew eager for independence. His imagination was filled with the adventures and voyages of which he had read in his grandfather's library and he was inspired with the deeds of his forefathers immortalized in family history. He yearned to become a mariner or a warrior, like his father and like the majority of his ancestors. His mother opposed him with an agony of dread which turned her cheeks pale and her lips blue. The last Febrer leading a life of danger far from her side! No! There had been heroes enough in the family. He must be a señor on the island, a gentleman of tranquil life who would raise a family to perpetuate the name he bore.

Jaime yielded to the prayers of his mother, that eternal invalid, in whom the slightest opposition seemed to precipitate the danger of death. Since she did not wish him to be a sea-faring man he must study for another career. He must live as did the other youths of his age with whom he mingled in the lecture halls of the Institute. At sixteen he set sail for the Peninsula. His mother wished that he should be a lawyer in order that he might disentangle the family fortune, burdened and oppressed with mortgages and other indebtedness.

The luggage with which he started was enormous—enough to furnish a house—and likewise his pocket was well lined. A Febrer must not live like any poor student! First he went to Valencia, his mother believing that city less dangerous for the young. For the next course of lectures he passed on to Barcelona, and thus several years were spent flitting from one University to another, according to the notions of the professors and their ready connivance with the students. He made no great progress in his career. He sneaked through certain courses by the cool audacity with which he talked of things of which he knew nothing, and passed examinations by some lucky chance. In others he flunked completely. His mother accepted his explanations in good faith on his return to Majorca. She consoled him, advising him not to exert himself too much over his studies, and she railed against the injustice of the times. Her implacable enemy, the Popess Juana, was right. These were no times for gentlemen; war had been declared against them; all manner of injustices were committed to keep them in the background.

Jaime enjoyed a certain popularity in the clubs and cafés of Barcelona and Valencia where he gambled. They called him "the Majorcan of the ounces," because his mother remitted his gold in gold ounces, which rolled with scandalous glitter across the green tables. Adding to the prestige given by this extravagance was his strange title of butifarra, which caused a smile in the Peninsula, yet at the same time it evoked in the imagination a picture of feudal authority, accompanied with the rights of a sovereign lord in those distant islands.

Five years passed. Jaime was now a man, but he had not yet compassed the half of his studies. His fellow-students from the island, when they came home in summer, entertained their cronies in the cafés on the Paseo del Borne with stories of Febrer's adventures in Barcelona; how he was frequently seen on the streets with luxurious women clinging to his arm; how the rude people who frequented the gambling houses showed respect for the "Majorcan of the ounces" on account of his strength and courage; they told how, one night, he had laid hands on a certain bully, lifting him off his feet in his athletic arms, and hurling him out of the window. The peaceful Majorcans, on hearing this, smiled with local pride. He was a Febrer, a genuine Febrer! The island still produced valiant youths as of old!

Good Doña Purificación, Jaime's mother, experienced grave displeasure and at the same time maternal joy on hearing that a certain scandalous woman had followed her son to the island. She understood it, and she forgave her. A youth as attractive as her Jaime! But with her dresses and her habits the young woman disturbed the tranquil customs of the city; the staid families became indignant, and, Doña Purificación, making use of intermediaries, came to an understanding with her, giving her money on the condition that she should leave the island. At other vacation times the scandal was even greater. Jaime, who had gone to Son Febrer on a hunting trip, had an affair with a pretty peasant girl and was on the point of shooting a rustic swain who pretended to her hand. His rural love adventures helped him to pass his summer exile. He was a true Febrer, like his grandfather. The poor lady had known how to deal with that ever grave and dignified father-in-law who nevertheless chucked young peasant girls under the chin without losing his sedate and lordly frigidity. In the vicinity of the estate of Son Febrer were many youths who bore the features of Don Horacio, but his wife, the Mexican lady, poetic soul, lived above such vulgarities, while, with her, harp between her knees and her eyes dilated she recited Ossian's poems. The rustic beauties with their snowy rebocillos, their hanging braids, and white hempen sandals, attracted the immaculate and lordly Febrers with an irresistible force.

When Doña Purificación complained of the long hunting excursions which her son took throughout the island, he would stay in the city and spend the day in the garden, practising shooting with a pistol. He called his mother's attention to a sack lying in the shade of an orange tree.

"Do you see that? It is a quintal of powder. I shall not stop until I have used it all up."

Mammy Antonia was afraid to peep out of her kitchen windows, and the nuns who occupied a portion of the ancient palace showed their white hoods for an instant, and then hid themselves immediately like doves frightened by the continual popping.

The garden with its battlemented enclosure, contiguous to the sea wall, rang from morning till night with the sound of the detonations. The astonished birds flew away; green lizards crept over the cracked walls hiding in the shelter of the ivy; cats leaped along the paths in terror. The trees were very old, venerable as the palace itself; centenarian oranges with twisted trunks, leaning on the support of a circle of forked sticks to hold up their ancient limbs; gigantic magnolias with more wood than leaves; unfruitful palms lifting themselves into blue space, seeking the sea which they greeted above the merlons with the fluttering plumes of their crested heads.

The sun made the bark of the trees creak, and forgotten seeds on the ground burst forth; insects buzzing across the bars of light which shot through the foliage danced like golden sparks; ripe figs loosened from the branches fell with soft patter; in the distance rose the murmur of the sea lashing the rocks at the foot of the wall. This calm was broken only by

Febrer who continued firing his pistol. He had become a master shot. When he aimed at the figure sketched on the wall he lamented that it was not a man, some hated enemy whom he must needs exterminate. Bang! That ball pierced his heart! He smiled with satisfaction at seeing the bullet hole outlined on the very spot at which he had aimed. The noise of the shooting, the smoke of the powder, aroused in his imagination warlike fancies, stories of struggle and death in which he was always the victorious hero. Twenty years old and yet he had never fought a duel! He must have a fight with someone to prove his courage. It was a disgrace that he had no enemies, but he would try to make some when he returned to the Peninsula. Continuing these vagaries of his imagination, excited by the cracking detonations, he pretended an affair of honor. His adversary wounded him with the first shot and he fell. He still had his pistol in his hand; he must defend himself while stretched on the ground; and to the great scandal of his mother and of Mammy Antonia who thought him crazy as they peeped out of the window, he continued lying face downward shooting in this position, preparing for the time when he should be wounded.

When he returned to the Peninsula to continue his interminable studies, he went refreshed by the country life, sure of himself after his practice in the garden and eager to have the longed for duel with the first man who should give him the slightest pretext. But as he was a courteous person, incapable of unjust provocation, with manners that inspired respect from the insolent, time passed and the duel did not take place. His exuberant vitality, his impulsive strength, were consumed in dark adventures, of which his fellow students afterward told on the island with admiration.

While in Barcelona he received a telegram announcing that his mother was seriously ill. He was delayed two days before sailing; there was no boat ready. When he reached the island his mother was dead. Of the ancient family which he had seen in his childhood none remained. Only Mammy Antonia could recall the past.

Jaime was twenty-three when he found himself master of the Febrer fortune, and in absolute liberty. The fortune had been diminished by the ostentation of his ancestors and burdened with encumbrances. The Febrer house was big. It was like vessels which when wrecked and lost forever enrich the coast where they are dashed to pieces. The remains and spoils, upon which his ancestors would have looked with scorn, still represented a fortune. Jaime did not wish to think. He did not wish to know. He must live; he must see the world! So he gave up his studies. What need had he for law, and for Roman customs, and for ecclesiastical canons, in order to lead a gay existence? He knew enough. In reality, the most delightful of his accomplishments he owed to his mother. When he was a child still living in the palace, before he had ever seen a schoolmaster, she had taught him something of French and had given him a little instruction on an ancient piano with yellow keys and a great red silk reredos almost touching the ceiling. Others knew less than he, and yet they were just as gentlemanly and they were much happier. Now for life! He stayed two years in Madrid; where he affected mistresses who gave him a certain notoriety, and drove famous horses. He became the intimate friend of a celebrated bull-fighter, and he gambled heavily in the clubs on Alcalá Street. He fought a duel, but with swords, instead of lying on the ground, pistol in hand, as he had formerly pictured to himself, and he came out of the affair with a scratch on his arm, something in the nature of a pin prick in the epidermis of an elephant. He was no longer "the Majorcan with the ounces." The hoard of round gold pieces treasured by his mother had vanished. He now flung bank bills prodigally upon the gaming tables, and when bad luck assailed him he wrote to his administrator, a lawyer, the scion of a family of old time mossons, retainers of the Febrers during many centuries.

Jaime wearied of Madrid, where he felt himself essentially a stranger. The soul of the ancient Febrers lingered within him—those travelers through all countries except Spain, for they had ever lived with their backs turned upon their sovereigns. Many of his ancestors were familiar with every one of the important Mediterranean cities, they had visited the princes of the small Italian states, they had been received in audience by the Pope and by the Grand Turk, but never had it occurred to them to visit Madrid. Moreover, Febrer was often irritated with his relatives in the court city—youths proud of their noble titles who smiled at his odd appellation of butifarra. With what indifference his family had allowed various marquisates to descend to relatives on the Peninsula while they clung to their supreme title of island nobility and the high knightly rank of Malta!

He began to run over Europe, fixing his residence in the autumn and during part of the winter in Paris; spending the cold months on the Blue Coast; spring in London; summer in Ostend; with various trips to Italy, Egypt, and Norway to see the midnight sun. In this new existence he was barely known. He was one traveler more, an insignificant circulating globule in the great arterial network which desire for travel extends over the Continent; but this life of continual movement, of tedious monotony, and unexpected adventures, satisfied his hereditary instinct, the inclinations transmitted from his remote ancestors, constant visitors among new peoples. This wandering existence, also, satiated his longing for the extraordinary. In the hotels at Nice, phalansteries of the most polite and hypocritical worldly corruption, he had been flattered in the seclusion of his room by unexpected visits. In Egypt he had been compelled to flee from the caresses of a decadent

Hungarian countess, a withered flower of elegance, with moist eyes and violent perfume.

He passed his twenty-eighth birthday in Munich. A short time before he had gone to Bayreuth to hear the Wagnerian operas, and now in the capital of Bavaria he attended the theater of the Residence, where the Mozart festival was celebrated. Jaime was not a melomaniac, but his vagrant existence forced him with the crowd, and his accomplishment as an amateur pianist had led him to make his musical pilgrimage for two consecutive years.

In the hotel in Munich he met Miss Mary Gordon, whom he had seen before at the Wagner theater. She was an English girl, tall, slender, with firm flesh and the body of a gymnast which exercise had developed into agreeable feminine curves, giving her a youthful figure, and the wholesome, asexual appearance of a handsome boy. Her beautiful head was that of a court page, with skin as transparent as porcelain, pink nostrils like those of a toy dog, deep blue eyes and blonde hair, pale gold on the surface and dark gold beneath. Her beauty was adorable but fragile; that British beauty which is lost at thirty beneath purplish flushes and blotches on the skin.

In the restaurant Jaime had several times surprised the gaze of her blue eyes, frankly, tranquilly bold, fixed upon him. She was attended by a fat, spongy woman with rouged cheeks, a traveling companion dressed in black with a red straw hat and a broad belt of the same color, which divided the bulky hemispheres of her breast and abdomen. Young and graceful, Mary Gordon resembled a flower of gold and nacre in her white flannel suits of masculine cut with a mannish cravat, and a Panama with drooping brim around which she wound a blue veil.

Febrer met the pair at every turn; in the picture gallery, standing before Durer's Evangelists; in the hall of sculpture examining Egina's marbles; in the rococo theater of the Residence, where Mozart was sung, an audience hall of a former century, with decorations of porcelain and garlands which seemed to require that the spectators wear the purple heel and the white wig. Accustomed to meeting each other, Jaime greeted her with a smile and she seemed to answer timidly with the flash of her eyes.

One morning, on coming out of his room, he met the English girl on a landing of the stairway. She was bending her boyish breast over the balustrade.

"Lift! Lift!" she called with her birdlike voice, summoning the elevator man to bring it up.

Febrer bowed as he entered the movable cage with her, and said a few words in French to start a conversation. The English girl stared at him in silence with her light blue eyes in which a star of gold seemed to be floating. She remained silent as if she did not understand, yet Jaime had seen her in the reading room turning the leaves of the Parisian dailies.

Stepping out of the elevator she turned with hasty step toward the office where sat the hotel clerk, pen in hand. He listened with obsequious mien, like a polyglot quick to understand each of his guests, and coming out from his enclosure he made straight toward Jaime, who, still embarrassed by his unsuccessful venture, was pretending to read the advertisements in the vestibule. Febrer at first did not realize that it was he who was being addressed.

"Señor, this lady asks me to introduce you to her," said the clerk.

Turning toward the English girl he added with Teutonic composure, like one fulfilling a duty, "Monsieur the hidalgo Febrer, Marquis of Spain."

He understood the part he was playing. Everyone who travels with good valises is an hidalgo and a marquis until the contrary be proven.

Then, with his eyes, he indicated the English girl who stood stiff and grave during the ceremony without which no well-bred woman may exchange a word with a man: "Miss Gordon, doctor of the University of Melbourne."

The young lady extended her white gloved hand and shook Febrer's with gymnastic vigor. Not till then did she venture to speak:

"Oh, Spain! Oh, 'Don Quixote'!"

Unconsciously they strolled out of the hotel together discussing the afternoon performances which they had attended. There was to be no function at the theaters that day and she was thinking of going to the park called Theresienwiese, at the foot of the statue of Bavaria, to see the Tyrolese fair and to listen to the folk-songs. After breakfasting at the hotel they went to the fair grounds; they climbed upon an enormous statue and viewed the Bavarian plain, its lakes and its distant mountains; they explored the Memorial Hall, filled with busts of celebrated Bavarians, most of whose names they read for the first time, and they finished by going from booth to booth, admiring the costumes of the Tyrolese, their gymnastic dances, their birdlike warbling and trilling.

They went about as if they had known each other all their lives, Jaime admiring the masculine liberty of Saxon girls who are not afraid of associating with men and who feel strong in their ability to take care of themselves. From that day they visited together museums, academies, old churches, sometimes alone, and again with the companion, who made strenuous exertions to keep pace with them. They were comrades who communicated their impressions without thinking of difference of sex. Jaime was disposed to take advantage of this intimacy by making gallant speeches, by risking little advances, but he restrained himself. With women like this action might be dangerous, they remain impassive, proof against all manner of impressions. He must wait until she should take the initiative. These were women who could go alone around the world, likely to interrupt passionate advances with the blows of a trained boxer. He had seen some in his travels who carried diminutive nickel-plated revolvers in their muffs or in their handbags along with powder box and handkerchief.

Mary Gordon told of the distant Oceanic archipelago in which her father exercised authority like a viceroy. She had no mother, and she had come to Europe to complete studies begun in Australia. She held the degree of Doctor from the University of Melbourne; a doctor of music. Jaime, suppressing his astonishment at this news from a distant world, told of himself, of his family, of his native land, of the curiosities of the island, of the cavern of Arta, tragically grand, chaotic as an ante-chamber of the inferno; of the Dragon's caves with their forests of stalactites, glistening like an ice palace, of its thousand placid lakes, from the deep crystal depths of which it seemed as if nude sirens would arise like those Rhine maidens who guarded the treasure of the Niebelungs. Mary listened to him, entranced. Jaime seemed to grow greater before her eyes, as she learned that he was a son of that isle of dreams, where the sea is always blue, where the sun is ever shining, and where blooms the orange flower.

Febrer began to spend his afternoons in the room of the English girl. The performances of the Mozart festival were ended. Miss Gordon needed daily the spiritual uplift of music. She had a piano in her reception room, and a roll of opera scores which accompanied her on her travels. Jaime sat near, before the keyboard, trying to accompany the pieces she was interpreting, ever those of the same author, the god, the only! The hotel was near the station, and the noise of drays, carriages and street cars annoyed the English woman and she closed the windows. Her stout companion had gone to her own apartment, rejoiced at being free from that musical tempest, the delights of which could not compare with those of making a good bit of Irish point lace. Miss Gordon, alone with the Spaniard, treated him as if she were a master.

"Come, do that again; let us repeat the theme of the sword. Pay attention!"

But Jaime was distracted, peeping out of the corner of his eye at the girl's long, white neck bristling with little golden locks, at the network of blue veins delicately outlined beneath the transparency of her pearly skin.

One afternoon it rained; the leaden sky seemed to graze the roofs of the houses; in the reception room there was the diffused light of a cellar. They were playing almost in the dark, bending their heads forward to read the score. Forth rolled the music of the forest of enchantments, moving its green and whispering tree tops before the rude Siegfried, the innocent child of Nature, eager to know the language of the soul and of inanimate things. The master-bird sang, his voice rising above the murmur of the foliage. Mary was trembling with excitement.

"Ah, poet! Poet!"

She continued playing. Then, in the growing darkness of the room, sounded the strong chords which accompanied the hero to the tomb; the funeral march of the warriors bearing upon the shield the muscular body of Siegfried, with his golden hair, interrupting the melancholy phrase of the God of gods. Mary continued trembling, until suddenly her hands fell from the keyboard and her head rested on Jaime's shoulder, like a bird folding its wings.

"Oh, Richard!... Richard, *mon bien aimée!*"

The Spaniard saw her wandering eyes and her tremulous lips offering themselves to him; in his grasp he felt her cold hands; her breath floated about him. Against his bosom were pressed hidden curves of firm elastic plumpness, the existence of which he had not suspected.

There was no more music that afternoon.

At midnight when Febrer retired, he had not yet recovered from his astonishment. After so many fears, this was the way things had happened, with the greatest simplicity, as one is offered a hand, without exertion on his part.

Another surprise had been to hear himself called by a name which was not his. Who could that Richard be? But in the hour of sweet and dreamy explanations which follow those of madness and forgetfulness, she had told him of the impression she had received in Bayreuth when she saw him for the first time among the thousand heads which filled the theater. It was he, the great musician, as he was portrayed in his youthful pictures! When she met him again in Munich beneath the same roof, she had felt that the die was cast and that it was useless to resist this attraction.

Febrer examined himself with ironical curiosity in the mirror in his room. What ideas a woman is capable of conceiving! Yes, he was something like that other one—the heavy forehead, the drooping hair, the beaked nose, and the prominent chin, which, in years to come would turn inward, seeking each other, and give him a certain witchlike profile.... Excellent and glorious Richard! By what miracle had Wagner brought to him one of the greatest joys of his existence! What an original woman was this!

Astonishment, mingled with a shade of annoyance, grew upon Febrer as the days passed. She seemed to forget what had taken place, and to grow constantly more unapproachable. She received him with grave rigidity, as if nothing had occurred, as if the past had left no trace upon her mind, as if the day before had never been. Only when music evoked the memory of the other man came tenderness and submission.

Jaime was irritated, and he determined to dominate her; he would prove himself a man! At last he triumphed to such an extent that the piano was heard less and she began to see in him something more than a living picture of her idol.

In their happy intoxication Munich and the hotel in which they had seen each other as strangers seemed to them offensive. They felt the need of flying far away, where they could make love freely, and one day they found themselves in a port which had a stone lion at its entrance, while beyond spread the liquid surface of an immense lake which mingled with the sky on the horizon. They were in Lindau. One steamer could convey them to Switzerland, another to Constance, but they preferred the tranquil German city of the famous Ecumenical Council, establishing themselves in the Island Hotel, an ancient Dominican Monastery.

Febrer was stirred as he contemplated this epoch, the happiest of his existence! Mary continued for him ever an original woman, in whom there was always something left to conquer; tolerant at certain hours, repellant and austere throughout the rest of the day. He was her lover, and yet she would not permit the slightest familiarity, nor any liberty which might reveal the confidence of their common life. The least allusion to their intimacy caused her to flush in protest. "Shocking!" Yet, every morning at daybreak Febrer sneaked into his room along the corridors of the old convent, unmade his bed so that the servants would not suspect, and he would show himself on the balcony. The birds were singing in the tall rose bushes in the garden below his feet. Beyond, the immense sheet of Lake Constance was flushing with purple tints caught from the rising sun. The first fishing barks were cleaving the orange tinted waters; in the distance sounded the cathedral bells, softened by the damp, morning breeze; the cranes began to creak on the quay where the waters cease to be a lake, and narrowing into a channel become the river Rhine; the footsteps of the servants and the swish of cleaning startled the monastic cloister with the noises of the hotel.

Near the balcony, adjoining the wall, and so close that Jaime could touch it with his hand, was a small tower with a slate roof and with ancient coats of arms on the circular wall. It was the tower in which John Huss had been imprisoned before going to the stake.

The Spaniard thought of Mary. At this time she must be in the perfumed shadows of her room, her blonde head clasped in her arms, sleeping her first real sleep of the night, her tired body still vibrant from fatigue. Poor John Huss! Febrer sympathized with him as if he had been his friend. To burn him in the presence of such a beautiful landscape, perhaps on a morning like this! To cast one's self into the wolf's mouth, and to give up one's life over the question whether the Pope were good or bad, or whether laymen should receive the sacrament with wine the same as priests! To die for such absurdities when life is so beautiful and the heretic might have enjoyed it so richly with any of the plump-breasted, big-hipped blonde women, friends of the cardinals, who witnessed his torture! Unhappy apostle! Jaime ironically pitied the simplicity of the martyr. He looked at life through different eyes. *Viva el amor!* Love was the only thing worth while in life.

They remained nearly a month in the ancient episcopal city, strolling out in the gloaming through the lonely, grass-grown streets with their crumbling palaces of the time of the Council; floating with the current down the river Rhine along its forest-clad banks; stopping to look at the tiny houses with red roofs and spacious arbors beneath which sang the bourgeoisie, stein in hand, with the Germanic joy of a subchanter, grave and reposeful.

From Constance they passed on to Switzerland and afterward to Italy. They traveled together for a year viewing landscapes, seeing museums, visiting ruins, the windings and sheltered nooks in which Jaime made use of for kissing Mary's pearly skin, reveling in the rush of color and the gesture of annoyance with which she protested "Shocking!"

The old traveling companion, unconscious as a suitcase of the points of interest in their journey, continued making the cloak of Irish point, beginning in Germany, and working at it while crossing the Alps, along the whole length of the Apennines, and in sight of Vesuvius and Ætna. Unable to talk with Febrer, who spoke no English, she greeted him with the yellowish glitter of her teeth and returned to her task, forming a conspicuous figure in the hotel lobbies.

The two lovers spoke of marriage. Mary summed up the situation with energetic decision. She need only write a few lines to her father. He was very far away, and besides she never consulted him in regard to her affairs. He would approve whatever she did, sure of her wisdom and prudence.

They were in Sicily, a land which reminded Febrer of his own island. The ancient members of his family had been here also, but with cuirasses on their breasts, and in worse company. Mary spoke of the future, arranging the financial side of the anticipated partnership with the practical sense of her race. It did not matter to her that Febrer had little fortune; she was rich enough for both; and she enumerated her worldly goods, lands, houses, and stocks like an administrator with accurate memory. On their return to Rome they would be married in the evangelical chapel and also in a Catholic church. She knew a cardinal who had arranged for her an audience with the Pope. His Eminence would manage everything.

Jaime passed a sleepless night in a hotel in Syracuse. Marriage? Mary was agreeable; she made life pleasant, and she would bring with her a fortune. But should he really marry her? Then the other man began to annoy him, the illustrious shade which had appeared in Zurich, in Venice, in every place visited by them which held memories of the maestro's past. Jaime would grow old, and music, his formidable rival, would be ever fresh. In a little while, when marriage should have robbed his relations of the charm of illegality, of the delight of the prohibited, Mary would discover some orchestra leader who bore a still greater resemblance to the other man, or some ugly violinist with long hair and possessed of youth who would remind her of Beethoven in his boyhood. Besides, he was of different race, different customs and passions; he was tired of her shamefaced reserve in love, of her resistance to final submission which had pleased him at first, but which had come at last to bore him. No; there was yet time to save himself.

"I regret it on account of what she will think of Spain. I regret it on account of Don Quixote," he said to himself while packing his suitcase one morning at sunrise.

He fled, losing himself in Paris, where the English woman would never seek him. She hated that ungrateful city for its hissing of Tannhäuser many years before she was born.

Of these relations, which had lasted a year, Jaime cherished only the memory of a felicity, increased and sweetened by the passing of time and by a lock of golden hair. Then, too, he must have somewhere among his papers, guide books, and post cards, lying forgotten in an old secretary in the great house, a photograph of the feminine doctor of music, strangely adorable in her long-sleeved toga with a square plate-like cap from which hung a tassel.

Of the rest of his life he remembered little; a void of tedium broken only by monetary worries. The administrator was slow and grudging in sending his remittances. Jaime would ask him for money and he would reply with grumbling letters, telling of interest which must be met, of second mortgages on which he could barely realize a loan, of the precariousness of a fortune in which nothing was left free of incumbrance.

Febrer, believing that his presence might disentangle this wretched situation, made short trips to Majorca, which always resulted in the sale of property, yielding him scarcely enough money to take flight again, heedless of his administrator's advice. Money aroused in him a smiling optimism. Everything would turn out all right. As a last resort he counted on recourse to matrimony. Meanwhile,—he would live!

He managed to exist a few years longer, sometimes in Madrid, or again in the great foreign cities, until at last his administrator brought this period of merry prodigality to an end by sending his resignation, with his accounts and his refusal to continue forwarding money.

He had spent one year on the island, buried, as he said, with no other diversion than nights of gambling in the Casino and afternoons on the Paseo del Borne, sitting around a table with a company of friends, sedentary islanders who reveled in the stories of his travels. Misery and want—this was the reality of his present life. His creditors threatened him with immediate legal process. He still outwardly retained possession of Son Febrer and of other estates derived from his forefathers, but property yielded little on the island; the rents, according to traditional custom, were no higher than in the time of his ancestors, for the families of the original renters inherited the right to farm the lands. They made payments directly to his creditors, but even this did not satisfy half of the interest due. The palace was but a storehouse for its rich decorations. The noble mansion of the Febrers was submerged, and no one could float it. Sometimes Jaime calmly considered the convenience of slipping out of his wretched predicament with neither humiliation nor dishonor by letting himself be found some afternoon in the garden asleep forever under an orange tree with a revolver in his hand.

One day in this frame of mind, a crony gave him an idea as he was leaving the Casino in the small hours of the night, one of those moments in which nervous insomnia causes a person to see things in an extraordinary light in which they stand out clearly. Don Benito Valls, the rich Jew, was very fond of him. Several times he had intervened, unsought, in his affairs, saving him from immediate ruin. It was due to personal liking for Febrer and to respect for his name. Valls had a single heiress, and, moreover, he was an invalid; the prolific exuberance characteristic of his race had not been fulfilled in him. His daughter Catalina, when she was younger, had wished to be a nun, but, now that she was past twenty, she felt a strong desire for the pomps and vanities of this world, and she expressed tender sympathy for Febrer whenever his misfortunes were discussed in her hearing.

Jaime recoiled from the proposition with almost as much astonishment as Mammy Antonia. A Chueta! The idea, however, began to fasten itself upon his mind, lubricated in its incessant hammering by the ever increasing poverty and necessity which grew with the passing days. Why not? Valls' daughter was the richest heiress on the island, and money possessed neither blood nor race.

At last he had yielded to the urging of his friends, officious mediators between himself and the family of the girl, and that morning he was on his way to breakfast at the house in Valldemosa where Valls resided the greater part of the year for relief from the asthma which was choking him.

Jaime made an effort to remember Catalina. He had seen her several times on the streets of Palma—a good figure, a pleasant face! When she should live far from her kindred and should dress better, she would be quite presentable. But—could he love her?

Febrer smiled skeptically. Was love indispensable to marriage? Matrimony was a trip in double harness for the rest of life, and one only needed to seek in the woman those qualities demanded of a traveling companion; good disposition, identical tastes, the same likes and dislikes in eating and drinking. Love! Every one believed he had a right to it, while love was like talent, like beauty, like fortune, a special gift which only rare and privileged persons might enjoy. By good luck, deception came to conceal this cruel inequality, and all human beings ended their days, thinking of their youth with melancholy longing, believing they had really known love, when they had in reality experienced nothing but a youthful delirium.

Love was a beautiful thing, but not indispensable to matrimony nor to existence. The important thing was to choose a good companion for the rest of the journey; to set the pace of the two to the same tune, so that there should be no kicking over the traces nor collisions; to dominate the nerves so that there should be no jar during the continual contact of the common existence; to be able to lie down together like good comrades, with mutual respect, without wounding each other with the knees nor jabbing each other in the ribs with the elbows. He expected to find all these things and to consider himself well content.

Suddenly Valldemosa appeared before his eyes above the crest of a hill, surrounded by mountains. The tower of La Cartuja, with its decorations of green tiles, rose above the foliage of the gardens and the cells.

Febrer saw a carriage standing in a turn of the road. A man alighted from it, waving his arms so that Jaime's driver would stop his horses. Then he opened the carriage door and climbed in, smiling, taking a seat beside Febrer.

"Hello Captain!" exclaimed Jaime in astonishment.

"You didn't expect me, eh? I'm going to the breakfast, too; I have invited myself. What a surprise it will be for my brother!"

Jaime pressed his hand. It was one of his most loyal friends, Captain Pablo Valls.

CHAPTER III
JEW AND GENTILE

Pablo Valls was known throughout all Palma. When he seated himself on the terrace of a café on the Paseo del Borne a compact circle of listeners would form around him, smiling at his forceful gestures and at his loud voice, which was ever incapable of discreet tones.

"I am a Chueta, and what of that? A Jew of the Jews! All of my family come from 'the street.' When I was in command of the Roger de Lauria, being one day in Algiers, I stopped before the door of the Synagogue, and an old man, after looking me over, said: 'You may enter; you are one of us!' I gave him my hand and answered: 'Thanks, fellow-believer.'"

His hearers laughed, and Captain Valls, proclaiming in a loud voice his Chuetan ancestry, glanced in every direction, as if defying the houses, the people, and the soul of the island, hostile to his race through the fanatical hatred of centuries.

His physiognomy revealed his origin. His gray-tinged ruddy side whiskers denoted the retired sea-faring man, but between these shaggy adornments projected his Semitic profile, the heavy, aquiline nose, the prominent chin, the eyes with elongated lids, and pupil of amber and gold according to the play of light, and in which here and there floated tobacco-colored spots.

He had been much on the sea; he had lived for long periods in England and in the United States; and as a result of his contact with those lands of liberty, free from religious tolerance, he had brought back a belligerent frankness which impelled him to defy the traditional prejudices of the island, socially and politically, unprogressive and stagnant. The other Chuetas, cowed by centuries of persecution and scorn, concealed their origin, or tried to make it forgotten through their humble demeanor. Captain Valls took advantage of every occasion to discuss the matter, parading the name of Chueta as a title of nobility, as a challenge which he hurled at the popular bias.

"I am a Jew, and what of that?" he shouted again. "A co-religionist of Jesus, of Saint Paul, of the other saints who are venerated on the altars. The butifarras boast of their ancestors, but they date scarcely further back than yesterday. I am more noble, more ancient! My forefathers were the patriarchs of the Bible!"

Then, waxing indignant over the antipathy to his race, he again became aggressive.

"In all Spain," he announced gravely, "there is not a Christian who can lift a finger. We are all descendants of Jews or of Moors. And he who is not—he who is not——"

Here he stopped, and after a brief pause affirmed resolutely, "He who is not, is the descendant of a priest!"

On the Peninsula the traditional odium for the Jew which still separates the population of Majorca into two antagonistic races, does not exist. Pablo Valls became furious discussing his fatherland. Openly orthodox Jews did not exist there. The last synagogue had been dissolved centuries ago. The Jews had all been "converted" en masse, and the recalcitrant were burned by the Inquisition. The Chuetas of the present day were the most fervent Catholics of Majorca, bringing to their profession of faith a Semitic zealotry. They prayed aloud, they made priests of their sons, they sought influence to place their daughters in the convents, they figured as moneyed people among the partisans of the most conservative ideas, and yet, against them lay the same antipathy as in former centuries, and they lived ostracized, with no allies in any social class.

"For four hundred and fifty years we have had the water of baptism on our pates," Captain Valls continued in loud tones, "and yet we are still the accursed, the reprobates, as before the conversion. Isn't that queer? The Chuetas! Look out for them! Bad people! In Majorca there are two Catholicisms—one for our people, and another for the rest."

Then with the concentrated odium gathered from centuries of persecution, the sailor said, referring to his racial brethren, "They are doing their best through cowardice, through too great love for the island, for this little rock, this Roqueta on which we were born; to not forsake it, they became Christians, and now, when they are really Christians at heart they are paid for it with kicks. Had they continued to be Jews, dispersing throughout the world as others have done, perhaps at this moment they would be great personages, bankers to kings, instead of sticking in their little shops on 'the street,' making silver hand bags."

Himself a skeptic, he scorned or attacked them all—the Jews faithful to their old beliefs, the converts, the Catholics, the Mussulmans, with whom he had lived on his journeys to the coasts of Africa and in the ports of Asia

Minor. Again he would be dominated by an atavistic tenderness, displaying a certain religious respect toward his race.

He was a Semite; he declared it with pride, beating his chest: "The greatest people in the world!"

"We were a lousy, starving crowd when we were in Asia, because there was no one in that land with whom to traffic, nor to whom we could loan our money. But no race has given the human flock more actual shepherds than has ours, which shall yet be for centuries and centuries masters of men. Moses, Jesus, and Mohammed are from my country. Three strong champions, eh, caballeros? And now we have given the world a fourth prophet, also of our race and of our blood, only that this one has two faces and two names. On the obverse he is called Rothschild, and is the captain of all who lay up money; on the reverse he is Carl Marx—the apostle of those who wish to wrest it from the rich!"

The history of the race on the island Valls condensed after his fashion into brief words. The Jews were many, very many in former times. Nearly all the commerce was in their hands; most of the ships were theirs. The Febrers, and other Christian potentates, had no objection to being their associates. The ancient times might be called the times of liberty; persecution and cruelty were relatively modern. Jews were the treasurers of kings, doctors, the courtiers of the courts of the Peninsula. When religious feuds broke out, the richest and most astute Hebrews of the island were wise enough to become converted in time, voluntarily, mixing with the native families, and sinking their origin into oblivion. These new Catholics were the very ones who, later on, with the fervor of the neophyte, had instigated the persecution against their former brethren. The Chuetas of the present time, the only Majorcans of recognized Jewish origin, were the descendants of the last to be converted, the offspring of the families persecuted by the Inquisition.

To be a Chueta, to spring from the street of the Silversmiths, which by antonomasia is called "the street," is the greatest disgrace which can happen to a Majorcan. In vain had revolutions been made in Spain, in vain had liberal laws been passed which recognized the equality of all Spaniards; the Chueta when he passed on to the Peninsula was a citizen like other people, but in Majorca he was a reprobate, a kind of pest who could marry none but his own kindred.

Valls commented ironically upon the social order, resembling the steps of a stairway, in which the different classes of the island had dwelt for centuries and where many steps still remained intact. Aloft, on the vortex, the proud butifarras; then the nobles, the caballeros; afterward the mossons; trailing along behind these came the merchants, the artisans, and finally the cultivators of the soil. Here opened an enormous gap in the order established by God in creating the classes; a vast open space which each one could people according to his caprice. Undoubtedly after the Majorcan nobles and plebeians came hogs, dogs, asses, cats, rats, and, at the tail of all these beasts of the Lord, the despised citizen of "the street," the Chueta, the pariah of the island. It mattered nothing if he were rich, like the brother of Captain Valls, or intellectual, like others. Many Chuetas who attained the dignity of state functionaries, army officers, magistrates, landed proprietors on the Peninsula, found on returning to Majorca that the meanest beggar considered himself superior to them, and on the slightest excuse poured insults upon their persons and their families. The isolation of this bit of Spain, surrounded by the sea, served to keep intact the spirit of earlier epochs.

In vain the Chuetas, fleeing from this odium which flourished despite the new era of progress, exaggerated their devotion to Catholicism with a blind and vehement faith, largely influenced by the fear absorbed into their souls and into their flesh during centuries of persecution. In vain they continued in imitation of their forefathers to recite their prayers in loud voices in their houses so that passersby might hear, and they cooked their food in their windows so that all should see that they ate pork. The traditional barriers could not be overcome. The Catholic Church, which entitles itself universal, was cruel and harsh with the Jews on the island, repaying their adherence with disdainful repulsion. The sons of the Chuetas who desired to become priests found no room in the seminary. The convents closed their doors against every novice proceeding from "the street." On the Peninsula the daughters of Chuetas married men of distinction and men of great fortune, but on the island they scarcely ever found one who would accept their hand and their riches.

"Bad people!" continued Valls sarcastically. "They are industrious, they lay up money, they live at peace in the bosoms of their families, they are more fervent Catholics even than the rest, but they are Chuetas; there must be something the matter with them to be so despised! Something there must be about them, do you understand? Something! He who wishes to know more let him find out for himself."

The seaman laughingly told of the poor peasants from the country who until a few years ago declared in good faith that the Chuetas were covered with grease and had tails, taking advantage of an occasion when they found a lonely child from "the street" to disrobe him and convince themselves whether the story of the caudal appendage were true.

"And how about what happened to my brother?" continued Valls. "To my sainted brother Benito, who prays aloud, and who is so devout that one might think he were going to actually devour the images?"

They all remembered the case of Don Benito Valls, and they laughed heartily, since his brother was ever the first to jest about the matter. The rich Chueta had found himself owner, on settling some accounts, of a house and valuable lands in a town in the interior of the island. On taking possession of the new property the most prudent citizens had given him good advice. He would be allowed to visit his property during the day, but as for spending the night in the house, never! There was no record of a Chueta having slept in the pueblo. Don Benito paid no attention to this counsel and he spent a night on his property, but scarcely had he gotten into bed than the domestics fled. When the master of the house had slept long enough he sprang from his couch. Not even the faintest ray of light entered through the crevices. He thought he must have slept at least twelve hours, yet it was still dark. He opened a window and his head bumped cruelly; he tried to open the door, but he could not. While he had been asleep the neighbors had walled up all the windows and doors, and the Chueta had to make his escape by way of the roof, to the accompaniment of shouts of laughter from the people who thus rejoiced over their work. This joke was merely by way of warning; if he persisted in going counter to the customs of the town, some night he would awake to find the house in flames.

"Very amusing, but very barbarous!" added the captain. "My brother! A good soul! A saint!"

They all laughed at this. He maintained friendly relations with his brother, although with some frigidity, and he made no secret of the grievances he had against him. Captain Valls was the bohemian of the family, ever on the high seas or in distant lands, leading the life of a gay bachelor. He had enough money on which to live. On the death of his father his brother had taken charge of the business of the house, defrauding him of many thousands of dollars.

"The same as the Christians of olden times!" Pablo hastened to add. "In matters of inheritance there is neither race nor creed. Money recognizes no religion."

The interminable persecutions suffered by his ancestors infuriated Valls. Advantage was taken of every circumstance for trampling under foot the people of "the street." When the peasants had grievances against the nobles or when foreigners descended in armed bands upon the citizens of Palma, the difficulty was always settled by a joint attack upon the ward of the Chuetas, killing those who did not flee, and looting their shops. If a Majorcan batallion received orders to march to Spain in case of war, the soldiers mutinied, broke out of their barracks and sacked "the street." When the reaction followed the revolutions in Spain, the royalists, to celebrate their triumph, assaulted the silversmiths' shops of the Chuetas, took possession of their riches, and made bonfires of their furniture, hurling even their crucifixes into the flames. Crucifixes belonging to old Jews, that, of course, must be false!

"And who are the people of 'the street'?" shouted the captain. "Everybody knows; those who have noses and eyes like mine; and there are many who are flat-nosed and present nothing of the common type. On the other hand, how many are there who pretend to be caballeros of antiquity, of proud nobility, with faces like Abraham and Jacob?"

There existed a list of suspicious surnames for identifying the genuine Chuetas, but these same surnames were borne by long-time Christians, and it was additional caprice which separated one from the other. Only the descendants of those families beaten or burned by the Inquisition had remained permanently marked by popular odium. The famous catalogue of surnames was made up undoubtedly from the autos of the Holy Offices.

"A joy indeed to become a Christian! The ancestors frizzled in the bonfire, and the descendants singled out and cursed for centuries upon centuries!"

The captain dropped his sarcastic tone upon recalling the harrowing story of the Chuetas of Majorca. His cheeks flamed and his eyes flashed with the effulgence of hatred. That they might dwell in tranquillity they had been converted en masse in the Fifteenth Century. There was not a Jew left on the island, but the Inquisition must do something to justify its existence, so there were burnings of persons suspected of Judaism in the Paseo del Borne, spectacles organized, as said the chroniclers of the epoch, "in accordance with the most brilliant functions celebrated by the triumph of the Faith in Madrid, Palermo, and Lima." Some Chuetas were burned, others were beaten, others went out to their shame wearing nothing but hoods painted as devils and with green candles in their hands; but all of them had their goods confiscated and the Holy Tribunal was enriched. After that, those suspected of Judaism, those who had no clerical protector, were forced to go to mass in the Cathedral with their families every Sunday under the command and custody of an alguacil, who herded them as if they were a flock of sheep, put mantles on them so that no one could mistake them, and thus he took them to the temple amidst catcalls, insults, and stonings from the devout populace. This happened every Sunday, and in this unceasing weekly torment fathers died, sons grew into manhood, begetting new Chuetas destined to public contumely.

A few families gathered together to flee from this degrading slavery. They met in an orchard near the sea wall, and were counselled and guided by one Rafael Valls, a valorous man of great culture.

"I don't know for sure that he was a relative of mine," said the captain. "It was more than two centuries ago; but if he were not, I wish he had been. It would be an honor to have him for an ancestor. Adelante!"

Pablo Valls had collected papers and books of the epoch of persecutions, and he talked of them as if they had occurred but yesterday.

"Men, women and children took passage on an English ship, but a storm drove them back on the coast of Majorca, and the fugitives were taken prisoners. This was during the reign of Charles II, the Bewitched. To wish to flee from Majorca where they were so well treated, and more than that, on a ship manned by Protestants! They were held three years in prison, and the confiscations of their property, yielded a million duros. Besides this, the Sacred Tribunal counted upon more millions wrested from former victims, and constructed a palace in Palma, the finest and most luxurious possessed by the Inquisition in any land. The prisoners were subjected to torment until they confessed what their judges desired, and on the seventh of March, 1691, the executions began. That event has as its historian such a one as no other part of the world has ever known, Father Garau, a pious Jesuit, a fount of theological science, rector of the Seminary of Mount Sion, where the Institute now stands, author of the book 'The Faith Triumphant,' a literary monument which I would not sell for all the money in the world. Here it is; it accompanies me everywhere."

Out of his pocket he drew "The Faith Triumphant," a small book bound in parchment, of antique and reddish print, which he fondled with a ferocious grip.

"Blessed Father Garau! Placed in charge of exhorting and encouraging the criminals, he had seen it all at close range, and he told of the thousands and thousands of spectators who flocked from many towns on the island to witness the festival, of the solemn masses attended by the thirty-eight criminals destined for the burning, of the luxurious trappings of caballeros and alguaciles mounted on prancing chargers at the head of the procession, and of the 'piety of the multitude, which burst into cries of pity when a highwayman was led to the gallows, but which remained dumb in the presence of these God-forgotten reprobates.' On that day, according to the learned Jesuit, the temper of soul of those who believe in God and of those who do not was displayed. The priests marched courageously, uttering shouts of exhortation unceasingly, while the miserable criminals were pale, exhausted and fainting. It was easy enough to see on which side lay celestial aid!

"The condemned were conducted to the foot of the Castle of Bellver for the final burning. The Marquis of Leganes, Governor of the Milanesado, chancing to be in Majorca with his fleet, took pity on the youth and beauty of a girl sentenced to the flames, and sued for her pardon. The tribunal praised the marquis for his Christian sentiments, but would not grant his petition.

"Father Garau was the one in charge of the conversion of Rafael Valls, 'a man of some letters, but one in whom the devil inspired an immeasurable pride, impelling him to curse those who condemned him to death, and refusing to reconcile himself with the Church.' But, as the Jesuit said, such boastfulness, the work of the Evil One, fails in the presence of danger, and cannot compare to the serenity of the priest who exhorts the criminal.

"The Jesuit father was a hero far from the flames! Now you shall hear with what evangelical pity he relates the details of the death of my ancestor."

Opening the book at a marked page, he read impressively: "'As long as nothing but the smoke reached him, he stood like a statue; when the flames came, he defended himself, he tried to shield himself, he resisted until he could bear no more. He was as fat as a sucking pig, and, being on fire inside in such a way that even before the flames reached him, his flesh was becoming consumed like half-burnt wood, and bursting in his middle, his entrails fell out like a Judas. *Crepuit medius difusa sunt oninia viscera ejus.*'"

This barbaric description always produced an effect. The laughter ceased, countenances darkened, and Captain Valls looked around with his amber-colored eyes, breathing satisfaction, as if he had achieved a triumph, while the small volume slipped back into his pocket.

Once when Febrer figured among his hearers, the sailor said to him rancorously, "You were there, too; that is, not yourself, but one of your ancestors, one of the Febrers, who carried the green flag as the chief ensign of the Tribunal; and the ladies of your family were in a carriage at the foot of the castle to witness the burning."

Jaime, annoyed by this reminder, shrugged his shoulders.

"Things of the past! Who ever remembers what is dead and gone? No one but some crazy fellow like you! Come, Pablo, tell us something about your travels—about your conquests of women."

The captain growled. Things of the past! The soul of the Roqueta was still the same as in those olden times. Odium of the Jewish religion and race still endured. For a good reason they dwelt apart, on this bit of ground isolated by the sea.

But Valls soon recovered his good humor, and, like all men who have knocked about the world, he could not resist the invitation to relate his past.

Febrer, another vagabond like himself, enjoyed listening to him. They both had led a turbulent, cosmopolitan existence, different from the monotonous life of the islanders; they both had squandered money prodigally, but Valls, with the active genius of his race, had known how to earn as much as he had spent, and now, ten years older than Jaime, he had enough to amply supply his modest bachelor needs. He still engaged in commerce occasionally, and he carried out commissions for friends who wrote to him from distant ports.

Of his eventful history as a mariner, Febrer disregarded the stories of hunger and storms, and only felt curiosity over his escapades in the great cosmopolitan ports where congregated the exotic vices and the women of all races. Valls, in his youth, when he was in command of his father's ships, had known women of every class and color, often finding himself involved in sailors' orgies, which ended in floods of whisky and stabbing affrays.

"Pablo, tell us of your love affairs in Jaffa, when the Moors came near killing you."

Listening to him Febrer laughed loudly, while the sailor said that Jaime was a good boy, worthy of a better fate, with no defect other than that of being a butifarra somewhat given to the family prejudices.

When he stepped into Febrer's carriage on the road to Valldemosa, ordering his own to return to Palma, he pushed back the soft felt hat which he wore on all occasions, the crown crushed in, and the brim tilted up in front and down in the back.

"Here we are! Really, didn't you expect me? I heard the news. I've been told all about it, and since there is to be a family gathering, let it be complete."

Febrer pretended not to understand. The carriage entered Valldemosa, stopping in the vicinity of La Cartuja before a dwelling of modern construction. When the two friends opened the garden gate they saw approaching them a gentleman with white whiskers, leaning on a cane. It was Don Benito Valls. He greeted Febrer with a weak, hollow voice, cutting short his words at intervals to gasp for air. He spoke humbly, laying great stress upon the honor which Febrer showed him by accepting his invitation.

"And how about me?" asked the captain, with a malicious smile. "Am I nobody? Aren't you glad to see me?"

Don Benito was glad to see him. He said so several times, but his eyes revealed uneasiness. His brother inspired him with a certain fear. What a tongue he had! It were better that they should not meet.

"We came together," continued the mariner. "Hearing that Jaime was breakfasting here, I invited myself, sure of giving you a great joy. These family reunions are delightful."

They had entered the house. It was simply decorated. The furniture was modern and vulgar. Some chromos and a few hideous paintings representing scenes in Valldemosa and Miramar hung on the walls.

Catalina, Don Benito's daughter, came down hurriedly. Her bosom was besprinkled with rice powder, revealing the haste with which she had given the last touch to her toilette on seeing the carriage arrive.

Jaime had opportunity to study her appearance for the first time. He had not been mistaken in his conjecture. She was tall, with pale brown coloring, black eyebrows, eyes like drops of ink, and a light down on her lip and on her temples. Her youthful figure was full and firm, announcing a greater expansion for the future, as in all the women of her race. She seemed of a sweet and gentle disposition, a good companion, not likely to be in the way during the journey of a common life. She kept her eyes lowered, and her face flushed as she greeted Jaime. Her manner, her furtive glances, revealed the respect, the adoration of one who is abashed in the presence of a being whom she considers her superior.

The captain caressed his niece with a certain familiar-it, adopting that air of a gay old man with which he spoke to the common girls of Palma in the small hours of the night in some restaurant on the Paseo del Borne. Ah! A smart girl! And how pretty she was! It seemed incredible that she came of a family of homely people!

Don Benito directed them all into the dining-room. Breakfast had been waiting for some time; in this house old customs were kept up; twelve o'clock sharp! They took their seats around the table, and Febrer, who sat next to the host, was annoyed by his heaving respiration, by the sharp gasps which interrupted his words.

In the silence which often reigns at the beginning of a dinner the wheezing of his unsound lungs was painfully noticeable. The rich Chueta pursed his lips, rounding them like the mouth of a trumpet, and drew in the air with a disagreeable rattle. Like all sick people he was eager to talk, and his sentences were long drawn out from a combination of stammering and pauses which left him with palpitating chest and eyes aloft, as if he were about to die of asphyxia. An atmosphere of uneasiness pervaded the dining-room. Febrer glanced at Don Benito in alarm, as if expecting to see him fall dead from his chair. His daughter and the captain, more accustomed to the spectacle, displayed indifference.

"It is asthma—Don Jaime," laboriously explained the sick man. "In Valldemosa—I am better—In Palma—I would die."

The daughter took advantage of the opportunity to put in her voice, which was like that of a timid little nun, contrasting strangely with her ardent, oriental eyes.

"Yes, papa is better here."

"You are more quiet in Valldemosa," added the captain, "and you commit fewer sins."

Febrer pictured to himself the torment of spending his life near that broken bellows. By good luck he might die soon. An annoyance of some months, but it did not alter his resolution of becoming one of the family. Courage!

The asthmatic, in his verbose mania, spoke of Jaime's ancestors, of the illustrious Febrers, the finest and noblest caballeros of the island.

"I had the honor—of being a great friend—of your—grandfather, Don Horacio."

Febrer looked at him in astonishment. It was a lie! Everyone in the island knew his grandfather, and he exchanged a few words with them all, but ever maintaining a gravity which imposed respect in others without alienating them; but as for being his friend! Don Horacio may have had business relations with the Chueta relating to loans needed for propping up his fortune in its decline.

"I also knew—your father—very well," continued Don Benito, encouraged by Febrer's silence. "I worked for him—when he was running—for deputy. Those were—different times—from these! I was young—and had not—the fortune which I have now. Then I figured—among the 'reds.'"

Captain Vails interrupted him with a laugh. His brother was a conservative now and a member of all the societies in Palma.

"Yes, I am," shouted the sick man, choking. "I like order—I like the old customs—and I think it right—for those who have—something to lose to be—in command. As for religion? Ah, religion! For that I would—give my life."

He pressed a hand against his breast, breathing painfully, as if choking with enthusiasm. He fixed aloft his pain-clouded eyes, adoring with a respect inspired by fear the sacred institution which had burned his forefathers alive.

"Pay no attention—to Pablo," he gasped, turning to Febrer when he had recovered breath. "You know him—a wild-headed fellow—a republican; a man who might be rich—but he won't have two pesetas—in his pocket—in his old age."

"Why not? Because you'll get them away from me?"

After this rude interruption by the sailor silence fell. Catalina looked alarmed, as if she feared that the noisy scenes which she had often witnessed when the two brothers fell into an argument would be reproduced in Febrer's presence.

Don Benito shrugged his shoulders and addressed his conversation to Jaime. His brother was crazy; he had a good head, a heart of gold, but he was mad, stark mad! With his exalted ideas, and his loud talk in the cafés, it was largely his fault that decent people felt a certain prejudice against—that they spoke ill of— —

The old man accompanied his mutilated expressions with gestures of humility, avoiding the word Chueta and refusing to name the famous street.

The captain, flushing with contrition for his violence, desired his hasty words to be forgotten, and he ate voraciously, keeping his head lowered.

His niece smiled at his good appetite. Whenever he ate at their table he amazed them with the capacity of his stomach.

"It is because I know what hunger is," said the sailor with a kind of pride. "I have suffered real hunger, the kind of hunger that makes men think of the flesh of their companions."

This reminiscence spurred him on to a vivid relation of his maritime adventures, telling of his younger days when he had been a supernumerary aboard a frigate which sailed to the coasts of the Pacific. When he insisted upon being a sailor, his father, the elder Valls, originator of the fortune of the house, had shipped him in a galley of his own which freighted sugar from Havana, but that was not a sailor's life because the cook reserved the best dishes for him; the captain dared not give him an order, seeing in him the son of the ship-owner. At this rate he would never have become a real sailor, rugged and expert. With the tenacious energy of his race he had taken passage unknown to his father on a frigate bound for the Chinchas Islands for a cargo of guano, manned by a crew of many races—deserters from the

English navy, bargemen from Valparaiso, Peruvian Indians, black sheep of every family, all under command of a Catalonian, a niggardly ruffian, more prodigal with blows than with the mess. The outbound trip was uneventful, but on the return voyage, after passing the Straits of Magellan, they ran into the calms, and the frigate lay motionless in the Atlantic almost a month, and the store of provisions soon ran low. The miser of a ship-owner had victualled the vessel with scandalous parsimony, and the captain, in his turn, had sailed with a scanty supply, appropriating to his own uses part of the money intended for stores.

"He gave us two sea biscuits a day, and those were full of worms. At first I used to busy myself scrupulously, like a well brought up boy, carefully picking out the little beasts, but after the housecleaning, there was nothing left except bits of crust as thin as wafers, and I was starving. Then— —"

"Oh, uncle!" protested Catalina, guessing what he was going to say, and pushing away her plate and fork with a gesture of repugnance.

"Then," continued the impassive sailor, "I gave up cleaning them out, and I swallowed them whole. It is true I ate at night—I've eaten lots of them, girl! Finally he only gave us one a day, and when I got back to Cadiz I had to go on a broth diet to get my stomach straightened out again."

Breakfast being over, Catalina and Jaime strolled out to the garden. Don Benito, with the air of a kindly patriarch, told his daughter to take Señor Febrer and show him some exotic rose bushes which he had recently planted. The two brothers remained in the room, which served as an office, watching the couple as they sauntered through the garden and finally seated themselves in the shade of a tree on two willow seats.

Catalina replied to her companion's questions with the timidity of a Christian maiden, piously educated, guessing the purpose concealed in his brusque gallantry. This man had come on her account, and her father was the first to welcome the suggestion. A settled affair! He was a Febrer, and she was going to tell him "yes." She thought of her youthful days in the college surrounded by poorer girls who took advantage of every opportunity to tease her, through envy of her wealth and hatred learned from their parents. She was a Chueta. She could only mingle with those of her own race, and even they, eager to ingratiate themselves with the enemy, played false to their own kind, lacking energy and cohesion for a common defense. When school let out the Chuetas marched in advance, by order of the nuns, to avoid insults and attacks from the other pupils out on the street. Even the servants who accompanied the girls quarreled among themselves, assuming the odium and prejudices of their masters. In the boys' school also the Chuetas were dismissed first to escape the stonings and whippings of those who had longer been Christians.

The daughter of Valls had suffered the torments of the treacherous pin-prick, of the stealthy scratching, of the scissors in her braids, and then, on becoming a woman, the odium and scorn of her old-time companions had followed her, embittering the pleasures of the young woman despite her riches. What was the use of being elegant? On the avenues none but her father's friends bowed to her; in the theater her box was visited only by people proceeding from "the street." At last she must marry one of them, as her mother and her grandmothers had done.

The despondency and mysticism of adolescence had urged her toward a monastic life. Her father almost choked with sorrow at the idea, but it was the call of religion, that religion to which she longed to devote her life! Don Benito consented to her entering a monastery in Majorca, where he could see his daughter every day, but not a convent would open its doors to her. The Superiors, tempted by the father's fortune, which would in the end revert to the order, showed themselves favorably disposed, but the monastic flock rebelled at receiving into its bosom a girl from "the street," and especially one who was not meek and resigned enough to submit to the superciliousness of the others, but rich and proud.

When she was left thus in the world by the resistance of the nuns, she did not know how to plan her future, and she spent her life near her father, like a nurse, ignorant of what was to be her fate, turning her back upon the young Chuetas who fluttered about her, attracted by Don Benito's millions, until the noble Febrer presented himself, like a fairy prince, to make her his wife. How good God is! She fancied herself in that palace near the Cathedral, in the ward of the nobles, along whose silent, narrow, blue-paved streets grave canons passed during the dreamy afternoon hours, summoned by the chime of bells.

She imagined herself in a luxurious carriage among the pines on the mountain of Bellver, or along the jetty, with Jaime at her side, and she revelled in the thought of the envious glances of her former companions, who would envy her, not only her wealth and her new position, but her possession of that man whom far-away adventures and a turbulent life had endowed with a certain halo of terrible seduction, dazzling and fatal to the quiet island señoritas. Jaime Febrer! Catalina had always seen him at a distance, but when she whiled away her monotonous hours with incessant novel reading, certain characters, the most interesting on account of their adventures and daring, always reminded her of that noble from the ward of the Cathedral who dashed about the world with elegant women dissipating his fortune. Then, suddenly, her father had spoken of this remarkable personage, giving her to understand that he was going to offer her his name, and with it the glory of his ancestors, who had been friends of kings! She did not know whether it were love or gratitude, but a wave of tenderness which dimmed her eyes drew her to the man. Ah! How she would love him! She listened to his words as to a sweet melody, not knowing what to say, intoxicated by its music, thinking at the same time of the future which he had suddenly opened to her, a rising sun bursting through the clouds.

Then, making an effort, she concentrated her mind and listened to Febrer, who was telling her about great foreign cities, of rows of luxurious carriages filled with women arrayed in the latest fashions, of broad stone steps in front of theaters down which came cascades of diamonds, ostrich plumes and nude shoulders, trying to place himself on a level of thought with the girl to allure her with these descriptions of feminine glory.

Jaime said no more, but Catalina guessed the purpose which had inspired these words. She, the unhappy girl from "the street," the Chueta, accustomed to seeing her people cringing and trembling beneath the weight of traditional odium, would visit these cities, would figure in the procession of riches, would have opened to her doors which she had always found closed, and she would pass through them leaning on the arm of a man who had ever seemed to her the personification of all terrestrial grandeur.

"When shall I see all that?" murmured Catalina with hypocritical humility. "I am condemned to live on the island, I am a poor girl who has never harmed anybody, and yet I have suffered great annoyances—I must be repulsive!"

Febrer rushed down the pathway which this feminine cleverness had opened for him. "Repulsive! No, Catalina." He had come to Valldemosa solely to see her, to speak to her. He offered her a new life. All these things at which she marveled she could experience and taste with but a word. Would she marry him?

Catalina, who had been waiting for an hour for this proposal, turned pale, tremulous with emotion. To hear it from his lips! She sat still for some time without answering, and at last stammered out a few words. It was a joy, the greatest she had ever known, but a well-educated girl like herself must not answer at once.

"I? Oh, I must have time! This is such a surprise!"

Jaime wished to insist, but at that very instant Captain Valls appeared in the garden, calling him vociferously. They must return to Palma; he had already given the driver orders to hitch up. Febrer protested stubbornly. But by what right did that busybody mix into his affairs?

Don Benito's presence cut off his protest. He was puffing painfully, with his face congested. The captain stirred about with nervous hostility, protesting at the coachman's delay. It was evident the brothers had been having a violent discussion. The elder one looked at his daughter, he looked at Jaime, and he seemed content in the belief that the two had reached an understanding.

Don Benito and Catalina accompanied them as far as the carriage. The asthmatic clasped Febrer's hand between his own with a vehement pressure. This was his house, and he himself a true friend desirous of serving him. If he needed his assistance he could dispose of him as he wished, just as if he were one of the family! He mentioned Don Horacio once again, recalling their former friendship. Then he invited Febrer to breakfast with them two days afterward, without remembering to include his brother.

"Yes, I will be here," said Jaime, giving Catalina a look which made her redden.

When the garden gate, behind which stood the father and daughter waving their hands, was lost to view, Captain Valls burst into a noisy laugh.

"So it seems that you would like to have me for an uncle of yours?" he questioned, ironically.

Febrer, who was furious at the intervention of his friend and the rudeness with which he had forced him to leave the house, gave expression to his choler. What business was it of his? By what right did he venture to meddle in his affairs? He was old enough not to need advisers.

"Halt!" said the sailor, leaning back in his seat and extending his hands near the musketeer's hat thrust on the back of his head. "Halt! my young gallant! I meddle in the affair because I am one of the family. I believe this concerns my niece; at least, so it looks to me."

"And what if I wished to marry her? Perhaps Catalina would think well of it; perhaps her father would consent."

"I don't say that he would not, but I am her uncle, and her uncle protests, and he says that this marriage is an absurdity."

Jaime looked at him in astonishment. An absurdity to marry a Febrer! Possibly he aspired to more for his niece?

"An absurdity for them and an absurdity for you," declared Valls. "Have you forgotten where you live? You can be my friend, the friend of the

Chueta, Pablo Valls, he whom you see in the café, in the Casino, and whom folks consider half crazy, but as for marrying a woman of my family!"

The sailor laughed as he thought of this union. Jaime's relatives would be furious with him, and would never speak to him again. They would be more tolerant with him if he were to commit a murder. His aunt, the Popess Juana, would scream as if she had witnessed a sacrilege. He would lose everything, and his niece, forgotten and tranquil until then, would give up the tediousness of her home, monotonous and sad, for an infernal life of misery, humiliation, and scorn.

"No, I say again; her uncle opposes it."

Even the people of the lower classes who declared themselves enemies of the rich would be indignant at seeing a butifarra marry a Chueta. The traditional atmosphere of the island must be respected, under penalty of death, as his brother Benito would die, for lack of air. It was dangerous to try to change all at once the work of centuries. Even those who came from outside, free of prejudices, after a short time suffered this repulsion of race, which seemed to permeate the very atmosphere.

"Once," continued Valls, "a Belgian couple came and established themselves on the island, bearing letters to me from a friend in Antwerp. I was attentive to them. I did all manner of favors for them. 'Be careful,' I told them; 'remember that I am a Chueta, and the Chuetas are very bad people.' The woman laughed. What barbarity! What out-of-date notions prevail here on the island! There were Jews everywhere and they were people like any other. After a while we met less frequently, they saw more of other people; at the end of a year they met me on the street and they glanced about in every direction before bowing to me; and now when they see me they always turn away their faces if they can, just the same as if they were Majorcans!"

Marriage! That was for a whole lifetime. In the first few months Jaime would try to face the murmurings and the scorn, but time runs on, and an odium dating from centuries does not wear out in the course of a few years, and finally Febrer would regret his ostracism, he would realize his mistake in running counter to the traditions of the grand majority, and the one to suffer the consequences would be Catalina, looked upon in her own house as a type of ignominy. No; in matrimony no chances must be taken. In Spain it is indissoluble, there is no divorce, and making experiments results dear. That was why he had remained a bachelor.

Febrer, irritated at these words, reminded Pablo of his vigorous propagandas against the enemies of the Chuetas.

"But don't you desire the elevation of your people? Doesn't it make you furious to have the people from 'the street' looked upon as different from ordinary human beings? What could there be better than this marriage to combat the prejudice?"

The captain waved his hands in sign of doubt. Ta! Ta! Such a marriage would accomplish nothing. During several epochs of tolerance and momentary forgetfulness some of the old-time Christians had married into the families of the people from "the street." There were many on the island who revealed this mixture by their surnames. And what was the result? Odium and separation continued the same. No, not the same; a little more tempered than in other days, but latent still. The things which would end this situation were the culture of the people, new customs, and this would be the work of years, and would not be accomplished by a marriage. Besides, experiments were dangerous and caused victims. If Jaime were eager to make the test let him choose someone besides his niece.

Valls smiled sarcastically on seeing Jaime's negative gestures.

"Are you enamored of Catalina?" he asked.

The captain's amber-colored eyes, malicious and focused steadily on Jaime, would not permit him to lie. Enamored?... No, not enamored; but love was not indispensable to marriage. Catalina was agreeable, she would make an excellent wife, a pleasant companion.

Pablo grinned even more widely.

"Let us talk like good friends, like men who know life. My brother is even more agreeable to you. No doubt he will set himself to arranging your business affairs. He will shed tears when he sees how much money you will cost him, but he has a mania for name; he respects and adores the past, and he will put up with anything. But don't trust him, Jaime. He is the type of those Jews represented in plays, with a fat pocketbook, helping people out in an hour of stress, but squeezing them afterward. They are the ones that discredit us; I am different. When he gets you into his power you will regret the business deal you have made."

Febrer looked at his friend with hostile eyes. The best thing he could do was to have no more to say about this matter. Pablo was a crazy fellow accustomed to saying whatever he thought, but he was not going to put up with it forever. If they were to continue friends, he must keep still.

"Well, we'll keep still," said Valls. "But understand once and for all that the girl's uncle opposes you, and that he does it for your sake and for hers."

They rode in silence the rest of the way. They separated on the Paseo del Borne with a frigid bow, without a handclasp.

Jaime returned to his house at dusk. Mammy Antonia had placed upon a table in the reception hall an oil lamp whose flame seemed to make the darkness of the vast room even more dense.

The Ivizans had just left. After breakfasting with her, and wandering about the city, they had waited until nightfall for the señor. They must spend the night on the boat; the master of the vessel wished to set sail before sunrise. Mammy spoke with kindly interest of these people who seemed to her to have come from another side of the world. "How they marveled at everything! They went about the island as if frightened; and Margalida! What a beautiful girl!"

Good old Mammy Antonia gave expression to one idea, but another persisted in her mind, and while she followed her master to his dormitory she looked him over with unconcealed curiosity, eager to read something in his face. What had taken place in Valldemosa, Virgin del Lluch? What had become of that absurd plan of which the señor had told her during breakfast?

But her master was in an ill humor, and he responded to her questions with brief words. He was not going to remain in the house; he would dine at the Casino. By the light of a lamp which but dimly illuminated his vast apartment, he changed his suit and brushed himself up a bit, taking an enormous key from Mammy's hands in order to open the door when he returned late at night.

At nine o'clock, on his way to the Casino, he saw his friend Toni Clapés, the smuggler, standing in the doorway of an inn. He was a large man with a round, shaven face, in peasant garb. He looked like a country curate dressed as a farmer to spend the night in Palma. With his white hempen sandals, his collar minus a cravat, and his hat thrust back, he entered the cafés and clubs, being received with profuse manifestations of friendship. In the Casino the men respected him for the calm way in which he drew handfuls of bank notes from his pockets. A native of a town in the interior, he had, by force of courage and dangers, become chief of a mysterious industry of which everyone had heard, but whose secret operations remained in shadow. He had hundreds of accomplices ready to die for him, and an unseen fleet which sailed by night, unafraid of storms, putting into port at inaccessible places. The worry and risk of these enterprises were never reflected in his jovial countenance nor in his generous impulses. He only seemed downcast when several weeks passed without news of some vessel which had sailed from Algiers in stormy weather.

"Lost!" he would say to his friends. "The bark and the cargo don't matter so much, but there were seven men in her; I've sailed that way myself—I must see to it that their families don't lack bread."

On other occasions his gloom was only pretended, with an ironic wrinkling of his lips. A government craft had just seized one of his vessels; and everyone laughed, knowing that nearly every month Toni allowed some old boat carrying a few bales of tobacco to be captured, to satisfy his pursuers by letting them boast of a triumph. When there was an epidemic in African ports the authorities of the island, powerless to guard so extensive a coastline, sent for Toni, appealing to his patriotism as a Majorcan, and the contrabandist promised to cease his navigation for the time, or he loaded at another point to avoid spreading the contagion.

Febrer had in this rough man, lighthearted and generous, a fraternal confidence. He had often told him his troubles, seeking the advice of his rustic astuteness. He, who would never dream of soliciting a loan from his friends in the Casino, in moments of stress accepted money from Toni which the contrabandist seemed to think no more about.

They shook hands when they met. Had Febrer been at Valldemosa? Toni had already heard about his trip, thanks to the facility with which the most insignificant news circulates through the calm, monotonous atmosphere of a Biscayan city open-mouthed for gossip.

"They are saying something more," said Toni in his provincial Majorcan dialect, "something that I can't believe. They say you're going to marry the atlota of Don Benito Valls!"

Febrer, surprised that the news had circulated so quickly, dared not deny it. Yes, it was true. He would acknowledge it to no one but Toni.

The smuggler made a gesture of repulsion, while his eyes, accustomed to the greatest surprises, revealed astonishment.

"You are making a mistake, Jaime, a serious mistake."

He spoke gravely, as if dealing with a solemn matter.

The butifarra maintained with this friend a confidence which he would not have risked with any one else. But he was ruined, dear Toni! Nothing that remained in his house was his! His creditors only respected him in the expectation of this marriage!

Toni shook his head with a negative expression. The rude native, the contrabandist who mocked at laws seemed stupefied by the news.

"Any way you look at it, you are making a mistake. You should get out of your money troubles any way you can, but not this way. We, your friends, will help you. *You* marry a Chueta?"

He took leave of Febrer with a vigorous handclasp, as if he imagined him in danger of death.

"You are making a mistake, think it over," he said with a reproachful expression. "You are making a mistake, Jaime!"

CHAPTER IV
THE TYRANNY OF THE DEAD

When Jaime got into bed three hours after midnight, he fancied he saw in the obscurity of his dormitory the faces of Captain Valls and Toni Clapés.

They seemed to be speaking to him as they had been doing the afternoon before.

"I oppose it," repeated the seaman with an ironic laugh.

"Don't do it," counseled the smuggler with a grave gesture.

He had spent the evening at the Casino, silent and ill humored under the obsession of these protests. What was there so strange and absurd about his plan that it should be rejected by that Chueta, notwithstanding that it would be an honor to his family, and by that peasant, rude and unscrupulous, who lived almost beyond the pale of the law?

It was true that this marriage would arouse scandal and protest on the island; but, what of that? Had he not a right to seek his salvation by any means? Was it perhaps a new idea for people of his class to try to reëstablish their fortune by means of matrimony? How about the dukes and high born princes who sought gold in America, giving their hand to daughters of millionaires of origin more censurable than that of Don Benito?

Ah, that crazy Pablo Valls was right in a way! These alliances might be made in the rest of the world, but Majorca, the beloved Roqueta, still possessed a living soul, the soul of former centuries, filled with odium and prejudice. The people were such as they were born, such as their fathers had been, and thus they must continue to be here in this calm atmosphere of the island which was unstirred by new thoughts slowly wafted from the outside world.

Jaime tossed restlessly in his couch. He was not sleepy. He thought of the Febrers, and of their glorious past! How it weighed upon him, like a chain of slavery which made his misery keener!

He had spent many afternoons in the archives of his house, in the apartment next to the dining-room opening the bronze doors of the cabinets and poring over the bundles of papers by the soft light filtering through the Persian blinds, dusty old papers which had to be shaken to keep them from being devoured by moths! Barbarous letters of marque with erroneous and capricious profiles which had served the Febrers in their early commercial campaigns. The whole array of them would barely bring in enough to eat for two days; and yet, the family had fought for centuries to make itself worthy this trust. How much dead glory!

The true fame of his family, spreading beyond the borders of the island, began in 1541 with the arrival of the great Emperor. An armada of three hundred ships manned by eighteen thousand marines assembled in the bay on their way to the conquest of Algiers. Here were the Spanish infantry commanded by Gonzaga, the Germans under the Duke of Alva, the Italians led by Colonna, two hundred knights of Malta at whose head marched the knight commander Don Priamo Febrer, the hero of the family, while the whole fleet sailed under the orders of the famous admiral Andrea Doria.

With festivities in representation of mythologic scenes, Majorca welcomed the Lord of Spain and the Indies, of Germany and of Italy, who now happened to be suffering from gout and other infirmities. The flower of Castilian nobility followed the Emperor on this holy enterprise and was duly lodged in the dwellings of the Majorcan caballeros. The house of Febrer received as guest a parvenu noble, but recently risen from obscurity, whose achievements in a far off country, and whose visible riches, aroused both enthusiasm and criticism. It was the Marquis del Valle de Huaxaca, Hernando Cortés, who, having just conquered Mexico, had come with the expedition in a galley equipped at his own expense, accompanied by his sons Don Martin and Don Luis, eager to figure now among the ancient nobles of the reconquest as an equal.

A royal magnificence distinguished this conqueror from distant lands, this possessor of fabulous wealth. Three enormous emeralds valued at over a hundred thousand ducats decorated the bridge of his galley; one was cut in the form of a flower, another in the figure of a bird, and another was shaped like a bell, with an enormous pearl serving as a clapper. He was attended by persons who had been his companions overseas, and who had adopted exotic customs; slender hidalgos of sickly color who silently whiled away the time lighting bundles of herbs resembling pieces of rope, and puffing smoke out of their mouths like demons who were on fire within.

The long line of Febrer's grandmothers had handed down from generation to generation a great uncut diamond, a souvenir from the heroic captain given in return for their gracious hospitality. The precious stone was described in the family documents, but Don Horacio's grandfather had not had the pleasure of seeing it, since it had disappeared during the course of centuries, as had so many riches swept away by the financial troubles of an ostentatious house.

The Febrers prepared refreshments for the armada, in the name of Majorca, defraying most of the expenses themselves. In order to arouse the Emperor's appreciation of the abundance and productiveness of the island, this "refreshment" included a hundred beeves, two hundred sheep, hundreds of pairs of chicken and peacocks, hundreds of cuarteras of oil and flour, hundreds of cuarterones of wine, more hundreds of cuarterolas of cheese, capers, olives, twenty bottles of arrayan, and four quintales of white wax. Moreover, the Febrers resident on the island and not members of the Order of Malta, embarked in the squadron with two hundred Majorcan gentlemen, eager to conquer Algiers, that nest of pirates. The three hundred galleys sailed out of the bay, their pennants streaming, accompanied by salutes discharged from cannons and bombards, cheered by the multitude crowded upon the walls. Never had the Emperor gathered together so imposing a fleet.

It was October. The able Doria was in bad humor. According to him there existed no other safe ports in the Mediterranean than "June, July, August and—Mahon." The Emperor had delayed too long in Tyrol and Italy. The Pope, Paul III, when he came out to meet him at Lucca, had prophesied misfortunes due to the lateness of the season. The expedition disembarked on the shore of Hama. The knight commander Febrer, with his caballeros of Malta marched in the vanguard, sustaining incessant onslaughts from the Turks. The army took possession of the heights surrounding Algiers and began the siege. Then Doria's predictions were fulfilled. A frightful storm arose with all the violence of the African winter. The troops, without shelter, drenched to the bone during the night of the torrential rain, were stiff with cold. A furious wind compelled the men to lie flat upon the ground. At sunrise, the Turks, taking advantage of this situation, fell suddenly upon the army, which became demoralized and scattered, but the knight commander Priamo, a demon of war, insensible alike to either cold or fire, vigorous, aggressive and untiring, restrained the advance with a handful of his caballeros. Spaniards and Germans rallied. Pursued by the besiegers the Turks had to fall back to the very walls of Algiers, and Don Priamo Febrer, wounded in the face and in the leg, dragged himself to the city gates and thrust his dagger deep into one of its panels in testimony of his attack.

In another sally against the Moors, the onset was so furious that the Italians were driven back, the Germans following their example, and the Emperor, flaming with fury at seeing his favorite soldiers in retreat, unsheathed his sword, called for his colors, set spurs to his war-horse, and shouted to the brilliant retinue of caballeros that followed him: "Forward, gentlemen! If you see me fall with the flag, save it before you do me!" The Turks fled before the charge of this squadron of iron. A Febrer from the island, entitled "the rich," a remote ancestor of Jaime's, had twice rushed in between the Emperor and the enemy, saving his life. At the exit of a narrow defile the fire from the Turkish culverins decimated the cavalry. The Duke of Alva grasped the bridle of his monarch's horse. "Sire, your life is more important than a victory!" and the Emperor, growing calmer, turned back, and with a stately gesture of gratitude re moved the gold chain from about his neck and hung it upon the shoulders of Febrer.

Meanwhile, the storm wrecked one hundred and sixty vessels, and the remainder of the fleet was forced to take refuge behind Cape Matifou. The majority of the nobles agreed upon an immediate retreat. Hernando Cortés, the Count of Alcaudete, governor of Oran, and the Majorcan gentlemen, with the Febrers at their head, begged the Emperor to save himself and to let the army carry forward the expedition alone. At last a retreat was decided upon, and over mountain summits and through rain-swollen streams, they achieved their sorrowful purpose, continually accosted by the enemy, leaving killed and prisoners in their wake. In the teeth of the storm those who were able boarded the ship; the raging sea swallowed up nine more vessels, and the Majorcan galleys sailed mournfully into the bay of Palma convoying the Emperor who left for the Peninsula without landing in Majorca. The Febrers returned to their house covered with renown even in defeat; one bearing the golden testimonial of the Cæsar's friendship; the other, the knight commander, lying on a litter, cursing like a pagan because the blockading of Algiers had been discontinued.

Priamo Febrer! Jaime could not think of him without sympathy and curiosity aroused by the tales he had heard in his youth. His was the heroic, and also the unconventional soul of the family. The ancient dames of the house never mentioned his name. On hearing it they lowered their eyes and blushed. Although a soldier of the church, a holy knight who had taken the vow of chastity on entering the Order, he always carried women in his galley—Christian women ransomed from the Mussulman, who were in no haste to return to their homes, or else infidels captured on his audacious buccaneering expeditions.

When it came to a division of the booty, he looked with indifference upon the pile of riches, leaving them for the Grand Master of the Order; he was only interested in appropriating the women. If threatened with excommunication, he laughed impishly in the faces of the ecclesiastics of the Order. If the Grand Master sent for him to administer a reproof for his carnality, Febrer would straighten himself arrogantly, reminding him of the glorious victories on the sea which the Cross of Malta owed to him.

Some of his letters, bundles of yellow paper with reddish characters, faded and indistinct, were written in a style which revealed the knight commander's lack of learning. He expressed himself with soldierly fluency, mixing religious phrases with the most shameless expressions.

His name was known along the whole Mediterranean coast where dwelt the infidels. The Mohammedans feared him as they feared the devil; Moorish mothers hushed their babes with threat of the knight commander Febrer. Dragut, the great Turkish corsair, considered him the only rival worthy of his valor. Each feared and respected the other, and, after several engagements in which both were wounded, they endeavored to avoid meeting, either on land or sea.

One day Dragut, on visiting a galley of his fleet anchored off Algiers, found Priamo Febrer, half naked, chained to a seat with an oar in his hands.

"Casualties of war!" exclaimed Dragut.

"Casualties of fortune!" replied the knight commander.

They clasped hands and said no more. One did not offer favor, nor did the other ask for mercy. The people of Algiers flocked to see the "Maltese Demon," now become a slave and fastened to a bench, but when they beheld him as fierce and glowering as a captive eaglet they dared not insult him. The Order paid as ransom for its heroic warrior hundreds of slaves, ships, and cargoes, as if he were a prince. Years afterward, Don Priamo, upon entering a Maltese galley found the intrepid Dragut in turn chained to a rower's seat. The scene was repeated in reverse, with no sign of surprise from either, as if the event were perfectly normal. They clasped hands.

"Casualties of war!" said Febrer.

"Casualties of fortune!" replied the other.

Jaime liked the knight commander because he had represented in the bosom of the noble family lawlessness, license, scorn of convention. What cared he for difference of race and religion when he fancied a woman?

When this noble ancestor had come to middle life he retired to Tunis among his good friends the rich corsairs, who, once hating and fighting him, now at last became his comrades. Of this period of his existence little was known. Some thought that he had become a renegade, and that as a diversion he even gave chase on the sea to the galleys from Malta. Enemies of his, gentlemen of the Order, swore to having seen him during a battle, dressed as a Turk, in the forecastle of a hostile ship. The only positive fact was that he lived in Tunis in a palace on the seashore with a Moorish woman of splendid beauty, a relative of his friend the Bey. Two letters in the archives testified to this incomprehensible liaison. When the Moslem woman died Don Priamo returned to Malta, deeming his career ended. The highest dignitaries of the Order desired to favor him if he would amend his conduct, and they talked of appointing him Commander of the Order of Malta at Negroponte, or else Great Castellan at Amposta, but the incorrigible Don Priamo would not better his ways, and continued a libertine, crusty, fickle in disposition toward his companions, but a beloved hero to his brothers in arms, men of the ranks belonging to the Order, mere soldiers who could display over their cuirasses no other decoration than that of the half cross.

Scorn for their intrigues, and the hatred of his enemies, caused him to abandon the archipelago of the Order, the Islands of Malta and Gozo, ceded by the Emperor to the warrior friars for no other price than the annual tribute of a goshawk such as are native to the island. Old and worn he retired to Majorca, living off the products of the estates belonging to his commandery situated in Catalonia. The impiety and the vices of the hero horrified the family and scandalized the island. Three young Moorish girls and a Jewess of great beauty were his companions in the guise of servants where they occupied a whole wing of the Febrer mansion, which was much larger at that time than today. Moreover, he kept several male slaves; some were Turks; others Tartars; these shook with fear whenever they saw him. He had dealings with old women who were held to be witches; he consulted Hebraic healers; he shut himself up in his dormitory with these suspicious characters, and the neighbors trembled at seeing his windows glow with an infernal fire in the small hours of the night. Some of his male slaves grew pale and languid as if their lives were being sucked away. The people whispered that the knight commander was using their blood for magic drinks. Don Priamo wished to renew his youth; he was eager to reanimate his body with vital fires. The Grand Inquisitor of Majorca hinted at the possibility of paying a visit, with familiars and alguazils, to the apartments of the knight commander, but the latter who was a cousin of the Inquisitor, communicated by letter his intention of knocking open his head with a boarding pike if he ventured to so much as set foot on the first step of his stairway.

Don Priamo died, or rather he burst under pressure of his diabolical beverages, leaving as a testimonial of his freedom from bias a will, the copy of which Jaime had read. The warrior of the church willed the main portion of his property, as well as his weapons and trophies, to his elder brother's children, as had likewise done all the second sons of the house; but in continuation there figured a long list of legacies, all for children of his whom he declared begotten of Moorish slave women or of Jewess friends, Armenians and Greeks, vegetating, wrinkled, and decrepit, in some port of the Levant; an offspring like that of a patriarch of the Bible, but all irregular, hybrid, the product of the crossing of hostile blood of antagonistic races. Famous knight commander! It seemed as if on breaking his vows he tried to minimize the offense by always choosing infidel women. To his sins of carnality was added the shame of traffic with females hostile to the true God.

Jaime looked upon him as a precursor who cleared away his doubts. What was strange about his marrying a Chueta, a woman like others in her customs, beliefs, and education, since the most famous of the Febrers in an epoch of intolerance had lived beyond the pale of the law with infidel women? Suddenly, however, family prejudices provoked in Jaime a twinge of remorse, causing him to recall a clause in the knight commander's will. He left legacies to the children of his slave women, hybrids of other races, because they were of his blood and he wished to shield them from the sufferings of poverty, but he prohibited them from using their father's name, the name of the Febrers which had always been kept legally free from degrading admixtures in their Majorcan house.

Recalling this, Jaime smiled in the darkness. Who could answer for the past? What mysteries might not be hidden at the roots of the trunk of his origin, back in the medieval times, when the Febrers and the rich of the Balearic synagogue trafficked together and loaded their ships in Puerto Pi? Many of his family, and even he himself, with other members of the ancient Majorcan nobility, had something Jewish in their faces. Purity of race was an illusion. The life of nations depends upon constant change, the great producer of mixtures and assimilations. But, ah, the proud family scruples! The dividing lines created by custom!

He himself, though pretending to jest at the prejudices of the past, experienced an irresistible feeling of haughtiness in the presence of Don Benito who was to become his father-in-law. He considered himself superior; he tolerated him with condescending courtesy; he had mentally revolted when the rich Chueta spoke of his pretended friendship for Don Horacio. No, the Febrers had never mingled with these people. When his ancestors were in Algiers with the Emperor, Catalina's forefathers were probably shut up in the ward of Calatrava, making objects of silver, trembling at the thought that peasant-farmers might descend upon Palma under pretext of war, groveling, white with terror, before the Great Inquisitor, undoubtedly some Febrer, to gain his protection.

Outside, in the reception hall, hung the portrait of one of his less remote ancestors, a señor with shaven face, fine colorless lips, white wig, and red silk coat, who, according to a memorandum on the canvas, had been perpetual governor of the city of Palma. King Carlos III sent a royal ordinance to the island prohibiting the insulting of the old-time Jews, "an industrious and honorable people," threatening with penalty of imprisonment whosoever should call them "Chuetas." The island council sniffed at this absurd order of the too kind monarch, and Governor Febrer settled the matter with the authority of his name. "File the ordinance; it will be noted, but it will not be complied with. Why should the Chuetas be given respect like any one of us? They are content so long as their pockets and their women are not touched." Then they all laughed, saying that Febrer spoke from experience, for he was extremely fond of visiting "the street," giving work to the silversmiths so as to be able to talk to their women.

In the reception room there was also another ancestral portrait—that of the Inquisitor Don Jaime Febrer, whose name he bore. In the garrets of the house he had found several visiting cards yellowed by time, bearing the name of the rich priest; cards engraved with emblems such as came into use in the Eighteenth Century. In the center of the card appeared a wooden cross, with a sword and an olive branch; on both sides two pasteboard coronets worn as a mark of infamy by those on whom punishment was to be inflicted, one with the cross of the Sacred Office, another with dragons and Medusa heads. Manacles, whips, rosaries, and candles completed the decoration. Below burned a bonfire around a post with a large iron ring, and there figured a conical hat decorated with serpents, toads, and horned heads. A sort of sarcophagus rose between these decorations, and on it was inscribed in ancient Spanish lettering: "The Senior Inquisitor, Don Jaime Febrer." The peaceful Majorcan who, on returning to his house, found this visiting card, must have felt his hair rise in terror.

Another of his ancestors came into his mind, the one mentioned by the choleric Pablo Valls when he recalled the burning of the Chuetas and Father Garau's little book. He was an elegant and gallant Febrer, who had kindled enthusiasm among the ladies of Palma at the famous auto de fe, with his new suit of Florentine cloth, embroidered in gold, mounted upon a charger as sightly as his master, carrying the standard of the Sacred Tribunal. In flights of lyric rapture the Jesuit described his genteel bearing. At sundown the knight had seen, there near the foot of the castle of Bellver, how the corpulent bulk of Rafael Valls had burned, and how his entrails had burst out and fallen into the coals, a spectacle from which the presence of ladies distracted his attention, making his horse caracole near the doors of their carriages. Captain Valls was right; it was barbarous; but the Febrers were his kindred; his name and the fortune he had squandered he had owed to them. Now he, the last descendant of a family proud of its history, was about to marry Catalina Valls, the offspring of the executed Jew!

The old wives' tales he had heard in childhood, the simple stories with which Mammy Antonia used to entertain him, now surged through his mind like dreams of the past, which had made a deep impression. He thought of the Chuetas, who, according to popular opinion, were not the same as other people; reputed to be creatures of sordid poverty and slimy to the touch, who, no doubt, concealed terrible deformities. Who could say that Catalina was like other women?

Then his thoughts turned to Pablo Valls, so merry and generous, the superior of nearly every other friend Jaime possessed on the island, but Pablo had lived little in Majorca; he had traveled widely; he was not like those of his race, working stationary like automatons in the same posture for centuries, reproducing themselves in their cowardice, lacking courage and unity to compel respect.

Jaime knew rich Jewish families in Paris and in Berlin. He had even solicited loans from the lofty barons of Israel, but as he came into contact with these true Hebrews who clung to their religion and their independence, he did not feel that instinctive repugnance aroused by the devout Don Benito and other Chuetas of Majorca. Was it atmosphere which influenced him? Was it that centuries of submission, and fear, and the habit of cringing, had made of the Jews of Majorca a different race?

Febrer at last sank into the darkness of sleep, with these thoughts whirling through his troubled mind.

While dressing next morning, he decided, by a great effort of the will, to make a certain call. This marriage was something extraordinary and risky, which demanded long reflection, as his friend the smuggler had pointed out.

"Before taking the step I must play my last card," thought Jaime. "I'll go and see the Popess Juana. I haven't seen her for many years, but she is my aunt, my nearest relative. In justice, I ought to be her heir. Ah, if only that idea would occur to her! If she would only bestir herself all my troubles would be over."

Jaime decided upon the most advantageous hour to visit the great lady. In the afternoon she held her famous salon of canons and austere gentlemen whom she received with the airs of a sovereign. These were to be the inheritors of her money, as agents and representatives of various corporations of a religious character. He must visit her immediately; surprise her in her solitude after mass and morning prayers.

Doña Juana lived in a palace near the Cathedral. She had remained unmarried, abominating the world after certain deceptions in her youth for which Jaime's father had been responsible. All the combativeness of her irrascible disposition, and the zeal of her cold and haughty faith, she had dedicated to politics and religion. "For God and for the King," Febrer had heard her say, on visiting her once when he was a boy. In her youth she had dreamed of the heroines of Vendée, she had been aroused by the heroic deeds and sufferings of the Duchess of Berry, and was eager, like those forceful women, devoted to their legitimate rulers and to religion, to mount a war horse, wearing an image of Christ on her breast, with a sabre hanging by her side. This desire, however, did not pass beyond vague dreams. In reality she had been on no other expedition than a trip to Catalonia, during the last Carlist war, to see at closer range the sacred enterprise which was absorbing a great part of her wealth.

The enemies of the Popess Juana declared that the young woman had kept concealed in her palace the Count of Montemolín, a pretender to the crown, and that she had drawn him into conspiracy with General Ortega, Captain General of the islands. To these rumors were added tales of the romantic love of Doña Juana for the pretender. Jaime smiled on hearing this gossip. It was all a lie; Don Horacio's grandfather, who had known the whole story, often mentioned these matters to his grandson. The Popess Juana had loved no other than Jaime's father. General Ortega was a deluded person whom Doña Juana received with extraordinary show of mystery, gowned in white, in a darkened salon, talking in a sweet voice which seemed to come from beyond the tomb, as if she were an angel of the past, concerning the necessity of turning Spain back to its ancient customs, sweeping away the liberals, and reëstablishing the government of caballeros. "For God and for the King!" Ortega was shot on the coast of Catalonia when his Carlist expedition failed, and the Popess remained in Majorca, ready to bestow her money upon new pious enterprises.

Many thought that she was ruined after her prodigality during the last civil war, but Jaime knew what a fortune the devout lady possessed. She lived as simply as a peasant; she still owned extensive estates, and the money she had saved by her economies went in the form of gifts to churches and convents and in donations to Saint Peter's treasury. Her old time motto, "For God and for the King!" had suffered mutilation. She no longer thought of the king. Nothing was left of her former enthusiasm for the exiled pretender except a great daguerreotype with a dedication adorning the darker part of her salon.

"A fine young man," she used to say, "but like all liberals! Ah, life in a foreign land! How it changes men! What sins— —!"

Now her enthusiasm was only for God, and her money made its way to Rome. One supreme hope dominated her life. Would not the Holy Father send her the "Golden Rose" before she died? It was a gift originally intended for none but queens, but some pious rich women of South America had received this distinction, and Juana gave a detailed account of her liberalities, living in holy poverty so that she might send still more money. The "Golden Rose," and then she would be ready to die!

Febrer arrived at the dwelling of the Popess: a zaguán resembling his own, but better kept, cleaner, with no grass between the paving stones, no cracks nor broken places in the wall, but all in monastic pulchritude! The door was opened to him by a servant, young and pale, dressed in a blue habit with a white cord, who made a gesture of surprise on recognizing Jaime.

She left him in the reception hall among a concourse of portraits, such as that in the house of the Febrers, and she ran with a light, rat-like trot to the interior rooms to announce this extraordinary visit which disturbed the monastic peace of the palace.

Long moments of silence followed. Jaime heard furtive footsteps in the adjoining apartments; he saw curtains which swayed lightly, as if moved by a gentle zephyr; he felt lurking forms behind them, unseen eyes spying upon him. The servant reappeared, bowing low to Jaime with grave courtesy, for was he not the señora's nephew? She left the great salon and disappeared.

Febrer amused himself while waiting by looking over the vast room, with its archaic luxury. His own house had been like this in his grandfather's time. The walls were covered with rich crimson damask forming a background for the ancient religious paintings in soft, Italian style. The furniture was of white and gilded wood, with voluptuous curves, upholstered in heavy embroidered silk. Polychrome figures of saints and Eighteenth Century hangings with mythological scenes were reflected in the deep azure mirrors above the consoles. The vaulted ceiling was painted in fresco, with an assemblage of gods and goddesses seated on clouds, whose rosy nudity and bold gestures contrasted sharply with the dolorous visage of a great Christ which seemed to preside over the salon, occupying a wide space on the wall between two doors. The Popess recognized the sinfulness of these mythological decorations, but as they were reminiscent of a happy epoch, of a time when the caballeros ruled, she respected them, and tried not to see them.

A damask curtain parted, and a woman who looked like an old servant entered the salon, dressed in black, wearing a plain skirt and a poor jacket, after the manner of a peasant woman. Her gray hair was partly concealed by a dark shawl to which time and grease had imparted a reddish tint. Beneath her skirt peeped forth feet shod in hempen sandals, with coarse white stockings. Jaime hastily arose. That old servant was the Popess!

The chairs were arranged in a certain disorder, which suggested the coterie which gathered there every afternoon. Each seat belonged by right of habit to a certain grave person, and stood motionless in its own particular place. Doña Juana occupied a great throne-like chair, from which seat she presided every afternoon over her faithful reunion of canons, old woman friends, and señoras of wholesome ideas, like a queen receiving her court.

"Sit down," she said to her nephew curtly.

She extended her hands, in the automatism of custom, across a monumental empty silver brazier, and stared at Jaime fixedly with her piercing gray eyes so accustomed to commanding respect. This authoritative stare gradually began to soften until it weakened in tears of emotion. She had not seen her nephew for nearly ten years.

"You are a true Febrer. You look like your grandfather—like all of the men of your family."

She concealed her real thoughts; she kept silent about the only resemblance which moved her, his likeness to his father. Jaime was the young naval officer, just as he used to come to see her in the old days! He lacked nothing but the uniform and the eyeglasses. Ah, that monster of liberalism and of ingratitude!

Soon her eyes recovered their accustomed hardness; her features became more dry, more pale and angular.

"What do you wish?" she said rudely; "because you certainly have not come merely for the pleasure of seeing me!"

The moment had arrived! Jaime lowered his eyes with childish hypocrisy, and, afraid of broaching his actual desires, he began his attack in a roundabout manner. He explained that he was good, that he believed in all the old ideals, that he desired to maintain the prestige of his family and to add to it. He had not been a saint; he confessed it; a wild life had consumed his wealth—but the honor of the house remained intact! This life of sin and wickedness had given him two things, experience, and the firm intention to mend his ways.

"Aunt, I want to change my way of living; I want to become a different man."

The aunt assented with an enigmatic gesture. Very well; thus Saint Augustine and other holy men who had spent their early lives in licentiousness, changed their ways and had become luminaries of the church.

Jaime felt encouraged by these words. He certainly would never figure as a luminary of anything, but he desired to be a good Christian gentleman; he would marry, he would educate his children to carry on the traditions of the house—a beautiful future! But, alas! lives as irregular as his were difficult to patch up when the moment came to direct them toward virtuous ends. He needed help. He was ruined; his lands were almost in the hands of his creditors; his house was a desert; he had protected himself by selling the mementoes of the past. He, a Febrer, was about to be thrust into the street, unless some merciful hand should assist him; and he had thought of his aunt, who, when all was said and done, was his nearest relative, almost like a mother, in whom he trusted to save him.

The imaginary motherhood caused Doña Juana to flush slightly, and augmented the hard glitter in her eyes. Ah, memory, with its haunting visions!

"And is it from me you hope for salvation?" slowly replied the Popess in a voice that hissed between the yellow rows of her parted teeth. "You are wasting your time, Jaime. I am poor. I have almost nothing—barely enough to live on and to make a few gifts to charity."

She said it with such an accent of firmness that Febrer lost hope and realized that it would be useless to insist. The Popess would not help him.

"Very well," said Jaime with visible discouragement. "But, lacking your assistance, I must seek another solution for my troubles, and I have one in view. You are now the head of my family, and it is right for me to seek your advice. I am considering a marriage which can save me; an alliance with a rich woman, but one who does not belong to our class; one of low origin. What ought I to do?"

He expected in his aunt a movement of surprise, of curiosity. Perhaps the announcement of his marriage would soften her. It was almost certain that, terrified at this great danger to the honor of her house and of her blood, she would smooth the way for him by conceding assistance, but the one to be surprised, to be dismayed, was Jaime as he saw the pale lips of the old woman part in a cold smile.

"I have heard," she said. "I was told all about it this morning in Santa Eulalia as I was coming away from mass. You were at Valldemosa yesterday. You are going to marry—you are going to marry—a Chueta!"

It cost her an effort to pronounce the word; she shuddered as she spoke it. After this a long silence reigned, one of those tragic and absolute silences which follow great catastrophes, as if the house had just tumbled down, and the echo of the last toppled wall had died away.

"And what do you think of it?" Jaime ventured to ask timidly.

"Do as you wish," said the Popess with frigidity. "You remember that we have lived many years without seeing each other, and we can go on in the same way for the rest of our lives. Do as you please. Henceforward you and I will be like people of different blood; we think along different lines; we cannot understand each other."

"So I ought not to marry?" he insisted.

"Ask yourself that question. For many years the Febrers have wandered on such crooked paths that nothing they do surprises me."

Jaime detected in his aunt's eyes and noted in her voice a repressed joy, a reveling in vengeance, the satisfaction of seeing her enemies fall into what she considered a dishonor, and this irritated him.

"But if I marry," he said, imitating Doña Juana's frigid manner, "will you come to my wedding?"

This put an end to the tranquillity of the Popess, who drew herself up haughtily. The romantic books of her youth rushed through her mind; she spoke like an injured queen at the end of a chapter of a historic novel.

"Caballero! I am a Genovart on my father's side. My mother was a Febrer, but one family is as good as the other. I renounce the blood that is to be mixed with a vile people, Christ killers, and I remain true to my own, to that of my father which will end with me pure and honorable!"

She pointed toward the door with arrogant mien, bringing the interview to a close, but soon she seemed to realize how abrupt and theatrical her protest had been, and she lowered her eyes; she grew more human, assuming an air of Christian meekness.

"Good-bye, Jaime; may the Lord enlighten you!"

"Good-bye, Aunt."

Impelled by custom he extended his hand, but she drew hers back, concealing it behind her. Febrer smiled as he recalled certain tales told by the gossips. It was not scorn nor hatred. The Popess had made a vow that as long as she lived she would touch the hand of no man except those of the priests.

When he found himself again on the street, he began to curse mentally, looking at the swelling balconies of the rococo mansion. Rattlesnake! How she rejoiced at his marriage! When it had become a fact she would pretend indignation and scandal before her coterie; perhaps she would get sick so that all the islanders would sympathize with her, and yet, her joy would be great, the joy of a vengeance nourished for many years, on seeing a Febrer, the son of the man she hated, submerged in what she considered the most ignominious of dishonors. Urged on by the certainty of ruin, he must give her this joy by carrying into effect his union with the daughter of Valls! Ah, poverty!

He wandered along the solitary streets near the Almudaina and the Cathedral until past midday. At last hunger instinctively turned his steps homeward. He ate in silence, without knowing what was put before him, not even seeing Mammy, who, worried and restless since the previous day, was eager to start a conversation in order to learn more news.

After luncheon he stepped out upon a small gallery with a crumbling balustrade crowned by three Roman busts which looked into the garden. At his feet spread the foliage of the figs, the varnished leaves of the magnolias, the green balls on the orange trees. Before him the trunks of the palms shut off the blue of space, and, farther away, the sharp-pointed merlons of the wall extended to the sea, the luminous, immense sea, trembling with life as if the barkentines with their wind-filled sails were tickling its greenish surface. At his right lay the port crowded with masts and surrounded with yellow chimneys; beyond, striding into the waters of the bay, the dark mass of the pines of Bellver, and on the summit the circular castle like a bull-ring, with its Torre de Homenaje apart, isolated, with no other link than a graceful bridge. Below lay the modern red houses of Terreno, and beyond, at the end of the cape, the ancient Puerto Pi with its signal towers and the batteries of Don Carlos.

Across the bay, losing itself in the sea, amid the fog floating upon the horizon, was a dark green cape with reddish rocks, gloomy and desolate.

Against the blue sky the Cathedral lifted its buttresses and arcades like a ship of stone bereft of masts, flung by angry waves between the city and the shore. Behind the temple the ancient alcazar, the Almudaina, flaunted its red, Moorish, almost windowless towers. In the bishop's palace the glass panes in the miradors shone like flames of reddened steel, as if reflected from a conflagration. Between this palace and the sea wall, in a deep, grass-grown fosse along whose walls crept windswept garlands of rosebushes, lay some cannons, a few of them very ancient and mounted upon wheels; others more modern, which had awaited for years the call to action, were scattered over the ground. The great iron guns were oxidized, as were the gun-carriages; the long-range cannons, painted red, and sunken in the herbage, resembled exhaust pipes of a steam engine. Neglect and the rust of disuse were aging these modern pieces. The traditional, monotonous atmosphere which, according to Febrer, enveloped the island, seemed to weigh upon these instruments of war, old and out-of-date almost before they were fashioned, and before ever having spoken.

Insensible to the joyousness of the sun, heedless of the luminous palpitation of the blue expanse, deaf to the chirping of the birds fluttering at his feet, Jaime was overcome by intense sadness, by overwhelming depression.

Why struggle with the past? How rid himself of the chain? At birth everyone found the place and the gesture for everything in the course of his existence already defined; it was useless even to wish to change one's situation.

Often in his early youth, on looking down from a height upon the city with its smiling environs, he had felt obsessed by gloomy thoughts. In the sunshine-flooded streets, under shelter of the roofs, swarmed an ant-like humanity, dominated by necessities and ideas of the moment which they considered all important, believing with consuming egotism in a superior and omnipotent being watching and directing their goings and comings, as insignificant as the infusoria in a drop of water. Beyond the town Jaime's imagination pictured cypress tops thrust above sombre walls, the white structures of a compactly built city, multitudes of tiny windows like the mouths of ovens, and marble slabs which seemed to cover the entrances to caves. How many were the inhabitants of the city of the living, in their plazas and on their broad streets? Sixty thousand—eighty thousand. Ah! In that other city but a short distance away, crowded, silent, packed into their little white houses beneath the gloomy cypresses, the invisible inhabitants numbered four hundred thousand—six hundred thousand, perhaps a million!

In Madrid, the same thought had flashed through his brain one afternoon while he was strolling with two women through the outskirts of the town. The crests of the hills near the river were occupied by silent villages, among whose white edifices rose pointed groups of cypress; and on the opposite side of the great city also existed other bivouacs of silence and oblivion. The city was surrounded by a closely drawn cordon of fortresses of the departed. Half a million living beings swarmed through the streets, imagining themselves alone in the mastery and direction of their existences, never heeding the four—six—eight millions of their kind, close beside them, but invisible.

The same thought had come to him in Paris, where four millions of stirring citizens dwelt, surrounded by twenty or thirty millions of whilom inhabitants now asleep. The same melancholy reflections had haunted him in all the great cities.

The living were nowhere alone; the dead ever surrounded them, and as the dead were more, infinitely more, they weighed upon the living with the heaviness of time and of numbers.

No; the dead did not depart, as the people thought. The dead remained motionless on the brink of life, spying upon the new generations, forcing upon them the authority of the past with a rude tug at the soul whenever they tried to step out of the beaten path.

What tyranny was theirs! What unlimited power! It was futile to turn away the eyes and to stifle memory; the dead are everywhere; they occupy the highways of the living, and they stride out to meet us and remind us of their benefactions, compelling us to a debasing gratitude. What servitude! The house in which we live was constructed by the dead; religions were created by them; the laws which we obey the dead dictated. Our favorite dishes, our tastes, our passions, came from them; the foods which nourish us, all are produced by earth broken up by hands which now are dust. Morality, customs, prejudices, honor—these are their work. Had they thought in some different way, the present organizations of men would not be as they are today. The things which are agreeable to our senses are so because thus the dead willed them; the disagreeable and useless are detested by the will of those who no longer exist; what is moral and what is immoral are sentences pronounced centuries ago by them.

Those men who make an effort to say new things do nothing but repeat in different words the same thoughts that the dead had been expressing for centuries. That which we consider most spontaneous and personal in ourselves has been dictated to us by unseen masters lying in their earthen couches, who, in their turn, had learned the lesson from other ancestors. The gleam of our eyes is but the glow of the souls of our forefathers, as the lines in our faces reproduce and reflect the traces of generations long disappeared.

Febrer smiled sadly. We imagine that we think our own thoughts, while in the convolutions of our brain stirs a force which has lived in other organisms, like the sap of the grafted shoot which carries energy from old and dying trees to new offshoots. Much of the thought which we express spontaneously, as the latest novelty of our mind, is an idea of those others, encysted in our brain at birth, and which suddenly bursts its bondage. Our tastes, our caprices, our virtues and our defects, our affinities and our repulsions—all inherited, all a work of those who have disappeared but who survive in us.

With what terror Jaime thought of the power of the dead! They concealed themselves to make their tyranny less cruel, but they had not really perished; their souls were lying within the confines of our existence, just as their bodies formed an entrenched field roundabout the man-made towns. They scrutinized us with arbitrary eyes; they followed us, guiding us with invisible clutch at the slightest indication of deviating from the path; they banded together with diabolic determination to lead the flocks of men who rush after some new and extraordinary ideal, reëstablishing with violent reaction, the order of life, which they love, silent and placid, amid rustle of dried grasses and the flutter of butterfly wings and the sweet peace of the cemetery, asleep in the sun.

The souls of the dead fill the world. The dead do not go away, they remain as masters. The dead command, and it is useless to resist.

The man of the great cities living a giddy life, knowing not who built his house, nor who makes his bread, seeing no other works of nature than the stunted trees adorning his streets, ignores these things. He does not even realize that his life is spent among millions and millions of his forefathers crowded together but a few steps away, spying upon him and directing him. He blindly obeys their tugging, without knowing where leads the cord fastened upon his soul. Poor automaton, he believes all his acts to be the product of his will, when they are nothing less than impositions of the omnipotent invisible horde.

Jaime, submerged in the monotonous existence of a tranquil island, thinking back upon his forefathers one by one, knowing the origin and history of all that surrounded him, objects of art, clothing, furniture, and the house itself which seemed possessed of a soul, could give account of this tyranny better than could others.

Yes; the dead command! The authority of the living, their startling novelties—illusion, deception, serving only to carry forward existence.

Gazing on the sea, on whose horizon the smoke from a steamer traced a slender column, Febrer thought of the great trans-Atlantic liners, floating cities, speeding monsters, the pride of human industry, which can make the round of the world in a few short weeks. His remote ancestors in the Middle Ages who went to England in a ship no better than a fishing smack, represented something more extraordinary, and the great captains of the present time with their swarming crews, had not achieved greater deeds than the knight commander Priamo with his handful of sailors. What deceptions, what illusions, we form concerning life, to conceal from ourselves the monotony of its shams. The brevity of its experiences was maddening. It mattered not whether one lived thirty years or three hundred. Men perfected the playthings which served their egoism and their well being, machines, means of locomotion; but aside from this, they lived the same. The passions, the joys, and the sorrows were the same; the human animal did not change.

Jaime had believed himself a free man, with a soul which he called modern, his, all his; and now he discovered in it a confused medley of the souls of his ancestors. He could recognize them, because he had studied them, because they were in the next room, in the archives, like dried flowers preserved between the leaves of an old book. The majority of humans retained at the most a memory of their great grandfathers; families which had been unable to scrupulously preserve the history of their past through the centuries gave no heed to the ancestral life perpetuated in their souls, taking as inspirations of their own the cries which their ancestors uttered through them. Our flesh was flesh of those who no longer exist; our souls combined fragments of the souls of many dead men.

Jaime felt within him his austere grandfather, Don Horacio, and along with him the animosities of the Inquisitor-general, he of the appalling visiting card, and the souls of the famous knight commander and other ancestors. In the mind of the man of today still lingered something of that "perpetual governor" who considered the Jewish converts on the island as a separate and degraded race.

The dead command! Now he understood the inevitable repugnance, the arrogance he had felt as he came into contact with the obsequious and humble Don Benito. Those sentiments were unconquerable, and his aversion irremediable. It was imposed upon him by others stronger than himself. The dead command, and they must be obeyed!

His pessimism caused him to reflect upon his present condition. All was lost! He was unfitted for the conduct of a small business, for the petty transactions and details which might suffice for one of meager wants. He would renounce the idea of that marriage which was his only salvation, and his creditors, as soon as they heard the news that this hope had vanished would fall upon him. He would find himself expelled from the house of his forefathers, pitied by everybody, with a pity that would sting more keenly than insult. He felt himself unequal to witness the final wreck of his house and of his name. What could he do? Where should he go?

He sat staring at the sea for a great part of the afternoon, watching the white sails until they hid themselves behind the cape, or vanished into the broad horizon of the bay.

Leaving the terrace without knowing how, Febrer found himself opening the door of the chapel, an old and forgotten door, which, as it creaked upon its rusty hinges, scattered dust and cobwebs. How long it had been since he had entered there! In the dense atmosphere of the closed room he thought he perceived a vague odor of essences, as from a bottle of perfume opened and long abandoned; an odor which brought back to his memory the solemn dames of the family whose portraits hung in the reception hall.

In the ray of light filtering through the tiny windows of the cupola millions of dust motes illuminated by the sun danced in an ascending spiral. The altar, with its antique carving, glowed faintly in the mellowed light with reflections of old gold. Upon it lay a duster and a pail, carelessly left since the last cleaning of the room, many years ago.

Two prayer stools of old blue velvet seemed to still retain the impression of lordly and delicate forms which no longer existed. Two prayer books with worn edges lay upon the rack before them, as if forgotten. Jaime recognized one of the books. It had belonged to his mother, poor lady, pale and sick, who divided her life between praying and the adoration of her son, for whom she dreamed an illustrious future. The other, perhaps, had belonged to his grandmother, that Mexican lady of the days of romanticism, who still seemed to thrill the great house with the rustling of her white garments and the melody of her harp.

The apparition from the past, vague and dim, arising in the deserted chapel, the memory of those two ladies, the one all piety, the other all idealism, aristocratic and dreamy, drove Febrer to distraction. To think that soon the rude hands of the usurer would profane so much that was old and venerable! He could not stay to witness it! Good-bye! Good-bye!

At dusk he sought out Toni Clapés in the Borne. With the confidence which the contrabandist inspired in him he asked him for money.

"I don't know when I can return it. I am leaving Majorca. Everything is going to ruin, but I must not stay to see it."

Clapés gave Jaime more money than he asked for. Toni was to stay awhile on the island, and with the help of Captain Valls he would try to straighten out Jaime's business affairs, if it were still possible. The captain was a good business man, and he knew how to disentangle the most hopeless complications. He and Jaime had quarreled the day before, but that was no matter; Valls was a true friend.

"Don't tell anyone that I am going away," added Jaime. "No one must know it but you—and Pablo. You are right; he is a friend."

"And when are you leaving?"

"On the first steamer for Iviza."

Jaime still had something left there; a pile of rocks covered with thickets and full of rabbits; a crumbling tower belonging to the time of the pirates. He had learned of it by chance the day before; some peasants from Iviza whom he had met in the Borne had reminded him of it.

"I shall be as well off there as anywhere else—better, much better! I will hunt and fish. I am going to live where I cannot see people."

Clapés, remembering the advice he had given the evening before, grasped Jaime's hand with satisfaction. That affair of the Chueta girl was a thing of the past. His peasant soul rejoiced at this solution.

"You are right in going. The other thing, the other thing would have been an act of madness."

PART SECOND

CHAPTER I
IVIZA

Febrer was contemplating his image, a transparent shadow of quivering contours on the changing waters, through which the bottom of the sea could be seen with milky spots of clean sand and dark blocks of stone broken from the mountain overgrown with a strange vegetation.

The seaweed floated backward and forward like waving green hair; fruits round as Indian figs hung in whitish clusters on the rocks; pearly flowers shone in the depths of the green waters, and among the mysterious growth star-fishes spread their colored points; sea-urchins formed balls like dark blots covered with spines; the hippocampi, those little "devil's horses," swam restlessly; and flashes of silver and purple, of tails and fins, passed swiftly among whirlpools and bubbles, dashing out of one cave to disappear into the mouth of another unfathomable mystery.

Jaime was leaning over a small boat, with its sail dropped. In one hand he held the volanti, a long line with several hooks, which almost reached the bottom of the sea.

It was nearly midday. The craft lay in the shade. In the rear extended the wide coast of Iviza with its broad sinuosities of projecting points and steep shores. Before him was the Vedrá, an isolated rock, a superb landmark a thousand feet in height, which, standing solitary, seemed even higher. At his feet the shadow of the colossus imparted to the waters a dense and yet transparent color. Beyond its azure shadow seethed the Mediterranean, flashing with gold in the sunlight, while the coasts of Iviza, ruddy and lonely, seemed to irradiate fire.

Every pleasant day Jaime came to the narrow channel between the island and the Vedrá to fish. In calm weather this was a river of blue water with submarine rocks which peeped their black heads above the surface. The giant allowed itself to be approached without losing its imposing appearance, harsh and inhospitable. When the wind blew fresh and strong, the half submerged heads were crowned with foam and roared ominously;

mountains of water rushed roaring and foaming through this maritime throat, and the fishermen must hoist their sails and hurry away from the narrow pass, from this growling chaos of whirlpools and currents.

In the prow of the boat was old Uncle Ventolera, a seaman who had sailed on ships of many nations, who had been Jaime's companion since he arrived in Iviza. "I am almost eighty, señor," but he never let a day pass without going out to fish. Neither illness nor fear of bad weather prevented him. His face was tanned by the sun and the salt air, but it had few wrinkles. His rolled up trousers displayed spare legs with fresh and healthy skin. His blouse, open on the chest, showed a gray coating of hair of the same color as that on his head, which was covered by a black cap, a souvenir of his last trip to Liverpool, boasting a red tassel on the top, and a broad white and red plaid ribbon. His whiskers were white, and from his ears hung copper earrings.

When Jaime first made his acquaintance he expressed curiosity in regard to these decorations.

"When I was a lad I was a ship's boy on an English schooner," said Ventolera in his Ivizian dialect, singing the words in a sweet little voice. "The master was a very arrogant Maltese, with whiskers and earrings; and I said to myself, 'When I get to be a man I'm going to be like the padrone.' Although you see me like this, I used to be a great swell, and I used to like to imitate persons of importance."

When Jaime first went but fishing to the Vedrá he forgot to watch the water and the line in his hand, while he stared at the colossus which stands high above the sea, broken off from the coast.

The rocks piled to a great height, wedged in one by another and mounting into space, compelled the spectator to throw back his head to see the pointed summit. The rocks at the water's edge were accessible. The sea swept over them, sinking in to the low arcades of submarine caves, a refuge of corsairs in former days, and now sometimes the depository of smugglers. One could leap at places from rock to rock among the sabinas and other wild plants along its base, but farther up the rock rose straight, smooth, inaccessible, with polished gray walls. At enormous heights were green-covered benches, and above these the cliff again rose vertically to its crest, sharp as a finger. A party of hunters had scaled a portion of this citadel, climbing along salient angles until they gained the lower benches. Beyond there no one had gone, according to Uncle Ventolera, except a certain friar exiled by the government as a Carlist agitator, who had built on the coast of Iviza the hermitage of the Cubells.

"He was a strong and daring man," continued the old sailor. "They say that he erected a cross on the summit, but the wind blew it down some time ago."

In the hollows of the great gray rock, shaded by the green sabinas and sea pines, Febrer saw points of color jumping about, something like red and white fleas, incessantly moving. They were the goats of the Vedrá; goats abandoned for some years which had become wild, and which reproduced beyond the reach of man, having lost all domestic habit, springing up the mountain side with prodigious leaps as soon as a boat approached the cliff. On calm mornings their bleating, increased by the impressive silence, could be heard far out upon the sea.

One morning, Jaime, having brought his gun, took a couple of shots at a cluster of goats a long distance away, not expecting to hit them, but merely for the fun of seeing them leap away. The reports, magnified by the echo within the narrow defile, filled the air with the screaming and flapping of wings of hundreds of enormous old gulls that flew out of their haunts, frightened by the noise. The startled island had given forth its winged inhabitants. Other huge birds emerged and flew from the summit and disappeared like black specks toward the larger island. These were falcons which roosted in the Vedrá and lived upon the doves of Iviza and Formentera.

The old sailor pointed out to Febrer certain window-like caves in the most sheer and inaccessible cliffs of the smaller island. Neither goat nor man could reach them. Uncle Ventolera knew what was hidden within those dark passages. They were beehives; beehives centuries and centuries old; natural retreats of bees that, crossing the straits between Iviza and the Vedrá, took refuge in these inaccessible caves after having gleaned the flowery fields of the island. At certain times of the year he had seen glistening streams trickling down the cliff from these openings. It was honey melted by the sun at the entrance of the cavern.

Uncle Ventolera tugged at his line with a grunt of satisfaction.

"That makes eight!"

Hanging from a hook, flapping its tail and kicking, was a species of lobster of dark gray color. Others of its kind lay inert in a basket at the old man's side.

"Uncle Ventolera, aren't you going to sing the mass?"

"If you will allow me."

Jaime knew the old man's habits, his fondness for singing the canticles of high mass whenever he was in a joyous mood. Having given up long voyages, his pleasure consisted in singing on Sundays in the church in the town of San José, or in that of San Antonio, and indulging in the same diversion during all the happy moments of his life.

"In a minute," he said with a tone of superiority, as if he were going to treat his companion to the greatest of delights.

Placing one hand to his mouth he quickly extracted his teeth and put them in his girdle. His face collapsed into wrinkles around his sunken mouth, and he began to sing the phrases of the priest and the responses of the assistant. The childish and tremulous voice acquired a grave sonorousness as it resounded over the watery expanse and was reproduced by the echoes from the rocks. The goats on the Vedrá responded from time to time with mild bleatings of surprise. Jaime smiled at the earnestness of the old man who, with eyes gazing aloft, pressed one hand against his heart, holding his fishline with the other. Thus they remained for some time, Febrer watching his line, on which he did not perceive the slightest movement. All the fish were taken by the old man. This put him in a bad humor, and he suddenly became annoyed at the singing.

"Enough; Tío Ventolera, that's enough!"

"You liked it, didn't you?" said the old man with candor. "I know other things, too; I could tell you about Captain Riquer—a true story. My father saw it all."

Jaime made a gesture of protest. No, he did not wish to hear about Captain Riquer. He already knew the tale by heart. They had been going out fishing together for three months, and rarely did they get through the day without a relation of the event; but Tío Ventolera, with his senile inconsequence, convinced of the importance of everything concerning himself, had already begun his story, and Jaime, his back turned to his companion, was leaning over the boat, gazing into the depths of the sea, to avoid hearing once again what he already knew so well.

Captain Antonio Riquer! A hero of Iviza, as great a mariner as Barceló, who fought at Gibraltar and led the expedition against Algiers, but as Barceló was a Majorcan and the other an Ivizan all the honors and decorations were bestowed upon the former. If there were such a thing as justice the sea ought to swallow the haughty island, the stepmother of Iviza. Suddenly the old man recollected that Febrer was a Majorcan and he was silent and confused.

"That is to say," he added, making excuses for himself, "there are good people everywhere. Your lordship is one of them; but, to come back to Captain Riquer——"

He was the master of a small three-masted vessel called a xebec, armed for privateering, the *San Antonio*, manned by Ivizans, engaged in constant strife with the galliots of the Algerian Moors and with the ships of England, the enemy of Spain. Riquer's name was known all over the Mediterranean. The event occurred in 1806. On Trinity Sunday, in the morning, a frigate carrying the British flag appeared off Iviza, tacking beyond the reach of the cannons of the castle. It was the *Felicidad*, the vessel of the Italian Miguel Novelli, dubbed "the Pope," a citizen of Gibraltar and a corsair in the service of England. He came in search of Riquer, to mock him in his very beard, sailing arrogantly in view of his city. The bells were rung furiously, drums were beat, and the citizens crowded upon the walls of Iviza and in the ward of "La Marina." The *San Antonio* was being careened on the beach, but Riquer with his men shoved her into the water. The small cannon of the xebec had been dismounted, but they hastily tied them with ropes. Every man from the ward of the Marina was eager to embark, but the captain chose only fifty men and heard mass with them in the church of San Telmo. While they were hoisting the sails, Riquer's father appeared. He was an old sailor, and, in spite of his son's opposition, he climbed into the boat.

The *San Antonio* took many hours and expert maneuvering to draw close to "the Pope's" ship. The poor xebec looked like an insect beside the great vessel manned by the wildest and most reckless crew ever gathered on the wharves of Gibraltar—Maltese, Englishmen, Romans, Venetians, Livornese, Sardinians, and Dalmatians. The first broadside from the ship's cannons kills five men on the deck of the xebec, among them the father of Riquer. He lifts up the old man's body, being bathed in his blood, and he runs to place it in the hold. "They have killed our father!" groan the brothers. "Let's get busy!" replies Riquer sternly. "Bring out the frascos! We must board her!"

The frascos, a terrible weapon of the Ivizan corsairs, fire-bottles, which, as they burst upon the enemy's decks, set it ablaze, begin to fall upon "the Pope's" vessel. The rigging begins to burn, the upper works shiver, and like demons Riquer and his men spring aboard among the flames, pistol in one hand, boarding axe in the other. The deck flows with blood, the corpses roll into the sea with broken heads. They find "the Pope" hiding, half dead with fear, in a locker in his cabin.

Tío Ventolera laughed like a boy as he recalled this grotesque detail of Riquer's great victory. Then, when "the Pope" was brought a prisoner to the island, the people of the city and the peasants gathered in crowds, staring at him as if he were a rare wild beast. This was the pirate, the terror of the Mediterranean! And they had found him stuck between decks, shaking with fear of the Ivizans! He was sentenced to be strung up on the island of the hanged men, a small islet where now stands the lighthouse in the Strait of the Freus; but Godoy ordered him to be exchanged for some other Spaniards.

Ventolera's father had seen great events; he was a cabin-boy on Riquer's ship. Later he had been captured by the Algerians, being one of the last captives enslaved before the occupation of Algiers by the French. There he ran a terrible risk of death once upon a time when one out of every ten of the captives was killed in revenge for the assassination of a wicked Moor whose body was found crammed into a latrine. Tío Ventolera remembered the stories his father used to tell of the days when Iviza produced corsairs, and when captured vessels were brought into port with captive Moors, both men and and women. The prisoners would be haled before the *escribano de presas*, the scrivener of the captives, as evidences of the victory, and he compelled them to swear "by Alaquivir, by the Prophet and his Koran, with hand and index-finger raised, his face turned toward the rising sun," while the fierce Ivizan corsairs, on dividing the booty, set aside a sum for the purchase of linen for binding up their wounds, and left another portion of the loot under pledge for celebration of daily mass by a priest every day while they were absent from the island.

Tío Ventolera passed from Riquer to earlier valorous corsair commanders, but Jaime, annoyed by his chatter, ever displaying a desire to overwhelm the island of Majorca, its hostile neighbor, at last grew impatient.

"It's twelve o'clock, grandfather. Let's go in; the fish have quit biting."

The old man glanced at the sun, which had passed beyond the crest of the Vedrá. It was not yet noon, but it lacked little. Then he looked at the sea; the señor was right; the fish would bite no longer, and he was satisfied with his day's work.

He tugged at the rope with his lean arms, hoisting the small triangular sail. The boat heeled over, pitched without making headway, and then began to cleave the water with a gentle ripple against her sides. They sailed out of the channel, leaving the Vedrá behind, coasting along the island. Jaime held the tiller, while the old man, clasping the fish-basket between his knees, began counting and fingering the catch with avaricious delight.

They rounded a cape and a new stretch of coast appeared. On the summit of a mountain of red rocks, dotted here and there by dark masses of shrubbery, stood a broad yellow squat tower, with no opening on the side toward the sea except a window, a mere black hole of irregular contour. The outlines of a porthole in the battlement of the tower, that had formerly served for a small cannon, was outlined against the blue sky. On one side the promontory rose sheer above the sea, and on the other sloped landward, covered with green, with low and leafy groves, among which peeped the white dots of a diminutive village.

The boat headed straight for the tower, and when near it they turned her toward a nearby beach, the bow grating upon the gravel. The old man struck the sail and warped the boat near a rock along shore from which hung a chain. He fastened the boat to it, and then he and Jaime sprang out. He did not wish to beach the boat; he was thinking of going out again after dinner, a matter of putting out a trawl which he would take up again the next morning. Would the señor accompany him? Febrer made a negative gesture, and the old man left him until the following day when he would awaken him from the beach singing the introit, while the stars still shimmered in the sky. Daybreak must find them at the Vedrá.

"Let us see how early you will come down from the tower!"

The fisherman turned toward the mainland, his fish-basket hanging on his arm.

"Give my regards to Margalida, Tío Ventolera, and tell her to have my dinner brought over right away."

The sailor replied with a shrug of his shoulders without turning his face, and Jaime walked along the beach in the direction of the tower. His feet, shod in hempen sandals, crunched on the gravel at the edge of the wash from the surf. Among the azure pebbles were fragments of pottery; portions of earthen handles; concave pieces of bowls bearing vestiges of decoration, which had, perhaps, belonged to swelling urns; small, irregular spheres of gray clay in which one seemed to make out, despite the corrosion of the salt water, human features worn by the passing centuries. They were curious relics of days of storm; suggestions of the great secret of the sea, which had come to light after being hidden thousands of years; confused and legendary history returned by the restless waves to the shores of these islands, which had been the refuge in ancient times of Phoenicians and Carthaginians, of Arabs and Normans. Tío Ventolera told of silver coins, thin as wafers, found by boys at play on the beach. His grandfather remembered the tradition of mysterious caves containing treasure, caves of the Saracens and Normans, which had been walled in with heavy blocks of stone, and long forgotten.

Jaime began to ascend the rocky slope leading to the tower. The tamarisk-shrubs stood erect like dwarf pines clothed in sharp and rustling foliage, which seemed to be nourished on the salt carried in the atmosphere, their roots embedded in the rock. The wind on stormy days, as it swept away the sand, left bare their multiple, entangled roots, black and slender serpents in which Febrer's feet were often caught. A sound of hurried flight and a crackling of leaves in the bushes answered to the echo of his footsteps, while a bunch of gray hair with a tail like a button scampered from bush to bush in blind haste. The startled rabbits roused dark emerald-colored lizards basking lazily in the sun.

Together with these sounds there floated to Jaime's ears a faint drumming, and the voice of a man intoning an Ivizan romance. He hesitated from time to time as if undecided, repeating the same verses over and over until he managed to pass on to new ones, uttering at the end of each strophe, according to the custom of the country, a strange screech like a peacock, a harsh and strident trill like that which accompanies the songs of the Arabs.

When Febrer gained the crest, he saw the musician sitting on a stone behind the tower, gazing at the sea.

It was a youth he had met several times at Can Mallorquí, the house of his old renter, Pèp. Resting on his thigh was the Ivizan tambourine, a small drum painted blue, decorated with flowers and gilded branches. His left arm was resting on the instrument, his chin in his hand, almost concealing his face. He beat the drum slowly with a little stick held in his right hand, and he sat motionless, in a reflective attitude, with his thoughts concentrated on his improvisation, peeping between his fingers at the immense horizon on the sea.

He was called the Minstrel, as were all those in the island who sang original verses at dances and serenades. He was a tall young man, slender, and narrow shouldered, a youth not yet eighteen. As he sang he coughed, his slender neck swelled, and his face, of a transparent whiteness, flushed. His eyes were large, the eyes of a woman, prominent and rose-colored. He always wore gala costume; blue velvet trousers; the girdle, and the ribbon which served him as a cravat, were of a flaming red, and above this he wore a little feminine kerchief around his neck, with the embroidered point in front. Two roses were tucked behind his ears; his hair, lustrous with pomade, hung like a wavy fringe beneath a hat with a flowered band, which he wore thrust on the back of his head. Seeing these almost feminine adornments, the large eyes and the pale face, Febrer compared him to one of those anemic virgins who are idealized in modern art. But this virgin displayed a certain suggestive bulk protruding beneath his red belt. Undoubtedly it was one of the knives or pistols made by the ironworkers of the island; the inseparable companion of every Ivizan youth.

Seeing Jaime, the Minstrel arose, leaving the tambourine hanging from his left arm by a strap, while he touched the brim of his hat with his right hand, still holding his drumstick.

"Good-day to you!"

Febrer, who, like a good Majorcan, had believed in the ferocity of the Ivizans, admired their courteous manners when he met them on the roadways. They committed murder among themselves, always on account of love affairs, but the stranger was respected with the same traditional scruples that the Arab possesses for the man who seeks hospitality beneath his tent.

The Minstrel seemed ashamed that the Majorcan señor had surprised him near his house, on his own land. He had come because he liked to look at the sea from this height. He felt better in the shadow of the tower; no friend was near to disturb him, and he could freely compose the verses of a romance for the next dance in the town of *San Antonio*.

Jaime smiled at the Minstrel's timid excuses, suggesting that perhaps the verses were dedicated to some maiden. The boy inclined his head. "Sí, señor."

"And who is she?"

"Flower of the Almond," said the poet.

"Flower of the Almond? A pretty name."

Encouraged by the señor's approbation, the youth continued talking. The "Flower of the Almond" was Margalida, the daughter of señor Pèp of Can Mallorquí. The Minstrel himself had given her this name, seeing her as white and beautiful as the flowers which the almond tree puts forth when the frosts are done and the first warm breezes blowing in from the sea announce the spring. All the youths roundabout repeated it, and Margalida was known by no other name. He had a certain gift for thinking of pretty sobriquets. Those which he gave lasted forever.

Febrer listened to the boy's words with a smile. In what a strange creature had the muse taken refuge! He asked the youth if he worked, and the boy replied negatively. His parents did not wish him to do so; a doctor from the city had seen him in the market place one day and advised his family that he must avoid all fatigue; and he, pleased at such counsel, spent the working days in the country in the shade of a tree, listening to the songs of the birds, spying on the girls walking along the paths, and when some new verse rung in his head he sat down on the seashore to quietly work it out and fix it in his memory.

Jaime took leave of him, saying that he might continue his poetic occupation, but a few steps away he stopped, turning his head at not hearing the tambourine again. The troubador was going down the hill, fearful of annoying the señor with his music, and seeking another solitary retreat.

Febrer reached the tower. All that which from a distance seemed to belong to a lower story was massive foundation. The door was on a level with the elevated windows; thus the guards in early days could avoid being surprised by the pirates. For ingress and egress they made use of a ladder which they drew up after them at night. Jaime had ordered made a rude wooden ladder by which to reach his room, but he never drew it in. The tower, constructed of sandstone, was somewhat eroded on its exterior by the winds from the sea. Many stones had fallen from their places, and these hollows simulated steps for scaling the tower.

The hermit ascended to his habitation. It was a round room with no other opening than the door and the window, which almost seemed to be tunnels, so great was the thickness of the walls. These, on the inside, were carefully whitewashed with the gleaming lime of Iviza, giving a transparency and milky softness to all the buildings, and to the modest little country houses the appearance of elegant mansions. Only on the ceiling, broken by a skylight, which told of the ancient ladder-way leading to the flat-roof above, did there remain any trace of the soot of the fires which used to be lighted in former days.

Rough boards, crudely fastened to wooden cross-pieces, which served to reinforce them, were used for door, window-shutter, and ceiling trap-door. There was not a pane of glass in the tower. It was still summer, and Febrer, undecided, and, in truth, indifferent as to his future, put off the details of actually settling down until some other time.

This retreat seemed to him romantic and pleasing, in spite of its crudity. He detected in it the skilful hand of Pèp and the grace of Margalida. He noticed the whiteness of the walls, the neatness of three chairs and of the deal table, all scrubbed by the daughter of his former tenant. Fish nets were draped upon the walls like tapestry; beyond hung the gun and a bag of cartridges. Long, slender sea-shells with the brown translucency of the tortoise were arranged in the form of fans. They were the gift of Tío Ventolera, as were two enormous periwinkles on the table, white, with erect points, and the interior of a moist rose-color, like feminine flesh. Near the window his mattress lay rolled up with his pillow and sheets—a rustic bed which Margalida or her mother made every afternoon.

Jaime slept there more peacefully than in his palace in Palma. When Tío Ventolera failed to awaken him at dawn by singing mass down on the beach or by climbing up the hill to fling stones at the door of the tower, the hermit rested on his mattress until late in the morning, listening to the music of the sea, the great crooning mother; watching the mysterious light, a mixture of golden sun and blue waters filtering through the cracks and trembling on the white walls; hearing the gulls scream outside, as they passed before the windows in joyous flight, flinging swift shadows within the room.

At night he retired early and lay open-eyed in the diffused starry light, wakeful in the glint of the moon as it shimmered through the half-opened door. It was that half hour in which all the past appears supernatural; that forerunner of sleep, in which the remotest memories are revived. The sea roared, strident calls of the night birds broke the stillness, the gulls complained with a lament like tortured children. What were his friends doing now? What were they saying in the cafés of the Borne? Who might be in the Casino?

In the morning these recollections brought a sad smile to his lips. The returning day seemed to gladden his life. Had he ever been like others who rejoiced in existence in the city? Here was where one could really live.

He glanced over the interior of his round tower. It was a veritable salon, more agreeable to him than the house of his forefathers; this was all his own, free from the dread of co-ownership with money lenders and usurers. He even had handsome antiquities which no one could claim. Near the door was a pair of amphoræ, drawn up by fishermen's nets—whitish earthern jars with pointed bases, indurated by the sea and capriciously decorated by Nature with garlands of adhering shells. In the center of the table, between the periwinkles, was another gift from Tío Ventolera, a terra cotta female head with a strange round tiara crowning her braided hair. The grayish clay was dotted with little, hard spherical concretions formed while lying for centuries in the salt water. As Jaime gazed at this companion of his solitude his imagination pierced the harsh outer crust and he recognized the serenity of feature, the strangeness and mystery of the almond-shaped, Oriental eyes. It appeared to him as to no one else. His long hours of silent contemplation had brushed away the mask, the work of centuries.

"Look at her! She is my sweetheart," he had said one morning to Margalida while she was cleaning his room. "Isn't she beautiful? She must have been a princess of Tyre or of Ascalon, I am not sure which; but the thing of which I am sure is that she was destined for me, that she loved me four thousand years before I was born, and that she has come down through the ages to seek me. She owned ships, robes of purple and palaces with terraced gardens, but she abandoned all to hide in the sea, waiting dozens of centuries for a wave to bear her to this coast so that Tío Ventolera might find her and bring her home to me. Why do you stare at me like that? You, poor child, cannot comprehend these things."

Margalida did, indeed, look at him in surprise. Imbued with her father's respect for this high-caste gentleman, she could only imagine him talking seriously. What things he must have seen in this world!

Now his words about this millenial sweetheart shook her credulity, causing her to smile nervously, while at the same time she looked with superstitious fear at the great lady of forgotten centuries who was nothing but a terra cotta head. How could Don Jaime talk like that? Everything about him was strange!

Whenever Febrer climbed up to the tower he sat down near the doorway and looked across the landscape. At the base of the hill spread recently ploughed fields, wooded areas belonging to Febrer which Pèp was clearing for cultivation. Then began the plantations of almonds, of a fresh green color, and the ancient and twisted olive trees, which lifted up their dark trunks with tufted branches bearing silver gray leaves. The house, Can Mallorquí, was a sort of Moorish dwelling, a cluster of buildings, all as square as dice, dazzling white, and flat-roofed. New white buildings had been added as the family increased, and as its necessities were augmented. Each of the dice constituted one room, and, taken together, they formed a house, which resembled an Arabian village. From without no one could guess which were the living rooms and which the stables.

Beyond Can Mallorquí lay the grove, and the high-banked terraces, separated by thick stone walls. The strong winds did not suffer the trees to grow tall, so they put out many luxuriant branches round about them, gaining in width what they lost in height. The branches of all the trees were upheld by numerous forked sticks. Some of the fig trees had hundreds of supports and spread out like an immense green tent ready to shelter sleeping giants. They were natural summer-houses in which nearly a whole tribe might be sheltered. The horizon in the background was shut out by pine-clad mountains, having here and there red, barren spots. Columns of smoke rose out of the dark foliage from the pits of the charcoal burners.

Febrer had now been on the island three months. His arrival had astonished Pèp Arabi, who was still busy telling his friends and relatives of his stupendous adventure, his unheard of daring, his recent voyage to Majorca with his children, his few hours in Palma, and his visit to the Palace of the Febrers, a place of enchantment, which held within its confines all the luxurious and regal splendor that existed in the world. Jaime's brusque declarations had astonished the peasant less.

"Pèp, I am ruined; you are rich compared to me. I have come to live in the tower; I don't know how long; perhaps forever."

He entered into the details of getting settled in his new quarters while Pèp smiled with an incredulous air. Ruined! All great gentlemen said the same thing, but what was left them in their misfortune was enough to enrich many poor men. They were like the vessels shipwrecked off Formentera, before the government established lighthouses. The people of Formentera, a lawless and God-forsaken crowd—they were natives of a smaller island—used to light bonfires to decoy the sailors, and when the ship was lost to them it was not lost to the islanders, for its spoils made many of them rich.

A Febrer poor? Pèp would not accept the money Febrer offered him. He was going to cultivate some of the señor's lands; they would settle accounts some other time. Since he was determined to live in the tower Pèp worked hard to make it habitable, besides ordering his children to carry the señor's dinner to him whenever he did not feel like coming down to the table.

These three months had been rustic isolation to Jaime. He did not write a letter, nor open a newspaper, nor read any book, except the half dozen volumes he had brought from Palma. The city of Iviza, as tranquil and dreamy as a town in the interior of the Peninsula, seemed to him a remote capital. Probably Majorca and the other great cities he had visited no longer existed. During the first month of his new life an extraordinary event disturbed his placid tranquillity. A letter came; an envelope bearing the mark of one of the cafés in the Borne and a few lines in large, crude script. It was Toni Clapés who had written. He wished him much joy in his new existence. In Palma everything was as usual. Pablo Vails did not write because he was angry with Febrer for going away without bidding him good-bye. Still he was a good friend, and he was busy disentangling Jaime's business affairs. He had a diabolical cleverness for that sort of thing—a Chueta, in fact! He would write more later.

Two months had gone by without the arrival of another letter. What did he care about news from a world to which he should never return? He did not know what destiny had in store for him; he did not even wish to think of it; hither he had come and here he would stay, with no other pleasures than hunting and fishing, enjoying an animal-like ease, having no other ideas or desires than those of primitive man.

He dwelt apart from Ivizan life, not mingling in their doings. He was a gentleman among peasants; a stranger! They treated him respectfully, but it was a frigid respect.

The traditional existence of these rude and somewhat ferocious people held for him that attraction which the extraordinary and the vigorous always exerts. The island, thrown upon its own resources, had been compelled century after century to face Norman pirates, Moorish sailors, galleys from

Castile, ships from the Italian republics, Turkish, Tunisian, and Algerian vessels, and in more recent times, the English buccaneers. Formentera, uninhabited for centuries after having been a granary of the Romans, served as a treacherous anchorage for the hostile fleets. The churches were still veritable fortresses, with strong towers where the peasants took refuge on being warned by bonfires that enemies had landed. This hazardous life of perpetual danger and ceaseless struggle had produced a people habituated to the shedding of blood, to the defense of their rights, weapons in hand; the farmers and fishermen of the present day possessed the mentality of their ancestors, and kept up the same customs. There were no villages; there were houses scattered over many kilometers, with no other nucleus than the church and the dwellings of the curate and the alcalde. The only town was the capital, the one called in ancient documents the Royal Fortress of Iviza, with its adjacent suburb of La Marina.

When a youth arrived at puberty his father summoned him into the kitchen of the farmhouse in the presence of all the family.

"Now you are a man," he said solemnly, handing him a knife with a stout blade. The youthful paladin lost his filial shrinking. In future he would defend himself instead of seeking the protection of his family. Later, when he had saved some money he would complete his knightly trappings by purchasing a pocket-pistol with silver decorations, made by the ironworkers of the country, who had their forges set up in the forest.

Fortified by possession of these evidences of citizenship, which he never laid aside as long as he lived, he associated with other youths similarly armed and the life of a swain with its courtings opened before him; serenades with the accompaniment of signal calls; dances, excursions to parishes that were celebrating the feast of their patron saint, where they amused themselves slinging stones at a rooster with unerring aim, and above all the festeigs, the traditional courtships when seeking a bride, the most respectable of customs, which gave occasion for fights and murders.

There were no thieves on the island. Houses isolated in the heart of the country were often left with the key in the door during the absence of their owners. The men did not commit murder over questions of gain. Enjoyment of the soil was equitably divided, and the mildness of the climate and the frugality of the people made them generous and but mildly attached to material possessions. Love, only love, impelled men to kill each other. The rustic caballeros were impassioned in their predilections, and as fatal in their jealousy as heroes in novels. For the sake of a maiden with black eyes and brown hands they hunted and challenged each other in the darkness of night, with outcries of defiance; they sighted each other from afar with a howl before coming to blows. The modern pistol which fired but one shot seemed to them insufficient, and in addition to the cartridge they rammed in a handful of powder and balls. If the weapon did not burst in the hands of the aggressor, it was sure to make dust of the enemy.

The courtings lasted for months and even for years. A peasant-farmer who had a daughter of suitable age for betrothal would see the youths of the district and others from all over the island offer themselves, for every Ivizan deemed it his privilege to court her. The father of the girl would count the suitors—ten, fifteen, twenty, sometimes even thirty. Then he would calculate the amount of time that could be devoted to the affair before he would be overcome by sleep, and, taking into account the number of aspirants, he divided it into so many minutes for each.

At twilight they would gather from every direction for the courting, some in groups, humming to the accompaniment of clucking and a sort of whinnying, others alone, blowing on the bimbau, an instrument made of small sheets of iron, which buzzed like a hornet, serving to lull them into forgetfulness of the fatigue of the journey. They came from far away. Some walked three hours, and must travel as many back again, crossing from one end of the island to the other on the courting days which were Thursdays and Saturdays, for the sake of talking three minutes with a girl.

In the summer they sat in the pòrchu, a kind of rural zaguán, or if it were winter they would go into the kitchen. The girl sat motionless on a stone bench. She had removed her straw hat with its long streamers that during the daytime gave her the air of an operetta shepherdess; she was dressed in gala attire, wearing the blue or green accordian-plaited skirt, which she kept during the remainder of the week compressed by cords, and hanging from the ceiling, in order to keep the plaiting intact. Under this she wore other and still other skirts; eight, ten or twelve petticoats, all the feminine clothing the house possessed, a solid funnel of wool and cotton that obliterated every sign of sex and made it impossible to image the existence of a fleshy reality beneath the bulk of cloth. Rows of filigree buttons glittered on the cuffs of her jacket; on her breast, crushed flat by a monastic corset which seemed made of iron, shone a triple chain of gold with its enormous links; from beneath the kerchief worn on the head hung her heavy braids tied with ribbons. On the bench, serving as a cushion for her voluminous body, made bulky by skirts, lay the abrigais, the feminine winter garment.

The suitors deliberated over the question of precedence in the courting, and one after another they took their places at the girl's side, talking to her the allotted number of minutes. If one of them, becoming too enthusiastic in conversation, forgot his companions and trespassed on their time, they reminded him by coughs, furious glances, and threatening words. If he persisted, the strongest of the band would grasp him by the arm and drag him away so that another might take his place. Sometimes when there were many suitors and time was at a premium, the girl would talk with two at once, trying to display no preference. Thus the courting continued until she manifested predilection for a youth, often without regard for her parents' choice. In this short springtime of her life the woman was queen. After marriage she cultivated the soil alongside her husband and was little better than a beast.

The rejected youths, if they felt no particular interest in the girls, would then retire, transferring their affections a few leagues farther on; but if they were really enamored, they would lurk about the house and the chosen one was forced to fight with his former rivals, achieving marriage only by a miracle after passing through a pathway strewn with knives and pistols.

The pistol was like a second tongue to the Ivizan; at the Sunday dances he would fire off shots to demonstrate his amorous enthusiasm. On leaving his sweetheart's house, to give her and her family a sign of his appreciation, he was accustomed to fire a shot as he crossed the threshold, then calling out, "Good-night!" If, on the contrary, he went away offended and wished to insult the family, he would invert this order, first calling out, "Good-night," and shooting his pistol afterwards; but he was obliged in that case to rush out at full speed, for the members of the household promptly replied to the declaration of war with answering shots, with clubs, and with rocks.

Jaime was living on the brink of this existence, burdened with its crude traditions, looking on from the outside at the Arabian customs which still prevailed in this lonely island. Spain, whose flag floated every Sunday over the few houses embraced within each parish, scarcely gave a thought to this bit of soil lost in the sea. Many countries of far-away Oceanica were in more frequent communication with the great centers of civilization than this island, in former times scourged by war and rapine, and now lying forsaken off the beaten track of ocean steamers, surrounded by a girdle of small, barren islets, reefs, and shallows.

In his new round of life Febrer felt the joy of one who occupies a comfortable seat from which he may witness an interesting spectacle. These farmers and fishermen, the warlike descendants of corsairs, were pleasant companions for him. He pretended to look upon them from afar, but gradually their customs were captivating him, drawing him into similar habits. He had no enemies, and yet, in strolling about the island when he did not have his gun upon his shoulder, he carried a revolver hidden in his belt, ready for an emergency.

In the early days of his life in the tower, as the exigencies of getting settled compelled him to go into the town, he dressed as in Majorca, but little by little he left off his cravat, his collar, his boots. For hunting he preferred the blouse and the velveteen trousers of the peasants. Fishing accustomed him to wearing hempen sandals for climbing rocks and for walking along the beach. A hat like that worn by the youths of the parish of San José covered his head.

Pèp's daughter, who was familiar with the island customs, admired the señor's hat with a kind of gratitude. The people of the different quarters, which formerly divided Iviza, were distinguished one from another by the style of wearing their head-dress and by the shape of the brim, almost imperceptible to any but a native of the island. Don Jaime wore his like the youths of San José, and unlike those worn by the inhabitants of other parishes. This was an honor for the parish of which she was a daughter.

Ingenuous and pretty Margalida! Febrer enjoyed talking with her, delighting in her surprise at his jests and at his tales of other lands.

She would be coming with his dinner any moment now. A slender column of smoke had been floating above the chimney of Can Mallorquí for half an hour. He imagined Pèp's daughter flitting from place to place preparing his noonday meal, followed by the glances of her mother, a poor peasant woman, silent in her dullness, who did not venture to set her hand to anything pertaining to the señor.

Any moment he might see her appear beneath the shadow of the pòrchu which gave entrance to the house, the dinner basket on her arm, her marvelously white face, which the sun slightly gilded with a faint tinge of old ivory, shaded by her straw hat with its long streamers.

Someone was stepping into the shelter of the portico, beginning to climb up to the tower. It was Margalida! No, it was her brother Pepet, Pepet who had been in Iviza for a month preparing to enter the Seminary, and whom the people had on this account given the sobriquet of Capallanet, the Little Chaplain.

CHAPTER II
ALMOND BLOSSOM

"Good day to you!"

Pepet spread a napkin over one end of the table and placed upon it two covered dishes and a bottle of wine which had the color and transparency of the ruby. Then he sat down on the floor, clasping his hands about his knees, and kept very still. His teeth shone like luminous ivory as a smile lighted his brown face. His mischievous eyes were fixed upon the señor with the expression of a happy, faithful dog.

"You have been in Iviza studying to become a priest, have you not?"

The boy nodded his head. Yes; his father had entrusted him to a professor in the Seminary. Did Don Jaime know where the Seminary was?

The young peasant spoke of it as a remote place of torture. There were no trees; no liberty; scarcely any air; it was impossible to live in that prison.

While listening to him Febrer recalled his visit to the elevated city, the Royal Fortress of Iviza, a dead town, separated from the district of Marina by a great wall, built in the time of Philip II, with its cracks now filled with waving green caper bushes. Headless Roman statues, set in three niches, decorated the gate, which opened from the city to the suburb. Beyond this the streets wound upward toward the hill occupied by the Cathedral and the fort; pavements of blue stone, along the center of which rushed a stream of filth; snowy façades half concealing beneath the whitewash escutcheons of the nobility and the outlines of ancient windows; the silence of a cemetery by the seashore, interrupted only by the distant murmur of the surf and the buzzing of flies above the stream. Now and then footsteps were heard along the pavement of the Moorish streets, and windows half opened with the eager curiosity aroused by some extraordinary event; a few soldiers climbing leisurely up to the castle on the hill; the canons coming down from the choir, the fronts of their cassocks shining with grease, their hats and mantles the color of a fly's wing, wretched prebendaries of a forgotten cathedral, too poor to support a bishop.

On one of these streets Febrer had seen the Seminary, a long structure with white walls, and windows grilled like a jail. The Little Chaplain, as he thought of it, grew serious, the ivory flash of his smile vanishing from his chocolate-colored face. What a month he had spent there! The professor was driving away the tedium of the vacation by teaching this young peasant, wishing to initiate him into the beauties of Latin letters with the aid of his eloquence and a strap. He wished to make a prodigy of him by the time he took up his classes again, and the blows grew more frequent. Besides this were the window grilles, which allowed glimpses of nothing but the opposite wall; the barrenness of the city, where not a green leaf was to be seen; the tiresome walks accompanying the priest through that port of dead waters that smelled of putrid mussels, and was entered by no other ships than a few sailing vessels that occasionally came for a cargo of salt. The day before a still more vigorous strapping had exhausted his patience. The idea of beating him! If it had not been a priest who had ventured it he would — —! He had run away, returning on foot to Can Mallorquí; but before leaving, he had taken revenge by tearing up several books which the maestro held in great esteem; he had upset the inkstand; and had written shameful inscriptions on the walls, with other pranks characteristic of a monkey at liberty.

The night had been one of storm in Can Mallorquí. Pèp was blind with fury, and had used a club upon his back until Margalida and her mother had been compelled to interfere.

The boy's smile reappeared. He told with pride of the punishment he had taken from his father without uttering a cry. It was his father who was beating him, and a father could chastise because he loved his children; but should anyone else try to beat him, that person was doomed! As he said this he straightened himself with the belligerent air of a race accustomed to seeing blood flow and to administering justice with their own hands. Pèp talked of taking his son back to the Seminary, but the boy put no faith in this threat. He would not go, even if his father tried to fulfill his vow of binding him with ropes and taking him on the back of a donkey like a sack of wheat; rather than that he would run away to the mountains or to the rock of Vedrá and live with the wild goats.

The master of Can Mallorquí had planned the future of his children high-handedly, with the energy of a rustic who gives no thought to obstacles when he believes he is doing right. Margalida should marry a peasant-farmer, and the house and land should be his. Pepet should be a priest, which would represent social ascension for the family, honor and fortune for them all.

Jaime smiled as he listened to the boy's protests against his fate. There was no other center of learning on the island than the Seminary, and the peasants and shipowners who desired for their children a better fortune than their own, enrolled them there. The priests of Iviza! What an incongruous class! Many of them, while carrying on their studies, had taken part in the courtings, using knife and pistol. Descendants of corsairs and of soldiers, when they donned the cassock they still retained the arrogance and the rude virility of their forefathers. They were not lacking in piety, for their simplicity of mind did not permit of this, but neither were they devout and austere; they loved life with all its sweetness, and were attracted by danger with inherited enthusiasm. The island turned out hardy and venturesome priests. Those who remained in Spain became army chaplains. Others, more bold, no sooner had they sung their first mass than they embarked for South America, where certain republics boasting a large Catholic aristocracy were the Eldorado of Spanish priests who had no fear of the sea. They sent home generous sums of money to their families, and they bought houses and lands, praising God, who maintains his priests in greater ease in the new world than in the old. There were charitable señoras in Chile and Peru who gave a hundred pesos as a gratuity for a single mass. Such news made their relatives, gathered in the kitchen on winter nights, open their mouths in amazement. Despite such greatness, however, their most fervent desire was to return to the beloved isle, and after a few years they did so with the intention of ending their days on their own lands; but the demon of modern life had bitten deep into their hearts; they wearied of the monotonous insular existence, with its narrow limitations; they could not forget the new cities on the other continent, and finally they sold their property, or gave it to their family, and sailed away to return no more.

Pèp was indignant at the obstinacy of his son, who insisted upon remaining a peasant. He blustered about killing him, as if the boy were on the road to perdition. The son of his friend Treufoch had sent almost six thousand dollars home from America; another priest who lived in the interior among the Indians, in some very high mountains called the Andes, had bought a farm in Iviza that his father was now cultivating; and this rascal Pepet, who was more quick at letters than any of these, refused to follow such glorious examples! He ought to be killed!

The night before, during a moment of calm, while Pèp was resting in the kitchen with the weary arm and the sad mien of the father who has been wielding a heavy hand, the youth, rubbing his bruises, had proposed a compromise. He would become a priest; he would obey Señor Pèp; but he wanted to be a man for a while first, to go out serenading with the other boys of the parish, go to the Sunday dances, join in the courtings, have a sweetheart, and wear a knife in his belt. This last desire was greatest of all.

If his father would only give him his grandfather's knife he would put up with anything.

"Grandfather's knife, father!" implored the boy. "Grandfather's knife!"

For his grandfather's knife he would become a priest, and even if necessary live in solitude, on the alms of the people, as did the hermits on the seashore in the sanctuary of Cubells. As he thought of the venerable weapon his eyes glowed with admiration, and he described it to Febrer. A jewel! It was an antique steel blade, keen and burnished. He could cut through a coin with it, and in his grandfather's hands— —! His grandfather had been a man of renown, a famous man. Pepet had never seen him, but he talked of him with admiration, giving him a higher place in his esteem than that evoked by his mediocre father.

Then, spurred on by his desire, he ventured to implore Don Jaime's assistance. If only he would help him! If he should ask just once for the famous knife his father would immediately hand it to him.

"You shall have the knife, my boy. If your father won't give you that one, I'll buy one for you the next time I go to the city," said Febrer good-naturedly.

This filled the Little Chaplain with joy. It was necessary for him to go armed so that he could mingle with men. His house was soon to be visited by the bravest youths of the island. Margalida was now a woman, and the courting was going to begin. Señor Pèp had been besieged by the young gallants, who demanded that he set the day and the hour for the suitors.

"Margalida!" cried Febrer in surprise. "Margalida to have sweethearts!"

The spectacle he had witnessed in so many other houses on the island seemed to him an absurdity for Can Mallorquí. He had not realized that Pèp's daughter was a woman. Could that child, that pretty, white doll, really care for men? He felt the strange sensation of the father who has loved many women in his youth, but who, later in life, judging by his own lack of susceptibility, cannot understand his daughter's fondness for men.

After a few moments of silence Margalida seemed changed in his eyes. Yes, she was a woman. The transformation pained him; he felt that he had lost something dear to him, but he resigned himself to reality.

"How many suitors are there?" he asked in a low voice.

Pepet waved one hand while at the same time he raised his eyes to the vaulted ceiling of the tower. How many? He was not sure yet; at least thirty. It was going to be such a courting as would make talk all over the island, despite the fact that many, although they devoured Margalida with their eyes, were afraid to join the courting, giving themselves up for conquered in advance. There were few like his sister on the island; trim, merry, and with a good slice of dowry, too, for Señor Pèp let it be known everywhere that he intended leaving Can Mallorquí to his son-in-law when he died. And his son might burst with his cassock on his back over there on the other side of the ocean, without ever seeing any girls but Indian squaws! Futro!

However, his indignation soon passed. He became enthusiastic thinking about the young men who were to gather at his house twice a week to make love to Margalida. They were coming even from as far away as San Juan, the other end of the island, the region of valiant men, where one avoided going out of the house after dark, well knowing that every hillock held a pistol and every tree was a lurking place for a firearm. They were capable, every man of them, of waiting for satisfaction for an injury committed years before—the home of the terrible "wild beasts of San Juan." Then, too, various notables would come from the other sections of the island, and many of them must walk leagues to reach Can Mallorquí.

The Little Chaplain rejoiced at the thought of the arrogant youths with whom he was to become acquainted. They would all treat him like a chum because he was the brother of the bride to be; but of all these future friendships the one which most flattered him was that of Pere, nicknamed Ferrer, on account of his trade as an ironworker, a man about thirty, much talked about in the parish of San José.

The boy looked upon him as a great artist. When he condescended to work he made the most beautiful pistols ever seen on the field of Iviza. Old barrels were sent to him from the Peninsula, and he mounted them to suit his fancy in stocks engraved with barbaric design, adding to the work ornate decorations of silver. A weapon of his make could be loaded to the muzzle without danger of bursting.

A still more important circumstance increased his respect for Ferrer. He declared in a low voice, with a tone of mystery and respect, "Ferrer is a vèrro."

A vèrro! Jaime was silent for a few moments, trying to coördinate his recollection of island customs. An expressive gesture from the Little Chaplain assisted his memory. A vèrro was a man whose valor was already demonstrated, one who has several proofs of the power of his hand, or the accuracy of his aim, rotting in the earth.

That his kindred might not seem beneath Ferrer, Pepet recalled his grandfather's prowess. He had also been a vèrro, but the ancients knew how to do things better. The skill with which the grandfather settled his affairs was still remembered in San José; a stab with his famous knife, and his well-laid plans sufficed, for people were always found who were ready to swear they had seen him at the other end of the island at the very moment when his enemy lay writhing in mortal agony far away.

Ferrer was a less fortunate vèrro. He had returned six months ago after having spent eight years in a prison on the Peninsula. He had been sentenced to fourteen, but he had received various exemptions. His reception was triumphal. A native of San José was returning from heroic exile! They must not fall behind the citizens of other parishes who received their vèrros with great demonstrations, and on the day of the arrival of the steamer even the most distant relatives of Ferrer, who composed half the town, went down to the port of Iviza to meet him, and the other half went out of pure patriotism. Even the alcalde joined in the expedition, followed by his secretary, to retain the sympathy of his political partisans. The gentlemen of the city protested with indignation at these barbaric and immoral customs of the peasantry, while men, women, and children assaulted the steamer, each striving to be first to press the hero's hand.

Pepet described the vèrro's reception on his return to San José. He had been a member of the party, with its long line of carts, horses, donkeys, and pedestrians, looking as if an entire people were emigrating. The procession halted at every tavern and inn along the way, and the great man was regaled with jugs of wine, tid-bits of roasted sausage and glasses of figola, a liquor made of native herbs. They admired his new suit, a suit suggesting the fine señor which had been made to his order on leaving the penitentiary; they inwardly marveled at his ease of manner, at the princely and condescending air with which he greeted his old friends. Many of them envied him. What wonderful things a man learns when he leaves the island! There is nothing like travel! The former ironworker overwhelmed them all with boasts of his adventures on his homeward voyage. For several weeks thereafter the evening gatherings in the tavern were most interesting. The words of the vèrro were repeated from house to house throughout all the little homes scattered through the cuarton, every peasant finding some luster for his parish in these adventures of his fellow citizen.

The Ironworker never wearied of praising the beauty of the penal establishment in which he had spent eight years. He forgot the misery and hardship he had endured there; he looked back upon it with that love for the past which colors one's recollections.

He had been more fortunate than those poor wretches who are sent to the penitentiary on the plains of La Mancha, where the men have to carry up the water on their backs, suffering the torments of an Arctic cold. Neither had he been in the prisons of old Castile where snow whitens the courtyards and sifts in through the barred windows. He came from Valencia, from the penitentiary of Saint Michael of the Kings, "Niza," as it was nicknamed by the habitual pensioners of these establishments. He spoke with pride of this house, just as a wealthy student recalls the years he has spent in an English or German university. Tall palm trees shaded the courtyards, their crested tops waving above the tiled roofs; standing in the window-grilles one could see extensive orchards, with the triangular white pediments of the farmhouses, and farther out stretched the Mediterranean, an immense blue expanse, behind which lay his native rock, the beloved isle; perhaps the breeze, laden with the salt smell and with the fragrance of vegetation, which filtered like a benediction through the malodorous cells of the penitentiary, had first passed over it. What more could a man desire! Life there was sweet; one dined regularly, and always had a hot meal; everything was orderly, and a man had only to obey and allow himself to be led. One made advantageous friendships; one associated with people of note, whom he would never have met had he remained on the island, and the Ironworker told of his friends with pride. Some had possessed millions, and had ridden in luxurious carriages there in Madrid, an almost fantastic city whose name rung in the ears of the islanders like that of Bagdad to the poor Arab of the desert listening to the tales of the "Thousand and One Nights;" others had overrun half the world before misfortune shut them up in this enclosure. Surrounded by an absorbed circle, the vèrro recounted the adventures of these associates in the lands of the negroes, or in countries where men were yellow, or green, and wore long womanish braids. In that ancient convent, as large as a town, dwelt the salt of the earth. Some of them had girded on swords and commanded men; others had been accustomed to handling papers bearing great seals and had interpreted the law. Even a priest had been a cell-companion of the Ironworker!

The vèrro's admirers heard him with wide-open eyes and nostrils palpitating with emotion. What joy! To be a vèrro, to have gained celebrity and respect by killing an enemy in the darkness of night, and, as a recompense, eight years in "Niza," a place of honor and delight. How they envied such good luck!

The Little Chaplain, who had listened to these tales, felt a great and enduring respect for the vèrro. He described the particulars of his person with the detail of one enamored of a hero.

He was neither as tall nor as strong as the señor; he would scarcely come up to Don Jaime's ear, but he was agile, and nobody surpassed him in the dance: he could dance whole hours until he tired out every girl in the parish. From his long season at the prison he had returned with a pale and waxy complexion, the complexion of a cloistered nun; but now he was dark like everybody else, with his face bronzed and tanned by the sea air and the African sun of the island. He lived in the mountain, in a hut at the edge of the pine woods near the charcoal-makers, who supplied fuel for his forge. This he did not light every day. With his pretensions at being an artist, he worked only when he had to repair a fire-lock, to transform a flintlock into a rifle, or to make one of those silver decorated pistols which were the admiration of the Little Chaplain.

The boy hoped that this man would be his sister's choice; that the vèrro, with his astonishing skill, would become a member of his family.

"Maybe Margalida will like him, and then Ferrer will give me one of his pistols. What do you think, Don Jaime?"

He plead the vèrro's cause as if he were already a relative. The poor fellow lived so wretchedly, alone in his shop with no other companion than an old woman always dressed in the black garb of long-past mourning; one of her eyes was watery, the other was shut. She would blow the bellows while her nephew hammered the red-hot iron. Ever working around the fire, she grew more bony and thin each day; the hollows of her eyes seemed to be turning into liquid in her old face, which was wrinkled like a withered apple.

That gloomy, smoky den in the pine forest would be embellished by Margalida's presence. Its only decorations at present were a few small, colored rush baskets woven in the shape of checker-boards, adorned with silk pompons, a friendly token from the unfamed artists who whiled away the time in their retreat in "Niza." When his sister should live at the forge Pepet would go to see her, and he counted on acquiring through the munificence of his brother-in-law, a knife as famous as his grandfather's, that is, if Señor Pèp unjustly persevered in refusing him this glorious heritage.

The recollection of his father seemed to cloud the boy's hopes. He realized how difficult it would be for the master of Can Mallorquí to accept the Ironworker as a son-in-law; the old man could say no ill of him; he acknowledged his fame as an honor to the town. The island not only had brave men in "the wild beasts of San Juan," but San José could also gloat over valiant youths who had undergone trying tests; Ferrer, however, was little skilled in agricultural affairs, and although all the Ivizans showed themselves equally predisposed to cultivating the soil, to casting a net into the sea, or to landing a cargo of smuggled goods, along with other little industries, skipping easily from one kind of work to another, he desired for his daughter a genuine farmer, one accustomed all his life to scrabbling the earth. His resolution was unbreakable. In his empty and inflexible brain, when an idea sprouted it became so firmly imbedded that no hurricane nor cataclysm could uproot it. Pepet should be a priest, and should travel over the world. Margalida he was keeping for some farmer who should add to the lands of Can Mallorquí when he inherited them.

The Little Chaplain thought eagerly of him who might be the one favored by Margalida. It would be a struggle for them all, having at their head a man like the Ironworker. Even if his sister should incline toward another, the fortunate one would be compelled to settle accounts with Pere, the glorious desperado, and must put him out of the way. Great things were going to be seen. The courting of Margalida was already discussed in every house in the cuarton; her fame would spread throughout the whole island; and Pepet smiled with ferocious delight like a young savage on his way to a massacre.

He looked up to Margalida, acknowledging her as a greater authority than his father for the reason that his respect was not based on fear of blows. She it was who managed the house; everyone obeyed her. Even her mother walked in her footsteps like a serving woman, not venturing to do anything without consulting her. Señor Pèp hesitated before making a decision, scratching his forehead with a gesture of doubt and murmuring, "I must consult the girl about that." The Little Chaplain himself, who had inherited the paternal obstinacy, quickly yielded at his sister's slightest word, a gentle insinuation from her smiling lips uttered in her sweet voice.

"The things she knows, Don Jaime!" said the boy with admiration, and he enumerated her talents, dwelling with a certain respect on her skill in singing.

"Do you know the Minstrel, the sick boy, Don Jaime? He has trouble with his chest. He cannot work, and he spends his time lying in the shade thumping on a tambourine and mumbling verses. He's a white lamb, a chicken, with eyes and skin like a woman's, incapable of standing up before a brave man. He aspires to Margalida, too," but the Little Chaplain swore that he would smash the tambourine over his head before he would accept him as a brother-in-law. He would only claim as a relative of his a hero. Yet, as for making up songs and singing them interspersed with cries like the peacock's, there was no one to equal the Minstrel. One should be just, and Pepet recognized the youth's merit. He was a glory to the cuarton, almost to be compared with the valorous Ironworker. At the summer gatherings on the pòrchu of the farmhouse, or at the Sunday dances, Margalida, blushing, urged on by her companions, would sometimes take a seat in the center of the circle, and, the tambourine on her knee, her eyes hidden behind a kerchief, would reply with a long romance of her own invention to the rhymes of the troubadour.

If, some Sunday, the Minstrel intoned a long harangue about the perfidy of woman and how dear her fondness for dress cost man, the following Sunday Margalida would reply with a romanza twice as long, criticizing the vanity and egoism of the men, while the crowd of girls chorused her verses with cluckings of enthusiasm, glorying in having an avenger in the girl of Can Mallorquí.

"Pepet!... Pepet!..."

A feminine voice sounded in the distance like a crystal, breaking the dense silence of the early afternoon hours vibrant with heat and light. The voice grew stronger, as if approaching the tower.

Pepet changed from the position of a young animal at rest, freeing his legs from his encircling arms, and sprang to his feet. It was Margalida calling him. No doubt his father needed him for some task, and he had made a long visit.

Jaime grasped his arm.

"Wait, let her come," he said, smiling. "Pretend you don't hear her."

The Little Chaplain's lustrous teeth glistened in his bronzed face. The young imp was pleased at this innocent duplicity, and he took advantage of it by speaking to the señor with bold confidence.

"You will really ask Señor Pèp for it—for my grandfather's knife?"

"Yes, you shall have it," said Jaime. "Or if your father will not give it to you I will buy you the best one I can find in Iviza."

The boy rubbed his hands, his eyes glowing with savage joy.

"Having that will make a man of you," continued Febrer, "but you must not use it! Just a decoration, nothing else."

Eager to realize his desire at once, Pepet replied with energetic nodding of his head. Yes, a decoration, nothing else! Yet his eyes darkened with a cruel doubt. A decoration it might be, but if anyone should offend him while he had such a companion, what ought a man to do?

"Pepet!"

The crystal voice now rung out several times at the foot of the tower. Febrer waited for her coming, hoping to see Margalida's head, and then her figure, appear in the doorway; but he waited in vain; the voice grew more insistent, with pretty quavers of impatience.

Febrer peeped through the doorway and saw the girl standing at the foot of the stairs, in her full blue skirt and her straw hat with its streamers of flowered ribbons. The broad brim of her hat seemed to form an aureole around the rose-pale face in which trembled the dark drops of her eyes.

"Greeting, Almond Blossom!" called Febrer, smiling, but with hesitation in his voice.

Almond Blossom! As the girl heard this name on the señor's lips a flush of color momentarily overspread the soft whiteness of her face.

Had Don Jaime heard that name? But did such a gentleman interest himself in nonsense of that kind?

Now Febrer saw nothing but the crown and brim of Margalida's hat. She had lowered her head, and in her confusion stood fingering the corners of her apron, abashed, like a girl listening to the first words of love, and suddenly realizing the significance of life.

CHAPTER III
LOVE AND DANCING

The next Sunday morning Febrer took a trip to town. Tío Ventolera could not go fishing with him, for he considered his presence at mass indispensable, that he might respond to the priest with his shrill voice.

Having nothing else to do, Jaime started for the pueblo, walking along the paths in the red earth which stained his white hempen sandals. It was one of the last days of summer. The snowy white farmhouses seemed to reflect the African sun like mirrors. Swarms of insects buzzed in the air. In the green shade of the spreading fig trees, low and round, like roofs of verdure resting on their circle of supports, figs opened by the heat, fell, flattening on the ground like enormous drops of purple sugar. Prickly pears raised their thorny, wall-like trunks on either side of the road, and among their dusty roots whisked flexible, little animals, with long emerald green tails, intoxicated by the sun.

Through the dark and twisted columns of the olive and almond trees groups of peasants, also on their way to town, could be seen in the distance, following other paths. The girls in their Sunday gowns walked in advance, wearing red or white kerchiefs and green skirts, their gold chains glittering in the sun; near them walked the suitors, a tenacious and hostile escort that disputed for every glance or word of preference, several of them laying siege to the girl at the same time. The procession was closed by the girls' parents, aged before their time by the hardships and cares of country life, poor beasts of the soil, submissive, resigned, black of skin, with their limbs as dry as vineshoots, and who, in the dullness of their minds, looked back upon their years of courting as a vague and remote springtime.

Febrer turned in the direction of the church when he reached the village, which consisted of six or eight houses with the alcalde's office, the school and the tavern, grouped about the temple of worship. This rose stately and imposing, the band of union of all the dwellings scattered through mountains and valleys for some kilometers roundabout.

Removing his hat to wipe the perspiration from his brow, Jaime took refuge beneath the arcade of a small cloister before the church. Here he experienced the sensation of well being as does the Arab when, after a journey across the burning sands, he takes asylum with the lonely hermit.

The snowy exterior of the whitewashed church with its cool arcade and its walled terraces crowned with nopals, reminded him of an African mosque. It had more resemblance to a fortress than a temple. Its roofs were concealed by the upper edge of the walls, a kind of redoubt over which fire-locks and catapults had frequently peered. The tower was a military turret still crowned with merlons. Its old bell had pealed forth with feverish clangor of alarm in other times.

This church, in which the peasants entered life with baptism and left it with the mass for the dead, had for centuries been their refuge in time of stress, their fortress of defense. When the atalayas on the coast announced with fires or smoke the approach of a Moorish vessel, families streamed to the temple from all the farmhouses in the parish; men carrying guns, women and children driving asses and goats or bearing on their backs all the fowls of their barnyards, their feet tied together like a bundle of faggots. The house of God was converted into a stable for the property of His followers. Off in one corner the priest prayed with the women, his prayers interrupted by screams of anguish and by crying children, while the fusileers on the roof explored the horizon until word came that the sea birds of prey had sailed away. Then normal existence began again, each family returning to its isolation, with the certainty of being compelled to repeat the agonizing journey within a few weeks.

Febrer continued standing under the arcade, watching the hurrying groups of peasants, spurred forward by the last stroke of the bell whirling in the tower-loft. The church was almost full. A dense effluvium of hot breath, perspiration, and coarse clothing floated out to Jaime through the half-open door. He felt a certain sympathy for these good people when he met them singly, but in a crowd they aroused aversion, and he kept away.

Every Sunday he came to the pueblo and stood in the doorway of the church. The loneliness of his tower on the coast made it necessary to see his fellow men. Besides, Sunday was, for him, a man without occupation, a monotonous, wearisome, interminable day. This day of rest for others was for him a torment. He could not go fishing for lack of a boatman, and the solitary fields, with their closed houses, the families being at mass or at the afternoon dance, gave him the painful impression of a stroll through a cemetery. He would spend the morning in San José, and one of his diversions consisted in standing under the arcade of the church watching the coming and going of the crowd, enjoying the cool shade of the cloister, while a few steps away the soil was burning in the sun. The branches of the trees writhed as if agonized by the heat and by the dust covering their leaves, and the hot air stifled one as it was drawn into the lungs.

Belated families began to arrive, passing Febrer with a glance of curiosity and a diffident greeting. Everyone in the cuarton knew him; they were kind folk, who, on seeing him out in the country opened their doors to him, but their affability went no further, for they could not get near to him. He was a "foreigner"; moreover a Majorcan! The fact of his being a gentleman aroused a vague distrust in the rustic people, who could not understand his living in the lonely tower.

Febrer remained solitary. He could hear the ringing of a little bell, the rustle of the crowd as the people knelt or struggled up to their feet, and a familiar voice, the voice of Tío Ventolera, giving the responses in sing-song tones, with the harsh stridor of his toothless mouth. The people accepted the old man's officious interference without a smile, attributing it to senile aberration. They had been accustomed for years and years to hearing the Latin jargon of the old sailor, who from his pew supported the responses of the assistant in a loud voice. They attributed a certain sacred character to these vagaries, like the Orientals who see in dementia a sign of piety.

Jaime lighted a cigarette to help while away the time. Doves were cooing on the arches, breaking the long silences with their tender calls. Jaime had cast, one after another, three cigarette stubs on the ground near his feet before a long drawn out murmur came from within the church, as from a thousand suspended breaths which finally exhaled a sigh of satisfaction. Then a noise of footsteps, scraping of chairs, creaking of benches, dragging of feet, and the doorway was thronged by people, all trying to crowd out at once.

The faithful exchanged friendly greetings as if they saw one another for the first time as they met out in the sunshine beyond the dim light of the temple.

"Bòn día! Bòn día!"

The women came out in groups; the elder ones dressed in black, emitting a stale odor from their innumerable skirts and petticoats; the young ones erect in rigid corsets which crushed their breasts and obliterated the prominent curves of their hips, displaying with stately pride, above the motley hued handkerchiefs, gold chains and enormous crucifixes. There were brown faces and olive, with great eyes of dramatic expression; coppery virgins with glossy, oily hair divided by a part which their rough combing was ever widening.

The men stopped in the doorway to adjust upon their tonsured heads the kerchief worn in womanish fashion under their hats, below which fell long curls over their foreheads. It was a relic of the ancient haick, or Arabian hood, now worn only on extraordinary occasions.

Then the old men drew from their belts their rustic, home-made pipes, filling them with the tobacco of the pòta, an acrid herb which was cultivated on the island. The young men strolled from the porch and adopted ferocious attitudes, their hands in their belts, and their heads held high, before the groups of women, among which were the beloved atlotas, the marriageable girls, who feigned indifference, but at the same time peeped at them out of the corners of their eyes.

Gradually the mass of people scattered.

"Bòn día! Bòn día!"

Many of them would not meet until the following Sunday. Along every path walked multi-colored groups; some dark, without any escort, moving slowly, as if dragging themselves along in the misery of old age; others energetic, with rustling skirts and fluttering kerchiefs, followed by a troop of boys, who shouted, whinnied like colts, and ran back and forth to attract the girls' attention.

Febrer saw a few black-clad figures leave the church, a somber group of shawled women, each affording a glimpse through the opening in the mantle of a nose reddened by the sun, and of one eye swimming in tears. They were covered by the abrigais, the winter shawl, the coarse wool wrap of ancient usage, the very sight of which on that sultry summer morning aroused sensations of torment and asphyxia. Then followed some hooded men, old peasants wearing the ceremonial cape, a gray garment of coarse wool, with broad sleeves and tight hood. The sleeves were loose and the hood was fastened under the chin, showing their brown, pirate-like faces.

They were relatives of a peasant who had died the week before. The large family, which dwelt in different parts of the cuarton, had gathered, according to custom, at the Sunday mass to honor the deceased, and when they saw one another they gave vent to their grief with African vehemence, as if the corpse still lay before their eyes. Tradition demanded that they cover themselves with the ceremonial garments, their winter dress serving to shut them up as it were in casques of mourning. They wept and perspired inside their wraps, and as each recognized a relative whom he had not seen for several days, his grief burst forth anew. Sighs of agony issued from within the heavy wrappings; the rude faces framed by the hood wrinkling and emitting howls like sick babies. They expressed their grief by melting into an incessant flood of mingled perspiration and tears. From every nose, the most visible part of these grief-struck phantoms, trembled drops which fell upon the folds of their heavy garments.

In the midst of the clamor of feminine voices, hoarse with pain, and the masculine lamentations sharpened by grief, a man began to speak with kindly authority, demanding calm. It was Pèp, of Can Mallorquí, a far-off connection of the dead man. In this island where everyone was more or less united by ties of blood, the distant relationship, although it required that he participate in the mourning, did not oblige him to don the haik worn on solemn occasions. He was dressed in black, and covered with a light wool mantle and a round felt hat that gave him a certain ecclesiastic air. His wife and Margalida, who did not consider themselves related to this family, stood at a distance, as if their bright Sunday apparel set them apart from this show of affliction.

Good natured Pèp pretended to be angry at the extremes of despair which were growing more and more vehement. Enough, enough! Let everyone return to his house, and live many years commending the dead to God's mercy.

The weeping grew louder beneath the shawls and hoods. Adios! Adios! They clasped each other's hands, they kissed each other's lips, they twisted each other's arms, as if saying farewell never to meet again. Adios! Adios! They departed in groups, each taking a different direction, toward the pine-covered mountains, toward the distant white farmhouses half hidden among fig and almond trees, toward the red rocks along the shore, and it was an absurd and incongrouous spectacle to see these heavy perspiring images, these tireless mourners, marching slowly through the resplendent green fields.

The return to Can Mallorquí was sad and silent. Pepet led the way, the bimbau between his lips buzzing like a gad-fly. From time to time he stopped to throw a stone at a bird or at a puffed-up black lizard darting among the opuntia cactus. Little impression did death make upon him! Margalida walked at her mother's side, silent, abstracted, her eyes opened very wide, beautiful bovine eyes, which looked in every direction reflecting not a single thought. She seemed to forget that behind her was Don Jaime, the señor, the revered guest of the tower.

Pèp, also abstracted, addressed an occasional word to Febrer, as if he felt need of one with whom to share his feelings.

"What an ugly thing is death, Don Jaime! Here we are, in a bit of land surrounded by the waters, unable to escape, unable to defend ourselves, awaiting the moment for the final weighing of the anchor."

The peasant's egoism rebelled at this injustice. It was all very well that over there on the mainland, where people are happy and enjoy life, Death should show himself; but here—here, too, in this far-away corner of the world, was there no limit, no exemption from the great meddler? It was useless to think of obstacles against Death's coming. The sea might be raging along the chain of islands and reefs lying between Iviza and Formentera; the narrow channels might be boiling caldrons, the rocks crowned with foam, and the rude men of the sea might acknowledge themselves vanquished and seek safety in the harbors, the passage might be closed against every living thing, the islands shut off from the rest of the world, but this signified nothing to the invincible mariner with the hairless head, to him who walks with fleshless legs, who rushes with gigantic strides over mountain and sea. No storm could detain him; no joy could make him forget; he was everywhere; he remembered everyone. The sun might shine, the fields might be in the fullness of their glory, the crops bountiful—they were deceptions to divert man in his tasks and to make these more endurable! Deceitful promises, like those made to children, so that they will submit to the torments of school! Nevertheless, one must allow himself to be deceived; the lie was good; one must not dwell upon this inevitable ill, this ultimate danger for which there was no remedy, and which saddened life, depriving the bread of its relish, the liquid of the grape of its merry sparkle, the white cheese of its succulency, the open fig of its sweetness, and the roasted sausage of its piquant strength, overshadowing and embittering all the good things that God has put on the island for the enjoyment of worthy people. "Ah, Don Jaime, what misery!"

Febrer dined at Can Mallorquí to save Pèp's children the climb up to the tower. The meal was begun in gloom, as if the lamentations of the hooded creatures on the porch of the church still vibrated in their ears; but gradually around the little low table, crowned with its great bowl of rice, joy began to spread. The Little Chaplain talked of the afternoon dance, absolutely forgetting his life in the Seminary, and venturing to meet Pèp's eyes. Margalida recalled the Minstrel's glances and the Ironworker's arrogant mien when she had walked past the youths on her way to mass. Her mother sighed.

"Alas, señor! alas, señor!"

She never said more than this, accompanying her confused thoughts of joy or of sorrow with the same exclamation.

Pèp had made numerous attacks upon the wine-jug filled with the rosy juice of grapes from the very vines which spread a leafy screen before the porch. His melancholy face was flushed with a merry light. "To the Devil with Death and all fear of him!"

Should an honorable man spend his whole life trembling at thought of Death's approach? Let him present himself whenever he wished! Meanwhile, let a man live! And he manifested this desire to live by falling asleep on a bench, and by loud snoring, which did not avail to frighten away the flies and wasps whirling about his mouth.

Febrer returned to his tower. Margalida and her brother barely noticed the señor. They had left the table that they might more freely discuss the dance, with the light-heartedness of children who were disturbed by the presence of a serious person.

In the tower he threw himself upon his couch and tried to sleep. All alone! He reflected upon his isolation, surrounded by people who respected him, who, perhaps, even loved him, but at the same time felt in irresistible attraction for their simple pleasures which were insipid to him. What a torment these Sundays were! Where should he go? What could he do?

In his determination to while away the time, to seek relief from an existence wanting in immediate purpose, he at last fell asleep. He awoke late in the afternoon when the sun was beginning slowly to descend beyond the line of islands in a shower of pale gold which seemed to impart to the waters a deeper and intenser blue.

On going down to Can Mallorquí he found the farmhouse closed. Nobody! His footsteps did not even arouse the dog that lived under the porch. The vigilant animal had also gone to the fiesta with the family.

"They've all gone to the dance," thought Febrer. "Suppose I go to the pueblo myself!"

He hesitated for awhile. What could he do there? He detested these diversions in which the presence of a stranger aroused animosity among the peasants. They preferred to remain by themselves. Should he, at his age, and with his austere appearance, that inspired only respect and chill, go and dance with an island maiden? He would have to keep near Pèp and the other men, breathing the odor of native tobacco, discussing the almond crop and the possibility of a frost, making an effort to bring his mind down to the level of these peasant farmers.

At last he decided to go. He dreaded solitude. Rather than spend the rest of the afternoon alone he preferred the dull, monotonous, conversation of the simple folk, a restful conversation, he said to himself, which did not compel him to think, and which left his mind in a state of sweet, animal calm.

Near San José he saw the Spanish flag floating over the roof of the alcalde's office, while the hollow beating of a drum, the bucolic quavering of a flute, and the snapping of castanets, reached his ears.

The dance took place in front of the church. The young people were formed into groups, standing near the musicians, who occupied low seats. The drummer, with his round instrument resting on one knee, beat the parchment with rhythmical strokes, while his companion blew on a long, wooden flute, carved with primitive designs. The Little Chaplain was flipping castanets as enormous as the shells brought in by Tío Ventolera.

The girls, their arms about each other's waists, or leaning against their shoulders, glanced with modest hostility at the young men, who strutted through the center of the plaza, hands in belts, broad felt hats thrust back to show the curls hanging over their foreheads, embroidered kerchiefs or ribbon cravats around their necks, wearing sandals of immaculate whiteness, almost concealed by the bell of the velveteen trousers cut in the shape of an elephant's foot.

At one side of the plaza, seated on a hummock or on chairs from the nearby tavern, were the mothers and old women; matrons anemic and saddened in their relative youth by excessive procreation and the hardships of rural life, with eyes sunken in a blue circle that seemed to reveal internal disorders, wearing on their breasts the gold chains of their youthful days, their sleeves decorated with silver buttons. The old women, coppery and wrinkled, wearing dark dresses, sighed grievously at sight of the merriment among the young girls and boys.

After gazing for some time at these people who scarcely yielded him a glance, he placed himself beside Pèp in a circle of old peasants. They received the gentleman from the tower with respectful silence, and after puffing a few mouthfuls of smoke from pipes filled with native tobacco, they resumed their stupid conversation about the probable severity of the approaching winter and the prospects of the coming crop of almonds.

The drum continued beating, the flute shrilled, the enormous castanets clanked, but not a couple sprang into the center of the plaza. The swains seemed to confer with indecision, as if each were afraid to venture first. Besides, the unexpected presence of the Majorcan gentleman somewhat intimidated the bashful girls.

Jaime felt someone nudge his elbow. It was the Little Chaplain, who whispered mysteriously into his ear, at the same time pointing with a finger: "There's Pere the Ironworker, the famous vèrro." He designated a youth of less than medium stature, but arrogant and ostentatious in his appearance. The young men were grouped around the hero. The Minstrel was talking animatedly with him, and he was listening with condescending gravity, spitting through his half-open lips, and admiring himself for the distance to which he sent the stream of saliva.

Suddenly the Little Chaplain sprang into the center of the plaza, flourishing his hat. What, were they going to spend the whole afternoon listening to the flute without dancing? He ran to the group of damsels and grasped the biggest one by the hands, dragging her after him: "You!" he called. This was invitation enough. The more rudely he slapped her arm the greater was the compliment.

The mischievous youth stood facing his partner, an arrogant and ugly girl with coarse hands, oily hair, and swarthy face, nearly a head taller than himself. Suddenly turning toward the musicians, the boy protested. He did not want to dance the "llarga"; he wanted to dance the "curta." The "long" and the "short" were the only two dances known on the island. Febrer had never been able to distinguish between them—a simple variation of rhythm, otherwise the music and the step seemed identical.

The girl, with one arm bent against her waist in the form of a handle, and the other hanging down, began to whirl slowly. She had nothing else to do; this was her entire dance. She lowered her eyes, curled her lips as if performing a vigorous task, and with a gesture of virtuous scorn, as if dancing against her will, she turned and turned, tracing great figure eights. It was the man who really did the dancing. This traditional reel, invented, doubtless, by the first settlers of the island, lusty pirates of the heroic age, illustrated the eternal history of the human race, the pursuing and hunting of the female. She whirled, cold and unfeeling, with the asexual hauteur of a rude virtue, fleeing from his springing and contortions, presenting her back to him with a gesture of scorn, while his fatiguing duty consisted in placing himself ever before her eyes, obstructing her path, coming out to meet her so that she should see and admire him. The dancer sprang and sprang, following no rule whatever, with no other restraint than the rhythm of the music, rebounding from the ground with tireless elasticity. Sometimes he would open his arms with a masterful gesture of domination, again he would fold them across his back, kicking his feet in the air.

It was a gymnastic exercise rather than a dance, the delirium of an acrobat, a phrenetic movement like the war dances of African tribes. The woman neither perspired nor flushed; she continued her turning, coldly, never accelerating her pace, while her companion, dizzy from his velocity, panted for breath with reddened face, at last retiring tremulous with fatigue. Every girl could dance with several men, exhausting them without effort. It was the triumph of feminine passiveness, laughing at the arrogant ostentation of the opposite sex, knowing that in the end she would witness his humiliation.

The appearance of the first couple drew out the others. In a moment the entire open space before the musicians was covered with heavy skirts, beneath whose rigid and multiple folds moved the small feet in white hempen sandals or yellow shoes. The broad bells of the pantaloons vibrated with the rapid movement of the springing or the energetic stamping which raised clouds of dust. Manly arms chose with gallant slap among the clustered maidens. "You!" And this monosyllable followed the tug of conquest, the blows which were equivalent to a momentary title of possession, all the extremes of a crude, ancestral predilection, of a gallantry inherited from remote forbears of the dark epoch when the club, the stone, and the hand-to-hand struggle were the first declaration of love.

Some youths who had allowed themselves to be preceded by others more bold in the choice of partners, stood near the musicians watching for a chance to succeed to their companions. When they saw a dancer red-faced and perspiring, making every effort to continue, they approached him, grasping him by the arm and flinging him aside, and calling, "Leave her to me!" And they took his place with no other explanation, springing and pursuing the girl with the ardor of fresh energy, while she did not seem to notice the change, for she continued her turning with lowered eyes and disdainful mien.

Jaime had not seen Margalida at first, as she was surrounded by her companions, but soon he recognized her among the dancers.

Beautiful Almond Blossom! Febrer thought her more lovely than ever as he compared her with her friends, brown and tanned by the sun and by toil. Her white skin, its flower-like delicacy, with the deep and brilliant eyes of a gentle little animal, her graceful figure, and even the softness of her hands, set her apart, as if she belonged to a different rāce from her dusky companions, seductive on account of their youth, lively, good-natured, but who seemed to be chopped out with an axe.

Looking at her, Jaime thought that in a different atmosphere she might have been an adorable creature. He divined in Almond Blossom countless delicate ways, of which she herself was unconscious. What a pity that she had been born in this island which she would never leave! And her beauty would be for some of those barbarians who admired her with a canine stare of eagerness! Perhaps she was destined for the Ironworker, that odious vèrro, who seemed to patronize them all with his gloomy eyes!

When she married she would cultivate the soil like the other women; her flower-like whiteness would fade and turn yellow; her hands would become black and scaly; she would be like her mother and all the old peasant women, a female skeleton, bent and knaggy, like the trunk of an olive tree. These thoughts saddened Febrer, as a great injustice. How had the simple Pèp, who stood beside him, produced this offspring? What obscure combination of race had made it possible for Margalida to be born in Can Mallorquí? Must this mysterious and perfumed flower of peasant stock fade as would the woodland buds growing beside her?

Suddenly something unusual distracted Febrer's mind from these thoughts. The flute, the tambourine, and the castanets continued playing, the dancers sprang, the girls turned, but a gleam of alarm shone in the eyes of all, an expression of defensive solidarity. The old men ceased their conversation, glancing in the direction of the women. "What is it? What is it?" The Little Chaplain ran about among the couples, whispering into the ears of the dancers. These dashed from the circle, their hands in their belts, and after disappearing for a few seconds returned immediately to take their places, while the girls continued turning.

Pèp smiled lightly as he guessed what had happened, and he whispered to the señor. "It is nothing; just what happens at every dance." There had been danger, and the boys had put their equipment in a safe place.

This "equipment" consisted of the pistols and knives which the boys carried as a testimony of citizenship. For an instant Febrer saw flash in the light stupendous and enormous weapons, marvelously concealed on those spare, thin bodies. The old women beckoned with their bony hands, eager to share the risk, the vehemence of an aggressive heroism shining in their eyes. "These accursed times of impiety in which decent people are molested when they were following ancient customs! Here! Here!" And grasping the deadly weapons they hid them beneath the circle made by their innumerable layers of petticoats and skirts. The young mothers settled themselves in their seats and broadened the angle of their bulky legs, as if to offer greater hiding space for the warlike implements. The women looked at each other with bellicose resolution. Let those evil souls dare to approach! They would suffer being torn to shreds before they would stir from their places.

Febrer saw something glittering down a roadway leading to the church. They were leather straps and guns, and above these the white brims of the three-cocked hats of a pair of civil guards.

The two defenders of the peace slowly approached, with a certain hesitation, convinced, no doubt, of having been seen in the distance and of arriving too late. Jaime was the only one who looked at them; the rest pretended not to see, holding their heads low or looking in a different direction. The musicians played more vehemently, but the couples began to retire. The girls deserted the young men and joined the group of women.

"Good afternoon, gentlemen!"

To this greeting from the elder of the guards the drum replied by ceasing to beat and leaving the flute unaccompanied. This whined a few notes which seemed an ironic answer to the salutation.

A long silence fell. Some answered the greeting with a light "Tengui!" but they all pretended not to see, and glanced in another direction, as if the guards were not there.

The painful silence seemed to annoy the two soldiers.

"Vaya! Go on with your diversion. Don't stop on our account!"

He gave a sign to the musicians, and they, incapable of disobeying authority in anything, produced a music more brisk and diabolically gay than before; but they might as well be playing to the dead! Everyone stood silent and glowering, wondering how this unexpected visit would end.

The guards, accompanied by the beating of the drum, the musical capering of the flute, and the dry and strident laughter of the castanets, began moving about among the groups of young men, looking them over.

"You young gallant," said the leader with paternal authority, "hands up!"

The one designated obeyed tamely without the slightest intent of resistance, almost vain of this distinction. He knew his duty. The Ivizan was born to work, to live, and—to be searched. Noble inconveniences of being valorous, and of being held in a certain fear! Every youth seeing in the searching a testimony of his worth, raised his arms and thrust forward his abdomen, lending himself with satisfaction to the fumbling of the guards, while he glanced proudly toward the group of girls.

Febrer noticed that the two officers pretended to ignore the presence of the Ironworker. They acted as if they did not recognize him; they turned their backs, making visible display of paying no attention to him.

Pèp spoke to Febrer in a low voice, with an accent of admiration. Those men with the tricorne hats knew more than the devil himself; by not searching the vèrro they almost offered him an insult; they showed that they had no fear of him; they set him apart from the rest, exempting him from an operation to which everyone else was compelled to submit. Whenever they met the vèrro in the company of other young men, they searched those, without ever touching him. For this reason the boys, through fear of losing their weapons, finally avoided going out with the hero, and they shunned him as an attractor of danger.

The searching continued to the sound of music. The Little Chaplain followed the guards on their evolutions, always placing himself before the elder one, with his hands in his belt, looking at him fixedly, with an expression half threatening, half entreating. The man did not seem to see him; he looked for the others, but he continually stumbled against the youngster, who barred his way. The man with the three-cocked hat finally smiled under his fierce mustache, and called his comrade.

"You!" he said, pointing to the boy. "Search that vèrro. He must be dangerous."

The Little Chaplain, forgiving the enemy's waggish tone, raised his arms as high as possible so that no one should fail to see his importance. The guard had moved away after giving him a tickling in the stomach, but the boy still maintained his position as a man to be feared. Then he rushed toward a group of girls to boast of the danger he had faced. Fortunately his grandfather's knife was at home, safely hidden away by his father. Had he borne it on his person they would have taken it from him.

The guards soon wearied of this fruitless search. The elder glanced maliciously toward the group of women, like a dog sniffing a trail. He knew well enough where the weapons were concealed, but let anyone venture to make the bronze matrons stir from their places! Hostility shone in the eyes of the ancient dames. They would have to be torn away by main force, and they were señoras!

"Gentlemen, good afternoon!"

They slung their guns over their shoulders, refusing the proffer of some youths who had run to a tavern to bring glasses. They were offered without fear or rancor; were they not all neighbors, living together on their little island? The guards, however, were firm in their refusal. "Thanks; it is against the rules." They strode away, perhaps to lie in ambush a short distance away and repeat the searching again at sunset when the party was broken up and the people returning to their lonely farmhouses.

After the danger had passed the instruments ceased playing. Febrer saw the Minstrel take the little drum and seat himself in the open space recently occupied by the dancers. The people crowded around him. The venerable matrons drew up their esparto-seated chairs in order to hear better. He was about to sing a romance of his own composition; a relación, accentuated, according to the custom of the country, by a quavering plaint, a cry of pain drawn out as long as the singer had air left in his lungs.

He beat the drum slowly to impart a gloomy solemnity to his monotonous song, dreamy and sad. "How can I sing for you, friends, when my heart is broken?" began the recitative; and then, in the midst of a general silence, came a strident trill, like the long continued lament of a dying bird.

The entire company gazed at the singer, not seeing in him the indolent, sickly youth, despicable on account of his uselessness for work. In their primitive minds stirred a vague something which impelled them to respect the words and complaints of the weakling. It was something extraordinary, which seemed to sweep, with rude beating of wings, over their simple souls.

The Minstrel's voice sobbed as it told of a woman insensible to his sighs, and as he compared her whiteness with the flower of the almond, they turned their eyes to Margalida, who remained impassive, with no sign of virginal flushing, being accustomed to this tribute of crude poesy which was a sort of prelude to gallantry.

The Minstrel continued his laments, reddening with the strain of the painful crowing which ended every strophe. His narrow chest heaved with the effort; two rosettes of sickly purple colored his cheeks; his slender neck dilated, the veins standing out in blue relief. In accordance with custom, he concealed part of his face under an embroidered kerchief, which he held with his arm resting on the drum. Febrer felt anxiety listening to this painful voice. It seemed to him that the singer's lungs would give way, that his throat would burst; but his hearers, accustomed to this barbaric singing, which was as exhausting as the dance, paid no attention to his fatigue, nor did they weary of his interminable narration.

A group of youths, moving away from the circle around the poet, seemed to be holding a consultation, and then they approached the older men. They were in search of Señor Pèp, of Can Mallorquí, to discuss an important matter. They turned their backs scornfully upon the Minstrel, an unhappy creature, good for nothing but to dedicate verses to the girls.

The most venturesome of the group faced Pèp. They wished to speak of the "festeig" of Margalida; they reminded the father of his promise to sanction the courting of the girl.

The peasant-farmer looked at the group deliberately, as if counting their number.

"How many are you?"

The leader smiled. There were many more. They represented other young men who had remained to hear the song. There were youths from every district. Even from San Juan, at the opposite end of the island, youths were coming to court Margalida.

Despite the mock gesture of an intractable father, Pèp reddened and compressed his lips with ill-concealed satisfaction, glancing out of the corner of his eye at the friends sitting near him. What glory for Can Mallorquí! Such a courtship had never been known before. Never had his companions seen their daughters so honored.

"Are there twenty of you?" he asked.

The youths did not reply immediately, being occupied in mental calculation, murmuring the names of friends. Twenty? More, many more! He might count on thirty.

The peasant persisted in his pretended indignation. Thirty! Maybe they thought he needed no rest, and that he was going to spend a whole night without sleep, witnessing their courting.

Then he grew calm, giving himself up to complicated mental calculations, while he repeated thoughtfully, with an expression of amazement, "Thirty! Thirty!"

In the end he gave his sanction. He would not give more than an hour and a half in one evening to the wooing. Since there were thirty, that made three minutes each; three minutes, counted, watch in hand, to talk to Margalida; not a minute more! Thursday and Saturday would be courting nights. When he had gone courting his wife the suitors were many less, and yet his father-in-law, a man who had never been seen to smile, did not concede more time than this. There must be much formality, understand! Let there be no rivalry nor fighting! The first one to break the agreement Pèp was man enough to beat out of the door with a club; and if it became necessary to use the gun, he would use it.

Good-natured Pèp, gratified at being able to assume unbounded ferocity at the expense of the respect due from his daughter's suitors, heaped bravado upon bravado, talking of killing anyone who should not keep to the agreement, while the youths listened with humble mien, but with an ironic grin under their noses.

The bargain was closed. Thursday next the first audience would be held at Can Mallorquí. Febrer, who had heard the conversation, glanced at the vèrro, who held himself aloof, as if his greatness prevented his condescending to wretched haggling over the arrangement.

When the boys moved away to join the circle, discussing in a low voice the order of precedence, the troubadour ceased his doleful music, crowing his last crow with a dolorous voice that seemed finally to rend his poor throat. He wiped away the perspiration, pressed his hands against his breast, his face becoming a dark purple, but the people had turned their backs and he was already forgotten.

The girls, with the solidarity of sex, surrounded Margalida with vehement gesticulations, pushing her, and urging her to sing a reply to what the troubadour had said about the perfidy of women.

"No! No!" replied Almond Blossom, struggling to rid herself of her companions.

So sincere was she in her resistance that at last the old women intervened, defending her. Let her alone! Margalida had come to enjoy herself, and not to entertain the others. Did they think it such an easy matter to suddenly compose a reply in verse?

The drummer had recovered the instrument from the Minstrel's hands and began to beat it. The flute seemed to be gargling the rapid notes before beginning the dreamy melody of an African rhythm. On with the dance!

The boys all began shouting at once with aggressive vehemence, addressing the musicians. Some demanded the "long" and others the "short"; they all felt themselves strong and imperious again. The deadly steel had come forth from beneath the women's petticoats and had returned to their belts, and contact with these companions imparted to each a new life, a recrudescence of their arrogance.

The musicians began to play what they pleased, the curious crowd made way, and again in the center of the plaza the white hempen sandals began to spring, the whorls of green and blue skirts began to turn stiffly, while the points of kerchiefs fluttered above heavy braids, or the flowers worn by the girls behind their ears shook like red tassels.

Jaime continued looking at the Ironworker with the irresistible attraction of antipathy. The vèrro stood silent and as if abstracted among his admirers, who formed a circle around him. He seemed not to see the others, fixing his eyes on Margalida with a tense expression, as if he would conquer her with this stare which inspired fear in men. When the Little Chaplain, with the enthusiasm of youth, approached the vèrro, he deigned to smile, seeing in the boy a future relative.

Even the boys who had ventured to discuss the wooing with Señor Pèp seemed intimidated by the Ironworker's presence. The girls came out to dance, led by the young men, but Margalida remained beside her mother, gazed at enviously by all, yet none of them dared approach to invite her.

The Majorcan felt the Camorrist tendencies of his early youth aroused in him. He loathed the vèrro; he felt the terror inspired by the man as a personal offense. Was there no one to give a slap in the face to this coxcomb from the prison?

A youth approached Margalida, taking her by the hand. It was the Minstrel, still perspiring and tremulous after his exertion. He held himself erect, trying to give the lie to his weakness. The white Almond Blossom began to turn on her small feet and he sprang and sprang, pursuing her in her evolutions.

Poor boy! Jaime felt an impression of anguish, guessing the effort of the pitiful attempt to dominate the fatigue of the body. He breathed laboriously, his legs began to tremble, but in spite of this he smiled, gratified at his triumph. He gazed tenderly at Margalida, and if he turned away his eyes it was to look haughtily at his friends who responded with looks of pity.

In making a turn he almost fell; as he gave a great leap his knees bent. Everyone expected to see him fall to the ground; but he went on dancing, displaying his will-power, his determination to die rather than confess his weakness.

His eyes were closing with vertigo when he felt a touch on his shoulder, according to usage, requiring him to yield his partner.

It was the Ironworker, who flung himself into the dance for the first time that afternoon. His leaping was received with a murmur of applause. They all admired him, with that collective cowardice of a timid multitude.

The vèrro, seeing himself applauded, increased his contortions, pursuing his partner, barring her way, surrounding her in the complicated net of his movements, while Margalida turned and turned with lowered gaze, avoiding the eyes of the dreaded gallant.

At times, the vèrro, to display his vigor, with his bust thrown back and his arms behind him, sprang to a considerable height, as if the ground were elastic and his legs steel springs. This leaping made Jaime think, with a sensation of repugnance, of escapes from prison or of surreptitious assaults with a knife.

Time passed, but the man did not seem to tire. Some of the girls had sat down, in other cases the dancer had been substituted several times, but the vèrro continued his violent dance, ever gloomy and disdainful, as if insensible to weariness.

Jaime himself recognized with a dash of envy the terrible vigor of the Ironworker. What an animal!

Suddenly the dancer was seen to feel for something in his belt, and reach downward with one hand, without ceasing his evolutions or his leaping. A cloud of smoke spread over the ground, and between its white film two rapid flashes were outlined pale and rosy in the sunlight, followed by two reports.

The women huddled together, screaming with sudden fright; the men stood undecided, but soon all were reassured, and burst into shouts of approbation and applause.

"Muy bien!" The vèrro had fired off his pistol at his partner's feet; the supreme gallantry of a valiant man; the greatest homage a girl on the island could receive.

Margalida, a woman at heart, continued dancing, without having been greatly impressed, like a good Ivizan, by the explosion of the powder; giving the Ironworker a look of gratitude for the bravado which made him defy persecution from the civil guards who might still be near; then turning to her friends who were tremulous with envy at this homage.

Even Pèp himself, to the great indignation of Jaime, displayed pride over the two shots fired at his daughter's feet.

Febrer was the only one who did not seem enthusiastic over this gallant deed.

Accursed convict! Febrer was not sure of the motive of his fury, but it was something spontaneous. He meant to settle accounts with that peasant!

CHAPTER IV
THIRTY AND ONE WOOERS

Winter came. There were days when the sea would lash furiously against the chain of islands and cliffs between Iviza and Formentera that form a wall of rock cut by straits and channels. The deep blue waters, which usually flow tranquilly through these narrows, reflecting the sandy bottoms, would begin to whirl in livid eddies, dashing against the coasts and the projecting rocks, which would disappear and then emerge again in the white foam. Vessels would struggle valiantly against the swift undertow and the spectacular, roaring waters between the islands of Espalmador and Los Ahorcados, where lies the pathway of the great ships. Vessels from Iviza and Formentera must spread all their canvas, and sail under shelter of the barren islands. The sinuosities of this labyrinth of channels permit navigators from the archipelago of the Pityusæ to go from one island to another by different routes, according to the direction of the winds. While the sea rages on one side of the archipelago, on the other it may be still and safe, lying heavy like oil. In the straits the waves may swirl high in furious whirlpools, but with a mere turn of the wheel, a slight shifting of her course, the vessel may glide into the shelter of an island where she will ride in tranquil waters, paradisiacal, limpid, affording views of strange vegetation, where dart fishes sparkling with silver and flashing with carmine.

Usually day dawned with a gray sky and an ashen sea. The Vedrá seemed more enormous, more imposing, lifting its conical needle in this stormy atmosphere. The sea rushed in cataracts through the caverns on its margin, roaring like the peals of gigantic cannons. The wild goats on their inaccessible heights sprang from one narrow footing to another, and only when thunder rolled through the gloomy heavens, and fiery serpents flashed down to drink in the immense pool of the sea, did the timid beasts flee with bleating of terror to seek refuge in the recesses covered by juniper.

On many stormy days Febrer went fishing with Tío Ventolera. The old sailor was thoroughly familiar with his sea. On the mornings when Jaime remained in his couch watching the livid and diffuse light of a stormy day filter through the crevices, he had to arise hastily on hearing the voice of his companion who "sang the mass," accompanying the Latin jargon by pelting the tower with stones. Get up! It was a fine day for fishing. They would make a good catch. When Febrer gazed apprehensively at the threatening sea, the old man explained that they would find tranquil waters in the shelter around the Vedrá.

Again, on radiant mornings, Febrer fruitlessly awaited the old man's call. Time dragged on. After the rosy tint of dawn the golden bars of sunlight stole through the cracks; but in vain the hours passed, he heard neither mass nor stone throwing. Tío Ventolera remained invisible. Then, on opening his window, he looked out upon the clear sky, luminous with the gracious splendor of the winter sun, but the sea was restless, a gloomy blue, undulating, without foam and without noise under the impulse of a treacherous wind.

The winter rains covered the island as with a gray mantle, through which the indefinite contours of the nearby range were vaguely outlined. On the mountain tops the pine trees dropped tears from every filament, and the thick layer of humus was soaked like a sponge, expelling liquid beneath the footsteps. On the barren rocky heights along the coast, the rain gathered, forming tumultuous brooks, which leapt from cliff to cliff. The spreading fig trees trembled like enormous broken umbrellas, allowing the water to enter the broad spaces beneath their cupolas. The almond trees, denuded of their leaves, shook like black skeletons. The deep gulleys filled with bellowing waters that flowed uselessly toward the sea. The roads, paved with blue cobbles, between high, rocky banks, were converted into cataracts. The island, thirsty and dusty during a great part of the year, seemed to repel this exuberance of rain from all its pores, as a sick man repels the strong medicine administered too late. On these stormy days Febrer remained shut up in his tower. It was impossible to go to sea and impossible also to go out hunting in the island fields. The farmhouses were closed, their white cubes spotted by torrents of rain, devoid of any other sign of life than the thread of blue smoke escaping from the chimney tops.

Forced to inactivity, the lord of the Pirate's Tower began to read over again one of the few books he had acquired on his trips to the city, or he smoked pensively, recalling that past from which he had endeavored to run away. What was happening in Majorca? What were his friends saying?

Given over to this enforced idleness, lacking the distraction of physical exercise, he thought over his former life, which was daily growing more hazy and indistinct in his memory. It seemed to him like the life of another man; something which he had seen and been familiar with, but which belonged to the history of another. Really was that Jaime Febrer who had traveled all over Europe and had had his hours of vanity and triumph the same person who was now living in this tower by the sea, rustic, bearded, and almost savage, with the sandals and hat of a peasant, more accustomed to the moaning of the waves and the screaming of gulls than to contact with men?

Weeks before he had received a second letter from his friend Toni Clapés. This also was written from a café on the Borne, a few hastily scrawled lines to attest his regard. This rude but kind friend did not forget him; he did not even seem to be offended because his former letter had remained unanswered. He wrote about Captain Pablo. The captain was still angry with Febrer, nevertheless he was working diligently to disentangle his affairs. The smuggler had faith in Valls. He was the cleverest of Chuetas, and more generous than any of them. There was no doubt that he would save the remains of Jaime's fortune, and he would be able to spend the rest of his days in Majorca, tranquil and happy. Later he would hear from the captain himself. Valls preferred to keep quiet until matters were settled.

Febrer shrugged his shoulders. Bah! It was all over! But on gloomy winter days his spirit rebelled against existing like a solitary mollusk, shut up in his stone shell. Was he always going to live like this? Was it not folly to have hidden himself away in this corner while still having youth and courage to struggle with the world?

Yes, it was folly. The island and his romantic shelter were all very pretty for the first few months, when the sun shone, the trees were green, and the island customs exercised over his soul the charm of a bizarre novelty; but bad weather had come, the solitude was intolerable, and the life of the rustics was revealed to him in all the crudity of their barbarous passions. These peasants, dressed in blue velveteen, with their bright belts and gay cravats and their flowers behind their ears, had at first seemed to him picturesque figures, created only to serve as a decoration for the fields, choristers for a pastoral operetta, languid and tame; but he knew them better now; they were men like others, and barbarous men, barely grazed by contact with civilization, conserving all the sharp angles of their ancestral rudeness. Seen from a distance, for a short time, they attracted with the charm of novelty, but he had penetrated their customs, he was almost one of them, and it weighed upon him like falling into slavery—this inferior existence which seemed to be clashing every instant with ideas and prejudices of his past.

He ought to get away from this atmosphere; but where could he go? How could he escape? He was poor. His entire capital consisted of a few dozens of duros which he had brought from Majorca, a sum which he retained, thanks to Pèp, who was firm in his refusal to accept any remuneration whatever. Here he must remain, nailed to his tower as if it were a cross, without hope, without desire, seeking in cessation of thought a vegetative joy like that of the junipers and tamarisks growing between the cliffs on the promontory, or like that of the shell fish forever clinging to the submerged rocks.

After long reflection he resigned himself to his fate. He would not think, he would not desire. Besides, hope, which, never forsakes us, conceived in his mind the vague possibility of something extraordinary that would present itself in its own good time, to save him from this situation; but while it was on its way, how the loneliness bored him!

Margalida had not been to the tower for some time. She seemed to seek pretexts for not coming, and she even went out of her way to avoid meeting Febrer. She had changed; she seemed to have suddenly awakened to a new existence. The innocent and trustful smile of girlhood had changed to a gesture of reserve, like a woman who realizes the dangers of the road and travels with slow and cautious step.

Since the courting had begun, and young men came twice a week to solicit her hand, according to the traditional "festeig," she seemed to have taken heed of great and unknown dangers before unsuspected, and she remained at her mother's side, shunning every occasion of being left alone with a man, and blushing as soon as masculine eyes met her own.

This courting had nothing extraordinary about it, according to island customs, and yet it aroused in Febrer a dumb anger, as if he saw in it an offense and a spoliation. The invasion of Can Mallorquí by the braggart and enamored young blades he took as an insult. He had looked upon the farmhouse as his home, but since these intruders had been cordially received he was going to take his leave.

Besides, he suffered in silence the chagrin of not being the only preoccupation of the family, as he had been at first. Pèp and his wife still looked up to him as their master; Margalida and her brother venerated him as a powerful lord who had come from far away because Iviza was the best place in the world; but in spite of this other thoughts seemed to be reflected in their eyes. The visit of so many youths and the change which this had wrought in their daily life, made them less solicitous in regard to Don Jaime. They were all worried about the future. Which one of the youths deserved in the end to be Margalida's husband?

During the long winter evenings Febrer, shut up in his tower, sat gazing at a little light shining forth in the valley below—the light of Can Mallorquí. On the nights not devoted to the courting, the family would be alone, gathered around the fireplace, but, in spite of this, he remained fixed in his isolation. No, he would not go down. In his chagrin he even complained of the bad weather, as if he would make the winter cold responsible for this change which had gradually taken place in his relations with the peasant family.

He wistfully recalled those beautiful summer nights when they used to sit until the small hours watching the stars tremble in the dark sky beyond the black border of the portico. Febrer used to sit beneath the pergola with the family and Uncle Ventolera who came, drawn by the hope of some gift. They never let him go away without a slice of watermelon, which filled the old man's mouth with its sweet red juice, or a glass of perfumed figola, brewed from fragrant mountain herbs. Margalida, her eyes fixed on the mystery of the stars, would sing Ivizan romances in her girlish voice, more fresh and soft to the ear of Febrer than the breeze which filled the blue tumult of the night with rustling. Pèp would tell, with the air of a prodigious explorer, of his stupendous adventures on the mainland during the years when he had served the king as a soldier, in the remote and almost fantastic lands of Catalonia and Valencia.

The dog, lying at his feet, seemed to be listening to his master with mild, gentle eyes, in the depths of which a star was reflected. Suddenly he would spring up with nervous impulse, and giving a leap, would disappear in the darkness, accompanied by the sonorous murmur of crashing vegetation. Pèp would explain this stealthy flight. It was nothing more than some animal wandering in the darkness; a jack rabbit, a cotton-tail, which the beast had scented with the delicate nose of the hunting dog. Again he would rise to his feet slowly with growls of vigilant hostility. Somebody was passing near the farmhouse; a shadow, a man walking quickly, with the celerity of the Ivizans, accustomed to going rapidly from one side of the island to the other. If the shade spoke, they all answered his greeting. If he passed in silence they pretended not to see him, just as the dark traveler seemed to be unconscious of the existence of the farmhouse and of the persons seated under the pergola.

It was a very ancient custom in Iviza not to greet each other out in the country after nightfall. Shadows passed along the roads without a word, avoiding a meeting so as not to stumble against nor recognize each other. Each was bound on business of his own, to see his sweetheart, to consult the doctor, to kill an enemy at the other end of the island, to return on a run and be able to prove an alibi by saying that at the fatal hour he had been with friends. Every one who traveled at night had his reasons for passing unrecognized. One shadow feared another shadow. A "bòna nit," or a request for a light for the cigarette, might be answered by a pistol shot.

Sometimes no one passed by the farmhouse, and yet, the dog, stretching out his neck, howled into the dark void. In the distance human howls seemed to answer him. They were prolonged and savage yells, which rent the mysterious silence like a war cry. "A-u-u-ú!" And much farther away, weakened by distance, replied another fierce exclamation: "A-u-u-ú!"

The peasant silenced his dog. There was nothing strange about these cries. They were the voices of youths howling in the darkness, guiding one another by their calls, perhaps that they might recognize each other and come together for a friendly purpose, or perhaps to fight, the cry being a challenging shout. It was not unlikely that after the howling a shot would ring out. Affairs of young bloods and of the night! They had no significance.

Then Pèp would continue the relation of his extraordinary journeys, while his wife, who heard these ever new marvels for the thousandth time, stared at him in amazement.

Uncle Ventolera, not to be outdone, narrated tales of pirates and of valorous mariners of Iviza, bearing them out with the testimony of his father, who had been cabin boy on Captain Riquer's xebec, and which assaulted the frigate *Felicidad*, captained by the formidable corsair "the Pope." Stirred by these heroic recollections, he hummed in his quavering old voice the ballad in which Ivizan sailors had celebrated the triumph, verses in Castilian, for greater solemnity, whose words Tío Ventolera mispronounced.

The toothless old sailor continued singing the heroic deeds of long ago, as if they dated from yesterday, as if he had witnessed them himself, as if a flash from the atalaya announcing a disembarcation of enemies might suddenly flare across this land of combat, enveloped in darkness.

Again, his eyes glittering with avarice, he would tell of enormous sums which the Moors, the Romans, and other red mariners whom he called the Normans, had buried in caves along the coast. His ancestors knew much about all this. What a pity that they had died without saying a word! He related the true history of the cavern of Formentera, where the Normans had stored the product of their freebooting expeditions throughout Spain and Italy—golden images of saints, chalices, chains, jewels, precious stones and coins measured by the peck. A frightful dragon, trained doubtless by the red men, used to guard the deep, dark cavern, with the treasure beneath his belly. The rash soul who should slip down a rope into the cave would serve the beast for nourishment. The red mariners had died many centuries ago; the dragon was dead also; the treasure must still be on Formentera. Who could find it? The rustic audience trembled with emotion, never doubting the existence of such treasure because of the respect inspired in them by the age of the narrator.

Placid summer evenings those, which were no longer repeated for Febrer! He avoided going down to Can Mallorquí after dark, fearful of disturbing by his presence the conversation of the family about Margalida's suitors.

On courting nights he experienced even greater uneasiness, and, without explaining to himself his motive, he stared longingly toward the farmhouse. The same light, the same appearance as ever—but he imagined that he could make out in the nocturnal silence, new sounds, the echo of songs, Margalida's voice. There would be the odious Ironworker, and that poor devil of a Minstrel, and the rude, barbarous youths, with their ridiculous dress. Gran Dios! How was it possible that these rustics had ever managed to interest him, after all that he had seen of the world?

The next day when the Little Chaplain would climb up to the tower to bring his dinner, Jaime would question him about the events of the previous evening.

Listening to the boy, Febrer pictured to himself the incidents of the courting. The family supped hurriedly at nightfall, so as to be ready for the ceremony. Margalida took down her gala skirt hanging from the ceiling in her room, and after donning it with the red and green kerchief crossed over her breast and a smaller one on her head, a long bow of ribbon at the end of her braid, she put on the gold chain her mother had turned over to her, and took her seat on the folded abragais on a kitchen chair. Her father smoked his pipe of tobacco de pòta; her mother sat in a corner weaving rush baskets; the Little Chaplain peeped out of the door to the broad porch, on which the youthful suitors were silently gathering. Some there were who had been waiting for an hour, for they lived near; there were others who came dusty or spattered with mud, after walking two leagues. On rainy nights, in the shelter of the porch they shook out their cowled Arabian capes of coarse weave, an inheritance from their forefathers, or the feminine mantles in which they were wrapped, as garments of modern elegance.

After briefly deciding upon the order to be followed in their conversation with the girl, the troop of rivals started for the kitchen, as it was too cold on the porch in winter. A knock on the door.

"Come in, whoever you are!" shouted Pèp, as if ignorant of the presence of the suitors and expecting an unusual visitor.

They entered tamely, greeting the family: "Bòna nit! Bòna nit!" They took seats on a bench, like schoolboys, or they remained standing, all gazing at the girl. Near her was a vacant chair, or if this were lacking, the suitor squatted on the ground, Moorish fashion, talking to her in low tones for three minutes, enduring the hostile gaze of his adversaries. The slightest prolongation of this brief term provoked coughing, furious glances, remonstrances and threats in undertones. The youth would retire and another would take his place. The Little Chaplain laughed at these scenes, seeing in the hostile tenacity of the suitors a motive for pride. The courting of his sister was not going to be like that of other girls. The suitors seemed to Pepet to be rabid dogs who would not easily give up their prey. This wooing smelled to him of gunpowder, and he affirmed it with a smile of joy and satisfaction which disclosed the whiteness of his wolf-cub teeth in his dark oval face. None of the suitors seemed to gain advantage over the others. During the two months that the courting had lasted, Margalida had done nothing but listen, smile, and respond to them all with words which confused the youths. His sister's talent was very great. On Sundays when they went to mass, she walked ahead of her parents accompanied by all her suitors—a veritable army. Don Jaime had met them several times. Her friends, seeing her come with this queenly retinue, paled with envy. The suitors besieged her, endeavoring to extract some word, some sign of preference, but she replied with astonishing discretion, keeping them all on the same footing, avoiding fatal clashes which might suddenly arouse the aggressive youths, who were always heavily armed.

"And how about the Ironworker?" asked Don Jaime.

Accursed vèrro! His name issued with difficulty from the señor's lips, but he had been thinking of him for some time.

The boy shook his head. The Ironworker was making no particular advance over his rivals, and the Little Chaplain did not seem to regret it keenly.

His admiration for the vèrro had cooled somewhat. Love emboldens men, and none of the youths who pretended to Margalida's hand, now that they came face to face with him as a rival, stood in fear of him any longer, and they even ventured disrespect to his formidable person. One evening he had appeared with a guitar, intending to employ a large part of the time which belonged to the others in playing. When his turn came he placed himself near Margalida, tuned his instrument and began to intone songs of the mainland learned during his retirement at "Niza"; but before beginning he had taken from his girdle a double-barreled pistol, cocked it, and had laid it upon one of his thighs, ready to grasp it and to let fly a shot at the first man to interrupt him. Absolute silence and impassive glances! He sang as long as he wished, he put up his pistol with the air of a conqueror, but later, when they went out, in the darkness of the fields, when the youths dispersed with cries of ironic farewell, two well-aimed stones issuing from the shadows struck the braggart to the ground, and for several days he failed to come to the courting so as not to show his bandaged head. He had made no effort to find out who the aggressor was. The rivals were many, and, moreover, he had to take into account their fathers, uncles, and brothers, almost a fourth part of the island, quick to mix in a war of vengeance for the honor of the family.

"I think," said Pepet, "that the Ironworker is less valiant than they say; and what is your opinion about it, Don Jaime?"

When it was growing late, and Margalida had talked with each of her suitors, her father, who was dozing in a corner, would break into a loud yawn. The man of the fields seemed to divine the passing of time even when asleep. "Half past nine! Bedtime! Bòna nit!" And all the youths, after this hint, would leave the house, their footsteps and their whinnying swallowed up by darkness.

Pepet, as he spoke of these reunions, in which he rubbed elbows with brave men, wearers of deadly weapons, again bethought him of his grandfather's knife. When would Don Jaime speak to his father about this family treasure? Since he had put off asking he must not forget his promise to present him another knife. What could a man like himself do, lacking such a companion? Where could he present himself?

"Don't worry," said Febrer. "One of these days I'll go to town. You may count on the gift."

One morning Jaime started for Iviza, eager for a fresh experience, and to renew and vary his impressions in a less rural atmosphere. Iviza seemed to him now like a great city, even to him who had traveled over all Europe. The houses in a row, the red brick sidewalks, the balconies with Persian blinds, he admired them all with the simplicity of a savage from the interior of a desert who arrives at a trading station on the coast. He paused before the shops, examining the goods exposed with the same enjoyment with which he used to contemplate the luxurious display windows on the boulevards or on Regent Street.

The jewelry shop of a Chueta held his attention a long while. He admired the filigree buttons with a stone in the center, the hollow gold chains made for the peasant girls, who deemed these objects the most perfect and marvelous works created by the art of man. Suppose he should go in and buy a dozen of those buttons! What a surprise for the girl of Can Mallorquí when he should present them to her for the decoration of her sleeves! Surely she would accept them from him, a grave gentleman upon whom she looked with filial respect. Detestable respect! That confounded gravity of his that hampered him like a crushing burden! But the scion of the Febrers, the descendant of opulent merchants and heroic navigators, was forced to resist, thinking of the money stowed away in his girdle. Probably he did not possess enough to make the purchase.

In another store he acquired a knife for Pepet, the largest and heaviest he could find, an absurd weapon, capable of making him forget the relic of his glorious grandfather.

At noon, Febrer, bored by objectless strolling through the ward of the Marina, and along the steep, narrow streets of the ancient Royal Fortress, entered a small inn, the only one in the city, situated near the port. There he met the customary patrons. In the vestibule a few youths dressed in peasant style, with military caps, soldiers of the garrison who served as orderlies; within the dining-room, subaltern officers of a batallion of light infantry, young lieutenants who were smoking with a bored mien and gazing through the windows at the immense blue expanse like prisoners of the sea. During the meal they lamented their bad luck at having their youth wasted by being chained to this rock. They spoke of Majorca as a place of joy; they recalled the provinces on the mainland, of which many of them were sons, as paradises to which they were eager to return. Women! It was a longing, a desire which made their voices quaver and brought a glow of madness into their eyes. The chaste Ivizan virtue, the exclusive islander, suspicious of foreigners, weighed upon them like the chain of an insufferable prison. There was no trifling with love here; no time was wasted; either hostile indifference or honest courting with a view to speedy marriage. Words and smiles led straight to matrimony; association with young girls was only possible for the purpose of the formation of a new household; and these lusty youths, gay, abounding in vitality, suffered a tantalizing torment discussing the most beautiful girls of the island, admiring them, yet living apart from them, in spite of moving in narrow limits which forced them to continual meetings. Their dearest hope was to get leave of absence, so that they might live a few days in Majorca or on the Peninsula, far from the cold-hearted and virtuous isle, which accepted the foreigner only as a husband.

Women! Those young bloods talked of nothing else, and seated at the long table, Febrer silently seconded their words and lamentations. Women! The irresistible tendency which binds us to them is the only thing that remains after the moral upheavals which change one's life; the only thing which remains standing among the ghosts of other illusions destroyed by the cataclysm. Febrer felt the same disgust as did the soldiers, the impression of being locked up in a prison of privations, surrounded by the sea as if it were a moat. Just now the island capital impressed him as a town of irresistible monotony, with its señoritas guarded in suspicious and monastic isolation. His mind reverted to the country as to a place of liberty, with its simple souled and natural women, restrained only by a defensive instinct like that of primitive females.

He left the city that same afternoon. Nothing remained of the optimism of a few hours before. The streets of the Marina were nauseating; an infectious odor escaped from the houses; in the arroyo buzzed swarms of insects, rising from the pools at the sound of the footsteps of a passerby. The recollection of the hills near his tower, perfumed by sylvan plants and by the salty odor of the sea, seemed to smile in his memory with idyllic sweetness.

A peasant's cart took him to the vicinity of San José, and after leaving it he started for the mountain, passing between the pine trees bent and twisted by the storms. The sky was overcast, the atmosphere warm and heavy. From time to time big drops fell, but before the clouds could settle into rain a gust of wind seemed to sweep them toward the horizon.

Near a charcoal burner's cabin Jaime saw two women walking rapidly among the pines. They were Margalida and her mother, coming from Cubells, a hermitage situated upon a hill on the coast, near a spring, which gave a vivid green to the abrupt cliffs, and nurtured oranges and palms in the shelter of the rocks.

Jaime overtook the two women, and next he saw Pepet spring out of the bushes where he had been walking outside the path, stone in hand, pursuing a bird whose cries had attracted his attention. They continued the journey to Can Mallorquí together, and, without realizing how it happened Febrer found himself in advance, walking by Margalida's side, while Pèp's wife trudged along behind with slow step, leaning on her son's arm.

The mother was ill; an obscure illness, which caused the doctor on his rare visits, to shrug his shoulders, and which excited the ambition of the island healers. They had been to make a promise to the Virgin of Cubells, and had left on her altar two fluted candles purchased in the city.

While Margalida talked in a sad voice of the old woman's aches and pains, the egoism of vigorous youth spurred her on with nervous haste until her cheeks became suffused with color, and her eyes betrayed a certain impatience. This was courting day. They must reach Can Mallorquí in time to prepare an early supper for the family before the suitors should arrive.

Febrer was admiring her with his serious eyes. He marveled now at the stupidity which had caused him to think of Margalida for all these months as a child, as an undeveloped creature, without realizing her graces. He remembered with scorn those señoritas of the city for whom the soldiers in the fonda sighed. Again he thought of the courting of Margalida with an annoyance resembling jealousy. Must this girl fall a prey to one of those dusky-faced barbarians who would subject her to slavery of the soil like a beast?

"Margalida!" he murmured, as if about to say something important. "Margalida!"

But he spoke no more. The old-time rake felt his instincts of libertinism aroused by the perfume exhaled by this woman, an indefinable perfume of flesh fresh and virginal, which he thought he inhaled, like a connoisseur, more with the imagination than through sense of smell. At the same time—a strange thing for him!—he experienced a timidity which deprived him of speech; a timidity like that he had felt in his early youth when, far from the easy conquests on his estate in Majorca, he ventured to address himself to worldly-wise women on the Continent. Was it not an unworthy act for him to speak of love to this girl whom he had considered a child and who respected him as if he were her father?

"Margalida! Margalida!"

After these exclamations, which aroused the girl's curiosity, making her raise her eyes to fix them questioningly on his, he at last began to speak, asking her about the progress of the courting. Had she decided on anyone? Who was to be the lucky man? The Ironworker? the Minstrel?

She lowered her eyes again, in her confusion picking up a corner of her apron and raising it to her bosom. She did not know. She hesitated and lisped like a child in her bashfulness. She did not wish to marry— neither the Minstrel or the Ironworker, nor anybody. She had acquiesced in the courting because all girls did the same when they reached a certain age. Besides (here she flushed vividly), it gave her a kind of satisfaction to humiliate her friends, who were raging with envy on seeing the great number of her suitors. She was grateful to the youths who came from great distances to see her, but as for loving one of them—or marrying——

She had slackened her pace as she spoke. Pèp's wife and his son passed on unconsciously, and as the two were left alone in the path, they at last stopped, without realizing what they were doing.

"Margalida! Almond Blossom!"

To the devil with shyness! Febrer felt arrogant and masterful as in his better days. Why this fear? A peasant girl! A child!

He spoke with a firm accent, trying to fascinate her with the impassioned fixedness of her eyes, drawing near her, as if to caress her with the music of his words. And how about him? What did Margalida think of him? What if he should present himself to Pèp some day, telling him that he wished to marry his daughter?

"You!" exclaimed the girl. "You, Don Jaime!"

She raised her eyes fearlessly, laughing at the absurdity—the señor was accustomed to fooling her with his jests. Her father said that the Febrers were all as serious as judges, but ever in a good humor. He was jesting at her expense again, as he had done when he had told about his clay sweetheart up there in his tower who had been waiting for him a thousand years.

But when her glance met Febrer's, seeing his pale face, tense with emotion, she turned white also. He seemed a different man; she saw a Don Jaime she had never known before. Instinctively, impelled by fear, she took a step backward. She remained on the defensive, leaning against the slender trunk of a small tree, which grew beside the path, its tiny sickly colored leaves almost loosened by the autumn wind.

She could still smile—a forced smile, pretending to believe it one of the señor's jokes.

"No," replied Febrer with energy, "I am speaking seriously. Tell me, Margalida, Almond Blossom, what if I should become one of your lovers; and if I should come to the courting, what would you answer me?"

She shrunk back against the yielding tree trunk, making herself smaller, as if she would escape those ardent eyes. Her instinctive backward step shook the flexible tree and a shower of yellow leaves, like flakes of amber, fell roundabout her, clinging to her hair. Pale, her lips compressed and blue, she murmured words scarcely more audible than a gentle sigh. Her eyes, enlarged and deep, bore the agonized expression of the humble of spirit who think many things, but who find no words to express them. He, the heir of the Febrers, a gran señor, to marry a peasant girl? Was he crazy?

"No; I am not a great señor; I am an unfortunate creature. You are richer than I, who am living off your charity. Your father wishes your husband to be a man who shall cultivate his lands. Will you marry me, Margalida? Do you love me, Almond Blossom?"

With bowed head, avoiding a glance that seemed to burn her, she continued speaking without listening to him. Madness! It could not be true! The señor to say such things! He must be dreaming!

Suddenly she felt on one of her hands a light, caressing touch. She looked at him again. She saw an unfamiliar face that thrilled her. She experienced a sensation of grave danger—the nervous start which gives a warning. Her knees shook, they contracted as if she were about to faint with fear.

"Do you think me too old?" he murmured in a supplicating voice. "Can you never come to love me?"

The voice was sweet and caressing, but those eyes seemed to devour her! That pale face, like that of men who kill! She longed to speak, to protest at his last words. She had never thought of Don Jaime's age; he was something superior, like the saints, who grow in beauty with the years. But fear held her silent. She freed herself from the caressing hand, she felt moved by the prodigious rebound of her nerves, as if her life were in danger, and she fled from Febrer as if he were an assassin.

"Heaven help me!"

Murmuring this supplication she sprang away, and began to run with the agility of the country girl, disappearing round a turn in the path.

Jaime did not follow her. He stood motionless in the solitude of the pine forest, erect in the pathway, unconscious of his surroundings, like the hero of a legend subjected to an enchantment. Then he passed a hand over his face, as if awakening from a dream, collecting his thoughts. His audacious words stung him with remorse, Margalida's alarm, the terrified flight which had terminated the interview. How stupid of him! It was the result of his going to the city; the return to civilized life which, had upset his bachelor calm, arousing passions of long ago; the conversation of the young soldiers, who lived with their thoughts ever fixed on women. But no; he did not repent what he had done. It was important for Margalida to know what he had so often vaguely thought in the isolation of his tower.

He continued slowly along his way to avoid meeting the family from Can Mallorquí. Margalida had joined her mother and brother. He saw them from a rise of ground, when they were journeying through the valley in the direction of the farmhouse.

Febrer changed his route, avoiding Can Mallorquí. He directed his steps toward the Pirate's Tower, but when he gained it he passed on, not stopping until he reached the sea.

The rock-bound coast, which seemed to overhang the waters, was broken by their incessant lashing for century upon century. The waves, like furious blue bulls, charged, frothing with anger, against the rock, wearing deep caverns, which were prolonged upward in the form of vertical cracks. This age-long battle was destroying the coast, shattering its stony armor, scale by scale. Colossal wall-like fragments loosened. They first separated by forming an imperceptible crevice which grew and grew with the passing of centuries. The natural wall leaned for years and years above the waves, which beat furiously at its base, until it would lose its balance some stormy night and topple like the rampart of a besieged citadel, crumbling into blocks, peopling the sea with new reefs soon to be covered with slimy vegetation, while the winding passages would seethe with foam and sparkle with the metallic gleam of fish.

Febrer seated himself on the edge of a great projecting rock, a ledge loosened from the coast that inclined boldly over the reefs. His fatalism impelled him to sit there. Would that the inevitable catastrophe might take place at that moment, and that his body, dragged down by the collapsing rock, might disappear in the bottom of the sea, having for its sarcophagus this mass, equal to the pyramid of a Pharaoh! What had he to look forward to in life?

Before sinking out of sight the setting sun peeped through an opening of stormy sky lying between riven clouds. It was a gory sphere, a wafer of purple which lightened the immensity of the sea with a fiery glare. The dark masses closing in the horizon were fringed with scarlet. A restless triangle of flames spread over the dark green waters. The foam turned red and the coast looked for an instant like molten lava.

In the glow of this stormy light Jaime contemplated the fluctuation of the waters at his feet, hurling their boisterous swirls into the hollows of the rock, roaring and writhing, frothing with anger in the winding passages between the reefs. In the depths of this greenish mass, illuminated by the setting sun with transparencies of opal, he saw strange vegetation growing on the rocks, diminutive forests among whose clinging fronds moved animals of fantastic form, nervous and swift or torpid and sedentary, with hard carapaces, gray and pinkish, bristling with defenses, armed with tentacles, with lances and with horns, making war among themselves and persecuting the weaker creatures which passed like white exhalations, flashing like crystal in the rapidity of their flight.

Febrer felt belittled by the solitude. Faith in his human importance destroyed, he considered himself no bigger than one of those tiny creatures swarming about in the vegetation of the submarine abyss—perhaps even smaller. Those animals were armed for life, they could sustain themselves by their own strength, never knowing the discouragement, the humiliations and the sorrows which afflicted him. The grandeur of the sea, unconscious of man, cruel and implacable in its anger, overwhelmed Febrer, arousing in his memory an endless chain of ideas which were perhaps new, but which he accepted as vague reminiscences of a former existence, as something which he had thought before, he knew not where nor when.

A thrill of respect, of instinctive devotion, swept over him, making him forget the event of a short time before, submerging him in religious contemplation. The sea! He thought, he knew not why, of the most remote ancestors of humanity, of primitive man, miserable, scarcely emerged from original animalism, tormented and repelled on every side by a nature hostile in its exhuberance, as a young and vigorous body conquers or throws off the parasites which endeavor to live at the cost of its organism. On the shore of the sea, in the presence of the divine mystery, green and immense, man should experience his most restful moments. The earliest gods sprung from the bosom of the waters; contemplating the fluctuation of the waves, and soothed by their murmur, man should feel that within him is born something new and powerful—a soul. The sea! The mysterious organisms which people it also live, as do those of the land, subjected to the tyranny of fear, immovable in their primitive existence, repeating themselves throughout the centuries as if ever the same entity. There also do the dead command! The strong pursue the weak, and are in their turn devoured by others more powerful, as in the times of their remote progenitors, when the waters were yet warm from the formation of the globe—ever the same, repeating themselves throughout hundreds of millions of years. A monster of prehistoric ages who might return to swim in these waters would find on all sides, in the dark chasms, and along the coasts, the same life and the identical struggles as in his youth. The animal of combat with his green carapace, armed with curving claws and with forceps for torture, implacable warrior of the dark submarine caverns, has never united with the graceful fish, swift and weak, which trails its rose and silver tunic through the transparent waters. His destiny is to devour, to be strong, and, if he should find himself disarmed, his defenses broken, to give himself up to misfortune without protest and to perish. Death is preferable to abdicating one's primal rights, the noble fatality of birth. For the strong of the land or of the sea there is no satisfaction nor life outside one's own sphere; they are slaves of their own greatness; birth brings them misfortunes as well as honors, and it will ever be the same! The dead are the only ones who rule the living. The first beings who initiated a plan for living wrought with their acts the cage in which succeeding generations must be imprisoned.

The tranquil mollusks which he now saw in the depths of the waters, clinging to the rocks like dark buttons, seemed to him divine beings who guard the mystery of creation in their stupid quiet. He imagined them great and imposing like those monsters worshipped by savages for their impassivity, and in whose rigidity they believe they divine the majesty of the gods. Febrer recalled his jests of other times, on nights of feasting, seated before a plate of fresh oysters, in the fashionable Parisian restaurants. His elegant companions thought him mad as they listened to the nonsensical ideas aroused by wine, the sight of the shell fish and the recollection of certain fragmentary reading in his youth. "We're going to eat our grandfathers like the merry cannibals that we are." The oyster is one of the primitive manifestations of life on the planet—one of the earlier forms of organic matter, still resting, uncertain and aimless in its evolution in the immensity of the waters. The sympathetic and slandered monkey only has the importance of a first cousin who has failed to make a career for himself, of an unfortunate and absurd relative whom one leaves outside the door, feigning ignorance of his family name, denying him a welcome. The mollusk is the venerable grandfather, the chief of the house, the creator of the dynasty, the ancestor crowned with a nobility of millions of centuries. These thoughts came back to Febrer's mind now with the vividness of indisputable truths.

Humanity is faithful to its sources. Nobody denies the traditions of those venerable ancestors who seemed to be asleep in the immense catacomb of the sea. Man thinks himself free because he can move from one side of the planet to the other; because his organism is mounted upon two agile and articulate columns which permit of his springing over the ground by the mechanism of walking—but, it is an error! One more of many illusions which deceptively gladden our lives, making us bearers of its misery and its triviality! Febrer was convinced that we are all born shut in between two valves of prejudices, of scruple, and of pride, an inheritance from those who proceeded us, and although man stirs about, he never manages to tear himself from the same rock to which his predecessors clung and vegetated. Activity, incidents of life, independence of character, all are illusions, the vanity of the mollusk which dreams while adhering to the rock, and imagines he is swimming through all the seas on the globe, while his valves continue fastened to the stone!

All creatures are as those who have gone before, and as those yet to come. They change in shape, but the soul remains stationary and immutable like that of those rudimentary beings, eternal witnesses of the first palpitation of life on the planet, which seemed to be sleeping the heaviest of sleeps; and thus will it ever be. Vain are great efforts to free oneself from this fatal environment, from the heritage of fear, from the circle in which we are forced to move, until at last comes death. Then other animals like ourselves appear, and begin whirling around the same circle, imagining themselves free because ever before their footsteps they have new space in which to run.

"The dead command!" Jaime once more declared to himself. It seemed impossible that men do not realize this great truth; that they dwell in eternal night, believing that they make new things in the glow of illusions which rise daily, as rises the great deception of the sun to accompany us through the infinite, which is dark, but which seems to us blue and radiant with light.

When Febrer thought this, the sun had already set. The sea was almost black, the sky a leaden gray, and in the fog on the horizon the lightning quivered and flashed. Jaime felt on his face and on his hands the moist kiss of drops of rain. A storm was about to break which perhaps would last throughout the night. The lightning flashes were coming nearer, a distant crashing was heard, as if two hostile fleets were cannonading beyond the curtain of fog on the horizon, and approaching each other behind its screen. The sheet of quiet water, glossy as crystal between reefs and coast, began to tremble with the widening undulations of the raindrops.

In spite of this he did not stir. He remained seated on the rock, experiencing a fierce anger against fate, rebelling with all the strength of his nature at the tyranny of the past. Why should the dead command? Why should they darken the atmosphere with the dust of their souls, like powdered bone lodging in the brains of the living, imposing the old ideas?

Suddenly Febrer experienced an overwhelming impression, as if he beheld an extraordinary light, never before seen. His brain seemed to dilate, to expand like a mass of water bursting an encompassing vessel of stone. At that instant a lightning flash colored the sea with livid light, and a thunder clap burst above his head, its echoes rattling with awesome reverberation over the expanse of the sea, in the caverns, and over the hilltops along the shore.

No, the dead do not command! The dead do not rule! As if he were a different man, Jaime ridiculed his recent thoughts. Those rudimentary animals which he had seen among the rocks, and with them all creatures of the sea and of the earth, suffer the slavery of fear. The dead rule them because they do the same things which their ancestors did, the same things their descendants will do. But man is not the slave of fear; he is its collaborator and sometimes its master. Man is a progressive and reasoning being, and can change his condition to suit his desires. Man was a slave to his surroundings in former times, in remote ages, but when he conquered nature and exploited her, he burst the fatal bondage in which other created things still remain prisoners. What matters to him the fear in which he has been born? He can make himself over anew if he will.

Jaime could not continue his reflections. Rain was streaming over the brim of his hat, running down his back. Night had suddenly come. By the glare of the lightning he saw the glazed surface of the sea trembling with the beating of the rain.

Febrer made all haste toward his tower, but he was happy, eager to run, with the overflowing joy of one emerging from long imprisonment and who has not before him space enough for his repressed activity.

"I will do what I please!" he shouted, rejoicing at the sound of his own voice, which was lost in the clamor of the storm. "Neither dead nor living shall rule me! What do I care for my noble forefathers, for my moth-eaten prejudices, for all the Febrers?"

Suddenly he was enveloped in a carmine light, and a cannon-shot burst above his head, as if the coast had been rent asunder by the shock of an immense catastrophe.

"That must have struck near here," said Jaime, referring to the electric flash.

His mind occupied with the Febrers, he thought of his ancestor the knight commander Don Priamo. The explosion of thunder recalled to his mind the combats of the diabolical hero, the religious cavalier of the Cross, a mocker of God and of the devil who always followed his sovereign will, fighting on the side of his kindred, or living among the enemies of the Faith, according to his caprices or his affections.

No! Febrer did not repudiate him. He adored the valorous knight commander; he was his true forbear, the best of them all, the rebel, the demon of the family!

Jaime entered the tower and struck a light; he flung around his shoulders the Arabian haik of coarse weave that served him for his nocturnal excursions, and taking a book he tried to distract himself until Pepet should bring his supper.

The storm seemed to be centered on the island. The rain fell on the fields, converting them, into marshes; it rushed down the declivities of the roadways, overflowing like rivers; it soaked the mountains like great sponges through the porous soil of the pine forest and thickets. The flare of the lightning gave hasty glimpses, like visions in a dream, of the blackish sea, the fretting foam, and flooded fields, which seemed filled with fiery fish, the trees glistening beneath their watery mantles.

In the kitchen of Can Mallorquí Margalida's suitors stood in a group, in damp, steaming clothing and muddy sandals. Tonight the courting lasted longer. Pèp, with a paternal air, had allowed the youths to remain after the time for the wooing had passed; he felt sorry for the poor boys who must walk home through the rain. He had been a suitor himself once upon a time. They might wait; perhaps the storm would soon pass; and if it did not they should stay and sleep wherever they could, in the kitchen, on the porch. "One wouldn't turn out a dog on such a night."

The youths, rejoicing in the event, which added more time to their courting, gazed at Margalida arrayed in her gala dress, seated in the center of the room, a vacant chair beside her. Each one had taken his turn at sitting upon it during the course of the evening, and now all looked at it eagerly, but lacked courage to occupy it again.

The Ironworker, wishing to outshine the others, was twanging a guitar, singing in low tones, accompanied by the rolling of the thunder. The Minstrel, sitting in a corner, was meditating new verses. Some boys hailed with mocking words the lightning flashes, which filtered through the cracks of the door, and the Little Chaplain smiled, sitting on the floor, his chin in his hands.

Pèp was dozing in a low chair, overcome by weariness, and his wife screamed with terror whenever a loud thunder clap shook the house, interjecting between her groans fragments of prayers, murmured in Castilian for greater efficacy: "*Santa Barbara bendita, que en el cielo estas escrita——*" Margalida, heedless of the glances of her suitors, seemed half dead with fright.

Suddenly there came two taps upon the door. The dog, who had scrambled to his feet scenting the presence of someone on the porch, stretched his neck, but instead of barking he wagged his tail in welcome.

Margalida and her mother glanced fearfully toward the door. Who could it be, at that time, on that night, in the solitude of Can Mallorquí? Had anything happened to the señor?

Aroused by the knocking, Pèp sat up straight in his chair. "Come in, whoever you are!" He gave the invitation with the dignity of a Roman paterfamilias, absolute master of his house. The door was not locked.

It opened, giving passage to a gust of rain-laden wind, which made the candle flicker, and refreshed the dense atmosphere of the kitchen. The dark rectangle of the doorway was lighted by the splendor of a lightning flash, and all saw in it, against the livid sky, a kind of penitent, with half-concealed face, a hooded figure, dripping rain.

He entered with firm tread, with no word of greeting, followed by the dog sniffing at his legs with affectionate growls. He strode directly toward the vacant chair beside Margalida, the place reserved for the suitors.

As he took his seat he flung back his hood and fixed his eyes on the girl.

"Ah!" she gasped, turning pale, her eyes widening in surprise.

So great was her emotion, so violent, her impulse to draw away from him, that she nearly fell to the floor.

PART THIRD

CHAPTER I
THE INTRUDER

Two days later, when Don Jaime was awaiting his dinner in the tower, having returned from a fishing excursion, Pèp presented himself and deposited the basket upon the table with an air of solemnity.

The rustic tried to make excuse for this extraordinary visit. His wife and Margalida had gone to the hermitage of the Cubells again, and the boy had accompanied them.

Febrer began to eat with a lusty appetite after having been on the sea since daybreak, but the serious air of the peasant at last claimed his attention.

"Pèp, you want to say something to me, but you are afraid," said Jaime, in the Ivizan dialect.

"That is true, señor."

Like all timid persons who doubt and vacillate before speaking, but rush into it impetuously when fear is overcome, Pèp bluntly unburdened his mind.

Yes, he had something to say; something very important! He had been thinking the matter over for two whole days, and he could keep silent no longer. He had taken it upon himself to bring the señor's dinner merely for the sake of speaking. Why did Don Jaime make fun of those who were so fond of him? What did he mean?

"Make fun of you!" exclaimed Febrer.

"Yes, make fun of us!" Pèp declared sadly. "How about what happened that stormy night? What caprice impelled the señor to present himself at the courting, taking the chair beside Margalida, as if he were a suitor? Ah, Don Jaime! The 'festeigs' are solemn occasions; men kill one another on account of them. I knew that fine gentlemen laugh at all this, and consider the peasants of the island about the same as savages; but the poor should be left to their customs, and they should not be disturbed in their few pleasures."

Now it was Febrer who assumed a serious countenance.

"But I am not making fun of you, my dear Pèp! It's all true! Listen! I am one of Margalida's suitors, like the Minstrel, like the detested Ironworker, like all other boys who gather in your kitchen to court her. I came the other night because I could bear no more, because I suddenly realized the cause of all that I have been suffering, because I love Margalida, and I will marry her if she will accept me."

His sincere and impassioned accent banished all doubt from the peasant's mind.

"Then it is really true!" he exclaimed. "The girl had told me something of this, weeping, when I asked her the motive of the señor's visit. I could not believe her at first. Girls are so pretentious! They imagine that every man is running mad after them; so it is really true!"

This knowledge caused him to smile, as at something unexpected and amusing.

"What a strange man you are, Don Jaime! It is very kind of you to make demonstrations of esteem for the household of Can Mallorquí; but it is not good for the girl, for she was giving herself airs, imagining herself worthy of a prince, and will not accept any of the peasants.

"It cannot be, señor. Don't you understand that it cannot be? I was young myself once, and I know what it is; how one takes a notion to chase after any girl who is not ugly; but later on one reflects, he thinks about what is good and what is not good, what is proper, and in the end he does not commit a foolish deed. Have you thought it over, really, señor? That was a joke the other night, a caprice — —"

Febrer shook his head energetically. No, neither a joke nor a caprice. He loved Margalida, the graceful Almond Blossom; he was convinced of his passion, and he would follow wherever she might lead. He intended in future to do as he pleased, laying aside scruples and prejudices. He had been a slave to them long enough. No; he would have no regret. He loved Margalida, he was one of her suitors, with the same right as any island youth. He meant every word he said.

Pèp, scandalized at these words, wounded in his most conventional and ancient ideas, raised his hands, while his simple soul showed in his eyes full of fear and surprise.

"Oh, Lord! Oh, Lord!"

He was compelled to call upon the ruler of heaven to give expression to his perturbation and astonishment. A Febrer wishing to marry a peasant of Can Mallorquí! The world was no longer the same; it seemed as if all the laws of the universe were turned upside down, as if the sea were about to cover the island, and that in future the almond trees would put forth their flowers above the waves; but had Don Jaime realized what this desire of his signified?

All the respect engendered in the soul of the peasant during long years of servitude to the noble family, the religious veneration his parents had infounded in him when, in his childhood, he saw the gentlemen from Majorca arrive at the island, was now revived, protesting at this absurdity, as something contrary to human custom and to the divine will. Don Jaime's father had been a powerful personage, one of those who made laws over there in Madrid; he had even lived in the royal palace. He still saw him in his memory, just as he had imagined him in the credulous illusions of boyhood, bending men to his will; able to send some to the gallows and pardoning others according to his caprice; seated at the table of monarchs and playing cards with them, just as Pèp himself might do with a crony in the tavern at San José; addressing one another by the familiar "thou"; and when he was not in the court city, he was an absolute seignior in vessels of iron— the kind that spit smoke and cannon balls. How about Jaime's grandfather, Don Horacio? Pèp had seen him but few times, and yet he still trembled with respect as he recalled his regal appearance, his grave, unsmiling face, and the imposing gesture which accompanied his benevolent acts. He was a king after the ancient style, one of those kings who are good and just fathers of the poor, offering bread with one hand and holding a rod in the other.

"And do you wish to have Pèp, the poor peasant of Can Mallorquí, become a relative of your father and of your grandfather and of all those great lords who were masters in Majorca and rulers of the world? Come, Don Jaime, I can't help thinking it all a joke; your seriousness does not deceive me. Don Horacio also used to say the funniest things without losing his judge's face."

Jaime swept his eyes around the interior of the tower, smiling at his poverty.

"But I am poor, Pèp! You are rich, compared to me. Why think of my family, when I am living on your generosity? If you were to cast me out I would not know where to go."

The gesture of incredulity with which Pèp always received such humble declarations, was renewed.

Poor? But was not this tower his? Febrer replied with a smile. Bah! Four old stones that were falling apart; an unproductive hill, which would be worth something only if the peasant should cultivate it. But the latter insisted; there was the property in Majorca, which, even though it were somewhat encumbered, was much—much!

And he extended his arms with a gesture indicating immensity, as if no one could measure the fortune of Jaime, adding convincingly:

"A Febrer is never poor. You can never be that. Better days will come."

Jaime ceased trying to make him realize his poverty. If he thought him rich so much the better. Thus those youths, who knew no broader horizon than that of the island, could not say that he was a ruined man seeking to marry into Pèp's family in order to recover the lands of Can Mallorquí.

Why should the peasant be so surprised at his desire to marry Margalida? In the end it was nothing more than the repetition of an eternal history, that of the disguised and vagabond king falling in love with the shepherdess and giving her his hand. He was no king, neither was he in disguise, but in a situation of absolute need.

"I have heard that story," said Pèp. "It was often told me when I was a child, and I have told it to my own children. I won't say that it never happened so, but that was in other times—other times, very long ago, when animals had speech."

According to Pèp, the most remote antiquity, and also the elysian state of man, was always that joyous time "when the animals had speech."

But now—now he, although he could not read, informed himself of the doings in the world when he went to San José on Sundays and talked with the secretary of the pueblo, and other lettered persons who read the newspapers. Now-a-days kings married queens, and shepherdesses married shepherds; everyone with his kind. The good old times were over.

"But do you know whether or not Margalida loves me? Are you sure that all this seems to her a wild dream as it does to you?"

Pèp maintained a long silence, one hand beneath his hat and the silk kerchief, which he wore in womanish manner, scratching his crisp gray curls. He smiled knavishly, with an expression of scorn, as if rejoicing over the inferiority in which dwells the woman of the fields.

"Women! How can one tell what they think, Don Jaime! Margalida is like all the rest of them, fond of vanities and strange things. At her age they all dream that some count or marquis is coming to take them, away in his golden chariot, and that all her friends will die of envy. I, too, when I was a boy, used often to think that the richest girl in Iviza would come to seek my hand in marriage, some girl, I did not know who, but beautiful as the Virgin and with fields as big as half the island—dreams of youth."

Then ceasing to smile, he added:

"Yes, maybe she does care for you without realizing it. Youth and love are so strange. She cries when anything is said to her about the other night; she declares it was madness, but she won't say a word against you. Ah, would that I could see into her heart!"

Febrer received these words with a smile of joy, but the peasant quickly dispelled it, adding energetically:

"It cannot be, and it must not be! Let her think as she pleases, but I am opposed because I am her father and I desire her welfare. Ah, Don Jaime, everyone with his kind! All this reminds me of a priest who used to lead a hermit's life at Cubells, a wise man, and like many wise men, half crazy; he was trying to raise a brood from, a rooster and a seagull; a gull the size of a goose."

With the interest which the rustic displays for the breeding of animals, he described the eagerness of the peasants when they went to Cubells, gathering curiously around the great cage, where the rooster and the gull were kept beneath the vigilance of the friar.

"The good man's work lasted for years—but—not a chick! Man's efforts avail nothing against the impossible. They were of different blood and of different breed; they lived together tranquilly, but they were not of the same sort, nor could they become so. Everyone with his kind!"

As he said this, Pèp gathered the plates and the remnants of the dinner from the table and put them into the basket, preparing to take his leave.

"We are agreed, Don Jaime," he said with his rustic tenacity, "that it was all a joke, and that you will not bother the girl any more with your notions."

"No, Pèp, we are agreed that I love Margalida, and that I am going to her courting with the same right as any of the island boys. The old customs must be respected."

He smiled at the peasant's ill-humored expression. Pèp shook his head in sign of protest. No; he repeated, that would be impossible. The girls of the district would laugh at Margalida, rejoicing over this strange suitor who broke the order of customs; the malicious would perhaps lie about Can Mallorquí, which had as honorable a past as the best family on the island; even his own friends, when he should go to mass at San José, and all gathered in the cloister of the church, would imagine him an ambitious man who desired to convert his daughter into a fine señorita. And this was not all. There was the anger of the rivals to be reckoned with, the jealousy of those youths, dumb with surprise when he came in that stormy night and sat down beside Margalida. Certainly by this time they had recovered from their astonishment and were talking about him, and would all join to oppose the stranger. The men of the island were as they were. They took life among themselves without disturbing the man from the outside world because they considered him foreign to their circle, and indifferent to their passions; but if the stranger meddled in their affairs, and especially if he were a Majorcan, what would happen? When had people of other lands ever disputed a sweetheart with an Ivizan?

"Don Jaime, for the sake of your father, for the sake of your noble grandfather! It is Pèp who begs you, Pèp who has known you ever since you were a boy. The farmhouse is at your service; everyone who lives in it is eager to serve you—but do not persist in this caprice! It will bring some dire misfortune upon us all!"

Febrer, who had at first listened with deference, straightened his figure when he heard Pèp's predictions. His rude nature rebelled, as if the peasant's fears were an insult. He afraid! He felt equal to fighting all the young men of the island. Not a man in Iviza could force him to change his mind. To the belligerent passion of the lover was joined the pride of race, that ancestral hatred which separated the inhabitants of the two islands. He would go to the courting; he had good companions to defend him in case of need; and he glanced at the gun hanging on the wall; then his eyes descended to his belt where his revolver was hidden.

Pèp bowed his head in despair. He had been just like this when he was young. For women the wildest deeds are done. It was useless to make further effort to convince the señor, who was determined and proud like all his kindred.

"Do as you please, Don Jaime; but remember what I tell you. A great misfortune awaits us—a great misfortune!"

The peasant left the tower, and Jaime watched him walking down toward the farmhouse, the points of his kerchief and the womanish mantle he wore over his shoulders fluttering in the breeze.

Pèp disappeared behind the fence of Can Mallorquí. Febrer was about to step away from the door when he saw rise from among the groups of tamarisks on the hillside a boy, who, after glancing cautiously about to convince himself that he was not observed, ran toward him. It was the Little Chaplain. He sprang up the stairway to the tower, and when he stood before Febrer he burst out laughing, displaying his ivory teeth, surrounded by a dark rose color.

Ever since that night when Febrer had presented himself at the farmhouse the Little Chaplain had treated him with greater confidence, as if he already considered him one of the family. He did not protest at the strangeness of the event. It seemed to him quite natural that Margalida should like the señor and that he should wish to marry her.

"But didn't you go to Cubells?" asked Febrer.

The boy began to laugh again. He had left his mother and sister half way on the road and had hidden among the tamarisks waiting for his father to leave the tower. No doubt the old man wished to have a serious talk with Don Jaime, and so he had sent them all away, and had taken it upon himself to bring him his dinner. For two days he had talked of nothing but this interview. His timidity, and his respect for the master, had made him vacillate, but at last he had decided. He was in ill humor over Margalida's courting. Had the old man scolded very hard?

Evading these questions, Febrer asked the boy with a certain anxiety, "How is Almond Blossom? What did she say when you talked to her about me?"

The boy straightened himself petulantly, happy in being able to defend the señor. His sister had not said anything; sometimes she smiled when she heard Don Jaime's name mentioned, again her eyes moistened, and she almost always brought the conversation to a close, advising the Little Chaplain not to meddle in this affair and to please his father by going back to his studies in the Seminary.

"It will turn out all right, señor," continued the boy, possessed of a fresh sense of his own importance. "It will turn out all right, I tell you. I am sure that my sister loves you dearly—only she is rather afraid of you—she feels a kind of respect. Who would ever have thought that you would notice her! At home everybody seems to be crazy; father looks cross and goes around grumbling to himself; mother sighs and calls on the Virgin, and meantime people imagine that we are rejoicing. But it will all come out right, Don Jaime, I promise you.

"But be careful, señor, be on your guard," added the boy, thinking of his former friends, the youths who were courting Almond Blossom. It seemed that the boys had lost confidence in him, and were cautious of speaking in his presence; but they were certainly plotting something. A week ago they seemed to hate one another and each kept to himself, but now they had joined forces in hatred of the stranger. They said nothing; they were merely taciturn; but their silence was disquieting. The Minstrel was the only one who shouted and displayed anger like an infuriated lamb, straightened his wasted figure, and declaring, between cruel fits of coughing, his intention of killing the Majorcan.

"They have lost respect for you, Don Jaime," continued the boy. "When they saw you come in and sit down beside my sister they were astounded. Even I could hardly believe my eyes, although for some time I knew that you were not indifferent to Margalida; you asked too many questions about her. But now they have waked up, and they are planning something. They have good reason, too. Who ever heard of such a thing as a stranger coming to San José and getting a sweetheart away from a crowd of the boys, the very bravest on the island?"

Local pride spurred the Little Chaplain to adopt for a moment the opinions of the others, but soon his gratitude and affection for Febrer were revived.

"Never mind. You love her and that is sufficient. Why should my sister have to wear out her life digging in the ground when a señor like yourself pays attention to her? Besides," here the young rascal smiled mischievously, "this marriage suits me. You are not going to till the fields, you will take Margalida away with you, and the old man, having no one to leave Can Mallorquí to, will let me marry and become a farmer, and, adios to the priesthood! I tell you, Don Jaime, you'll win. Here am I, the Little Chaplain, to fight half the island in your defense."

He glanced about as if expecting to encounter the severe eyes and the mustaches of the Civil Guard, and then, after a moment's hesitation, like that of a great but modest man trying to conceal his importance, he drew from his belt a knife the brilliancy and glitter of which seemed to hypnotize him.

"See that?" he asked, admiring the smoothness of the virgin steel, and looking at Febrer.

It was the knife which Jaime had presented him the day before. Jaime had been in a good humor and he had made the Little Chaplain kneel. Then, with jesting gravity, he had struck him with the weapon, proclaiming him invincible knight of the district of San José, of the whole island, and of the channels and cliffs adjacent. The little rascal, tremulous with emotion at the gift, had taken the act with all gravity, thinking it an indispensable ceremony among gentlemen.

"See that?" he asked again, looking a Don Jaime as if protecting him with all the immensity of his valor.

He passed a finger lightly along the edge, pressing the fleshy tip against the point, delighting in the sharp prick. What a jewel!

Febrer nodded his head. Yes, he recognized the weapon; it was the one he had brought from Iviza.

"Well, with this," continued the boy, "not a brave will dare to face us. The Ironworker? He is a fraud! The Minstrel and all the rest? Frauds also. I'm only waiting for a chance to use this! Anybody who attempts anything against you is sentenced to death."

Finally, with the sadness of a great man who is wasting his time without an opportunity to display his valor, he said, lowering his eyes:

"When my grandfather was my age they say that he had already killed his man, and that half the island stood in fear of him."

The Little Chaplain spent part of the afternoon in the tower talking of Don Jaime's supposed enemies, whom he now considered as his own, putting up his knife and drawing it forth again, as if he enjoyed contemplating his disfigured image in the polished blade, dreaming of tremendous battles which always terminated by the flight or death of the adversaries, and by his valorously rescuing the embattled Don Jaime, who took as a jest his appetite for conflict and destruction.

In the evening Pepet went down to the farmhouse to get Don Jaime's supper. He had found the suitors who came from a distance sitting on the porch awaiting the beginning of the festeig. "See you later, Don Jaime!"

As soon as night closed in, Febrer made his preparations, his face set, his mien hostile, his hands thrilling with an imperceptible homicidal twitch, like a primitive warrior starting on an expedition from the mountain top to the valley. Before throwing his haik over his shoulders, he drew his revolver from his belt, scrupulously examining the cartridges, and the working of the trigger. Everything all right! The first man to make an attempt against him would get all six shots in the head. He felt like a savage, implacable, like one of those Febrers, lions of the sea, who landed on hostile shores, killing to avoid being killed.

With one hand in his belt fondling the butt of his revolver, he walked down the hill among the clusters of tamarisks, which waved their undulating masses in the darkness. He found the porch of Can Mallorquí full of young men standing about, or seated on the benches, waiting while the family finished supper in the kitchen. Febrer detected them in the dim light by the odor of hemp emanating from their new sandals, and from the coarse wool of their mantles and Arabian capes. The red sparks of cigarettes at the lower end of the porch indicated other waiting groups.

"Bòna nit!" called Febrer in greeting.

They responded only with a careless grunt. The low-toned conversations ceased, and a painful and hostile silence seemed to settle around each man.

Jaime leaned against a pillar of the porch, his head held high, his bearing arrogant, his figure standing erect against the horizon, and it seemed as if he could feel the hostile eyes fixed on him under cover of the darkness.

He felt a certain emotion, but it was not fear. He almost forgot the enemies who surrounded him. He was thinking uneasily of Margalida. He experienced the thrill of the enamored man when he divines the proximity of the beloved woman and is in doubt as to his fate, fearing and at the same time desiring her approach. Certain memories of the past returned, causing him to smile. What would Mary Gordon say if she could see him surrounded by this rustic crowd, tremulous and vacillating as he thought of the proximity of a peasant girl? How his women friends in Madrid and in Paris would laugh if they should come upon him engaged in this rustic project, ready to take life over the conquest of a woman almost on a level with their servants!

A door opened, outlining in its rectangle of ruddy light the silhouette of Pèp.

"Come in, men!" he said, like a patriarch who understands the desires of youth and laughs good-naturedly at them.

The young men entered one after the other, greeting Señor Pèp and his family, taking their seats on benches or chairs like schoolboys.

As the peasant of Can Mallorquí recognized the señor he started in surprise. Don Jaime there, waiting like the others, like an ordinary suitor, without venturing to enter this house, which was his own! Febrer replied with a shrug of the shoulders. He preferred to do as did the others. He imagined that thus it would be easier to accomplish his purpose. He did not wish to have his former condition recalled—he was a suitor, nothing more.

Pèp forced him to sit beside him, and tried to entertain him with conversation, but Febrer did not take his eyes off Almond Blossom, who, faithful to the ritual of such occasions, was seated in a chair in the center of the room, receiving the admiration of her suitors with the demeanor of a timid queen.

One after another took his place beside Margalida, who responded to their words in a low voice. She pretended not to see Don Jaime; she almost turned her back upon him. The suitors, awaiting their turns, were silent, not keeping up the merry chattering with which they had whiled away the time on other nights. Gloom seemed to weigh upon them, compelling them to silence, with lowered gaze and compressed lips, as if a dead man were lying in the adjoining room. It was the presence of the stranger, the intruder, foreign to their class and to their customs. Accursed Majorcan!

When all the youths had sat in the seat beside Margalida, the señor arose. He was the last one to present himself as a suitor, and, according to rule, it was his turn. Pèp, who had been talking to him ceaselessly to distract his attention, suddenly remained open-mouthed in surprise at seeing him move away.

He sat down beside Margalida, who seemed not to see him, her head bowed and her eyes lowered. The young men remained silent in order to catch the stranger's faintest words, but Pèp, realizing their plan, began to speak in a loud voice to his wife and son about some work to be done the next day.

"Margalida! Almond Blossom!"

Febrer's voice sounded like a caressing whisper in the girl's ear. He had come to convince her that what she had considered a caprice was love, true love. Febrer hardly knew how it had come about. He had felt ill at ease in his solitude, experiencing a vague desire for better things, which perhaps lay within his reach, but which he in his blindness could not recognize, until suddenly he had seen clearly where joy was to be found. That joy was herself. Margalida! Almond Blossom! He was not young, he was poor, but he loved her so much! Only a word, some sign to dissipate his uncertainty!

But the girl gently shook her head. "No; no. Go! I am afraid!" She raised her eyes and glanced uneasily at all the brown youths with their tragic mien, who seemed to scorch the pair with their blazing eyes.

Afraid! This word sufficed to arouse Febrer from his beseeching attitude and to cause him to stare defiantly at the rivals seated before him. Afraid? Of whom? He felt equal to fighting all those rustics and their innumerable relatives. Afraid! No, Margalida! She need not fear either for herself or for him. He begged her to answer his question. Could he hope? What did she intend to reply?

Margalida remained silent, her lips colorless, her cheeks a livid pallor, winking her eyes to conceal her tears. She was going to cry. Her efforts to restrain her tears were apparent; she sighed with anguish. Tears, suddenly bursting forth in this hostile atmosphere, might be a sign for battle; they would bring about the explosion of all that restrained anger which she divined around her. No, no! This effort of her will served only to enhance her misery, compelling her to bow her head like those sweet and gentle animals who think to save themselves from danger by hiding their heads.

Her mother who sat in a corner weaving baskets, grew alarmed. With feminine intuition she realized Margalida's suffering. Her husband, seeing the anxiety in her sad, resigned eyes, intervened opportunely.

"Half past nine!" There was a movement of surprise and protest from the youths. It was early yet; it lacked many minutes of the hour; the agreement should rule. But Pèp, with the stubbornness of the rustic, would not listen. Repeating the words, he arose and strode toward the door, opening it wide. "Half past nine!" Every man was master of his own house, and he did as he thought best in his. He had to get up early the next morning. "Bòna nit!"

He spoke courteously to each of the suitors as they filed out of the house. As Jaime passed, gloomy and crestfallen, Pèp grasped his arm. He must remain; Pèp would accompany him to the tower. He glanced uneasily at the Ironworker, who was behind him, the last to take his leave.

The señor did not reply, freeing his arm with a brusque movement. Accompany him! He was furious on account of Margalida's silence, which he considered crushing; on account of the hostile attitude of the young men; on account of the strange way in which the evening had been brought to a close.

The young suitors dispersed in the darkness, without shouts, or whistling, or songs, as if returning from a funeral. Something tragic seemed to be floating on the dark wings of night.

Febrer walked on until he arrived at the foot of the hill, where the tamarisk shrubs were thickest; then he turned, and stood motionless. His silhouette stood out against the whiteness of the path in the pale light of the stars. He held his revolver in his right hand, nervously clutching the breech, caressing the trigger with a feverish finger, eager to fire. Was no one following him? Did not the Ironworker or any of his other enemies lurk behind him?

Time passed, and no one appeared. The wild vegetation around him, enlarged by shadow and by mystery, seemed to laugh sarcastically at his anger. At last the fresh serenity of drowsy Nature seemed to penetrate his soul. He shrugged his shoulders scornfully, and holding his revolver before him walked on until he locked himself in his tower.

He spent the whole of the next day on the sea with Tío Ventolera. Returning to his dwelling he found the supper, which the Little Chaplain had brought him, cold on the table.

The following day the boy of Can Mallorquí appeared with a mysterious air. He had important things to tell Don Jaime. The afternoon before, when he had been hunting a certain bird in the pine forest near the Ironworker's forge, he had seen the man from a distance talking with the Minstrel beneath the porch of the blacksmith shop.

"And what else?" asked Febrer, wondering that the boy had no more to say.

Nothing else. Did that seem unimportant? The Minstrel was not fond of the mountains, for climbing made him cough. He always traveled through the valleys, sitting under the almond and fig trees to compose his verses. If he had gone up to the blacksmith shop it was undoubtedly because the Ironworker had sent for him. The two were talking with great animation. The Ironworker seemed to be giving advice, and the sick boy was listening with affirmative gestures.

"And what of that?" Febrer asked.

The Little Chaplain seemed to pity the señor's simplicity.

"Be careful, Don Jaime. You don't know the men of the island. This conversation at the forge means something. This is Saturday, courting night. I am sure they are plotting to do you harm if you come down to Can Mallorquí."

Febrer received these words with a gesture of scorn. He would be there, in spite of everything. Did they imagine they could frighten him? The only thing he regretted was that they delayed so long in attacking him.

He spent the rest of the day in a state of nervous anger, eager for night to come. He avoided approaching Can Mallorquí in his walks, gazing at it from a distance, in the hope of catching a glimpse of the slender figure of Margalida. Since he had become a suitor he could not present himself as a friend. A visit from him might prove embarrassing for Pèp's family, and also he feared that the girl might conceal herself on seeing him approach.

As soon as the sun had set and the stars appeared in the clear winter sky with the keenness of points of ice, Febrer descended from the tower.

During his brief walk to the farmhouse, recollections of the past returned again with ironic precision, as they had done on the former courting night.

"If Mary Gordon should see me!" he thought. "Perhaps she would compare me to a rustic Siegfried going forth to slay the dragon, which guards the treasure of Iviza. If certain cynical women I have known should see me!"

But his love immediately effaced these recollections. What if they should see him! Margalida was better than all the women he had ever known; she was the first, the only one. All his past life seemed to him false, artificial, like the life presented on the stage, painted and covered with tinsel beneath a deceptive light. He would never return to that world of fiction. The present was reality.

Arrived at the porch, he found all the suitors, who seemed to be talking in smothered voices. When they saw him they instantly became silent.

"Bòna nit!"

No one replied. They did not even receive him with the grunt of the other night.

When Pèp, opening the door, gave them entrance to the kitchen, Febrer saw that the Minstrel had a small drum hanging from one arm and was carrying the drum stick in his right hand.

It was to be an evening of music. Some of the youths smiled with a wicked expression when they took their places, as if rejoicing in advance over something extraordinary. Others, more serious, showed in their faces the noble disgust of those who fear to witness an inevitable evil deed. The Ironworker remained impassive in one of the farthest corners, shrinking down so as to remain unnoticed among his comrades.

A few of the youths had talked with Margalida, when suddenly, the Minstrel, seeing the chair unoccupied, approached and took his seat in it, holding the drum between his knee and his elbow, and resting his forehead in his left hand. He slowly beat the drum, while a prolonged hissing demanded silence. It was a new song; every Saturday the Minstrel came with fresh verses in honor of the daughter of the house. The charm of wild and barbarous music, admired since childhood, compelled all to listen. The sacred emotion of poesy made these simple souls thrill in advance.

The poor consumptive began to sing, accompanying each verse with a final clucking which shook his chest and reddened his cheeks. Tonight, however, the Minstrel seemed to have more strength than usual; his eyes had an extraordinary brilliancy.

An outburst of laughter greeted the first verses, hailing the sarcastic cleverness of the rural poet.

Febrer did not understand much of it. When he heard this monotonous and neighing music, which seemed to recall the primitive songs scattered over the Mediterranean by the Semitic sailors, he took refuge within his thoughts to pass away the time, and to be less bored by the extraordinary length of the ballad.

The loud laughter of the young men attracted his attention as something which he vaguely comprehended as directed against himself with hostile intent. What was that angry lamb saying? The singer's voice, his rustic pronunciation, and the continual clucking with which he ended the verses, were scarcely intelligible to Jaime, but he gradually began to realize that the ballad was directed at young women who desired to abandon the field, to marry caballeros, and who longed to wear the same ornaments as city ladies. The singer described feminine fashions in extravagant terms, which made the peasants laugh.

The simple Pèp also laughed at these jests, which flattered both his rural pride and his masculine vanity, which was inclined to see in the female nothing but a sharer of his burdens. "True! True!" And he joined his laughter to that of the boys. What an amusing fellow was that Minstrel!

After a few verses the improvisatore no longer sang of young women in general, but of a particular one, ambitious and heartless. Febrer glanced instinctively at Margalida, who remained motionless, with lowered eyes, her cheeks colorless, as if frightened, not at what she had already heard, but at what was undoubtedly yet to come.

Jaime began to stir uneasily in his chair. The idea of that rustic annoying her like that! A louder and more insolent outburst of laughter again attracted his attention to the verses. The singer was making fun of the girl, who, in order to become a lady, wished to marry a poor ruined man possessed of neither home nor family; a foreigner, who had no lands to cultivate.

The effect of this was instantaneous. Pèp, in the denseness of his dull brain, saw something like a spark of light, a luminous divination, and he extended his hands imperatively, while at the same instant he arose.

"Enough! Enough!"

But it was too late; a form interposed between himself and the candle light; it was Febrer, who had leaped forward.

He grasped the drum from the singer's knees and hurled it at his head with such force that the parchment gave way and the frame fitted itself down over the bleeding forehead like a shapeless cap.

The youths sprang impulsively from their seats, their hands reaching into their girdles. Margalida, screaming, took refuge at her mother's side, and the Little Chaplain felt that the time had come to draw his knife. His father, with the authority of his years, shouted:

"Outside! Outside!"

They all obeyed, and went out into the fields in front of the farmhouse. Febrer went also, in spite of the resistance of Pèp.

The young men seemed to be divided among themselves, and were carrying on a heated discussion. Some were protesting. The idea of striking the poor Minstrel, an unfortunate sick boy who could not defend himself! Others shook their heads. They had been expecting it. A man could not be insulted gratuitously without something happening. They had opposed the singing; they believed that when a man had something to say to another man he should say it face to face.

In the heat of their contrary opinions and in their jealous rivalry they were about to resort to blows when their attention was distracted by the Minstrel. He had removed the drum from his head and was wiping the blood from his forehead, weeping with the fury of a weak man who longs to wreak direct vengeance, and yet realizes himself a slave to his impotence.

"I'll settle with him!" he cried. Suddenly stooping to pick up stones in the darkness, he began to throw them at Febrer, each time receding a few steps as if to defend himself against a new aggression. The stones, flung by his forceless arms, fell into the shadows or rebounded against the porch.

The Minstrel's friends surrounded him and led him away. His cries could be heard in the distance, shouting defiance, swearing vengeance. He would kill the stranger! He alone would put an end to the Majorcan!

Jaime stood motionless among his enemies, with one hand in his belt. He was overcome with shame at having lost his temper, and having struck the poor consumptive. To stifle his remorse he muttered arrogant threats. He only wished it had been another man who had done the singing. His eyes sought the Ironworker, as if defying him; but the dreaded man-slayer had disappeared.

Half an hour afterward, when the tumult had subsided and Febrer returned to his tower, he stopped on the way several times, revolver in hand, as if expecting someone.

Nobody!

CHAPTER II
LOVE AND PISTOLS

The next morning just after sunrise the Little Chaplain ran in search of Don Jaime, revealing in his manner as he entered the tower, the importance of the news which he was bearing.

In Can Mallorquí they had all passed a bad night. Margalida wept; her mother lamented the occurrence; what would the people of the district think of them when they heard that men had come to blows in her house as in a tavern? What would the girls say about her daughter? But Margalida gave little heed to the opinion of her friends. Something else seemed to worry her, something of which she said nothing, but which caused her to shed copious tears. Señor Pèp, after closing the door on the suitors, had paced up and down the kitchen for an hour muttering to himself and clenching his fists. "That Don Jaime! Why should he persist in trying to obtain the impossible? Obstinate, like all his kindred!"

The Little Chaplain had not slept either. In the mind of the young savage, astute and sagacious, a suspicion tad gradually assumed the reality of fact.

On entering the tower he immediately communicated his thoughts to Don Jaime. Whom did he imagine had conceived the offensive song? The Minstrel? No, señor; it was the Ironworker! The Minstrel had made the rhymes, but the theme originated with the malicious man-slayer. He it was who had conceived the idea of insulting Don Jaime in the presence of all the suitors, relying on the certainty that he would not let the affront pass unheeded. Now the boy understood the reason for the interview between the two suitors which he had surprised in the mountain.

Febrer received this news, to which the Little Chaplain attached great importance, with a gesture of indifference. What of that? He had already punished the insolent Minstrel, and as for the man-slayer, he had sneaked off when he had challenged him at the door of the farmhouse. He was a coward.

Pepet shook his head incredulously.

"Be careful, Don Jaime! You do not know the ways of the braves around here, the cunning they employ to avoid being caught when wreaking vengeance. You must be on your guard now more than ever. You know what the jail-bird is, and he doesn't want to get sent back to prison. What he has just done is a trick which other man-slayers have played before."

Jaime lost patience at the boy's mysterious air and confused words.

"Why don't you speak out? Come!"

At last the Little Chaplain gave voice to his suspicions. Now the Ironworker could attempt anything he liked against Don Jaime; he could lie in ambush for him among the tamarisks at the foot of the tower and shoot him as he passed. Suspicion would at once be directed against the Minstrel, in view of the quarrel at the farmhouse and his threats of vengeance. With this, and with the man-slayer establishing an alibi by taking a short cut to some distant place where he could be seen by many persons, it would be easy for him to avenge himself with impunity.

"Ah!" exclaimed Febrer seriously, as if suddenly realizing the importance of these words.

The boy, delighting in his superior knowledge, continued giving advice. Don Jaime must be more careful; he must lock the door of his tower and pay no attention to calls from outside after dark. Surely the man-slayer would try to induce him to come out by challenging cries, with howls of defiance.

"If you hear any cries of challenge during the night, Don Jaime, you must keep still. I know their ways," continued the Little Chaplain with the importance of a hardened man-slayer. "They hide in the bushes, with weapon aimed, and if their man comes out, they fire without ever showing themselves. You must stay in after dark."

This advice was for the night. By day the señor could go abroad without fear.

"Here am I to accompany you wherever you wish."

The boy straightened himself with an aggressive air, moving one hand to his belt to convince himself that his knife had not disappeared, but he was immediately undeceived by Febrer's mocking expression of gratitude.

"Laugh, Don Jaime; make fun of me if you will; but I can be of some use to you. See how I warn you of danger! You must be on your guard. The Ironworker planned that singing with evil intent."

He glanced about like a chieftain preparing for a long siege. His eyes encountered the gun hanging on the wall among the decorations of shells. Very good; both barrels must be loaded with ball, and on top of this a good handful of lead slugs or coarse bird-shot. It would be no more than prudent. Thus his glorious grandfather had done. Seeing Jaime's revolver lying on the table, he frowned.

"Very bad! Small arms should be worn on one's person at all hours. I sleep with my knife on my breast. What if an enemy should rush in suddenly without giving a man time to look for his weapon?"

The tower, which, in former centuries, had been the scene of executions and battles between pirates, a stone vault suggestive of tragedies, the walls covered by gleaming whitewash, then claimed the boy's attention.

He cautiously made his way to the door as if an enemy were lying in wait for him at the foot of the stairway, and concealing his body behind the thick wall, he advanced, nothing but an eye and part of his forehead being visible. Then he shook his head with despair. If one looked out at night, even with these precautions, the enemy, lying in ambush below, could see him, could aim at him with the greatest facility, resting his arms on a branch or on a stone with no fear of missing him. It would be even worse to step outside the door and venture to go down. No matter how dark the night, the enemy could point his gun at a cluster of leaves, at a star on the horizon, at anything standing out conspicuously in the dusk near the stairway, and when a dark form should pass before it, momentarily obscuring the object sighted at—bang! It was sure game! He had heard grave men tell of having spent whole months crouching behind a hillock or a tree trunk, the butt-end of a musket close to the cheek and the eyes fixed on the end of the barrel, from sunset till daybreak, lying in wait for some old-time enemy.

No, the Little Chaplain did not like this door with its stairway in the open. He must find another exit, and he inspected the window, opened it, and looked out. With simian agility, laughing with joy at his discovery, he sprang over the embrasure and disappeared, seeking with feet and hands the irregularities of the rubble-work, the deep, stair-like sockets left by the stones when they had fallen loose from the mortar. Febrer looked out and saw him picking up his hat and waving it with a triumphant expression. Then the boy ran around the base of the tower, and soon his steps resounded, trotting noisily up the wooden stairs.

"That's easy enough!" he shouted, as he entered the room, red with excitement over his discovery. "That's a stairway fit for a gentleman!"

Realizing the importance of his discovery, he assumed a grand air of mystery. This must be kept between them—not a word to anyone. It was a precious means of exit, the secret of which must be jealously guarded.

The Little Chaplain envied Don Jaime. How he longed to have an enemy himself to come and call a challenge to him in the tower during the night! While the Ironworker lay howling in ambush, his eyes glued upon the stairway, he would descend by means of the window, at the rear of the tower, and, creeping cautiously around, he would hunt the hunter. What a stroke! He laughed with savage glee, as if on his dark red lips trembled the ferocity of his glorious ancestors who considered the hunting of man the most noble of exercises.

Febrer seemed to be infected by the boy's exhilaration. He would try going down by the window route himself! He flung his legs over the sill, and carefully, clumsily, began feeling with his toes for the irregularities in the wall until he found the holes which served as steps. He slowly made his way down, loose stones slipping beneath his feet, until he reached the ground, giving a sigh of satisfaction. Very good! The descent was easy; after a few more trials he would be able to get down as nimbly as the Little Chaplain. Pepet, who had followed him agilely, almost hanging over his head, smiled, like a master pleased at the lesson, and repeated his advice. Don Jaime must not forget! When he heard the challenge he must climb out of the window and down the wall, getting around behind his adversary.

At noon when Febrer was left alone he felt himself possessed of a warlike ferocity, of an aggressiveness which caused him to look long at the wall on which hung his gun.

At the foot of the promontory, from the shore where Tío Ventolera's boat was beached, rose the voice of the old fisherman singing mass. Febrer looked out the door, carrying both hands to his mouth in the form of a trumpet.

Tío Ventolera, with the help of a boy, was shoving his boat into the water. The furled sail trembled aloft on the mast. Jaime did not accept the invitation. "Many thanks, Tío Ventolera!" The old fisherman insisted in his puny voice, which, wafted in on the wind, sounded like the plaintive crying of a child. The afternoon was fine; the wind had changed; they would catch fish in abundance near the Vedrá. Febrer shrugged his shoulders. No, no, many thanks; he was busy.

He had scarcely ceased speaking when the Little Chaplain presented himself at the tower for the second time, carrying the dinner. The boy seemed gloomy and sad. His father, choleric over the scene of the previous night, had chosen him as the victim on whom to vent his displeasure. An injustice, Don Jaime! Pèp had been striding up and down the kitchen, while the women, with tearful eyes and cringing air, shrank away from his gaze. Everything that had happened he attributed to the weakness of his character, to his good nature, but he intended to apply a remedy at once. The courting was to be suspended; he would no longer receive suitors nor visits. And as for the Little Chaplain—this bad son, disobedient and rebellious, he was to blame for everything!

Pèp did not know for a certainty how the presence of his son had brought on the scandal of the night before, but he remembered his resistance against becoming a priest, his running away from the Seminary, and the recollection of these annoyances inflamed his anger and caused it to be concentrated on the boy. Monday next he was going to take him back to the seminary. If he tried to resist, and if he should run away again, it would be better for him to embark as a cabin boy and forget that he had a father, for in case he returned home Pèp would break his two legs with the iron bar which fastened the door. To let off steam, to get his hand in, and to give a sample of his future temper, he gave him a few blows and kicks, getting even in this way for the wrath he had felt when he saw the boy appear as a fugitive from Iviza.

The Little Chaplain, submissive and shrinking through habit, took refuge in a corner behind the defense of skirts and petticoats which his weeping mother opposed to Pèp's fury; but now, up in the tower, recalling the event with glaring eyes, livid cheeks and clenched fists, he gnashed his teeth.

What injustice! Should a man stand being beaten like that, for no reason whatever except that his father might work off his ill humor! The idea of his having to take a beating, he who carried a knife in his belt, and was not afraid of anyone on the island. Paternity and filial respect seemed to the Little Chaplain at the moment the inventions of cowards, created only to crush and mortify brave-hearted men. Added to the blows, humiliating to his dignity as a man of mettle, the thought of being shut up in the Seminary, dressed in a black cassock, like a woman in petticoats, with shaven head, losing forever those curls which peeped arrogantly beneath his hat brim; having a tonsure which would make the girls laugh, and—farewell to dancing and courting! Farewell to the knife!

Soon Jaime would see him no more. Within a week the trip to Iviza was to be taken. Others would bring his dinner up to the tower. Febrer saw a ray of hope. Perhaps then Margalida would come as in former days! The Little Chaplain, in spite of his grief, smiled maliciously. No, not Margalida; anyone but her. Pèp was in no mood to consent to that. When the poor mother, to plead her son's cause, had timidly suggested that the boy was needed in the house to wait on the señor, Pèp burst forth into fresh raving. He would carry Don Jaime's meals up to the tower every day himself, or else his wife should do so, and if need be they would get a girl to act as servant for the señor since he was determined to live near them.

The Little Chaplain said no more, but Febrer guessed the words which the good peasant had doubtless hurled against him, forgetting all respect in his anger, enraged over the trouble brought upon the family by his presence.

The boy returned to the ranchhouse with his basket, muttering revenge, swearing that he would not return to the Seminary, although he knew no means of avoiding it. His resistance took the turn of knightly valor. Abandon his friend Don Jaime now that he was surrounded by dangers! Go and shut himself up in that house of gloom, among black-skirted gentlemen who spoke a strange language, now that out in the open, in the light of the sun, or in the mystery of night, men were going to kill one another! Should such extraordinary events occur, and he not witness them!

When Febrer was left alone he took down his gun, and stood near the door for a long time examining it absent-mindedly. His thoughts were far away, much farther than the ends of the barrels, which seemed to point toward the mountain. That miserable Ironworker! That insufferable bully! Something had stirred within him, an irresistible antipathy, the first time he had seen him. Nobody in the island aroused his ire as did that gloomy jail-bird.

The cold steel weapon in his hand brought him back to reality. He resolved to go into the mountains hunting. But what should he hunt? He extracted two cartridges from the barrels, cartridges loaded with small shot, suitable for the birds which crossed the island returning from Africa. He introduced two other cartridges into the double barrel and filled his pockets with more, which he took from a pouch. They were loaded with buckshot. He was going hunting for big game!

Slinging his gun over his shoulder, he walked with arrogant step down the stairway of the tower building, as if his resolution filled him with satisfaction.

As he passed Can Mallorquí the dog leaped out to meet him, barking joyously. No one peeped out of the door, as in the past. Surely he had been seen, but no one came out of the kitchen to greet him. The dog followed for some time, but turned back when he saw him take the road to the mountain.

Febrer strode hurriedly between the stone walls which retained the sloping terraces, following the walks paved with blue pebbles, converted by the winter rains into high-banked ravines. Then he passed beyond the lands furrowed by the plow. The compact soil was covered with wild and spiny vegetation. Fruit trees, the tall almonds and the spreading fig trees, were succeeded by junipers and pines, twisted by the winds blowing from the sea. As Febrer stopped for a moment and looked behind, he saw at his feet the buildings of Can Mallorquí, like white dice shaken from the great rocks by the sea. The Pirate's Tower stood like a fortress on its hill. His ascent had been swift, almost at full speed, as if he feared to arrive too late at some meeting-place with which he was unfamiliar. He continued on his way. Two wild doves rose from the shrubbery with the feathery swish of an opening fan, but the hunter seemed not to see them. Stooping black figures in the bushes caused him to lift his right hand to the stock of his gun to sling it from his shoulder. They were charcoal burners piling wood. As Febrer passed near them they stared at him with fixed eyes, in which he thought he noticed something extraordinary, a mixture of astonishment and curiosity.

"Good afternoon!"

The grimy men replied, but they followed him a long time with their eyes, which shone with a transparency of water in their soot-blackened faces. Evidently the lonely mountain dwellers had heard of the events of the evening before at Can Mallorquí and were surprised at seeing the señor of the tower alone, as if defying his enemies and believing himself invulnerable.

Now he no longer met people along his path. Suddenly, above the murmur of dry leaves caressed by the wind, he heard the faint ring of beaten iron. A slender column of smoke was rising from among the verdure. It was the blacksmith's forge.

Jaime, with his gun half supported on his shoulder, as if the weapon were about to slip off, stepped into a clearing, which formed a broad square in front of the smithy. It was a miserable little adobe hut of a single story, blackened by smoke and covered by a hip roof, which, in places, sunk in as if about to collapse. Beneath a shed gleamed the flaming eye of a forge and near it stood the Ironworker beside the anvil, beating with his hammer on a bar of red-hot iron, which looked like the barrel of a carbine.

Febrer was not displeased with his theatrical entrance into the open square. The man-slayer raised his eyes on hearing the sound of steps in the interval between two blows. He stood motionless, with raised hammer as he recognized the señor of the tower, but his cold eyes conveyed no impression.

Jaime passed by the forge, staring at the Ironworker, giving a look of challenge which the other seemed not to understand. Not a word, not a greeting! The señor walked on, but once outside the square he stopped near one of the first trees and sat down on a projecting root, holding the gun between his knees.

The pride of virile arrogance invaded the soul of Febrer. He was rejoiced at his own assurance. That bully could easily see that he had come to seek him in the solitude of the mountain, at his own house; he must be convinced that he was not afraid of him.

To better demonstrate his serenity, he drew his tobacco box from his belt and began to roll a cigarette.

The hammer had begun to ring upon the metal again. From his seat on the tree trunk Jaime saw the Ironworker, his back turned with careless confidence, as if ignorant of his presence and intent on nothing but his work. This calmness disconcerted Febrer somewhat. *Vive Dios!* Had the man not guessed his intention?

The Ironworker's coolness was exasperating, but at the same time his calmly turning his back, confident that the señor of the tower was incapable of taking advantage of this situation to fire a treacherous shot, inspired a vague gratitude.

The hammer ceased ringing. When Febrer looked again in the direction of the shed he did not see the Ironworker. This caused him to pick up his gun, fingering the trigger. Undoubtedly he was coming with a weapon, annoyed by this provocation of one who came to seek him in his own house. Perhaps he was going to shoot out of one of the miserable windows which gave light to the blackened dwelling. He must be prepared against stratagem, and he arose, trying to conceal his body behind a tree trunk, leaving nothing but an eye visible.

Someone was stirring inside the hut; something black cautiously peeped out. The enemy was coming forth. Attention! He grasped his gun, intending to fire as soon as the muzzle of the hostile weapon should appear, but he stood motionless and confused on seeing that it was a black skirt, terminated by naked feet in worn and tattered sandals, and above it a withered bust, bent and bony, a head coppery and wrinkled, with but one eye, and thin gray hair, which allowed the gloss of baldness to shine between its locks.

Febrer recognized the old woman. She was the Ironworker's aunt, the one-eyed woman of whom the Little Chaplain had told him, the sole companion of the Ironworker in his wild solitude. The woman stood near the forge, her arms akimbo, thrusting forward her abdomen, bulky with petticoats, focusing her single eye, inflamed by anger, on the intruder who came to provoke a good man in the midst of his work. She stared at Jaime with the fiery aggressiveness of the woman who, secure in the respect produced by sex, is more audacious and impetuous than a man. She muttered threats and insults which the señor could not hear, furious that anyone would venture to oppose her nephew, the beloved whelp on whom, in her sterility, she had lavished all the ardor of frustrated motherhood.

Jaime suddenly realized the odiousness of his behavior in coming to antagonize another in his own house in broad daylight. The old woman was right in insulting him. It was not the Ironworker who was the bully; it was himself, the señor of the tower, the descendant of so many illustrious dons, he, so proud of his origin.

Shame intimidated him, overcoming him with stupid confusion. He did not know how to get away, nor which way to escape. At last he flung his gun across his shoulder, and, gazing aloft, as if pursuing a bird which sprang from branch to branch, wandered among the trees and through thickets, avoiding the forge.

He walked down toward the valley, escaping from the forest to which a homicidal impulse had drawn him, ashamed of his former purpose. Again he passed the grimy men making charcoal.

"Good afternoon!"

They replied to his greeting, but in their eyes which shone peculiarly white in their blackened faces, Febrer felt something like hostile mockery of objectionable strangeness, as if he were of a different race and had committed an unheard of deed which forever placed him beyond friendly contact with the islanders.

Pines and junipers were left behind on the skirt of the mountain. Now he walked between terraces of ploughed ground. In some fields he saw peasants at work; on a sloping bank he met several girls stooping over the ground gathering herbs; coming along a path he met three old men traveling slowly beside their burros.

Febrer, with the humility of one who feels repentant for an evil deed, greeted them pleasantly.

"Good afternoon!"

The peasants who were working in the field responded to him with a low grunt; the girls turned away their faces with a gesture of annoyance so as not to see him; the three old men replied to his greeting gloomily, looking at him with searching eyes, as if they found something extraordinary about him.

Under a fig tree, a black umbrella of interlaced boughs, he saw a number of peasants listening intently to someone in the center of the group. As Febrer approached there was a movement among them. A man arose with angry impulse, but the others held him back, grasping his arms and trying to restrain him. Jaime recognized him by the white kerchief under his hat. It was the Minstrel. The robust peasants easily overpowered the sickly boy, but, although he could not get away, he vented his fury by shaking his fist in the direction of the roadway, while threats and insults gurgled from his mouth. No doubt he had been telling his friends of the events of the night before when Febrer appeared. The Minstrel shouted and threatened. He swore that he would kill the stranger; he promised to come to the Pirate's Tower some night and set it on fire and rend its owner into shreds.

Bah! Jaime shrugged his shoulders with a scornful gesture and continued on his way, but he felt depressed and almost desperate on account of the atmosphere of repulsion and hostility, growing steadily more apparent round about him. What had he done? Where had he thrust himself? Was it possible that he had fallen so low as to fight with these islanders, he, a foreigner, and, moreover, a Majorcan?

In his gloomy mood he thought that the entire island, together with all things inanimate, had joined in this mortal protest. When he passed houses they seemed to become depopulated, their inhabitants concealing themselves in order not to greet him; the dogs rushed into the road, barking furiously, as if they had never seen him before.

The mountains seemed more austere and frowning on their bare, rocky crests; the forest more dark, more black; the trees of the valleys more barren and shriveled; the stones in the road rolled beneath his feet as if fleeing from his touch; the sky contained something repellant; even the air of the island would finally shrink away from his nostrils. In his desperation Febrer realized that he stood alone. Everyone was against him. Only Pèp and his family were left to him, and even they would finally draw away under the necessity of living at peace with their neighbors.

The foreigner did not intend to rebel against his fate. He was repentant, ashamed of his aggressiveness of the night before and of his recent excursion to the mountain. For him there was no room on the island. He was a foreigner, a stranger, who, by his presence, disturbed the traditional life of these people. Pèp had taken him in with the respect of an old time retainer, and he paid for his hospitality by disturbing his house and the peace of his family. The people had received him with a somewhat glacial courtesy, but tranquil and immutable, as if he were a foreign gran señor, and he responded to this respect by striking the most unfortunate one among them, the one who, on account of his illness, was looked upon with a certain paternal benevolence by all the peasants in the district. Very well, scion of the Febrers! For some time he had wandered about like a mad man, talking nothing but nonsense. All this for what reason? On account of the absurd love for a girl who might be his daughter; for an almost senile caprice, for he, despite his relative youth, felt old and forlorn in the presence of Margalida and the rustic girls who fluttered about her. Ah, this atmosphere! This accursed atmosphere!

In his days of prosperity, when he still dwelt in the palace in Palma, had Margalida been one of his mother's servants, no doubt he would have felt for her only the appetite inspired by the freshness of her youth, experiencing nothing which resembled love. Other women dominated him then with the seduction of their artifices and refinements, but here, in his loneliness, seeing Margalida surrounded by the brown and rural prettiness of her companions, beautiful as one of those white goddesses which inspire religious veneration among peoples of coppery skin, he felt the dementia of desire, and all his acts were absurd, as if he had completely lost his reason.

He must leave; there was no place on the island for him. Perhaps his pessimism deceived him in rating so high the importance of the affection which had drawn him to Margalida. Then again perhaps it was not desire, but love, the first real love of his life; he was almost sure of it, but even if it were, he must forget and go. He must go at once!

Why should he remain here? What hope held him? Margalida, as if overcome by surprise on learning of his love, avoided him, concealed herself, and did nothing but weep, yet tears were not an answer. Her father, influenced by a lingering sentiment of traditional veneration, tolerated in silence this caprice of the gran señor, but at any moment he might openly rebel against the man who had so disarranged his life. The island, which had accepted him courteously, seemed to rise up now against the foreigner who had come from afar to disturb their patriarchal isolation, their narrow existence, the pride of a people apart, with the same fierceness with which it had risen in former centuries against the Norman, the Arab, or the Berber, when disembarking on their shores.

It was impossible to resist; he would go. His eyes lovingly beheld the enormous belt of sea lying between two hills, as if it were a blue curtain concealing a rent in the earth. This strip of sea was the saving path, the hope, the unknown, which opens to us its arms of mystery in the most difficult moments of existence. Perhaps he would return to Majorca, to lead the life of a respectable beggar beside the friends who still remembered him; perhaps he would pass on to the Peninsula and go to Madrid in search of employment; perhaps he would take passage for America. Anything was preferable to staying here. He was not afraid; he was not intimidated by the hostility of the island and its inhabitants; his keenest feeling was remorse, shame over the trouble he had caused.

Instinctively his feet led him toward the sea, which was now his love and his hope. He avoided passing Can Mallorquí, and on reaching the shore he walked along the beach where the last palpitation of the waves was lost like a slender leaf of crystal among the tiny pebbles mixed with potsherds.

At the foot of the promontory of the tower he climbed up the loose rocks and seated himself on the wave-worn and almost detached cliff. There he had sat lost in thought one stormy night, the same on which he had presented himself as suitor at the house of Margalida.

The afternoon was calm. The sea had an extraordinary and deep transparency. The sandy bottoms were reflected like milky spots; the submarine reefs and their dark vegetation seemed to tremble with the movement of mysterious life. The white clouds floating on the horizon traced great shadows as they passed before the sun. One portion of the blue expanse was a glossy black, while beyond the floating mantle the luminous waters seemed to be seething with golden bubbles. Now and again the sun, concealed behind these curtains, flung beneath its border a visible strip of light, like a lantern ray, a long triangle of hoary splendor, resembling a Holland landscape.

Nothing in this appearance of the sea reminded Febrer of that stormy night, and yet, from the association which forgotten ideas form in our minds with old places when we return to them, he began to think the same thoughts, only that now, in place of progressing, they passed in an inverse direction with a confusion of defeat.

He laughed bitterly at his optimism then, at the confidence which had caused him to scorn all his ideas of the past. The dead command; their power and authority are indisputable. How had it been possible for him, impelled by the enthusiasm of love, to repudiate this tremendous and discouraging truth? Clearly do the dark tyrants of our lives make themselves felt with all the overwhelming weight of their power. What had he done that this corner of the earth, his ultimate refuge, should look upon him as an alien? The innumerable generations of men whose dust and whose souls were mingled with the soil of their native isle had left as a heritage to the present the hatred of the stranger, the fear and the repulsion of the foreigner with whom they had lived at war. He who came from other lands was received with a repellant isolation, decreed by those who no longer exist.

When, scorning his old-time prejudices, he had thought to join his life with that of a native woman, the woman had shrunk away, mysterious, frightened at the idea, while her father, in the name of servile respect, opposed such an unheard of union. Febrer's idea was that of a mad man; the mingling of the rooster and the gull, the vagary of the extravagant friar which so amused the peasants. Thus had men willed in former times when they founded society and divided it into classes, and thus it must ever be. It is useless to rebel against the established order. The life of man is short, and it is not enough to contend with hundreds of thousands of lives before it and which spy upon it unseen, crushing it between material fabrications which are tokens of their passage over the earth, weighting it down with their thoughts, which fill the atmosphere, and are taken advantage of by all those who are born without will power to invent something new.

The dead command, and it is useless for the living to refuse obedience. All rebellions to escape this servitude, to break the chain of centuries, all are lies! Febrer recalled the sacred wheel of the Hindoos, the Buddhist symbol which he had seen in Paris once when he attended an oriental religious ceremony in a museum. The wheel is the symbol of our lives. We think we advance because we move; we think we progress because we go forward, but when the wheel makes the complete turn we find ourselves in the same place. The life of humanity, history, are but an interminable "recommencement of things." Peoples are born, they grow, they progress; the cabin is converted into a castle and afterward into a mart; enormous cities of millions of men are formed; then catastrophes come, the wars for bread which people lack, the protests of the dispossessed, the great massacres; then the cities are depopulated and are laid waste. Weeds invade the proud monuments; the metropoli gradually sink into the earth and sleep beneath hills for centuries and centuries. The untamed forest covers the capital of remote epochs; the savage hunter stalks over ground where in other times conquering chieftains were received with the pomp of demigods; sheep graze and the shepherd blows his reed above ruins which were tribunes of dead laws; men group together again, and the cabin rises, the village, the castle, the mart, the great city, and the round is repeated over and over, with a difference of hundreds of centuries, as identical gestures, ideas, conceptions, are repeated in man succeeding man throughout the course of time. The wheel! The eternal recommencement of things! And all the creatures of the human flock though changing the sheep-fold, never change shepherds; the shepherds are ever the same, the dead, the first to think, whose primordial thought was like the handful of snow which rolls and rolls down the hill-slopes, growing larger, bearing along everything which clings to it in its descent!

Men, proud of their material progress, of the mechanical toys invented for their well-being, imagine themselves free, superior to the past, emancipated from original servitude, yet all that they say has been said hundreds of centuries before in different words; their passions are the same; their thoughts, which they consider original, are scintillations and reflections of other remote thoughts; and all acts which were held to be good or bad are considered as such because they have been thus classified by the dead, the tyrannical dead, those whom man would have to kill again if he desired to be really free!

Who would be courageous enough, to accomplish this great liberating act? What paladin would there be with sufficient strength to kill the monster which weighs upon humanity, as the enormous and overwhelming dragons of legend guarded useless treasures beneath their mighty forms?

Febrer remained motionless on the rock for a long time, his elbows on his knees and his forehead in his hands, lost in thought, his eyes appearing hypnotized by the gentle rise and fall of the fluctuating waters.

When he aroused himself from this meditation the afternoon was waning. He would fulfill his destiny! He could live only on the heights, although it might be as a proud mendicant. All descending paths he found barred. Farewell to happiness which might be found by retrocession to a natural and primitive life! Since the dead did not wish him to be a man, he would be a parasite.

His eyes, wandering over the horizon, became fixed on the white clouds massed above the rim of the sea. When he was a little lad and Mammy Antonia used to accompany him in his walks along the beach at Soller, they had often amused themselves by indulging their imagination in giving form and name to the clouds which met or scattered in an incessant variety of shapes, seeing in them now a black monster with flaming jaws, now a virgin surrounded by blue rays.

A group of clouds, dense and snowy as white fleece, attracted his attention. This luminous whiteness resembled the polished bones of a cranium. Loose tufts of dark vapor floated in the mist. Febrer's imagination pictured in it two frightful, black holes; a dark triangle like that which the wasted nose leaves in the skull of the dead; and below it an immense gash, tragic, identical with the mute grin of a mouth devoid of lips and teeth.

It was Death, the great mistress, empress of the world, displaying herself to him in broad daylight in her white and dazzling majesty, defying the splendor of the sun, the blue of the sky, the luminous green of the sea. The reflection of the sinking orb imparted a spark of malignant life to the bony countenance of wafer-like pallor, to the gloom of her dark eye-sockets, to her terrifying grin. Yes, it was she! The mist clinging to the surface of the sea was as plaits and folds of a garment which concealed her enormous frame; and other clouds which floated higher formed the ample sleeve from which escaped vapors more subtle and vague, making a bony arm terminating in an index finger, dry and crooked, like that of a bird of prey, pointing out far, far away, a mysterious destiny.

The vision disappeared with the rapid movement of the clouds, obliterating the hideous figure, assuming other capricious forms, but as it vanished from his sight Febrer did not awake from his hallucination.

He accepted the command without rebellion; he would go! The dead command, and he was their helpless slave! The late afternoon light brought out objects in strange relief. Strong shadows seemed to palpitate with life, imparting animation and giving animal shapes to the rocks along the coast. In the distance a promontory resembled a lion crouching above the waves, glaring at Jaime with silent hostility. The rocks on a level with the water raised and lowered their black heads, crowned with green hair, like giant amphibia of a monstrous humanity. In the direction of Formentera he saw an immense dragon which slowly advanced across the horizon, with a long tail of clouds, to treacherously swallow the dying sun.

When the red sphere, fleeing from this danger, sank into the waters, enlarged by a spasm of terror, the depressing gray of twilight aroused Febrer from his hallucination.

He arose, picked up his gun, and started for the tower. He was mentally arranging the programme of his departure. He would not say a word to anyone. He would wait until some mail steamer from Majorca should touch at the port of Iviza, and only at the last moment would he tell Pèp of his resolution.

The certainty of soon forsaking this retreat caused him to look with interest around the tower by the glow of a candle he had lighted. His shadow, gigantically enlarged, and vacillating in the flickering light, moved about on the white walls, eclipsing objects which decorated them, or glinting from the pearly shells or from the gleaming metal of the gun on its rack.

A familiar grating sound attracted the attention of Febrer, who looked down the stairway. A man, wrapped in a mantle, stood on the lower steps. It was Pèp.

"Your supper," he said shortly, handing him a basket.

Jaime took it. He saw that the peasant did not wish to talk, and he, for his part, felt a certain fear of breaking the silence.

"Good-night!"

Pèp started on his return journey after this brief salutation, like a respectful but angry servant who only allows himself the indispensable words with his master.

Jaime set the basket upon the table and closed the door. He had no appetite; he would eat his supper later. He caught up a rustic pipe, carved by a peasant from a branch of cherry, filled it with tobacco and began to smoke, following with distracted eyes the winding spirals, whose subtle blue assumed a rainbow transparency before the candle.

Then he took a book and tried to fix his mind upon it, but he could not concentrate his attention.

Outside this husk of stone night reigned, a night dark and filled with mystery. This solemn silence, which fell from on high, and in which the slightest sounds seemed to acquire terrifying proportions, as if the murmur were listening to its own self, appeared to filter through the very walls.

Febrer thought he heard the circulation of his blood in this profound calm; from time to time he caught the scream of a gull, or the momentary swaying of the tamarisks in a gust of wind, a rustling like that of theatrical mobs concealed behind the wings. From the ceiling resounded at intervals the monotonous cric-cric of a wood-borer gnawing the beams with incessant toil which passed unheeded during the day. The sea filled the darkness with a gentle moan whose undulations broke on all the projections and windings of the coast.

Suddenly, Febrer, who sat silently listening with a quiet resembling that of timid children who are afraid to turn over in bed in order not to augment the mystery which surrounds them, stirred in his chair. Something extraordinary rent the air, dominating with its stridor the confused sounds of night. It was a cry, a howl, a whinny, one of those hostile, mocking voices with which vengeful youths call one another in the shadows.

Jaime felt an impulse to arise, to run to the door, but something held him motionless. The traditional cry of challenge had sounded some distance away. They must be young bloods of the district who had chosen the vicinity of the Pirate's Tower to meet, weapon in hand. That was not intended for him; in the morning the event would be explained.

He opened his book again, intending to amuse himself by reading, but after a few lines he sprang from his chair, flinging the volume and his pipe upon the table.

A-u-u-u-ú! The whinny of challenge, the hostile and mocking cry, had resounded again, almost at the foot of the stairway, prolonged by the strong draft of a pair of bellows-like lungs. At the same instant the harsh noise of opening wings whistled in the dark; the marine birds, aroused from sleep, flew out from among the rocks to seek a new shelter.

This call was meant for him! Someone had come to challenge him at his very door! He glanced at his gun; with his right hand he felt the steel of the revolver in his belt, warmed by contact with his body; he took two steps toward the door, but he stopped and shrugged his shoulders with a smile of resignation. He was no native of the island; he did not understand this language of yells, and he considered himself superior to such provocations.

He returned to his chair and picked up his book, making an effort to smile.

"Yell, my good fellow, shriek, howl! My sympathy is with you, you may catch cold in the night air while I am here in my house taking things easy!"

This mocking complacency, however, was only on the surface. The howl rent the air again, not at the foot of the stairway now, but farther off, perhaps among the tamarisks which grew around the tower. The challenger seemed to have settled down to wait for Febrer to come out.

Who could it be? Perhaps the miserable Ironworker—the man-slayer, whom he had been seeking that afternoon; perhaps the Minstrel, who had publicly sworn to kill him immediately. Night and cunning, which equalize the forces of enemies, might have given courage to the sick boy to appear against him. It was also possible that there might be two or more lying in wait for him.

Another howl sounded, but Jaime shrugged his shoulders again. His unknown challenger might howl as long as he wished.

Reading was now out of the question! It was useless to pretend tranquillity!

The challenges were repeated fiercely now, like the crowing of an infuriated rooster. Jaime imagined the neck of the man, swollen, reddened, the tendons vibrating with anger. The guttural cry gradually acquired the inflection and the significance of language. It was ironic, mocking, insulting; it taunted the foreigner for his prudence; it seemed to call him a coward.

He tried not to hear. A mist formed before his eyes; it seemed as if the candle had gone out; in the intervals of silence the blood hummed in his ears. He remembered that Can Mallorquí was not far away, and that perhaps Margalida stood trembling at her little window, listening to the cries near the tower, wherein was a timid man, hearing them also, but with barred door, as if he were deaf.

No; it was enough! This time he flung his book definitively upon the table, and then, as by instinct, scarcely knowing what he did, he blew out the candle. He took a few steps, with hands outstretched, completely forgetting the plans of attack he had hastily conceived a few moments before. Anger transformed his ideas. In this sudden blindness of spirit he had but one thought, like a final splutter from a vanishing light. Now he touched the gun with palpitating hands, but he did not pick it up. He must have a less embarrassing weapon; perhaps he would need to go down and make his way through the bushes.

He tugged at his belt, and his revolver slipped out of its hiding place with the ease of a warm and silky animal. He groped in the dark toward the door and cautiously opened it, barely wide enough to get his head through, the heavy hinges creaking faintly.

Emerging suddenly from the darkness of his room to the diffused clarity of the sidereal light, he saw the clump of bushes near the tower, and farther on, the dim white farmhouse, and opposite stood the black hump of the mountains piercing the sky, in which flickered the stars. This vision lasted but an instant; he could see no more. Suddenly two tiny flashes, two serpents; of fire leaped from the bushes, one after the other, cutting luminous streaks through the dark, followed by two almost simultaneous reports.

Jaime perceived an acrid odor of burnt powder. At the same time he felt just above his scalp a numbing, violent shock, something abnormal, which seemed to touch him, and yet not touch him, the sensation of a blow from a stone. Something dropped upon his face like a light, impalpable shower. Blood? Earth?

The surprise lasted only an instant. Someone behind the bushes close to the stairway had fired at him. The enemy was there—there! In the darkness he saw the point from which the flashes had emerged, and, reaching his right arm outside the door, he fired, one, two, five times; all the cartridges contained in the cylinder.

He fired almost blindly, uncertain of his aim in the dark, and trembling with anger. A faint sound of crashing branches, an almost imperceptible undulation in the bushes, filled him with savage joy. He had hit the enemy undoubtedly, and he raised his hand to his head to convince himself that he was not wounded.

As he passed his fingers over his face something small and granulated fell from his cheeks. It was not blood; it was sand, dust, and mortar. He felt along the wall just above his head and discovered two small, funnel-like holes, still warm. The two balls had grazed his scalp, and had lodged in the wall, an almost imperceptible distance above his head.

Febrer was rejoiced at his good luck. He, safe, unharmed; but his enemy, how about him? Where was he at that moment? Ought he to go down and search among the tamarisks for him, to taunt him in his agony? Suddenly the shout was repeated, the savage howl, far, very far away, somewhere near the farmhouse; a howl triumphant, mocking, which Jaime interpreted as an announcement of an early return.

The dog of Can Mallorquí, aroused by the gunshots, was barking dismally. Other dogs in the distance answered. The howling of the man moved farther away, with incessant repetitions, steadily growing more remote, more faint, merging into the mysterious night.

CHAPTER III
THE CHALLENGE IN THE NIGHT

No sooner had day dawned than the Little Chaplain appeared at the tower.

He had heard everything. His father, who was a heavy sleeper, had perhaps not yet been informed of the event. The dog might bark, and a fierce battle might rage near the farmhouse, but good old Pèp, when he went to bed, tired out with his day's work, became as insensible as a dead man. The other members of the family had spent a night of anguish. His mother, after several attempts to arouse her husband, with no better success than to draw forth incoherent mumbling, followed by yet louder snoring, had spent the night praying for the soul of the señor of the tower, believing him dead. Margalida, who slept near her brother, had called him in a stifled and agonized voice when the first shots rang out: "Do you hear, Pepet?"

The poor girl had arisen and lighted the candle, by the dim radiance of which the boy had seen her pale face and terrified eyes. Forgetting everything, she had flung her arms about, lifting her hands to her head. "They have killed Don Jaime! My heart tells me that they have!" She trembled at the echo of the fresh shots. "A regular rosary of reports," according to the Little Chaplain, had answered the first discharges.

"That was you, wasn't it, Don Jaime?" continued the boy. "I recognized your pistol at once, and so I said to Margalida. I remember that afternoon you shot off your revolver on the beach. I have a good ear for such things."

Then he told of his sister's despair; how she had gathered her clothing, intending to dress so that she might rush to the tower. Pepet would accompany her. Then, suddenly becoming timid, she refused to go. She did nothing but weep, and she would not allow the boy to make his escape by climbing over the barnyard fence.

They had heard the howling near the farmhouse, some time after the shooting, and, as he spoke of this war-cry, the boy smiled mischievously. Then Margalida, suddenly tranquilized by her brother's words, had become silent, but during the whole night the Little Chaplain heard sighs of anguish and a gentle whispering as of a low voice murmuring words and words with tireless monotony. She was praying.

Then, when daylight came, everyone arose except his father, who continued his placid sleep. As the women timidly peeped out from the porch, full of gloomy thoughts, they expected to behold a terrifying picture—the tower in ruins, and the Majorcan's corpse lying above the wreck. But the Little Chaplain had laughed on seeing the door open, and near it, as on other mornings, Don Jaime, with naked chest, splashing in a tank which he himself brought from the beach filled with sea water.

He had not been mistaken when he laughed at the women's terror. No one living could kill his Don Jaime—that was what he said, and he knew something of men.

Then, after Jaime's brief account of the events of the night before, screwing up his eyes with the expression of a very wise person, Pepet examined the two holes made in the wall by the bullets.

"And your head was here, where mine is? Futro!"

His eyes reflected admiration, devout idolatry, for this wonderful man, whose life had just been saved by a veritable miracle.

Trusting in his knowledge of the people of the country, Febrer questioned the boy about the supposed aggressor, and the Little Chaplain smiled with an air of importance. He had heard the war-cry. It was the Minstrel's manner of howling; many might have imagined it was he. He howled that way at the serenades, at the afternoon dances, and on coming away from a wooing.

"But it was not he, Don Jaime; I am sure! If anyone should ask the Minstrel he would be free to say 'Yes,' just to give himself importance. But it was the other, the Ironworker; I recognized his voice, and so did Margalida!"

In continuation, with a grave expression, as if he wished to test the Majorcan's mettle, he spoke of the silly fear of the women, who declared that the Civil Guard of San José must be notified.

"You won't do that, will you, Don Jaime? That would be foolish. The police are only needed by cowards."

The deprecatory smile, and the shrug of the shoulders with which Febrer answered him, reassured the boy.

"I was certain of that; it's not the custom on the island—but, as you are a foreigner—you are right; every man should defend himself; that's what he's a man for; and in case of need, he counts on his friends."

As he said this, he strutted about, as if to call attention to the powerful aid on which Don Jaime might count in moments of danger.

The Little Chaplain wished to work this situation to his own advantage, and he advised the señor that it would be a good idea to have him come and live in the tower. If Don Jaime were to ask Señor Pèp, it would be impossible for his father to refuse. It would be well for Don Jaime to have him near; then there would be two for the defense; and, to strengthen his petition, he recalled his father's anger and the certainty that he intended to take him to Iviza at the beginning of next week, to shut him up in the Seminary. What would the señor do when he found himself deprived of his best friend?

In his desire to demonstrate the value of his presence, he censured Febrer's forgetfulness of the night before. Who would think of opening the door and looking out when someone was there with weapon prepared, challenging him? It was a miracle that he had not been killed. What about the lesson he had given him? Did he not remember his advice about climbing down from the window, at the back of the tower, to surprise the enemy?

"That is true," said Jaime, really ashamed at his forgetfulness.

The Little Chaplain, who was proudly enjoying the effect of this advice, started with surprise as he looked through the doorway.

"My father!"

Pèp was slowly climbing the hill, his arms clasped behind his back, seemingly in deep meditation. The boy became alarmed at the sight of him. Undoubtedly he was very cross over the latest news; it would not be well for them to meet just now, and repeating once again the advisability of Febrer's having him as a companion, he flung his legs out of the window, turning upon his belly, resting a second on the sill, and disappeared down the side of the wall.

The peasant entered the tower and spoke without emotion of the happenings of the night before, as if this were a normal event which but slightly altered the monotony of country life. The women had told him—he was such a heavy sleeper——. So it had not amounted to anything?

He listened, with lowered eyes, twiddling his thumbs, to the brief tale. Then he went to the door to examine the two bullet holes.

"A miracle, Don Jaime, a genuine miracle."

He returned to his chair, remaining motionless a long time, as if it cost him a great effort to make his dull mind operate.

"The devil has broken loose, señor. It was sure to happen; I told you so. When a man makes up his mind to have the impossible, everything goes wrong, and there's an end to peace."

Then, raising his head, he fixed his cold, scrutinizing eyes on Don Jaime. They would have to notify the alcalde; they must tell the whole business to the Civil Guard.

Febrer made a negative gesture. No, this was an affair between men, which he would handle himself.

Pèp sat with his eyes fixed enigmatically on the señor, as if struggling with opposing ideas.

"You are right," said the phlegmatic peasant.

Foreigners usually had other notions, but he was glad that the señor said the same as would his poor father (may he rest in peace!). Everyone on the island thought the same; the old way was the best way.

Then Pèp, without consulting the señor, exposed his plan for helping in the defense. It was a duty of friendship. He had his gun at home. He had not used it for some time, but when he was young, during the lifetime of his famous father (may he rest in peace!) he had been a fair shot. He would come and spend the nights in the tower, to keep Don Jaime company, so that he should not be taken unaware.

Neither was the peasant surprised at the firm negative of the señor, who seemed to be offended by the proposition. He was a man, not a boy, needing companionship. Let everyone sleep in his own house, and let happen what fate decreed!

Pèp assented also with nods of his head to these words. The same would his father have said, and like him all good people who followed ancient customs. Febrer seemed a true son of the island. Then, softened by the admiration this courage of Don Jaime's inspired in him, he proposed another arrangement. Since the señor did not wish company in his tower, he might come down to Can Mallorquí to sleep. They could fix him up a bed somewhere.

Febrer felt tempted by the opportunity to see Margalida, but the tone of weakness in which the father gave the invitation, and the anxious glance with which he awaited a reply, caused him to refuse.

"No, thank you very much, Pèp. I will stay here in the tower. They might think I had moved down to your house because I was afraid."

The peasant nodded assent. He understood. He would do the same in a like situation. But Pèp would try to sleep less at night, and if he heard shouts or shots near the tower he would come out with his old fire-lock.

As if this self-imposed obligation of sleeping on guard, ready to expose his skin in defense of his old-time patron broke the calm in which he had maintained himself until then, the peasant raised his eyes and clasped his hands.

"Oh, Lord! Oh, Lord!

"The devil is let loose!" he repeated, "there will be no more peace; and all for not believing what I told you, for going against the current of old customs, which have been established by wiser people than those of the present day. And what is all this leading to?"

Febrer tried to reassure the peasant, and a thought escaped him which he had intended to keep concealed. Pèp might rejoice. He was going to leave forever, not wishing to disturb the peace of himself and family.

Ah! was the señor really going away? The peasant's joy was so keen, and his surprise so lively that Jaime hesitated. He seemed to see in the peasant's little eyes a certain malice. Did the islander imagine that his sudden determination was caused by fear of his enemies?

"I am going," he said, looking at Pèp with hostility, "but I am not sure when. Later—when it suits my convenience. I can't leave here until the man who is looking for me finds me."

Pèp made a gesture of resignation; his gladness vanished, but he was about to assent to these words also, adding that thus would his father have done, and thus he himself thought best.

When the peasant arose to take his leave, Febrer, who was standing near the door, saw the Little Chaplain by the farmhouse, and this recalled the boy's desire to his mind. If the request would not put Pèp out, he might let the youngster keep him company in the tower.

But the father received this suggestion with displeasure.

No, Don Jaime! If he needed company, here he was himself, a man! The boy must study. The devil was let loose, and it was high time to impose his authority so that order should be maintained in the family. Next week he intended taking him back to the Seminary. That was final.

On being left alone Febrer went down to the beach. Uncle Ventolera was caulking the seams of his beached boat with tow and pitch. Lying in it as if it were an enormous coffin, with his weak eyes he sought out the leaks, and on finding one he would begin singing his Latin jargon in a loud voice.

Feeling the boat move and seeing the señor leaning over the edge, the old man smiled with amusement, and ended his canticles.

"Holloa, Don Jaime!"

Uncle Ventolera was informed of everything. The women of Can Mallorquí had told him the news, and by this time it had circulated all over the district, but only from ear to ear, as these things must be spoken in order to keep them from the police who muddle everything. So someone had come after him the night before, challenging him to step outside the tower? He, he, he! The same thing had happened to him in times gone by, when, between voyages, he was making love to the girl he married. A certain comrade who had become a rival had howled at him; but he had gotten the girl, because he was the more clever; to sum it all up, he had given his friend a stab in the breast, which held him for a long time between life and death. Then he had lived on his guard whenever he was in port, to avoid the vengeance of his enemy; but the years pass, old grudges are forgotten, and finally the two comrades took up the smuggling trade together, sailing from Algiers to Iviza, or along the Spanish main.

Uncle Ventolera laughed with a childish giggle, enjoying these recollections of his youth, recalling the memory of shooting scrapes, stabbing affrays, and provocations in the night. Alas! No one challenged him any more! This was only for young bloods. His accent betrayed melancholy at being no longer mixed up in these affairs of love and war, which he judged indispensable to a happy existence.

Febrer left the old man singing mass as he went on with his task of repairing the boat. In the tower he found the basket containing his supper upon the table. The Little Chaplain had left it without waiting, obeying, no doubt, some urgent call of the ill-humored father. After eating, Jaime went out again to examine the two holes which the projectiles had made in the wall. Now that the excitement of the danger was over, and he coldly appreciated the gravity of the situation, he felt a vengeful anger, more intense than that which had impelled him to rush to the door the night before. Had his enemy aimed a few millimeters lower, he would have rolled into obscurity, at the foot of the steps, like a hunted beast. Cristo! And could a man of his class die thus, the victim of treachery, ambushed by one of these rustics!

His anger assumed a vengeful impulse; he felt the necessity of taking the offensive, of making his appearance, serene and threatening, in the presence of the men among whom were numbered some of his adversaries.

He took down his gun, examined the action, slung it over his shoulder and descended from the tower, taking the same road as on the previous afternoon. As he passed Can Mallorquí the barking of the dog brought Margalida and her mother to the door. The men were in a distant field which Pèp was cultivating. The mother, tearful, and with her words broken by sobs, could only grasp the señor's hands.

"Don Jaime! Don Jaime!"

He must be very careful, he must stay close in his tower, and be constantly on guard against his enemies. Margalida, silent, her eyes extraordinarily wide open, gazed at Febrer, revealing admiration and anxiety. She did not know what to say; her simple soul seemed to shrink humbly within itself, finding no words to express her thoughts.

Jaime continued on his way. Several times he turned and saw Margalida standing on the porch, looking after him anxiously. The señor was going hunting, as he had done before, but, ay! he was taking the mountain trail; he was going to the pine forest where stood the forge.

During his walk Febrer thought over plans of attack. He was determined to try conclusions at once. The moment that the man-slayer should appear at the door of his house, he would let him have the two shots from his gun. He, Jaime Febrer, carried on his business in the light of day, and he would be more fortunate; his balls would not lodge in the wall!

When he arrived at the forge he found it closed. Nobody at home! The Ironworker had disappeared; neither was the old woman there to receive him with the hostile glare of her single eye.

He seated himself at the foot of the tree as before, his gun ready, sheltered behind the trunk, in case this apparent desertion of the premises was only a trick. A long time passed. The wild doves, emboldened by the stillness of the surrounding forge, fluttered about in the little clearing unheeding the motionless hunter. A cat crept cautiously over the rickety roof, and crouched like a tiger, trying to capture the restless sparrows.

Delay and inaction calmed Febrer. What was he doing here, far from home, in the heart of the forest, twilight about to fall, lying in wait for an enemy of whose active hostility he had only vague suspicions? Perhaps the Ironworker had locked himself in his house on seeing him approach, so that further waiting would be useless. It might be that he and the old woman had gone on some long excursion and might not return until night. He must go!

Gun in hand, ready to attack in case he should meet the enemy, he began his return to the valley.

Once more he passed the fields and again he met the peasants and the girls, who looked at him with eager curiosity, barely replying to his greeting. Again, in the same place as before, he met the Minstrel with his bandaged head, surrounded by friends to whom he was talking with violent gesticulations. When he recognized the señor of the tower, before his comrades could prevent him, he bent down to the hardened furrows of the earth and picked up two stones and flung them at him. These missiles, thrown by a forceless arm, did not make half their intended journey. Then, exasperated by the contemptuous serenity of Febrer, who continued on his way, the boy broke into threats. He would kill the Majorcan; he declared it at the top of his voice! Let them all hear that he had sworn to destroy this man!

Jaime smiled gloomily. No; the angry lamb was not the one who had come to the Pirate's Tower to kill him. His outrageous boasting was enough to prove that.

The señor spent a peaceful evening. After supper, when Margalida's brother had said good night, depressed by the certainty that his father would never desist from his determination of taking him back to the Seminary, Jaime closed the door, piling the table and chairs against it. He did not intend to be surprised while he was asleep. He blew out the light and sat smoking in the dark, amusing himself by watching the tiny brand on the end of his cigar widen and shrink as he drew upon it. His gun was near him and his revolver was in his belt ready for use at the slightest sound at the door. His ear was habituated to the murmurs of the night and to the surging of the sea, but he sought beyond them for some sound, some evidence that in this lonely retreat there were other human beings than himself.

Finally he looked at the face of his watch by the light of his cigar. Ten o'clock! Far away he heard barking, and Jaime thought he recognized the dog of Can Mallorquí. Perhaps it indicated the passing of someone on his way to the tower. Now the enemy might be near. It was not unlikely that he was dragging himself cautiously outside the path among the tamarisks.

He arose, reaching for his gun, feeling in his belt for his revolver. As soon as he should hear a cry of challenge, or a voice near the door, he would climb out of the window, make his way cautiously around the tower, and get behind the enemy.

More time passed. Still nothing! Febrer wished to look at his watch, but his hands would not obey his will. The ruddy point no longer glowed on the end of his cigar. His head had at last fallen back upon the pillow; his eyes closed; he heard cries of challenge, shots, curses, but it was in his dreams, as if in another world, where insults and attacks do not arouse one's sensibilities. Then—nothing! A dense shadow, a night of profound sleep. He was awakened by a ray of sunshine which filtered through a crack in the window and shone upon his eyes. The morning light again brought into relief the whiteness of the walls which during the night seemed to sweat the shadows and barbaric mysteries of former centuries.

Jaime arose in good spirits, and as he removed the barricade of furniture which obstructed the doorway, he laughed, somewhat ashamed of his precautions, considering them almost a sign of cowardice. The women of Can Mallorquí had worked upon his nerves with their fears. Who would be likely to seek him in his tower, knowing that he was on the alert and would meet a trespasser with shots! The Ironworker's absence when Jaime had presented himself at the forge, and the calm of the night before, gave food for thought. Was the man-slayer wounded? Had some of Jaime's balls reached their mark?

He spent the morning on the sea. Tío Ventolera took him to the Vedrá, praising the lightness and other merits of his boat. He repaired it year after year, not a splinter of its original construction being left in it. They fished in the shelter of the rocks until mid-afternoon. On their way back Febrer saw the Little Chaplain running along the beach waving something white.

Before landing, while the prow of the boat was scraping along the gravel, the boy called to him with the impatience of one who has great news:

"A letter, Don Jaime!"

A letter! Actually, in that remote corner of the world, the most extraordinary event that could disturb the everyday life was the arrival of a letter. Febrer turned it over in his hands, examining it as something strange and rare. He looked at the seal, then at the address on the envelope.... He recognized it—it aroused in his memory the same impression as a familiar face with which we cannot associate a name. From whom was it?

Meanwhile the Little Chaplain gave detailed explanations of the great event. The letter had been brought by the foot postman in the middle of the morning. It had come by the mail steamer from Palma, arriving in Iviza the night before. If he wished to answer it he must do so without loss of time. The boat would return to Majorca the following day.

On his way to the tower Jaime broke the seal and looked for the signature. Almost at the same moment his recollection grew clear and a name surged to his mind—Pablo Valls! Captain Pablo had written to him after a year of silence, and his letter was long, several sheets of commercial paper covered with close writing!

At the first few lines the Majorcan smiled. The captain himself seemed there in those written words, with his vigorous and exuberant personality, turbulent, kindly, and aggressive. Febrer almost saw in the page before him his enormous, heavy nose, his gray whiskers, his eyes the color of oil speckled with flecks of tobacco color, his dented, chambergo hat thrust on the back of his head.

The letter began, "Dear, shameless, fellow;" and the opening paragraphs continued in the same style.

"Something worth while," he murmured, smiling. "I must read this leisurely."

He put it in his pocket with the eagerness of one who sharpens a pleasure by deferring it. Jaime climbed to the tower, after taking leave of the boy.

He seated himself near the window, his chair tilted back against the table, and began to read. An explosion of mock fury, of affectionate insults, of indignation over events Jaime had actually forgotten, filled the first pages. Pablo Valls overflowed with amusing incoherency, like a charlatan condemned for a long time to silence who suffers the torture of his repressed verbosity. He flung into Febrer's face his origin and his pride, which had impelled him to run away without telling his friends good-bye. "In the last analysis you are descended from a race of inquisitors." His ancestors had burned the ancestors of Valls; let him not forget that! But the good must distinguish themselves from the bad in some way, and so he, the reprobate, the Chueta, the heretic hated by everybody, had responded to this lack of friendship by busying himself with Jaime's affairs. Very likely he had already heard about this through his friend Toni Clapés, whose business was thriving, as usual, although he had suffered some set-backs of late. Two of his vessels carrying cargoes of tobacco had been captured.

"But—to the gist of the matter! You know that I'm a practical man, a regular Englishman, an enemy to the wasting of time."

And the practical man, the "Englishman," in order to waste no words, covered two pages more with the explosions of his indignation at everything around him; at his racial brothers, timid and humble, who covered the hand of the enemy with kisses; at the descendants of the old-time persecutors; at the ferocious Padre Garau, of whom not even dust remained; against the whole island, the famous Roqueta, to which his people were held in subjection through love for its soil, a love returned with ostracism and insults.

"But let us not waste words; order, method, and clarity! Above all let us write practically. Lack of practical character is our ruination."

Finally he came to the Popess Juana, that imposing señora, whom Pablo Valls had only seen at a distance, as he seemed to her the personification of all the revolutionary impieties and of all the sins of his race. "There is no hope for you in that direction." Febrer's aunt remembered him only to lament his bad end and to praise the justice of the Lord, who punishes those who travel crooked paths, and depart from sacred family traditions.

Sometimes the good lady thought him in Iviza; again she declared she knew for a certainty that her nephew had been seen in America, engaged in the meanest employments. "Anyway, whelp of an inquisitor, your pious aunt will not remember you, and you need not expect the slightest assistance from her." It was now being whispered about the city that, definitely renouncing the pomps of this world and perhaps even the pontifical Golden Rose, which never arrived, she was about to turn over all her property to the priests of her court, going to shut herself up in a convent, with all the advantages of a privileged lady. The Popess was going away forever; it was impossible to expect anything from her. "And here is where I come in, young Garau: I, the reprobate, the Chueta, the long-tailed, who desire to be reverenced and adored by you as if you were Providence himself."

Finally the practical man, the enemy of useless words, fulfilled his promise, and the style of the letter became concise, with a commercial dryness. First a long statement of the properties still possessed by Jaime at the time of his leaving Majorca, burdened with all manner of incumbrances and mortgages; then a list of his creditors, which was longer than that of his properties, followed by lists of interest due and other obligations, an entangled skein in which Febrer's mind became wholly confused, but through which Valls made direct headway, with the confidence of those of his race for disentangling jumbled business affairs.

Captain Pablo had allowed half a year to pass without writing to his friend, but he had occupied himself daily over his affairs. He had haggled with the most ferocious usurers of the island, insulting some, outwitting others in finesse, resorting to persuasion or to bravado, advancing money to satisfy the more urgent creditors, who threatened attachment. In conclusion, he had left his friend's fortune free and sound, but it emerged from the terrible battle shrunken and comparatively insignificant. There only remained to Febrer some thousands of duros; perhaps it would not amount to fifteen thousand, but this was better than to live in his former position as a gran señor without anything to eat, and subjected to the persecution of his creditors. "It is time that you come home! What are you doing there? Are you going to spend the rest of your life like a Robinson Crusoe, in that pirate's tower?" He could live modestly; living is cheap in Majorca. Besides, he could solicit an office from the Government. With his name and pedigree it would not be difficult to accomplish that. He might devote himself to commerce under the direction and advice of a man like himself. If he wished to travel it would not be difficult for Valls to secure him a position in Algiers, in England, or in America. The captain had friends everywhere. "Come back soon, young Garau, dear old inquisitor. I have no more to say."

Febrer spent the rest of the afternoon reading the letter or strolling about the environs of the tower, deeply stirred by this news. Recollections of his past existence, dimmed by his rural and solitary life, stood out now with the same vividness as if they were the events of yesterday. The cafés on the Borne, his friends in the Casino! How strange to return there, passing at a bound into city life after his half savage seclusion in the tower! He would go at once! His mind was made up! He would start the next morning, taking advantage of the return trip of the same steamer which had brought the letter.

The memory of Margalida rose in his mind as if to detain him on the island. She appeared in his imagination with her white face, her adorable figure, her timid and lowered eyes, which seemed to conceal the dark ardor of her pupils as if it were a sin. Should he leave her? Never see her again? Then she would become the wife of one of those rough peasants who would make no better use of her beauty than to waste it in daily tasks in the field, gradually converting her into a farm animal, black, calloused, and wrinkled!

A pessimistic thought soon aroused him from this cruel doubt. Margalida did not love him; she could not love him. Disconcerting silence and mysterious tears were the only response he had succeeded in eliciting by his declarations of love. Why should he persist in trying to conquer that which seemed to everybody to be impossible? Why continue the senseless struggle against the whole island for a woman he was not as yet sure loved him?

The joy of the recent news turned Febrer into a skeptic. "Nobody dies of love." Yet it would cost him a great effort to abandon this country on the morrow; he would experience profound sorrow when the African whiteness of Can Mallorquí should fade from his view, but, once he had shaken himself free of the atmosphere of the island, no longer living among rustics, and had gone back to his old life, perhaps Margalida would linger only as a vague memory, and he would be the first to laugh at this passion for a peasant girl, the daughter of a former retainer of his family.

He hesitated no longer. He would spend the night in the solitude of his tower, like a primitive man, one of those who live lying in ambush against danger, ready to kill. Tomorrow night he would be seated at a table in a café beneath the light of an electric chandelier, seeing carriages beside the pavements, and gazing at women more beautiful than Margalida strolling along the Paseo del Borne. Back to Majorca, then! He would not live in a palace; the Febrer mansion he would lose forever, according to the arrangement made by his friend Valls; but he would not fail to have a neat little house in the ward of Terreno or somewhere near the sea, and in it the motherly care of Mammy Antonia. No sorrow, no shame would await him there. He would even be rid of the presence of Don Benito Valls and his daughter, from whom he had so discourteously fled, without a word of excuse. The rich Chueta, according to his brother's letter, now lived in Barcelona for the sake of his health, so he said; but undoubtedly, as Captain Pablo believed, this journey was taken for the purpose of finding a son-in-law unhampered by the prejudices which persecuted those of his race on the Island.

As night closed in the Little Chaplain came with his basket of supper. While Febrer was greedily eating, with the appetite aroused by his gladsome news, the boy's eager eyes roved about the room to see if he could discover the letter which had so piqued his curiosity. Nothing was in sight. The señor's good spirits finally enlivened him also, and he laughed without knowing why, feeling obliged to be in a good humor since Don Jaime was so.

Febrer joked him about his approaching return to the Seminary. He was thinking of making him a present, an extraordinary gift, he could never guess what; compared to it the knife would be worthless. As he said this his eyes traveled toward the gun hanging on the wall.

When the boy took his leave Febrer closed the door and diverted himself by taking an inventory and making a distribution of the objects which filled his dwelling. Within an old crudely carved wooden chest, laid away between fragrant herbs, was the clothing carefully folded by Margalida in which he had come to Majorca. He would put them on in the morning. He thought with a kind of terror of the torture of the boots and the torment of the stiff collar after his long season of rustic freedom, but he intended to leave the island as he had come to it. Everything else he would present to Pèp, except the gun, which would go to his son; he smiled as he thought of the expression of the young seminarist when he should receive this gift, which came rather late. By the time he could go hunting with it he would be a priest of one of the island districts.

He drew Valls' letter from his pocket again, taking pleasure in reading it over and over, as if each time he found fresh items of interest. While reading these paragraphs, which were already familiar, his mind was dwelling on the good news. His loyal friend Pablo! How timely was his advice! It called him from Iviza at the most opportune instant, when he was in open war with all these rude people, who were eager for the death of the stranger. The captain was right. What was he doing there, like a new Robinson Crusoe, and one who could not even enjoy the peace of solitude? Valls, opportune, as ever, delivered him from his danger.

His life of a few hours before, when he had not yet received the letter, seemed to him absurd and ridiculous. He was a new man now. He smiled with shame and pity for that mad man who, the day before, with his gun across his shoulder, had journeyed up the mountain to seek a former prisoner, challenging him to a barbarous duel in the solitude of the forest, as if all the life of the planet were concentrated on this little island and one must kill in order to live! As if there were no life nor civilization beyond the sheet of blue which surrounded this bit of land, with its primitive-souled inhabitants clinging to the customs of former centuries! What folly! This was to be the last night of his savage existence. On the morrow everything which had occurred would be but an interesting recollection, with tales of which he could entertain his friends on the Borne.

Febrer suddenly cut the trend of these thoughts, raising his eyes from the paper. As his gaze encountered half the room in shadow and the other half in a ruddy glow, which made objects flicker and tremble, he seemed to return from the long journey on which his imagination had drawn him. He was still living in the Pirate's Tower; he was still in the midst of darkness, of solitude peopled with whispers of Nature, in the interior of a cube of stone, the walls of which seemed to sweat dark mystery.

He had heard something outside; a cry, a howl, different from that of the other night, more stifled, more indistinct. Jaime received the impression that the cry came from very near, that perhaps it was uttered by someone hidden in the clusters of tamarisks.

He concentrated his attention and the howl came again. It was the same wild yell he had heard the other night, but low, repressed, hoarse, as if he who uttered it feared that the cry would scatter too much, and had placed his hands around his mouth in order to send it directly by means of this natural trumpet.

His first surprise subsided, he laughed softly, shrugging his shoulders. He did not intend to stir. What did primitive customs matter to him now, these peasant challenges? "Howl, my good man; yell until you're tired! I'm deaf!"

To divert his mind he returned to the reading of his letter, enjoying with particular zest the long list of creditors, many of whose names evoked choleric visions or grotesque recollections.

The howl continued at long intervals, and each time that the hoarse stridency pierced the silence Febrer thrilled with impatience and choler. Must he spend the whole night without sleep on account of this serenade of threats?

It occurred to him that perhaps the enemy concealed in the bushes saw his light through the cracks of the door and that this caused him to persist in his provocations. He blew out the candle and laid down on the bed, experiencing a sensation of comfort at being in the dark, with his back sunk into the soft, yielding mattress. That barbarian might howl for hours, or until he lost his voice. He did not intend to stir. What did the insults matter to him now? And he laughed with a joy of physical comfort, lying in his soft couch, while the other was making himself hoarse out there in the bushes, with his weapon ready and his eye alert. What a disappointment for the enemy!

Febrer was almost lulled to sleep by these cries of challenge. He had barricaded the door as he had done the night before. As long as the shouts continued he knew that he was in no danger. Suddenly, by a supreme effort, he sat up, flinging off a stupor which preceded sleep. He no longer heard howls. It was the mystery of silence which had awakened him, a silence more threatening and disquieting than the hostile shouts.

By listening intently he thought he could perceive a movement, a faint creaking of wood, something like the insignificant weight of a cat creeping from step to step, climbing up the stairway to the tower, with long intervals of waiting.

Jaime felt for his revolver, and he sat holding it with a tight clutch. The weapon seemed to tremble between his fingers. He began to feel the anger of the strong man who realizes the presence of an enemy at his door.

The cautious ascent ceased, perhaps half way up the stairs, and after a long silence, Febrer heard a low voice, a voice meant for him alone. It was the voice of the Ironworker. It invited him to step outside, it called him coward, uniting to this insult outrageous indignities against the detested isle of Majorca where Jaime was born.

Jaime sprang from his couch with a sudden impulse, the springs creaking loudly beneath him. As he arose to his feet in the dark, with his revolver in his hand, he began, to feel nothing but scorn for his challenger. Why heed him? It were better to go back to bed. There was a long pause, as if the enemy, when he heard the creaking springs, stood waiting for the inhabitant of the tower to come out. Time passed, and the hoarse and insulting voice once more pierced the calm of night. It called him coward again; it invited the Majorcan to come out. "Come out, you son of a— —"

At this insult Febrer trembled, and thrust his revolver back into his belt. His mother, his poor mother, pale and sick, and as sweet as a saint, whose memory was evoked by the greatest of infamies in the mouth of that criminal!

He started instinctively toward the door, colliding after a few steps with the barricade of tables and chairs. No; not the door. A rectangle of blue and hazy light was framed by the dark wall. Jaime had opened the window. The starry light faintly illuminated the contraction of his countenance, a cold grin, desperate, cruel, which gave him resemblance to the knight commander Don Priamo and other navigators of war and destruction whose dust-covered portraits were hanging in the great house in Majorca.

He seated himself on the window, threw his legs over the sill, and cautiously began to descend, feeling with his toes for the hollows in the wall.

As his feet touched earth he drew his revolver from his belt, and bending low, one hand on the ground, he crept around the base of the tower. His feet became entangled in the roots of the tamarisks which the wind had bared, and which sunk in the earth like a tangled skein of black serpents. Each time that he was stopped by a mesh of roots, each time that a stone rolled down or made a sound, he stopped, holding his breath. He was trembling, not with fear, but with the eagerness of the hunter who fears he may arrive too late. He longed to fall upon the enemy, to lay hands upon him while he stood near the door muttering his deadly insults!

Dragging himself along the ground, he came to where he could see the lower end of the stairway, then the upper steps, and finally the door, which stood out white in the light of the stars. Nobody! The enemy had fled.

In his surprise he stood erect, intently watching the black and undulating spot of bushes which extended around the foot of the stairway. Suddenly a red serpent, a streak of flame, followed by a tiny cloud and a thunder clap, leapt from out the tamarisks. Jaime thought he had been struck in the breast by a stone, a hot pebble, perhaps flung into the air by the concussion from the detonation.

"It's nothing!" he thought.

But at the same instant he found himself lying on the ground flat on his back.

He turned instinctively, lying with his breast on the earth, resting on one hand, extending the other which grasped the revolver. He felt strong; he repeated to himself that it was nothing; but suddenly his body almost refused to obey his will. He seemed to be glued to the ground. He saw the bushes move, as if stirred by some dark animal, cautious and malignant. There was the enemy! It thrust out first its head, then its trunk, and finally its legs from the crackling bushes.

With the rapid vision which accompanies the drowning man, a vision in which are concentrated fleeting recollections of all his former life, Febrer thought of his youth, when he used to fire off his pistol while lying on the ground in the garden at Palma as if rehearsing for a deadly encounter. The preparation of long ago was going to stand him in good stead now.

He clearly saw the black bulk of the enemy, motionless and in the line of sight of his revolver. His vision was becoming more hazy, more indistinct, as if the night were steadily growing darker. The enemy was approaching cautiously, also with a weapon in his hand, no doubt with the intention of finishing his deadly work. Then Febrer pulled on the trigger, once, twice, and again, believing that the weapon did not work, failing to hear the detonations, telling himself in his desperation that his enemy was going to fall upon him while he was without means of defense. He no longer saw the enemy. A white haze spread before his eyes; his ears buzzed—but when he thought he felt his adversary near, the mist cleared away, he saw the calm blue light of night again, and, a few steps away, also stretched on the ground, lay a body writhing, arching itself, clawing the earth, emitting a harsh groan, a hiccough of death.

Jaime could not understand this marvel. Really was it he himself who had fired a shot?

He tried to get up, but as he touched the ground his hands dabbled in a thick, warm clay. He touched his breast and he also found it wet by something warm and thick, dripping ceaselessly in slender streams. He tried to contract his legs in order to kneel, but his legs would not obey him. Only then was he convinced that he was wounded.

His eyes lost clearness of vision. He saw the tower double, then triple, then a curtain of cubes of stone extending along the coast, sinking into the sea. An acrid taste spread from his palate to his lips. It seemed to him that he was drinking something warm and strong, but that he was drinking it wrong way about, by a caprice of the mechanism of his life, the strange liquor reaching his palate from the depths of his vitals. The black bulk which lay writhing and moaning a few steps away, seemed to grow larger every time he touched the ground in his contortions. Now he was an apoplectic animal, a monster of the night, which, as it arched its body, reached the stars.

The barking of dogs, and the voices of human beings dissolved this phantom of solitude. Out of the darkness appeared lights.

"Don Jaime! Don Jaime!"

Whose voice was this? Where had he heard it before?

He saw dark figures stirring about, bending over him, carrying red stars in their hands. He saw a man holding back another smaller one who carried in his hand a white lightning flash, perhaps a knife, with which he tried to finish the kicking monster.

He saw no more. He felt a pair of soft arms lift his head. A voice, the same one he had heard a moment ago, tremulous and tearful, sounded in his ears, thrilling him to the depths of his soul.

"Don Jaime! Alas, Don Jaime!"

He felt on his mouth a sweet touch, something which caressed him with a silky sensation; gradually the contact pressed more close, until it became a frantic kiss, desperate, mad with grief.

Before sight forsook him he smiled weakly as he recognized near his own a pair of eyes tearful with love and pain; the eyes of Margalida.

CHAPTER IV
LIFE AND LOVE COMMAND

When Febrer found himself in a room in Can Mallorquí, lying on a white bed—perhaps Margalida's bed—he began to recall the events of a short time before.

He had walked to the farmhouse supported by Pèp and the Little Chaplain, feeling on his back sympathetic, trembling hands. His recollections were vague, dim, surrounded by a nimbus of white haze; something resembling the confused memory of acts and words after a day of intoxication.

He recalled that his head had fallen on Pèp's shoulder with mortal weariness; that his strength was deserting him, as if his life were escaping with the warm and sticky stream trickling down his breast and his back. He recollected that behind him sounded deafening groans, broken words imploring the aid of all the celestial powers; and he, in his weakness, his temples palpitating from the buzzing that accompanied the dizziness, made strenuous efforts to steady himself, advancing step by step, with the fear of falling in the roadway and remaining there forever. How interminable seemed the journey down to Can Mallorquí! It appeared to have lasted hours, days; in his dulled memory the walk seemed as long as the whole of his former life.

When at last friendly hands helped him climb into bed and began removing his clothing by the light of a candle, Febrer experienced a sensation of well-being and rest. He wished never to arise from this soft couch; he desired to remain here for all time!

Blood! The brilliant red of blood everywhere—on his jacket and shirt which were tossed at the foot of the bed as if they were rags, on the stiff white sheets, in the basin of water which reddened as Pèp wet a cloth to bathe Febrer's chest. Each garment removed from his body was dripping. His underclothing separated from his flesh with a wrench which made him shiver. The light of the candle, with its trembling flame, drew from the shadows a prevailing tone of red.

The women began to wail. Margalida's mother, forgetting all prudence, clasped her hands and raised her eyes with an expression of terror. Reina Santísima!

Febrer wondered at these exclamations. He was all right; why were the women so alarmed? Margalida, silent, her eyes enlarged by terror, moved about the room, turning over clothing, opening chests with the precipitation of fear, but never becoming confused at the furious cries of her father.

Good old Pèp, frowning, a greenish pallor on his dark countenance, attended the wounded man, while at the same time he gave orders.

"Lint! Bring more lint! Silence, women! Why so many cries and lamentations?"

He ordered his wife to go in search of a little pot of marvelous unguent treasured up ever since the times of his glorious father, the formidable man-slayer accustomed to wounds.

And when the mother, astounded at these abrupt orders, started to join Margalida in search of the remedy, her husband called her back to the bedside. She must hold the señor. Pèp had turned him on his side in order to examine and wash his breast and back, declaring that he had seen worse sights than this in his younger days, and that he understood something about wounds. When the blood was wiped off with a wet cloth two orifices were left exposed, one in the chest and the other in the back. Good! The ball had passed through his body; it would not have to be extracted, and this was an advantage.

With his rustic hands, to which he endeavored to impart a feminine tenderness, he tried to form tampons of lint to introduce into the wounds, which continued gently emitting the red liquid. Margalida, wrinkling her brows and turning away to avoid meeting Febrer's eyes, at last brushed Pèp aside.

"Let me do it, father. Perhaps I can do it better."

Jaime thought he felt on his bare flesh, sensitive, vibrating from the cruel wound, a sensation of coolness, of sweet calm, as the tampons were pressed into it by the girl's fingers.

Jaime remained motionless, feeling against his back and on his breast the cloths piled up by the two women in their horror at the blood.

The optimism which had animated him when he sank and fell near the tower, reappeared. Surely it was nothing, an insignificant wound; he felt better already. He was troubled by the sad expressions and the silence of those around him, and he smiled to encourage them. He tried to speak, but his first attempt at words produced extreme fatigue.

The peasant restrained him with a gesture. Silence, Don Jaime; he must keep perfectly still. The doctor would soon be here. Pepet had mounted the best horse on the place and had ridden to San José to call him.

On seeing Don Jaime's eyes opened wide in astonishment, persisting in his encouraging smile, Pèp continued speaking in order to divert Febrer's mind. He told him that he had been sound asleep when suddenly he was awakened by his wife calling him, and by the cries of the children, who made a rush for the door. Outside the farmhouse, in the direction of the tower, sounded shots. Another attack on the señor, the same as two nights before! When Pepet heard the two last shots he seemed to rejoice. Those were from Don Jaime; he recognized the sound of his revolver.

Pèp had lighted a lantern, his wife took the candle, and they all rushed up the hill to the tower, without giving a thought to danger. The first one they found was the Ironworker, his head streaming blood, writhing and howling like a demon.

His sinful life was ended, God have mercy on his soul! Pèp had been compelled to lay hands on his son, who had turned, furious and malignant as a monkey, when he saw who it was, and drew a great knife from his belt, with the intention of finishing him. Where had Pepet found that weapon? Boys are the very devil! A fine plaything for a seminarist!

The father glanced significantly at the knife presented to the Little Chaplain by Febrer, which was lying on a chair.

They had discovered the señor lying face downward near the tower stairway. Ah, Don Jaime, what a fright he and his family had! They thought him dead. In circumstances like this one realizes his affection for a person; and the good peasant glanced tenderly at Jaime, and was accompanied in this mute caress by the two women, who pressed close to the bed.

This glance of affection and of sorrowful anxiety was the last thing Febrer saw. His eyes closed, and he gradually fell into a stupor, without dreams, without delirium, in the gray softness of the void.

When he opened his eyes again the light which illuminated the room was no longer red. He saw the candle hanging in the same place with its wick black and dull. A cold, gloomy light penetrated through the little window of the sleeping room; the light of dawn. Jaime experienced a sensation of chill. The covers were being withdrawn from his body; agile hands were touching the bandages of his wounds. The flesh, numb a few hours before, now flinched at the lightest touch with the excruciating vibration of the pain, arousing an irresistible desire to groan.

Following with his clouded eyes the hands which were torturing him, Febrer saw a pair of black sleeves, then a cravat, a shirt collar different from those used by the peasants, and above all this a face with a gray mustache, a face he had often seen on the roads, but which failed to arouse in his memory a name; however, gradually he came to recognize it. It must be the doctor from San José whom he had seen frequently on horseback or driving along in a buggy; an old practitioner, wearing sandals like a peasant, and differing from them only in his cravat and his stiff collar, signs of superiority which he carefully maintained.

How the man tormented him as he touched his flesh, which seemed to have grown tense, becoming more sensitive, with a sickly and timid sensitiveness, as if it would contract at the mere contact with air! When this face was lost to his view and he no longer felt the torture of the hands he sank again into restful sleep. He closed his eyes, but his hearing seemed to be sharpened. He heard low voices in the next room, but he could only catch a few phrases. An unknown voice was congratulating himself that the ball had not remained in the body; undoubtedly in its trajectory it had passed through the lung. Here arose a chorus of exclamations of astonishment, of repressed sighs, and then of protest from the unfamiliar voice. Yes, the lung; but there was no cause for alarm.

"The lung heals readily. It is the most tractable organ of the whole body. The only thing to be feared is traumatic pneumonia."

Hearing this, Febrer persisted in his optimism. "It is nothing: it is nothing." And again he fell gently into the hazy sea of sleep, a sea immense, smooth, heavy, in which visions and sensations sank without causing a ripple or leaving a trace.

From that instant Febrer lost count of time and reality. He still lived; he was sure of it, but his life was abnormal, strange, a long life of shadow and inconsequence with short intervals of light. He opened his eyes and it was night; the little window was black and the candle flame colored everything with flickering red spots which joined the shadows in a merry jig. He opened them again, imagining that only a few moments had passed, and it was day once more; a ray of sunshine entered the room, tracing a circle of gold at the foot of the bed. In this way day and night succeeded each other with strange rapidity, as if the course of time had become forever reversed; or it seemed to remain stationary, with a maddening monotony. When the sick man opened his eyes it was night, eternally night, as if the globe were overwhelmed by unending darkness. Again it seemed that the sun were forever shining, as in the Arctic regions.

During one of his waking spells his eyes met those of the Little Chaplain. Thinking him suddenly better, the boy spoke in a low voice so as not to incur the ire of his father, who had commanded silence.

The Ironworker had already been buried. The bully lay rotting in the earth. What a true shot Don Jaime was! What a hand he had! He had broken the braggart's head.

The boy recalled what had taken place afterward with the pride of one who has enjoyed the honor of witnessing an historic event. The judge had come from the city with his tasselled staff, the chief of the Civil Guard and two gentlemen carrying papers and bottles of ink; all with an escort of men wearing three-cornered hats and carrying guns. These omnipotent personages, after a rest at Can Mallorquí, had climbed up to the tower, examining everything, prying all around, running over the ground as if to measure it, compelling him, the Little Chaplain, to lie down in the very spot where Don Jaime had been found, adopting a similar posture. After the visit of the magistrate some pious neighbors had borne the body of the Ironworker to the cemetery of San José, and the powerful representatives of the law had come down to the farmhouse to quiz the wounded man. It was impossible to make him speak. He was sound asleep, and when they aroused him he looked at them with a vague stare, and immediately closed his eyes again. Really did not the señor remember? They would question him again some other time when he was well. There was nothing to worry about; the magistrates and all honorable people were in his favor. As the Ironworker had no near relatives to avenge his death and as he had made himself obnoxious, the people had no reason for keeping silent, and they all spoke the truth. The Ironworker had gone two nights in search of the señor in his tower, and the señor had defended himself. It was certain that nothing would be done to him. Thus declared the Little Chaplain, who, on account of his warlike tendencies, possessed some of the characteristics of a juris consult. "Self defense, Don Jaime — —" It was the sole topic of conversation on the island. It was discussed in the cafés and casinos throughout the city. They had even written to Palma, giving news of the affair so that it would be published in the daily papers. By this time his friends in Majorca would have heard all about it.

The trial would be short. The only one who had been taken to Iviza and thrust into jail was the Minstrel, on account of his threats and lies. He tried to make the people believe that it was he who had gone in search of the detested Majorcan; he extolled the Ironworker as an innocent victim; but he was to be set at liberty at any time by the magistrate who was tired of his deceptions and his lying tales. The boy spoke of him with scorn. That chicken could not pride himself on having wounded a man. A mere farce!

Sometimes when the injured man opened his eyes he saw the motionless and muffled figure of Pèp's wife who sat staring at him with expressionless eyes, moving her lips as if in prayer, and giving vent to profound sighs. No sooner did she encounter the glassy gaze of Febrer than she ran to a small table covered with bottles and glasses. Her affection was manifested by an incessant desire to make him drink all the liquids ordered by the doctor.

When, in moments of turbid wakefulness, Jaime found Margalida's face bending over him, he experienced a joy which helped to dispel his drowsiness. The girl's eyes wore an adoring and timorous expression. She seemed to be imploring forgiveness with her tearful orbs outlined with blue against the nunlike delicacy of her skin. "For me! All on account of me!" she seemed to say tacitly, with a gesture of remorse.

She approached him timidly, vacillating, but without a flush of color, as if the strangeness of the circumstances had overcome her former shrinking. She arranged the disordered covers of his couch, she gave him to drink, and she raised his head to smooth his pillows. When Febrer tried to speak she raised her index finger to impose silence.

Once the wounded man grasped her hand as she passed and pressed it against his lips, caressing it with a prolonged kiss. Margalida dared not draw it away. She turned her head as if she wished to hide her tear-filled eyes. She groaned with anguish, and the sick man thought he heard expressions of remorse such as he had divined in her manner. "On account of me! It happened on account of me!" Jaime experienced a sensation of joy at her tears. Oh, sweet Almond Blossom!

Now he no longer saw the fine, pale face; he could distinguish only the flash of her eyes, surrounded by white mist, as one sees the splendor of the sun on a stormy morning. His temples throbbed cruelly, his sight grew turbid. The sweet stupor, soft and empty as nothingness, was succeeded by a sleep peopled with incoherent visions, of fiery images vibrating against a background of intense blackness, by torture which wrung from his breast groans of fear and cries of anguish. He was delirious. Often he would awake from one of his frightful nightmares for an instant, barely long enough to find himself sitting up in bed, his arms pinned down by other arms, which endeavored to hold him. Then he would sink back into that world of shadows, peopled with horrors. In this fleeting consciousness, like a hasty vision of light from a breathing-hole in the darkness of a tunnel, he recognized near his bed the sorrowful faces of the family of Can Mallorquí. Again his eyes would encounter those of the doctor, and once he even thought he saw the gray whiskers and the oil-colored eyes of his friend, Pablo Valls. "Illusion! Madness!" he thought, as he sank once more into lethargy.

Sometimes while his eyes remained sunk in this world of gloom, furrowed by the red comets of nightmare, his ear vibrated weakly with words which seemed to come from far, very far away, but which were uttered near his bedside. "Traumatic pneumonia—delirium." These words were repeated by different voices, but he doubted that they referred to himself. He felt well. This was nothing; a strong desire to continue lying down; a renunciation of life; the voluptuosity of keeping still, of lying there until the approach of death, which did not arouse in him the slightest fear.

His brain, disordered by fever, seemed to whirl and whirl in mad rotation, and these cycles evoked in his confused mind an image which had often filled it. He saw a wheel, an enormous wheel, immense as a terrestrial sphere, its upper part lost in cloud, its lower arc merging in the sidereal dust which glittered in the darkness of the heavens. The tire of this wheel was composed of human flesh; millions and millions of human beings soldered together, welded, gesticulating, their extremities free, moving them to convince themselves of their activity and of their liberty, while the bodies were joined one to another. The spokes of the wheel attracted Febrer's attention by their diverse forms. Some were swords, their blood-stained blades wound with garlands of laurel, the symbol of heroism; others seemed golden scepters tipped by crowns of kings or emperors; rods of justice; ingots of gold formed by coins laid one upon another; shepherd's crooks set with precious stones, symbols of divine guidance ever since men grouped themselves into flocks to timidly bawl with their gaze fixed on high. The hub of this wheel was a skull, white, clean, shiny, as if made of polished ivory; a skull as big as a planet, which seemed to remain stationary while everything turned around it; a skull luminous, moon-like, which seemed to leer malignantly from its dark eye-sockets, silently mocking at all this movement.

The wheel turned and turned. The millions of human beings fastened to it in its continual revolution shouted and waved their hands, aroused to enthusiasm and enkindled with fervor by the velocity. Jaime saw that no sooner did they rise to the highest point than they began to descend head downward; but, in their illusion they imagined themselves traveling forward, admiring at each revolution new spaces, new things. They fancied the very point through which they had passed but a moment before an unfamiliar and astounding region. Ignorant of the immovability of the center around which they were turning, they believed with the best of faith that the movement was an advance. "How we are running! Where are we going to stop?" they cried. And Febrer pitied their simplicity, seeing their elation at the rapidity of their imagined progress when they were actually remaining in the same place; rejoicing in the velocity of an ascension on which they started for the millionth time and which inevitably must be followed by the downward plunge.

Suddenly Jaime felt himself pressed forward by an irresistible force. The great skull smiled at him mockingly. "You, also! Why resist your destiny?" And he found himself fastened to the wheel, jumbled with that credulous and childish humanity, but lacking the consolation of their fond delusion; and his traveling companions insulted him, spat upon him, beat him in their indignation when they learned of his absurd denial of their movement, believing him insane for holding in doubt something which was visible to all.

At last the wheel exploded, filling the black space with flames, with thousands of millions of cries and tremulous vibrations from the human beings hurled through the mystery of eternity; and he fell and fell, for years, for centuries, until he dropped upon the soft bed. Then he opened his eyes. Margalida stood near, gazing at him by the candle light with an expression of terror. It must be the early morning. The poor girl gave a gasp of fear as she grasped his arms with her trembling little hands.

"Don Jaime! Ay, Don Jaime!"

He had cried out like an insane man; he was leaning over the bed with an evident desire to fall to the floor, he had been talking about a wheel and a skull. "What is the matter, Don Jaime?"

The invalid felt the loving touch of gentle hands, which smoothed his disordered clothing, drew up the covers and tucked them around his shoulders, maternally, with the same caressing care as if he were a child.

Before sinking back into a state of mental confusion, before again passing through the fiery gateway of delirium, he saw close to his face the moist eyes of Margalida, which were ever growing more sad and tearful within their circles of blue. He felt the warm gust of her breath on his lips, and then he felt their thrill at a silky, moist contact, a light, timid caress, similar to the brushing of a wing. "Sleep, Don Jaime." The señor must sleep. And despite the respect with which she addressed him, her words possessed a murmur of affectionate intimacy, as if Don Jaime were to her a different man since the misfortune which had drawn them together.

The delirium of fever dragged the sick man through strange worlds, where not the slightest vestige of reality remained. He was in his solitary tower again. The gloomy fortress was no longer constructed of stone; it was formed of skulls joined like blocks of stone by a mortar of bonedust. Of bones also were the hill and the cliffs along the coast; white skeletons the lines of foam which crowned the breakers from the sea. Everything that his view embraced, trees and mountains, ships and distant islands, became an ossified, glacial landscape. Craniums with wings similar to those of cherubims in religious pictures fluttered through the heavens uttering through their fleshless jaws hoarse hymns to the great divinity who filled the whole space with the folds of his shroud, and whose bony head was lost in the clouds. He felt that invisible beings were ripping off his flesh in bleeding tatters, which, having adhered to him throughout a whole lifetime, drew from him shrieks of pain as they were torn away. Then he beheld himself a white skeleton, bleached and polished, and a far away voice seemed to murmur a horrible consecration in his ear-cavities. The moment of true greatness had arrived; he had ceased being a man to become converted into a corpse. The slave had passed through the great initiation, and had changed to a demigod. The dead command! It was only necessary to see with what superstitious respect, with what servile fear, the city dwellers saluted those who were passing into the great beyond. The powerful bare their heads in the presence of the dead beggar.

With the potent vision of his black and eyeless sockets, for which there was neither distance nor obstacle, he gazed upon the entire world. Dead, dead on every side! They filled everything. He beheld tribunals of men dressed in black, their eyes haughty and their gesture imposing, listening to the woes of their fellow creatures, while behind them stood an equal number of enormous skeletons, endowed with the grandeur of centuries, wrapped in togas, who were those who moved the hands of the judges as they wrote, and who dictated their sentences over their heads. The dead judge! He saw great halls of vertical light with concentric rows of seats, and on them hundreds of men speaking, vociferating and gesticulating, in the noisy task of making laws. Behind them crouched the real legislators, the dead, the deputies in their winding sheets, whose presence was unguessed by these men of grandiloquent vanity, who imagined that they ever spoke by their own inspiration. The dead legislate! In a moment of doubt it was sufficient for someone to recall what had been the opinion of the dead in former times in order to reëstablish calm, everyone accepting their opinion. The dead, eternal and immutable, were the only reality! Men of flesh and blood were a mere accident, an insignificant bubble bursting with ostentatious pride!

He saw white skeletons guarding like gloomy angels the gates of cities which they had built, watching the flock hemmed within, repelling as accursed the irresponsible madmen who refused to recognize their authority. He saw at the foot of great monuments, museum paintings, and shelves of books in the libraries, the mute grin of the craniums which seemed to say to men: "Admire us! This is our work, and all which you do will be after our example!" The entire world belonged to the dead. They reigned. The living, as they opened their mouths to receive food, masticated particles of those who had preceded them along the pathway of life; when they wished to feast their eyes and ears on beauty, art offered them works and precedents established by the dead. Even love suffered this servitude. Woman in modesty or in bursts of passion, which she deems spontaneous, unconsciously imitated her grandmothers, who had been temptresses with hypocritical modesty or frankly voluptuous, according to the epochs in which they lived.

In his delirium the sick man began to feel oppressed by the density and number of these beings, white and bony, with eyeless sockets and malevolent grins, skeletons of a vanished life, obstinately determined to continue to subsist, dominating everything. They were so many, so many! It was impossible to even stir. Febrer stumbled against their bare and prominent ribs, against the sharp angles of their hips; his ears vibrated with the dry creaking of their knee-pans. They overpowered him, they asphyxiated him; there were millions upon millions; all the ancestors of the human race! Finding no space whereon to set their feet, they stood in rows one upon another. They were a kind of in-coming tide of bones which rose and swelled until it reached the summit of the highest mountains and touched the clouds. Jaime was choking in this white inundation, hard and crackling. They trampled him underfoot; they weighed upon his chest with the heaviness of dead things. He was going to die! In his despair he clutched a hand which seemed to come from far away, appearing out of the shadows; the hand of a living being, a hand of flesh! He tugged at it and gradually in the fog the pale spot began to assume the form of a countenance. After his existence in a world of empty craniums and bleached bones this human face caused him the same sense of grateful surprise as that experienced by the explorer on meeting with one of his race after a long sojourn among savage tribes.

He tugged harder at the hand; the vagueness of the countenance became condensed, and he recognized Pablo Valls bending over him, moving his lips as if murmuring affectionate phrases which he could not hear. Again? The captain was always appearing in his delirium!

After this rapid vision the sick man sank back into unconsciousness. Now his stupor was more tranquil. His thirst, that horrible thirst, which had impelled him to reach his hands outside the bed and to draw his lips away from the emptied glass with a gesture of unsatisfied eagerness, now began to diminish. In his delirium he had seen clear streams, great silent rivers, which he could never reach, his limbs overcome by a painful paralysis. Now he beheld a luminous and foaming cataract rolling down against the background of his dream, and at last he could walk, he could approach it, seeing it more clearly at each step, feeling the cool caress of the moisture on his face.

From out the noise of this waterfall stifled voices reached his ears. Someone was talking of traumatic pneumonia again. "It is conquered." And a voice added joyfully: "That is good! We have a man again!" The invalid recognized this voice. Pablo Valls was ever reappearing in his delirium!

He continued on his way, attracted by the coolness of the water. He stood beneath the sonorous torrent and he thrilled with voluptuous shivers as he received on his back the force of the falling stream. A sensation of freshness overspread his body, causing him to sigh with pleasure. His limbs seemed to relax beneath the icy touch. His chest broadened, overcoming the oppression which had tortured him until a moment ago, as if the whole earth weighed upon his body. He felt the haze clearing away from his brain. He was still delirious, but his delirium was not pierced by scenes of terror and cries of anguish. It was, instead, a placid sleep, in which the body relaxed, and his thoughts took wing through pleasant horizons of optimism. The foam of the cascade was white, reflecting the colors of the rainbow on its facets of liquid diamonds. The sky was a rose tint, with distant music and mild perfumes. Something trembled mysteriously, invisible, and at the same time smiling, in this fantastic atmosphere; a supernatural force which seemed to beautify it with its contact. It was returning health!

The incessant waters falling over the cliffs, aroused in his memory former dreams. Once more the wheel, the immense wheel, the image of humanity, which turned and turned in its identical place, beginning one ascent after another, ever passing the same places.

The sick man, revived by the sensation of coolness, thought that he possessed a new sense of understanding.

Again he saw the wheel revolving through the infinite, but was it really stationary?

Doubt, the beginning of new truths, caused him to look with closer attention. Was it not a deception of his own eyes? Was it he who was mistaken, and were not those millions of beings who uttered shouts of joy in their whirling prison right in thinking that they realized a fresh advance with each whirl?

It was cruel for life to go on developing for hundreds of centuries in this deceptive agitation, concealing an actual inactivity. For what then the existence of created things? Had humanity no other purpose than to deceive itself, turning by its own effort the cylinder which imprisoned it, as birds by their springing cause the cage which is their prison to vibrate?

Now he no longer saw the wheel. Before his vision passed an enormous globe of bluish color, on which were marked the seas and continents with outlines like those he had seen on maps. It was the Earth! He, an imperceptible molecule in the immensity of space, an abject spectator of the stupendous representation of Nature, beheld the blue globe with its girdle of clouds.

It also was revolving like the fatal wheel. It turned and turned upon itself with exasperating monotony, but this movement which was the nearest, the most visible, that which all could appreciate, was insignificant. Another movement was the one of real importance. Above that of the monotonous rotation, ever around the same axis, was that of translation, which dragged the globe through the infinitude of space in eternal travel, never re-passing through the same place.

Curses on the wheel! Life was not an eternal revolution through identical situations! Only the shortsighted, seeing no farther beyond, as they contemplated this movement, could imagine that it was the only one. The earth itself was the image of life. It ever rotated through determined spaces of time; days and seasons were repeated, as, in the history of mankind, greatness and decline follow each other; but there was something more than all this; the movement of translation, which drew toward the infinite, ever forward, ever forward!

The theory of "the eternal re-beginning of things" was false. Men and events were repeated as are days and seasons on earth; but although everything seemed alike it was not really so. The outer form of objects might be similar, but the soul was different!

No; the wheel had vanished! Perish inactivity! The dead could not command! The world, in its forward movement, ran so fast that they could not sustain themselves upon its surface. They clutched at the crust with their bony claws, struggling for years, perhaps for centuries, to keep firm hold, but the velocity of the race finally cast them off, leaving in their wake a trail of broken bones, of dust, of nothing!

The world, filled with the living, traveled straight forward, never passing over the same place twice. Febrer had seen it appear on the horizon like a tear of luminous blue, then grow larger and larger, until it filled the whole of space, passing near him with the velocity of a rotating projectile; and now it was becoming smaller again, fleeing through the opposite extreme. Now it was a drop, a point, nothing—becoming lost in obscurity! Who knew whither it was bound, and why?

Futilely his ideas of a moment before, being now overcome, returned with the purpose of making a final protest, shouting that this movement of translation was equally false, and that the Earth turned like a wheel around the sun—no; neither was the sun stationary, but with all its familiar company of planets, it fell and fell, if it is possible in the infinite to fall without rising; it traveled on and on—who knows toward what destination, or for what purpose?

Definitely, abominating the wheel, he rent it to bits in his imagination, experiencing the joy of the convict who passes out through the door of his prison and breathes the air of freedom. He thought that scales fell from his eyes as from those of the Hebrew Apostle at Damascus. He beheld a new light. Man is free, and he can liberate himself from the dead by an effort, cutting the knot of slavery that has soldered him to these invisible despots.

He ceased dreaming; he sank into oblivion with the silent and intimate joy of the laborer resting after a profitable day's work.

When, after a long time, he re-opened his eyes, he found those of Pablo Valls fastened upon his. Valls was holding one of his hands, gazing at him affectionately with his amber pupils.

He could no longer doubt; it was reality! He detected the odor of English tobacco, which always seemed to float around his mouth and beard. Was it not then an illusion? Had he really seen him in the course of his delirium? Was it his actual voice which he had heard in the midst of his nightmares?

The captain burst into a laugh, displaying his long teeth, yellowed by the pipe.

"Ah, my fine fellow!" he exclaimed. "You're better, aren't you? The fever has gone; there is no longer any danger. The wounds are healed. You must feel the itching of a thousand demons in them; something as if you had a thousand wasps under the bandages. That is the formation of tissue, the new flesh which hurts as it grows."

Jaime realized the truth of these words. In the region of his wounds he felt an itching, a tension which contracted his flesh.

Valls read a supplication of curiosity in the eyes of his friend.

"Do not talk! Do not tire yourself! How long have I been here? About two weeks. I read about your accident in the Palma newspapers, and I came immediately. Your friend the Chueta will always be the same. What anxiety you have given us! Pneumonia, my boy, and in a dangerous form! You opened your eyes and you did not recognize me; you raved like a madman. But it's all over now! We have given you the best of care. Look! See who's here!"

He stepped away from the bed so that Febrer might see Margalida, hidden behind the captain, shrinking and timid, now that the señor could look at her with eyes free from fever. Ah, Almond Blossom! Jaime's glance, tender and sweet, brought a flush to her cheeks. She feared that the sick man might remember what she had done in the most critical moments, when she was almost sure that he was going to die.

"Now you must keep still," continued Valls. "I will stay here until we can go back to Palma together. You know me. I understand everything; I'll arrange it all. Eh? Do I make myself clear?"

The Chueta winked one eye and smiled mischievously, sure of his cleverness in guessing the desires of his friends.

Famous captain! Ever since his arrival at Can Mallorquí the entire family seemed dependent upon his orders, admiring him as a personage of immense power, tempered by eternal joviality.

Margalida blushed at his words and winks, but she was fond of him for being so devoted to his friend. She remembered his eyes brimming with tears one night when they thought Don Jaime was going to die. Valls had wept, while at the same time he muttered curses. The Little Chaplain adored that great gentleman from Majorca ever since he saw him burst out laughing on learning that his parents intended him to be a priest. Pèp and his wife followed him like obedient and submissive dogs.

Several afternoons Pablo and the sick man discussed past events.

Valls was a man quick in his decisions.

"You know that I never tire of doing for my friends. When I landed in Iviza I went to see the judge. Everything can be satisfactorily arranged. You are in the right, and everybody knows it—self defense! A few annoyances when you get well, but they won't amount to much. The matter of your health is decided also. What else is there? Ah, yes! There is something else, but I have that about settled also."

He laughed knowingly as he said this, pressing the hands of Febrer, who, on his part, wished to ask no more; fearful of suffering a disappointment.

Once, when Margalida entered the room, Valls grasped her by the arm and drew her near the couch.

"Look at her!" he said, with burlesque gravity, turning toward the sick man. "Is this the girl you love? They haven't succeeded in changing her, have they? Then give her your hand, stupid! What are you doing there, staring at her with those frightened eyes?"

Febrer clasped Margalida's right hand with both of his. Was it really true? His eyes sought those of the girl, which remained lowered, while emotion whitened her cheeks and made her nostrils palpitate.

"Now kiss each other," said Valls, gently shoving the girl toward Febrer.

But Margalida, as if she felt threatened by a danger, freed her hands, fleeing from the room.

"Good!" said the captain. "You'll kiss each other before very long— when I'm not around."

Valls declared himself in favor of this union. Did Febrer love her? Then go ahead. This was more logical than the marriage with his niece for her father's millions. Margalida was a fine woman. He understood these things; when Jaime should take her away from the island, and accustom her to different ways and to different dress, with the adaptability of woman, it would soon be impossible to recognize the former peasant girl.

"I have arranged your future, young inquisitor. You know that your friend the Jew always accomplishes what he undertakes. You have enough left in Majorca so that you can live modestly. Don't shake your head; I know that you want to work, and now more than ever since you are in love and mean to raise a family. You will work. We'll set up a business together; we can decide on that later. I always have my head crammed with projects. That's characteristic of my race. If you prefer to leave Majorca, I'll look for a situation for you abroad. You must think it over."

In all matters relating to the family of Can Mallorquí the captain spoke with the authority of a master. Pèp and his wife dared not disobey him. How could they argue with a señor who knew everything? The peasant farmer offered little resistance. Since Don Pablo desired the marriage of Margalida to the señor and gave his word that it would not bring misfortune to the girl, they might marry. It was a great sorrow for the two old people to see her leave the island, but they preferred this to having Febrer with them as a son-in-law, for he inspired them with a respect which they could not outlive.

The Little Chaplain was almost ready to kneel before Vall's. "And yet they say in Palma that Chuetas are bad!" he murmured. It was clear that those who said so were Majorcans—a people unjust and proud! The captain was a saint. Thanks to him, he would not have to go to the Seminary. He would be a peasant-farmer. Can Mallorquí would be left to him. He had even received the knife from his father, at the intercession of Don Pablo, and he was counting on the gift of a modern pistol promised by the captain, one of those marvelous weapons which he had admired in Palma in the show windows along the Borne. As soon as Margalida's marriage had taken place he would go throughout the district in search of a bride, wearing in his girdle two noble companions. The race of brave men must not die out on the island. In his veins coursed the heroic blood of his grandfather!

One sunny morning Febrer, leaning on Valls and Margalida, made his way with the step of a convalescent as far as the porch of the farmhouse. Seated in a great armchair he gazed fondly upon the tranquil landscape outspread before him. Upon the summit of the headland rose the Pirate's Tower. How much he had dreamed and suffered there! Now he loved it as he remembered that within it, alone and forgotten of the world, this passion, destined to fill the rest of a once aimless life, had originated.

Enfeebled by the long weeks in bed and by the loss of blood, he breathed in the warm atmosphere of the luminous morning pierced by the breezes which blew in from the sea.

Margalida, after contemplating Jaime with loving eyes, which still held something of timidity, went into the house to prepare the morning meal.

The two men remained long in silence. Valls had taken out his pipe, filling it with English tobacco, and expelling fragrant mouthfuls.

Febrer, with his gaze fixed on the landscape, his dazzled eyes embracing the sky, the hills, the fields, and the sea, spoke in a low voice, as if talking to himself.

Life was beautiful. He affirmed it with the conviction of one arisen from the grave who returns unexpectedly to the world. Man could move freely, the same as the bird and the insect, on the bosom of Nature. There was a place for all. Why confine oneself by the bonds which others had invented, tyrannizing over the future of the men who were to come after them? The dead, ever the accursed dead, trying to meddle in everything, complicating our existence!

Vall's smiled, looking at him with mischievous eyes. Several times he had heard him in his delirium talking of the dead, waving his arms as if fighting, trying to repel them with frightful struggles. As he listened to Jaime's explanations, as he realized his respect for the past and his submission to the influence of the dead that had stultified his life, and had banished him to a remote island, Vall's remained silent and lost in thought.

"Do you believe that the dead command, Pablo?"

The captain shrugged his shoulders. For him there was nothing absolute in the world. Perhaps the dominion of the dead was tottering and was already in its decadence. In other times they commanded like despots; there was no doubt of that. It might be that now they commanded only in some places, in others losing forever all hope of power. In Majorca they still governed with a strong hand; he said it, he, the Chueta. In other lands, perhaps not.

Febrer experienced deep annoyance as he recalled his mistakes and his worries. Accursed dead! Humanity could never be happy and free until they should cast off their power.

"Pablo, let us kill the dead!"

The captain looked at his friend for an instant with a certain anxiety, but seeing the serenity of his eyes he was reassured and said, smiling:

"Kill them, for all I care!"

Then, recovering his gravity, and leaning back in his chair, while he puffed a mouthful of smoke, the Chueta added: "You are right. Let us kill the dead! Let us crush beneath our feet all useless obstacles, old things that obstruct and complicate our pathway. We live according to the word of Moses, to the word of Jesus, of Mohammed, or of other shepherds of men, when the natural and logical thing would be to live according to what we ourselves think and feel."

Jaime glanced behind him, as if his eyes would seek in the interior of the house the sweet figure of Margalida. Then he thought over all his old anxieties and all the new truths to which he had awakened, repeating the same vigorous declaration: "Let us kill the dead!"

Pablo's voice aroused him from his reflections.

"Would you have married my niece in your present state of mind, without fear or compunction?"

Febrer hesitated before replying. Yes, he would have married her, regardless of the scruples which had caused him so much suffering; yet something was lacking for the fulfillment of that union; something which was above the will of man, superior to his power, something which could not be bought and which ruled the world; something which the humble Margalida unconsciously brought with her.

His troubles had ended. Now for a new life!

No; the dead do not command! It is life that commands, and above life, love!